BENJAMIN MYERS

TURNING BLUE

MOTH

First published in 2016 by Moth, an imprint of Mayfly Press, a partnership between New Writing North and Business Education Publishers Limited, Chase House, Rainton Bridge, Tyne and Wear, DH4 5RA

Cover design by Courage, UK

A CIP catalogue record for this book is available from the British Library

Paperback ISBN 978 1 911356 00 4
Ebook ISBN 978 1 911356 03 5

Printed and bound by Martins the Printers Ltd, UK

www.mayfly.press

'Sacred love is selfless, seeking not its own. The lover serves his beloved and seeks perfect communion of oneness with her.'

– D. H. Lawrence

TURNING
BLUE

THE BLACK WATER shot through with silver. Scraps of the moon on the surface like a shoal of fish floating belly up. The slow rock and tip and the slap of the water on the side of the boat.

It is too dark for silhouettes but the hot glow of his cigarette seems brighter than the sun as he takes a final draw and sees the last burning shreds of tobacco fall down to the tarpaulin sheet and sit there just long enough to singe tiny holes in its cracked glaze.

He is down to the filter. He throws it away. He has nothing left.

There are no buildings on the reservoir's shoreline; no cars in the car park. The wind turbines sit over the brow on the crest of the valley. No hills surround the body of water either – only the flat moor-tops flush with the late spring's first sprouting of heather not yet purple.

It is not raining.

He lifts the clanking chain and feels the weight of it first in one hand and then the other. He throws it down and then lifts an oar from the rowlock. Steadies his feet. He throws the paddle out into the water. He waits for the splash then does the same with the second one at the other side of the boat. Swimming is the only way back now and that distance would challenge any man on a night like this.

A breeze picks up.

He has drifted and with no markers to guide the way he has no way of knowing if he is in the same spot as last time. Probably he is some metres off his target. Maybe many. But this is close enough to put him into that next dimension. To bring the two of them together.

He sits down and the boat rocks again. The tin in his breast pocket rattles. He waits until the boat has settled and then he feeds the chain through the hole in the centre of the first breeze block. He loops it through twice. He wraps rusting steel around powder dry coke and cinder.

He knots it. Pulls it tight. He does the same with a second breeze block. He does it slowly. He does it meticulously. He has to get this right.

The chain is the same length as the one he used last time but the extra knots that he ties take six inches off it. Their difference in height will not matter. They will stand together. Side to side or eye to eye. Weightless like flight or eternal suspension. Hovering between sky and earth. Angelic in the water until the sun rises and its rays beam down. The water keeping their secrets.

It will be silent down there; it will be the most beautiful graveyard imaginable.

He takes the chain and he threads one end through his belt-loops. When he has done that he crosses it over and threads it under then he runs it down one trouser leg. He snaps it tight and then wraps it around his ankles once twice three times again. He ties it. Binds his ankles and feet. Locks them in. Strapped. Bound.

He reaches into his pockets and he takes out the padlock and then brings the chain together and he puts the arm of the lock through the two ends of the chain and he snaps it into place. The sound of the mechanism locking is satisfying. Finite. He throws the key. Chucks it far out. The lack of hesitation makes his heart race. He doesn't hear it hit the water.

The breeze picks up.

He turns and puts his legs over the side of the boat. He dangles his feet in the reservoir. The cold snaps at him. He hefts the first breeze block into his lap. The second one follows. One on top of the other. Stacked. He is a human hod.

He straightens the chain out on the floor of the boat. Makes sure there are no snags.

He holds the blocks in place.

Thinks of her face.

That day in the snow.

In winter.

Up top.

He thinks of her face. Her scent.

He thinks of all their faces. All of their faces.

All those secrets trapped inside him. He'll take them with him. He thinks of other men thwarted. He thinks of victory – finally. Victory over the hills and the hamlet and the town and the city. Victory over everyone and everything.

He thinks of his mother.

Then he pushes the breeze blocks into the water and hears the rusting chain accelerating into the black and silver.

PART I

WINTER

1

MIRRORS. THERE ARE mirrors everywhere.

Brindle lets the water run hot and then he washes his hands. He scrubs each finger in turn using the soap that he keeps in the type of plastic case that campers and frequent travellers use. The cheap industrial stuff that the force buys makes his skin itch. It bothers him. So he brings his own. He looks at his face – briefly.

Mirrors. Mirrors and masks.

Brindle touches his hair. He runs his comb beneath the tap and then he confirms the neat side parting.

He washes the comb. He washes between each tooth and then uses a paper towel to dry it. Replaces it in his pocket.

The toothbrush. It is new. He adds paste and cleans his teeth in a circular motion as advised by the hygienist who remarked that his gums were in exceptionally good condition. He spits and swills spits and swills. Sees his face again.

Mirrors masks and memories.

He tries to avoid them all. Especially mirrors. It is not easy. His face follows him everywhere. It confronts him around corners and is reflected in computer monitors and handheld devices. In rear-view mirrors and shop windows. The sunglasses of strangers on the street even.

His flawed face introduces Brindle to the world and neither the world nor he likes what they see: the crude imperfection of a birth defect. He wears a red mark caused by the haemangioma that signifies more than just mutant pigmentation and increased vessels filled with blood while still in the womb. The darkened strawberry shape on his cheek has marked him out as different since it was first pointed out to him with horror by a fellow toddler.

He does not need mirrors to remind him of this but mirrors masks and memories are to be avoided all the same.

None lead you anywhere good.

The bathroom door opens.

Brindle says a voice. He looks up from the sink. Sees his face. Mirrors masks and memories. Sees a colleague.

What is it?

You're wanted.

HAT GLOVES SCARF.

Phone. Lighter. Papers. A cigarette half-emptied of its contents and the paper twisted at the end. Her old metal pencil case with some coins and photographs and bus tickets and a few small blims of hash in it. Squidgy black. Easy to burn and roll. Melanie Muncy puts them all into her pocket.

The house makes her anxious now. Since she has returned for Christmas she has been experiencing the unpleasant feeling of something fluttering and then tightening inside her and when this happens she has to get out. She needs air and space and the moors.

Keys?

She goes into the kitchen. Her mother is at the table. She is moving toast crumbs around with the edge of her hand. Sweeping them into lines.

Are you going to be here in a bit Mam?

Her mother looks up and offers a wan smile but says nothing.

Mam.

Yes?

Do I need to take my keys with me? I'll only be half an hour.

Take them where?

Mungo needs a walk.

Why?

Melanie sighs.

Because he's a dog she says. That's what they do.

June Muncy looks back to the table. To the line of crumbs.

Her parents especially make Melanie Muncy anxious. They wear masks all the time now. Her father that of respectability and confidence and her mother that of balance and normality. Her fear and quiet despair seep through the edges though. It is like trying to trap liquid beneath an upturned glass. Only now coming home for the holidays does she see just how bad it has become. This house way up the valley with its land and outbuildings and endless extensions and conservatory and paddock might outwardly be a sign of Ray Muncy's business-success but for only the first time Melanie sees it for what it really represents: his insecurity and isolation. It is a fortress from the outside world; a retreat from reality. Even the campsite fields that they let out by plot during spring and summer are a strictly controlled area that her father polices with authority.

I'll take them then shall I? says Melanie.

Yes says her mother. You walk the dog love. It'll soon be Christmas.

Turning away Melanie rolls her eyes.

See you later then.

She calls the dog who leaps out of his basket in the utility room. She hears his claws scratching at the lino as he comes skittering through to the hall. He puts his paws up onto her thighs and she holds them for a moment and then takes his lead from the hook by the door and attaches it to his collar.

Come on then she says. Shall we go out for a walk up top?

The dog cocks his head at the mention of these familiar words. His ears prick up.

She leaves by the back door and follows the path round the side garden and across the front lawn that is deep with snow. It coats the large ornamental urns and the potted plants. It hangs top-heavy from the kissing gate and two garden benches.

Viewed from a distance the garden is a neat landscaped space in miles of rough and uneven terrain. It is a sanitised section with a rockery and a fountain now turned off for winter and decking around the back. Behind the house the camping fields run down to the river and round the other side are the outbuilding and the stable-door hatch from which they sell refreshments to the walkers during camping season.

The dog tugs at the lead eager to hit the higher ground and run free. Melanie walks down the lane and sinks deeper into the fresh snow. It comes up to her shins. The air is fresh and thin and her lungs feel tight as if they are coated with tiny motes of glass. She realises she has not brought her inhaler.

She goes through the old stone gate and round past the post office and the turning circle and through the newer gate with the rabbit-run gap to one side and onto the short path that leads to the old horse track curving up the hillside. She unhooks the dog from his lead and lets him run panting through the snow. Excited by winter he hops four-footed through the thickest drifts like a spring lamb.

Halfway up the hill Melanie Muncy turns right where the wall has tumbled down into a pile of old stones and into a field where a disused shepherd's bothy sits in the corner. She has been coming here for years. Once men would take refuge in it when they found themselves caught out on the fells during whiteout storms or in the lambing month of March but it had not been used for that purpose in decades.

Now the sloped tiled roof has holes in it where slates have slid away but the walls are still sound and the view across the hamlet and down the valley always breathtaking. Always different.

A fallen piece of roof timber provides a bench on which to sit as the dog sniffs around the edges of the stone chamber with his ears pricked and wet nose roving close to the ground. In one corner is an old roll of carpet matted into a single grey heap that she has never dared move in case she dislodges a rat's nest. There is also one shoe there and some twisted empty cans. Broken glass. A hairbrush. All the same stuff as when she was last here in early September. A whole term ago.

She plays some music on her phone and with cold hands Melanie begins to make a joint. When it is rolled and licked and twisted she lights the end and takes a hit. She calls the dog over and scratches behind his ears until he wanders off to urinate on the carpet. She plays with the lighter wheel. She flicks it so that the flint shoots sparks. She stands and stretches and then leans in the doorway.

From here the hamlet below seems impossibly small. Drawn down to miniature. It is nothing more than a cluster that could fit into the grounds of her school three times over though of course she understands that it isn't the hamlet that is shrinking but she who is growing.

Once it was her entire world but Melanie Muncy knows that soon she will be too big for this backwater entirely.

She takes the smoke into her lungs and lets the feeling of it wash over her body. Through her. She feels her eyelids drop. She feels that anxious flutter inside of her finally slow to a manageable thrum. She breathes out and lets the smoke take her tension with it.

She imagines it floating high above the valley. Her tension released as smoke like a grey swan silently rising.

HE WALKS THE old Corpse Road. No map marks it as that but that's what the locals call it. The Corpse Road.

It is the long back walk up from town where coffins would be dragged from the coffin-makers to be buried in plots on the tiny hillside cemetery that is now grown over so infrequent is its use.

The rocks are frosting and the sky is coming in. It has that weighted feeling like it cannot hold its snow for long. A dusting is already circulating and there'll be a heavy fall by sunset. He walks slowly.

Up ahead beyond his house wind turbines spin on the valley's crest. Their blades thrash at the sky.

He picks his way along the top path through the trees. He walks a hundred feet or more above the glistening levels of the river and the slow pools that form as it drops down a series of elongated shelves. There are six falls of varying heights along this stretch and each sounds different. His ears are long since tuned to the wavelengths of the upper end of the dale and now he can recognise each waterfall with his eyes closed.

There are trout in the pools. Over the years he has fished them all. Not for a while but. Not for half a lifetime but. There are strange associations with fishing since the last time. Memories of the place have become polluted.

He peaks the valley and walks the final mile or so along the moor-edge. It's easier than clambering across the rocks that have fallen down the gorge to the gill or scrambling the slippy dirt banks of the wood.

He comes out of the trees and walks up a ways then is out in the open amongst the stiff heather and blackened soil. It's like pushing up through the clouds into a purer more rarefied atmosphere.

The snow is circulating in spirals of light dust that falls to dot the ground; an advance party for what is to follow.

Up top the moors are punctuated by irregular scars. They are half-healed wounds that reveal the bedrock and clay that lie beneath the skin of the earth. They are the negative imprints of houses down in the hamlet built from the rock that has been mined and hewn and dragged and shaped from these gaping holes.

They exist unseen from any distance as the moorland

heather around them suddenly plunges away to nothing. Their sides steep and treacherous like waterless tarns or quarries reclaimed by nature. The scars are not signposted. There is no wayfinding for the walkers. They are obscure and occasionally dangerous relics from the industrial past. Hidden worlds. Subterranean.

Trees grow in some of these excavations and in places large fallen boulders lie where they have landed when the shifting of the soil and slurry has unearthed them during the wet months. Rocks the size of cars or larger are set in moss. Rooted and immoveable. Sunken and sculptural.

It is always silent in these many basins. Some do not see people for months or years. In the absence of human disturbance it is the rabbits that have taken up residence. Scores of them in each scar their complex warrens running wide and deep. They are not threatened by humans because they have never seen humans. In others – in the bigger excavations – there are deer and foxes and badgers too and many birds nesting in the steep rock sides around the jagged rim.

Even in winter the wind barely penetrates these remote amphitheatres.

The biggest is his favourite. It is so big it has a name: Acre Dale Scar. That sits further along. A mile past his house up the back way. He will not pass it today.

Acre Dale is its own world. A sunken forest supporting its own infrastructure and hierarchy of animals; its own wet and windless climate.

A child died in one of the base pools there. Years back. Since then it has been fenced off and condemned. Hewn and plundered then abandoned. A doomed space. In his mind he has assumed ownership. He treats it as his place alone. His barren fiefdom.

He cuts through the heather of the moor-lip and sees the

chimney of the house as if it is protruding from the stiff earth. A shape against the sky. Home.

Then the sky can no longer hold itself and the snow falls and lays thick. White on black filling in the gaps. He walks towards it.

ON BRINDLE'S DESK there is: a MacBook and a bottle of water that he fills every morning at home with filtered water to avoid the dusty-tasting water from the office cooler. There is a box of tissues. There is a Tupperware tub containing dried apricots dried cranberries dried pineapple goji berries banana chips macadamia nuts cashew nuts peanuts raisins sultanas and shavings of dried coconut. There is a yellow legal notepad. A phone and charger. And there is a framed photo of a kitten in a wellington boot given to him as a joke by his colleagues on his last birthday.

He always assumed it was meant as a wry dig at his contempt for sentimentality and a counterpoint to the brutality of the case he was working on at the time – that of a rhubarb-picking Pole who had put his slicing knife through the throat of a colleague before going home and doing the same to his wife and child. The press had erroneously dubbed him the Rhubarb Killer and though for James Brindle there was no case at all the sight of the wife and especially the child – a girl – punctured like a mongrel puppy's cheap rubber toy had stayed with him for a long time. The Pole got life and survived three years in Monster Mansion before some of the younger lads got to him with the boiling sugar-water and then with an HMP shiv. The Rhubarb Killer never saw Katowice again.

Brindle finds himself inadvertently looking at the photo of the kitten in the wellington boot quite often.

From his desk in the corner of Cold Storage Brindle can see across the rooftops of the adjacent warehouses. The way the early spring sun beams down and reflects on their corrugated roofs makes them look like a series of rippling swimming pools. Rectangular pools filled with mercury. Sometimes he imagines stepping into one of those imaginary bodies of water and never resurfacing.

The new detective culture now is one of sparseness and minimalism. Lots of light and clean straight lines. Open-plan spaces to encourage communication and quickness of mind.

Cold Storage as it is dubbed is discreetly tucked away in a vast business park. It is not like other police departments. This is no red-brick post-war village building or vast municipal behemoth. It is at the vanguard of policing and its anonymity and obscure positioning is wholly deliberate; its exterior reveals nothing about the building's contents. The architecture is vehemently twenty-first century – a projection of ideals manifested in tinted windows and syphonic drainage and a temperature-controlled climate plus well-maintained common green spaces. A manmade lake has been dug in to provide a tranquil ambience and there is enough parking to ensure that no worker need stray more than ten paces from the designated building's entrance to ensure maximum productivity. There is a nearby gymnasium whose interior Brindle has never seen though from the outside he has watched the faceless shadows of bodies on treadmills flattened beneath opaque glass and ghostlike forms lunging and shadow-boxing. Apparitions fighting themselves.

The adjoining organisations are similarly enigmatic and low-key. Here companies called Plexus and Remit and Forward do business.

The correctness and uniformity of his everyday surroundings should appeal to Brindle. Sparse surfaces should be soothing to him; should put him at ease. Yet somehow for reasons he has not yet determined it does not.

Increasingly nothing does.

THAT FIRST DAY after his transfer James Brindle made sure he took a corner desk which he has now surreptitiously positioned in such a way that the towers of empty box-files form a sort of wall to keep his colleagues out. He does not want to encourage undue interaction. That might be the Cold Storage way but it is not his way.

Brindle's drawers are full of print-outs. He likes to file copies of all correspondence and keep notes on everything. Everything. He files and he stores and he cross-references continuously. He has a complex system that involves colour codes and marker pens. Every case every conversation. Documented. Every scrap every suspicion every statement. Recorded. Every journey every receipt. Every crumb consumed. Secretly he calls them his Archives of Everything.

And they call the emerging department Cold Storage because this is where the bodies go. Or the memories of them anyway. Those trapped in that silent vortex somewhere between murder and justice. Here their bodies have been replaced by – or reduced to – open files. Missing persons. They are piles of paper now; they are the odd photograph or photocopied bank statement. They are notable by their absence. They are gaps in the lives of those living left behind.

Cold Storage for cold cases. These are the people who have upped and left under suspicious circumstances. Those whose trails are scant. The gone.

Sometimes there are bodies but only the bloodiest ones. And when there are the Cold Storage detectives retrace the steps from death back into life. They walk backwards from tragedy through the strange lives of these people. They start at the final breath and end at their birth and somewhere along the way they find out where it all went wrong.

They are at the centre of that great unseen grid of national policing information and in years to come history will view Cold Storage's creation as a leap forward in information-gathering and modern British policing.

This is what they are told anyway.

He keeps his work-surface spotless. Just because the world exists in a state of chaos it does not mean that he has to. A small amount of order imposed is the best that he can strive for – that and closed cases. Cracked cases. Concluded cases. This is James Brindle's philosophy: to bring order and conclusion and justice for those that lie forgotten in files by all but those few who work here; those who have excelled in their different departments and have now been shipped in to improve the statistics. Those detectives tasked with solving those cases once deemed high-profile enough for a co-headliner slot on the evening news but have now been left to fester. Sudden disappearances. Kids. The unexplained and inexplicable.

Big cases like these need big men. Stone-turners and stat men. Dirt-diggers. The emotionally stunted. The obsessives. The spectrum-dwellers. The pragmatists. The scientists of crime with the brilliant minds. Those who fail at everything in life except detective work.

Brindle knows this. They all know this. In Cold Storage they revel in their outlier status and do little to dispel the myths surrounding those that exist on the periphery of the police force.

THE SNOW CAPTURES the deer tracks. It marks them out. It finds evidence. Leaves a trail.

The snow makes it harder for them to hide on the open hillsides. The snow is the hunter's ally.

Against snow all things dark become vulnerable.

More has fallen in the night and the first layer has packed down to a hard crust with another layer of powder sitting on top.

It is still dark when he sets out.

He eats a bowl of porridge and then makes a pack-up of bread and cheese. Oatcakes. Banana. He cleans and oils his rifle.

He throws a couple of stiff rabbits to the dogs on the way out. They're shivering in their nest of straw.

The dogs are too noisy for where he is going. The dogs never stand still always fussing. They get a scent and they're gone. No. They'll stop at home today.

He leaves the back way. Leaves his home. Past the pens and the stone sheds; past the old grain store and the pig sheds and the chicken coop and the barn that has no roof.

He hoofs the back gate open. It was makeshift twenty years; now it is a distorted lattice of rotting wood hanging on one rusted hinge. Symbolic rather than functional.

Then he is straight up onto the slopes below the moor where the wind turbines watch over the farm and cast it in ever-shifting shadows and the hum of them penetrates his sleep.

He bears left. His rifle is held across his chest by his backpack straps. He walks up the narrowing valley. Up into the throat of it.

After a mile or so he comes to the first concrete drain.

There are a dozen of them dotted in a wide circumference all around the moor edge a mile or so apart. They sit below the reservoir. Gaping grey concrete orifices built into the hillside. Some of the locals call them the portals; an ominous name already woven into the mythology of the upper valley.

Each is a doorway beneath a curved concrete carapace. Concrete steps climb down into the stiff Yorkshire peat at a diagonal then take a turn into dank dark corridors that lead to the covered metal grids of the underground culverts. They were installed with the reservoir to act as run-offs for the conduits that are buried deep beneath the moor. In the event of flooding their purpose is to drain the reservoir overflow away from the flat moor-tops that surround the body of water. Unseen these swelling pools are then filtered away via a complex network of channels to join streams and rivers miles further down the dale.

In spring and autumn when the rainfall is at its most persistent hard copper-coloured water runs through the channels and rises up through the culverts and then the entrances to the portals overflow with brackish peat-heavy water and thick silt. It washes up the steps and then runs in rivulets and streams and channels down the valley sides to join the river at the flat base. Gravity takes care of the rest.

The portals are not for public access. During the first few years that they were open local kids would dare each other to descend the darkening steps and wade through the stagnant water that sits shallow on the floor taking care not to cut their legs on the twisted strips of metal and rocks that lay beneath. Inevitably accidents happened. Parents became more protective. Now fewer children wander the fells or moors or build camps in the scars or makeshift houses up trees in copses. They have been scared off by fearful adults glad that their kids prefer the safety of their televisions and computers.

So the portals are closed off to the world now. Condemned. Gated. Sealed off locked up shut down. Still in use but inaccessible. Signs warn of DANGER and PRIVATE PROPERTY KEEP OUT.

Now dawn snow has gathered in drifts. It has blown in to block up these dark toothless mouths and inside the stagnant water has frozen over and mineral deposits have formed the beginnings of small stalactites on the stone ceilings as the moor tightens around them like the skin of a drum.

The soil has frozen too and the gaping mouths seem to purse and close a little.

The man passes the first drain. He views himself as if from a mile away and feels what he is: a tiny figure moving sideways against a great canvas. The gate is padlocked and drift-blocked. He sees a length of timber poking through the ice that covers the drain floor. Beyond that – darkness.

A mile later he passes the next one.

WHEN SHE HAS finished smoking and put the butt of the joint back in her tin – she once read that a cigarette end can take something like six hundred years to rot away – Melanie Muncy makes snowballs and rolls them down the field for the dog to chase. He throws himself down the slopes and then runs back wide-eyed and panting for more.

Her mouth is dry so she scoops up more snow and sucks on it until her tongue and cheeks go numb.

She does not want to return to the silence of the house and her mother sitting there being weird and saying random things or sometimes not saying anything at all. She wonders whether it is the new medication she has been prescribed or just further disintegration. Nor can she handle her father's mock sincerity – the permanent smile that is plastered on his face but which fails to hide the tightness of his jaw and the desperation in his eyes.

When she is at school she misses the dog and she misses these open spaces but she does not miss her parents. Where once she was alone and without siblings she now has friends and allies. People who have actually grown up around other functioning humans rather than animals and anguished unwashed farmers. They can hold conversations that aren't about the weather.

And she has civilisation on her doorstep now rather than a walk and then a bus ride and then a train journey away. Beyond the classroom there are shops and pubs and boys and drugs and music to keep her occupied. Being sent to board was the best thing her parents did for her. They gave her freedom.

Melanie Muncy leaves the bothy and decides to walk off the shadowed remains of her anxiety. She wants to enjoy the high as she has ten whole days here with only a small amount of the hash left. She can't even think about spending new year with her parents.

She leaves the field and takes the track uphill. The dog runs up ahead. The sky is almost as white as the land. There will be more snow later. It is certainly cold enough. The roads up from town will harden and ice over and the drifts will freeze and people won't be able to get in or out of the hamlet without a snowplough to clear the route.

She will be stuck here. Snowed in – and not for the first time. She will be going nowhere but on foot for the coming days.

Melanie Muncy has a feeling she will be taking the dog out for a lot of walks.

HE CONTINUES UP top. Past the end of the reservoir and onto the moor before he circles down and round to the edge of Acre Dale Scar.

There were always deer round that way and often in groups. Whole families of them. The buck and the doe and their fawns. They are solitary creatures but in winter they tended to band together. In his lifetime he's seen all kinds around here.

He has seen roe deer. Red deer too. He once saw two great stags gouging at each other's faces in the rut.

He's bagged a few over the years. Popped most of them without them even knowing about it. Dead before they hit the ground.

It is clear and cold but the smudged figure against the landscape doesn't feel it. He has his farmer's layers on. Long johns vest t-shirt shirt padded shirt. A beanie on top. The walking keeps him warm.

As he approaches Acre Dale he stops. The incline leading

down to it is covered in untouched snow before dropping away to a vast hole in the moor edge. A chunk bitten from the spine of the valley. Some of the quarried holes are no bigger than fifty feet across but Acre Dale is a good half-mile at its narrowest point and even longer lengthwise. Deep too. A hundred maybe even a hundred and fifty feet below land-level.

Tracks worn by the footfall of dog walkers and ramblers lead around the rim of Acre Dale but none enter it. He follows one to an escarpment that gives him a view down the rocks and mudslides into the trees below.

He rubs some snow away and lays flat on his belly looking down into the great wooded cavity.

Here he waits and watches and feels the cold permeating his knees his chest and his elbows.

Without leaves on the trees visibility is much better in winter and he can see right through that which in summer will be a dense canopy and provide cover for the creatures.

Fallen trunks half-rotted now lie frozen at angles and the branches reach out to one another. They are bare bones clasping desperately in fleeting connections. He sees two plump squirrels scurry across a limb. Their backs are arched and their bellies distended as they cross Acre Dale without touching ground. As a boy he would pop them for fun. For fur. But not now. Now they are too easy; they are too obvious. Now he seeks something bigger. A more noble kill.

HE WALKS FURTHER around the edge of the quarry to where the moors slip away and trees grow out of the cliff face and the large supplanted boulders of many decades' rock-fall sit way down below.

He climbs down through the brittle frosted furze. The bank levels out. He slips on the hard ground.

He takes his pack off his back and slots his rifle through the flap then finds a stout stick to help his balance. He digs it into the soil.

He is below the treeline now. He is on the prowl and in his element.

He sees frozen prints: the clear markings of a two-toed ungulate. He squats and examines them. He looks left and he looks right. The tracks follow a line through the rotten leaves. A path. It goes uphill one way and downhill towards the bottom of the scar the other.

The tracks overlap and are of different sizes. These are the prints of more than one animal.

He takes the deer-run down the slope and spots more clear signs: a snag of fur. A nibbled bud. A broken branch with its papery bark scratched and stripped. The deer are near. He knows. Senses it.

Above him there is a small bluff comprised of a series of stalled boulders where the smaller rocks have come to rest against the larger ones when caught mid fall.

He cuts back uphill and climbs out onto the rocks. He removes his gun from his straps and takes a tarp from his pack. He puts the tarp down and then rolls himself in it and lays on the slab of rock. He settles in he settles on he settles down. Turns himself into a statue and lets his mind drift.

IT APPEARS AS a solitary roe; a reward for his patience.

It has wandered up out of the trees and onto the open heath. Right onto the path below. It is unwitting it is unknowing it is in his sights.

He inhales. Holds.

Then: a gentle squeeze and a crack and a slow slump.

Legs folding head bowing eyes glazing. Crumpled.

He exhales.

Now it is his. The bullet has made it so. The bullet exchanged ownership of the deer from the woods to him. Death is the currency. It is something to sell to a man in the

Dales who pays money and asks no questions but for the time of the kill and can you get any more? A man who knows what to do with death. How to deal with it. A cold man of the countryside. A man a little like him in fact. Discreet and deft and quiet and part of a chain of events where life and death are muted by grey areas. It's living off the land. The way it has always been.

There is no morality in dead meat but there is new life when consumed. It is a magic of sorts – that a dead creature can fuel a man. Feed a family. Fill a freezer.

It is hit in the neck and the bullet has severed major arteries and stopped the heart in seconds. A nice clean drop.

The man sees that it is male. He sees the stubbed beginnings of antlers flowering through its scalp like fossilised blossom. Its fur is in good condition too: smooth and glistening and so shiny it appears wet. The deer's dark face placid. At peace.

A narrow chimney of steam rises from the wound.

He checks the gums and the teeth and finds them to be straight and clean and good and strong. He feels around and finds jagged canines. He is glad it is a roe – the smallest of the deer to be found round here. Yet still it will be heavy to carry back. He looks at it for a moment and weighs it with his eyes and then he decides to dress it where it has fallen. He folds out his tarp and lays the deer on it. He takes a machete and a field knife from his backpack. Then he rolls a cigarette and smokes it. When he has finished smoking he draws up the sleeves of his padded shirt and takes a paring knife and he makes three incisions in the creature's lower abdomen.

He draws first through fur then meat and then he sees the intestines coiled like a beautiful puzzle. He turns the knife around and folds out a gut hook from the end of it. He puts the hook into the incision then guides it up the creature's belly splitting fur and skin and meat and membrane along the way.

A new world opens up. The creature steams. He feels its warmth on his face. The final plumes of life escaping like a sorrowful exhalation. The intestines bulge. He marvels at the economy of space and nature's engineering.

He severs through fat and grey sinew. He lifts the hot intestines in one hand and cuts around and beneath them then puts the blade down and pulls the bloody balloon of guts out. It flops beside him on the tarpaulin. An amorphous thing like a pillow full of blood. A drowned accordion.

It is still early. It is colder today. Later there will be more snow.

He moves around the carcass and then crouches and reaches into the back of the cavity and takes the blade to its oesophagus.

He feels like climbing inside it and staying there for the winter.

He tugs at the oesophagus and pulls it free.

The deer is gutted.

He stands and stretches and catches his breath. Then he takes the machete and begins to work on removing the creature's head and limbs. He'll only take the best parts for himself – the choice cuts – those he can hang and cure and dry or cook. The four leg primals: the rump and the topside. The silverside and the knuckle. He's after the shortloin the tenderloin the striploin. The ribrack and double chop too if he can get a clean cut on them. Poacher's privilege. He packs what he can carry on his back and caches the rest for later. And that is when he sees her: a solitary smudged figure against the wash of sunless sky.

He ducks out of sight and ditches his cargo and then leopard-crawls through the heather. Through the snow. Stays low. Stops. Raises his head. Sees here again. She is closer this time and her back is to him.

He has seen her face grow towards maturity but always

from a distance just as he views her now; unseen and unknown. To her a man like him would be invisible. He has seen her become a little princess. Her father's greatest achievement.

But she has come too early. She should not be up here on the moor just yet. Not today.

And then suddenly there is a streak of colour and a dog is lunging at him from nowhere. Barking. Lips peeled back and stained teeth flashing. It is wide-eyed. The man hears the snap of its terrier jaws. He leans forward. Raises a blood-smeared backhand and shoos it. *Geeit.* Shoos it again. It lunges for his wrist and finds a cuff. Snags on it and shakes it as if his arm were a creature caught. A neck to be snapped or back to be broken. He swings wide and tries to fling it away but the dog locks on harder now. It finds the bone angle where hand joins arm. Where the skin is thin. Teeth puncturing. Teeth finding flesh and something beyond it. Agony. Jolts of electricity up his arm. Like nothing he has felt. His arm and shoulder and neck are screaming.

There's something viscous beneath him and around him and under him and his hand is grabbing out at the sheath on his belt in desperation now and when it finds what it wants what he needs – what he desperately needs – he slips out his knife and he swings it but mainly he slices air as the dog holds fast but then suddenly she arrives from nowhere. The girl nearly stumbling upon him nearly stumbling into him nearly stumbling over him.

She is wearing headphones. Big headphones that look life ear muffs. She sees him before she hears him. Sees a blood-smeared man with a knife. Bent double like a hideous troll. A golem of the hills. The dog has let go and is rearing up. It is part of this grim tableau. The girl gasps and reels and then she screams and she doesn't stop screaming.

This is not what he intended he thinks. She's spoiling it all he thinks.

The girl falls silent and she is gasping for breath and her breath is a hot plume and it's like she is biting chunks from the air but only for a moment because then she screams again and she sounds strangulated and this was not how he planned it he thinks. No. Not this way.

He scrambles. He scrambles backwards. He slips and flails.

He leaps up and says *shhh* it's OK but her eyes are wide with horror and there's blood on the snow and his heart is thumping in his ears and the moor is a wide and white frozen plane and the knife is in his hand.

And the girl. Between short gulps of air she just won't stop screaming.

He reaches for her he lunges at her he says *shhh* it's OK stop your screaming but she doesn't she won't she can't so he tries to clamp a hand over her mouth but she stumbles and he stumbles and they both stumble falling backwards into the snow as he covers her as he squashes her as he flattens her as he enfolds her.

For a moment they are eye to eye and around them there's blood on the snow. Deer blood or dog blood. His blood or her blood. And then like her dog the girl bites his hand and he strikes her.

He strikes her and he strikes her. And this was not how he planned it. Not how he planned it all.

And then there's more blood on the snow.

His blood.

Her blood.

And he hits her and he hits her again. He thinks: snow ice flesh fist bones hair legs spread cold beasts breasts blood bite eat hold touch kiss love mother oil men shit bruise burst.

The snow. It's white.

And he strikes her.

The blood. It's red.

And he strokes her.
Strikes her.
Strokes her.
Then silence.

THE EVENING DARKNESS brings phonecalls. Ray Muncy is loath to call the local force in but his daughter has been gone eight hours now and her phone is going straight to voicemail and there is no sign of the dog and it is winter. The temperature is dropping further and the forecast is not in their favour. He knows the landscape up there; knows the snow can blanket its pitfalls. It can create bear traps out of frozen bogs and stretch time and distance into new shapes. It is a moor of quarries and shafts and endless heather – a place scarred by early industry and shot through with secrets. From the old industries of pick-axe and dynamite; of slate sheets and ugly stone. The secrets of deceits and trysts and lies and mistakes.

Only rabbits and hawks and deer and mice thrive there now.

And she knows the place too – Melanie. That's what worries him. That she knows it well yet still has not returned. It is not like her.

So the town force sends up some of the lads; Roy Pinder's lot.

They arrive with torches and boots and flak jackets. Three of them. They do not seem in a hurry and they do not have a plan. They ask for tea from Ray Muncy and he says no bloody tea my girl is missing what are you asking me for tea for? They shrug and one of them produces a hip flask and they swig from it and Ray Muncy says is that even allowed? and one of them – PC Jeff Temple – says yes it's bloody allowed. Round here it's allowed. You should know that.

Then they search the moors together. Muncy and the three policemen. It is up to him to suggest that they fan out and be methodical about this – that they hold the line while they sweep certain sections of the moor in turn. They do this but they see nothing. Ray takes one end of the line and he shouts out his daughter's name and he whistles for the dog and he scours the snow with his high-beam torch and he wonders what is so funny to cause the policemen to laugh on a subzero night during the search for a missing teenage girl. He can hear them. They are not holding the line. The hip flask is out again. The local lads are passing it. The local lads. The boys. And him. Ray Muncy. On the end on the outside holding the line. Alone and apart. Not a part of it.

SOMETIMES SHE WOULD stick him in the chicken coop. His mother. That's what she'd do. The chicken coop. Enclosed.

Only now is he beginning to learn that it all started in the coop. Before the cinema before the girls before the shovelling of shit and the school-yard fists. Before all of that the journey started there.

Shoved him in when she was entertaining she did. In the big one. Stick him in there when she was having one of her special parties. One of Black Tits' legendary all-nighters. Because that's what they called her. The men. Black Tits. Or sometimes just Tits. Behind her back.

It came from a rumour that had long passed into valley mythology.

A man – then a boy – had been up at the farm one day running an errand. Fetching eggs for his father. This was when the place was a working farm a good farm a proper operation with produce and life; a place of growing and cropping; of birthing breeding and slaughtering.

There was no answer when he knocked on the door and no one out back either. No sign of anyone round any of the outbuildings so he walked to the front window and there he saw her with her top off having herself a wash in front of the fire.

A whore's bath. And where her big sagging breasts sat on her chest there was a crust of grime. Two dark smiles of farm scum. Black tits.

Stories stick. And so:

Black Tits was born.

It didn't put the men off though. No. She was known to give it away cheap. A barrow of coal or a half-tank of diesel or some shoes for the boy and she was anyone's. Maybe just a ride home from town. Cheap at half the price.

One two three at a time. She could take all-comers. His mother. Up in the quarry or out the back in one of the barns. They'd gather round and then she'd do them in turn or all at the same time. Made no difference to her. Any which way for Black Tits.

Black Tits who would put her son in a box with the beasts when she wanted him out of the house for a while. When his watching eyes weren't required. Get in with them peckers she would say and then shove him down one end with the green shit and the feathers and the constant flapping. Just boot him in there and lock the gate and leave the lad with the commotion.

Then when the birds had calmed down he'd get himself under the ramp slide beneath the chicken walk and put his sleeve to his nose to mask the acrid ammonia stench and he would curl up. His eyes closed his fists balls his lips locked.

And then they would arrive. He would hear them. First their engines down the valley and then the raising of voices. Voices of men climbing out of cars and down from flatbeds. The odd tractor. Some came on foot.

They would scrub themselves sore and bring food and booze. Starched shirts and work boots buffed with spittle. Made a night of it some of them. Made a weekend of it sometimes.

They would roll up with their plastic containers of cider and home-brew beer and their sides of ham and their cartons of cigarettes and they'd turn it into a party. Four men six men eight men more men.

Men from across the Dales.

Farmhands. Pickers and.balers. Quarry men. Pig men. Married men single men old men. Young men too.

And boys he recognised from his school. Bigger boys. Three four five years above him but still young themselves.

He grew to hate those chickens.

He hated their twitching ducking heads those pink blank eyes staring at him and their beaks blunt from pecking at ground and gravel. Beady-eyed and endlessly clucking. Stupid bloody things.

And still more cars and trucks and tractors would arrive. More doors slamming. Men sharing greetings with long lost friends.

Old men young men. Plastic jugs and glass cider bottles clinking. Smoke and laughter. Throat oysters spat into the yard.

Pissing up the barn doors.

She'd go all night and right through to morning. His mother.

Four men six men eight men. Drovers and diggers and dairy men.

Lined up laughing. Drunk and ready.

Get to the back of the line you. Right. Who's next?

And the next day there would be meat and there would be milk and there would be logs and money for school dinner and empty plastic jugs of cider placed around the house and empty beer bottles and hay for the horse – plenty of hay – and his mother would be laid up all day resting in silence sore and spent and he – he would have to do even more of the slopping out and the fetching of water and the gathering of eggs and the whole lot of it. The smudges of pecker shit still on his jumper and the feathers of those stupid twitching creatures jammed in his hair and the yard pitted and churned from the tyres of all that heavy machinery. All that coming and going and coming.

IT'S A GIRL. Missing. A teenager.

Brindle's heart sinks when he's briefed by Chief Superintendent Alan Tate. Great. Another spoiled little runaway pissed off because her pocket money's been stopped. He already knows how these play out. These are not murder cases. He should not be having to deal with cases like this one. Not Brindle. Not him. He knows he's better than these cases knows he's wasted on these cases doesn't care about these cases.

Tate is at his desk but he's refusing to look up from his laptop.

Where? he says.

Tate passes him the call sheet. Brindle's hand receives it.

Way up in the Dales. Last seen heading towards the moors.

Not my jurisdiction.

You're Cold Storage. You don't have jurisdiction.

Brindle looks at the sheet and sighs.

Where in the Dales?

What does it matter where in the Dales? The Dales. The backwoods. It's all the same up there. Sheep shit and rain. We've been called in and I'm sending you. That's all you need to know.

Brindle considers Tate but says nothing.

Look says his superior. You have to take the meat and potatoes from time to time. I know you like wading waist-deep through blood but it can't all be high-profile headless torsos and dead minor celebrities you know. Even for you.

Brindle had been a strange child and not because of the birthmark. Darkness had fascinated him. He liked to draw the curtains and read by torchlight. Crime and horror and detective stories mainly. But especially true crime. While others read sci-fi comics or fantasy stories if they read at all by his teenage years James Brindle had read all the books on the Ripper and the Black Panther and the Moors Murderers; he had read the cuttings about Hannibal the Cannibal and

Dennis Nilsen and the Acid-bath Murderer and the Railway Killers. All of them. These were the myths of Britain; the folk crimes from the dark side. Secrets unearthed.

I know that says Brindle. But it'll be a waste of time this one.

You don't know that.

I have a nose for it.

You're not too good to take the simple cases.

Cold Storage was built for this?

James Brindle flaps the sheet at his boss.

Cold Storage was built to solve crimes more quickly and efficiently and whenever necessary by utilising the most up-to-date technologies says Tate. Twenty-first century detective work. You know that. We're the privileged pricks who everyone else hates. Or do I have to personally flatter you to get this done? Do I need to tell you one more time that Cold Storage is only for the best of the best and James Brindle is top of the pile the man to watch the one they're tipping for the top – is that what you want? More smoke up your anally retentive hole? I'm not sure I can fit any more up there.

Brindle looks at the sheet.

She's a runaway.

So find her then. What are you afraid of – mud?

You should send a uniform out on this because it isn't murder. This is not the type of case I work.

Look says Tate. I just need you to get up there and check out the lay of the land. It's one day. Two tops. Find the girl wherever she is and let's get this all wrapped up so that her parents know whether to prepare for a happy Christmas homecoming – or the worst they'll ever know. You'll get a gold star for effort and a nice juicy corpse case as a new-year reward.

Now?

Yes now.

LATER AT HOME Brindle lifts up the final lid and carefully places it on the container of cooling steamed rice and vegetables and presses it into place. He puts it on top of the others in the bag. He reaches into the fridge and takes out two bottles of distilled water and puts them into the bag too. From the cupboard he reaches for packets of dried fruits – cranberries and raisins and apricots – and cradles them in the crook of his arm as he pauses frowning for a moment and then he opens another cupboard and takes out a packet of Earl Grey tea and a spherical metal strainer. A small tea glass. His spoon – the same spoon he has used since he was a student; the spoon he has to use otherwise the tea might poison him or his car might crash or the world might end in great eruptions of molten lava followed by disease and pestilence.

Brindle wraps them in newspaper and then adds them to the bag. He pats them down to make sure they cannot fall and break.

The remnants of the soy milk that is in a carton in the fridge he pours into the sink and then turns the tap on to swill it away. There are vegetables in there too. Broccoli and asparagus. Sweet potatoes. They should keep. He lifts his plants from the window sill and places them in the sink. He waters them.

Brindle goes into his bedroom and stands in the doorway. He looks at everything and then he turns the light off and then he turns it on and then he turns it off again. He does this eight times. An even number. Has to be even. Even is solid even is divisible even has corners and straight lines.

He goes into the kitchen and checks that the power switch for the cooker and range is turned off. It is. He turns it on and off again to be sure. Eight times he does this. Eight is even. Even is solid even is good. Eight is good because eight plus eight is sixteen and eight times eight is sixty-four. Six plus four is ten. An even number. Good. Solid. Good.

He takes the bag with the food and drink and puts it by the front door next to his suitcase. He does a sweep of the downstairs. He quickly checks each room though for what he is not sure. Irregularities perhaps. Oversights. He moves through the rooms and he feels the rooms move through him. His breath is quickening now. Outside. Soon he will be outside.

He returns to the front door and opens it and he sees outside but he decides to check the cooker one more time. He clicks the light switch eight times and then makes sure the tap is off. If it was left dripping and the plants were blocking the plug hole the room could flood. If the gas was on the whole place could blow.

If a light was left on or a curtain was folded over or a lamp tilted at the wrong angle or the television left on standby or his CDs and records not put away or his shoes not lined up in parallel lines then the entire universe would be in disarray. And if he never returned what would this space left behind say about him in his absence?

Brindle walks to the front door and surveys the hallway.

He will be back tomorrow.

Brindle leaves.

2

THERE IS BANGING. There is footfall and voices out back.

Someone is shouting his name.

Rutter. Are you in there Steven Rutter?

He's upstairs. He looks down and sees someone cupping a hand to his back kitchen window and looking in. He sees only the one person but hears other voices. A mumbling. His name being said again: Steven Rutter. It sounds alien to him – like they are looking for someone else; someone from his past who he once vaguely knew.

He walks downstairs and opens the door. His rifle is in his hand.

Well you can put that away for a start.

It's his nearest neighbour. Ray bloody Muncy. Muncy and a policeman in a hi-vis patrol jacket.

Steven Rutter? asks the policeman.

Of course it's Steve Rutter says Muncy.

What do you want?

For you to put that gun down.

Alright.

Rutter turns and leans the gun against the door frame.

I'm PC Temple says the policeman and I only hope for your sake that you've got registration for that.

He's alright Jeff says Muncy – that gun's as old as these hills. Look at it. He's had it since he was a kid. Then to Rutter he says: it's our Melanie. She's missing. Have you seen her?

Rutter shakes his head.

You've not seen her out and about on your walks. With the dog like. Up top maybe?

No.

Have you been out today? says Temple.

Aye.

Where?

Rutter shrugs.

Sorting the peckers mainly.

The policeman is peering into the house.

Peckers?

He means chickens says Muncy.

Live here alone do you? asks the policeman.

Of course he does says Muncy. You know he does. It's Rutter.

I was asking him.

Aye says Rutter.

You'll not mind if we have a look around.

Rutter shrugs again then steps aside.

Temple comes in. He stops to look at the gun. He touches it lightly and then steps into the kitchen and is followed by Muncy.

Listen – she's been gone all day Steve says Muncy. You know I wouldn't come up here if it wasn't serious. It's just not like her. I'm bloody worried.

Am I under suspicion? says Rutter.

Under suspicion says Temple. For what?

Whatever it is you're suspecting.

Who says we're suspecting. Are you always this cagey? Is he always this cagey Ray?

They're sending someone up Muncy says to Rutter. From the city.

So what do you need me for?

They are in the kitchen now. The policeman looks to the top corner of the room.

What's that – is that a bird's nest?

Rutter nods.

Indoors?

Aye says Rutter. A wren.

It's nesting indoors.

Aye that's what I said.

Well how does it get in and out?

Rutter points.

She comes in through the top of the door. Where it's all rotted like.

Temple turns and looks at the back door.

And you don't mind?

Why would I mind?

Shitting everywhere like that says the policeman as much to himself as anyone.

Rutter's top lip twitches at one corner but he says nothing.

Temple shakes his head and mutters Christ and then walks down the passage and into the front room. He has to stoop to mind his head catching the thick stone lintel above the doorless doorway. Rutter follows then Muncy. The policeman walks to the window and wipes a finger through the grime.

Nice view I'd bet.

Rutter says nothing.

I bet you can see your place from here Ray. In daylight. Through clean windows. God man it stinks in here.

THE SKELETON STAFF are unsure of their roles.

Usually they are defined but not enough drink has been consumed yet for their workplace inhibitions to have been shed and boundaries to become blurred but just enough of the cheap wine has gone down for ties to have been loosened and the radio turned up. The incidents of future regret will come later in the evening.

It is the festive season. The office party for a dwindling workforce demoralised by the slashed budgets for a dying medium.

There are too few of them left for festering grudges or

distant flirtations to bubble up to the surface because the *Valley Mercury* is a newspaper struggling and save for the remaining half-dozen staff the team has been reduced to part-timers passing through. Subs and designers mainly. A production crew comprised of a desperate graduate and two old-timers returning from retirement after careers on Women's Institute newsletters or the National Trust members' magazine or the free news-sheets the postmen are paid to shove crumpled through letterboxes. Most of them don't even live in the valley. They drive in from far-flung suburbs and recently they have even had interns filing pages to the repro house. The old bonds are no longer there and the medium is dying; paper they whisper is pointless.

They have gone to print an hour early today. The annual Christmas party – four boxes of warm wine and cheese sticks; Classic FM on the radio – has started. Dennis Grogan has dipped into petty cash especially.

December the 22nd.

Across the office a phone rings. Production editor Anne Byron answers it then holds it aloft. Looks around the room.

Roddy. I'd say this one is for you.

What is it?

A potential something or other.

He sighs and mutters: fucksake.

When London had turned sour Roddy Mace had scoured the job market. Fired off his CV to dozens of papers and decided to take whatever came up first. *If* anything came up.

He got offered a staff job in the upper Dales; a surprise posting in a far-flung market town. Apparently experience on a tabloid still counted for something. Had he even heard of the place? He can no longer remember. What he did know: the wage that the *Valley Mercury* paid was only half of what he was used to in London but so was the rent and – he hoped – the pressure.

Fresh air. That's what he needed. Easy work.

The job and the Soho scene had wrecked him within eighteen months. Left him in tatters. London had been ruthlessly efficient in its near-destruction of both body and mind and this move he reasoned would be a holiday from life – from himself. Sobriety and fewer sexual encounters would be refreshing and it would give him a chance to make headway with the novel he was writing. Yes. He would regroup and rejuvenate. Yes. Maybe disguise his past indiscretions and reinvent himself slightly. Oh yes.

London had been where he had bottomed out but up here he would get the work done during the day and work on the novel at night. Hill walks at weekends for mental clarity and physical refinement. A more wholesome existence. All of that. Put in a stint for a few months and then think about moving on. Down in the capital he was the northern oik who'd got a lucky break but up in the Dales he could be whoever he wanted to be. He would – he told himself only half-convincingly – get it together in the country and then return with all guns blazing. He was still young. He just needed the hunger to return.

He took the job and had barely looked at the novel since.

Mace took the call. He held the phone in one hand and the cheap warm wine in the other.

Hello?

Roddy?

Yes.

Les.

It was Les Bunker. One of his newfound drinking buddies in the Magnet. A roofer and fully committed broth-hound.

Les. Is everything alright?

I thought I might have a little something for you.

I'm at our Christmas party.

You're not interested in a story then?

Of course I bloody am.

I just heard that Ray Muncy's girl has gone missing.

Ray Muncy?

Yeah. He lives up the back of beyond. He's worth a packet. Used to sit on all the boards. All that shite.

I know of him.

Thinks he's about something but really he's just a bit of an arsehole. Still.

Go on says Mace.

His Melanie's gone missing and now the cops are out looking.

For how long?

Long enough to treat it as serious judging by the number of blue lights they've got up there. I'm surprised you've not seen them heading out.

I'm still in the office. How old is she?

I don't know. Fourteen or fifteen. I'm not sure. They send her away to school. She's just back for the holidays.

How long has she been gone?

Since first thing.

It's not really a story yet then is it?

Don't ask me.

How do you know all this anyway? asks Mace.

Our lass ran in to Sheila just now.

Who's she?

Sheila Laidlaw. Our lass's' cousin. She runs the Post Office up there.

And?

And nothing Roddy. That's your story. It's fucking freezing and pitch black the snow is yay deep and a wee lass has gone missing on the moors. They're got a search party going and everything – what else do you need?

You never mentioned the moors.

I'm mentioning them now.

Maybe she's got lost up there then. Gone for a wander with her boyfriend.

I doubt it Roddy. I'm no copper but people from round here don't get lost up there. That's for the mumpers and the yompers. There's been cops everywhere. Ray Muncy's going spare.

Mace sighed.

Alright Les. I appreciate you letting me know. I owe you a pint.

Or two.

Or two says Mace.

I mean she might be alright but she might turn up dead an all. You know what it's like up top when the storm sets in.

OK Les.

THERE IS ONLY one chair so they all stand. Rutter and Muncy and Temple. There are pictures on the walls. Horse brasses too. Everything is coated in dust. The fireplace is an explosion of black on the back wall. A sooted grimace. Temple's face a pious twist.

What's that smell? he says.

Rutter shrugs. The policeman turns to Muncy.

Ray – can you smell that?

Aye. It's fairly ripe.

It's vile is what it is. You can't smell that? the policeman asks again.

I can't smell owt says Rutter. No smell.

What do you mean no smell.

No sense of it.

You've no sense of smell?

Aye.

That's right says Muncy. It's true.

Temple: how come?

I took a few knocks to my head when I was a bairn says

Rutter.

What happened?

Rutter shrugs.

Different things.

Like what.

I fell out of a tree one time. Fell off a roof another. Lost me sense of smell and my hair. The hair came back. The smell stopped away.

Consider yourself lucky then because it smells like a butcher's slop-bucket in here. You need to get the place aerated.

Muncy interjects.

Look – don't fuck about Jeff. Melanie's missing.

You're sure you've not seen her? the policeman says to Rutter. About five-three. Five-four. Mousy hair.

I know what she looks like says Rutter.

Only because Ray tells me you're always lurking about and you're the person most likely to have seen something.

Lurking?

Aye. Lurking. Up there. Like a weirdo.

Rutter says nothing.

Aye says Temple. Bet he can see right into the back of yours Ray.

Maybe.

My boss Roy Pinder said you were alright but I'm not so sure.

What's it got to do with Roy Pinder? says Rutter.

Everything in the valley has got something to do with Roy Pinder says Muncy. You should know that by now.

Do you always answer the door with a gun in your hand? says the policeman.

Only when folk are knocking on it like idiots.

Go shooting do you?

It's not a crime but.

What do you shoot?

Pests.

Like what?

Owt says Rutter.

Poacher are you?

No.

Where's your bloody furniture at?

What bloody furniture?

The PC is incredulous.

What bloody furniture he says. The furniture to sit on you clot.

Rutter stiffens at this and Rutter stares. Stares back at the policeman that is in his living room.

That there chair's enough. What of it?

Looks like it's seen better days says the policeman. And so's this house.

There's nowt wrong with it.

You're off your rocker you are. He's off his nut Ray.

It's just his way Jeff. The farm's not been the same since your mother's day – that right Steve? You're not so used to minding the place on your own that's all.

Rutter shrugs and reaches for his packet of tobacco.

What about them buildings out back? says the policeman.

What about them says Rutter.

You'll not mind if we have a look around.

Do what you like.

There's a pause.

No missus? says Temple.

Rutter snorts some phlegm from his nose to the back of his throat then slowly shakes his head.

Muncy looks at his watch. Rutter looks at it too. It is large. Too big for his wrist.

Never been married? says Temple.

Rutter's eye twitches.

The valley's most eligible bachelor is it.

Rutter stares back.

What is it you *do* up here? says the policeman.

Come on Jeff says Ray Muncy. He's answered your questions – this is getting us nowhere.

Farming says Rutter. What does it look like?

What is it you farm?

Coconuts says Rutter.

Are you getting smart? Is he getting smart Ray?

I told you – it's just his way Jeff. And you are asking stupid questions.

Rutter lights his cigarette.

There's another pause. Rutter exhales smoke then speaks to the floor.

Is she seeing anyone?

What? says the policeman.

Is she seeing anyone – your girl? A lad like.

No says Muncy. Not that I know of. She's only fifteen.

You think we haven't already considered that? says the policeman. It's me that asks the questions not you Norman Bates.

Lasses can get up to all sorts says Rutter.

She's not like that says Muncy. Not our Melanie. No.

They all fall silent again.

Maybe you should look on the moors says Rutter.

We've looked on the bloody—

Muncy snaps but then composes himself. He points a finger at Rutter. He wags it.

You better not have owt to do with this Steve he says. I mean it. I'll put you in the ground myself.

BRINDLE SAW IT laid out already. From the moment he got given the file containing her photo and family details. The last sighting and so forth.

He knew the status of the case. These hillbilly plods would barely have managed the basics. That would be a certain. Some door-to-door and a search of the moors maybe. They would have checked the nearest train and bus stations too. Token gestures for the family.

But they'd have done bugger-all else of worth. Nothing beyond the standards of procedure. Brindle would bet his life on the fact that they'd have shot the case in the crucial first twenty-four hours. This lot – the detectives assigned the Muncy case – would be living in the last century. Reading between the lines the notes told him as much.

He'd had dealings with some of these backwater boys before. North Yorkshire born and North Yorkshire bred. Real-ale-and-a-round-of-golf types. Relics; the last of a breed. Murders were as rare as sirloin up there in the Dales so they never had to challenge themselves whereas as he lived breathed and had nightmares about cases that would turn the local coppers' hair grey.

So now they were bringing him in to stick him in a coffin room above a grotty pub where he would be forced to play catch-up with nothing but a laptop a phone and a slim file of notes and the prospect of a cold turkey dinner and his multitude of demons. To hell with it. Christmas is for the birds anyway. To hell with it all.

AS HE WALKS back up to the moor in darkness he thinks about how even then – even then years ago before this internet business took off – the Odeon X Adult Cinema was one of the very last of its kind in the north of England. A relic. A throwback. A place for men stuck in a sordid past. Men like him.

Men not fully formed or functional.

Once a month he made the pilgrimage to his flesh Mecca. Every month and always a Saturday. Salvation Saturday away from the farm.

Saturdays you could stay all day. Saturdays was when the action was. It quelled the loneliness and released a certain tension. Made you forget. Made them all forget.

He was twenty that first time. Half a lifetime ago now. So young he was. So green.

A day off from the buckets of feed and the slopping out and the swill and the slurry and the silage and the poaching and the hunting. It promised this and more.

And he never veered from the same route down there; he never even considered going anywhere else. No shops or galleries or parks interested him. No. Not he. Hell no. Not there.

He knew the quickest route all the way down from the dale to the car park nearest to the X and he always took it. He knew how much it cost and the shortest way through the back streets on foot. He never strayed from his route. And he never told his mother.

He walks now and he remembers all those years ago.

How you had to be a member.

How you registered and then they gave you a laminated card that had your name on it and a strip and inside the films were imported projections of writhing bodies enlarged on the screen. The bodily sounds – the pants and moans – were amplified and the lights always kept low to create a dreamlike state and the seats were velvet covered flip-up ones bought as a job lot from one of the great old cinemas across the city when it had closed. The Alhambra perhaps. Or the Rex. Now the seats were worn and threadbare. Indelibly stained.

There were booths out back then and the place was never cleaned – only sprayed twice a day with cheap air freshener.

Synthetic strawberry.

Entry was five pounds and tea was free but soft drinks had to be paid for.

The Odeon X was a place for men. Men like him. Hooked on the blueys.

Lonely men frustrated men repressed men.

And a place for men who dressed as women too.

A place for watching and lurking and jerking in the dark. He took to it straight away. He became a regular. And so it began.

He cuts through the darkness of the moorland night and when he reaches her he hears a crystalline tinkling sound like the cracking of thin ice. It is distant and minuscule like the dripping of cool water on frozen rock.

He cocks an ear then squats. The sound is coming from the girl's headphones. He picks them up and holds one to his ear. He hears a metallic echo and the voice of a man singing.

The drain water is frozen over. The smashed padlock tells him that he must have jemmied it off the storm gate as he had hoisted her over his shoulder one more time and carried her in. Scratch marks and tiny hardened shavings of ice tell him she was dragged rather than carried. He barely remembers anything.

He hopes for more snowfall later. He needs that.

There are things he knows or implicitly understands have happened. How earlier galvanised by adrenaline and pain and fear and blood he carefully laid her on the iced-over grill-covering of the drain then propped her up against the stonework of the portal.

How his eyes took a few moments to adjust to the darkness.

How he thought she was dead but she was not dead but perhaps she is dead now.

Now he has got her gagged. Now he has got her trussed.

Tied and tangled.

Bound and bloody.

Knotted.

They're in the dark concrete corridor that leads into the

hillside to the drain that drops deep down into the guts of Yorkshire.

Twenty-some hours she has been here and the girl's temple is bruised. Swelling rapidly. He can see it coming up. Turning crimson. Perhaps she has chipped teeth too. Perhaps she is badly concussed. Certainly her nose is broken. She is alive but not conscious.

There is blood though not all of it has come from inside of the girl. Some is from a cut to his hand. Not much of it appears to be hers. She is swollen – yes. Bruising rapidly – yes.

And she is alive – just. He thinks perhaps he can see the pulse in her temple.

She could almost be sleeping. Yes he thinks. Possibly she is just tired like he is tired and one day they'll look back and laugh about this. Yes that's it. Years in the future when they are a couple they will laugh about how they met.

Panic. He's trying not to. Not to panic.

Clean thoughts. A clear plan.

This wasn't meant to happen he thinks.

A clear plan. That's what needed. Clear thoughts.

Christ. Not again.

Christ.

Again.

It's dark down there it's remote down there and it's cold down there. But there's no breeze and there's no snow and –

Christ. Panic. Again.

Breathe.

Just the two of them. Alone. Man and girl.

The girl has a name. He knows she does.

Be practical though he thinks. Forget names. Be practical and use the head they said you never had.

But he knows the decision is made for him. There's no way – no way – he can let her out alive.

That's not happening.

No way.

Stupid girl but. Stupid girl but he thinks. Springing up on him like that. Stumbling up on him like that. No warning or nothing. Enough to give a man a bloody heart attack. So young as well. Only a teenager. Young and stupid and out wandering the moors creeping up on people in the bloody snow in the bloody cold in the bloody middle of winter not minding her own bloody business like she should be.

Nice coat she's wearing but. Nice and thick and warm and hugging.

And the dog. It was the dog's fault going for him. It could have had his throat out. The dog is to blame for all of this really.

He is considering the girl now. He is looking now. Chewing his lip. Here they are entombed and he is reaching out. He is touching.

Moans and groans and echoes she makes. Her soft sounds ricocheting in this dark wet concrete chamber.

Christ. Oh Christ.

She is definitely not dead.

He is toying with her buttons.

And humming.

HE SEES HIMSELF at two. At three.

In the abattoir. In the yard.

As a little lad naked thirsty and dipping a finger into the rainbow swirl of petrol atop what's left of a dirty puddle.

Dipping and stirring it then taking a taste. Gagging and coughing at the throatburn.

The summer sun blazing down the summer sun burning down and beating down. No cloud cover or shade to be found no fresh water to drink. A pig hanging hooked at its heel. Its throat slit and great gouts of blood dripping and gathering and pooling. Spreading and stagnating. Red blood turning to black blood. A permanent stain on the ground like a target from the thousands of hung trunks of meat before it.

Another lies splayed out on the closed lid of a broken freezer its head sitting separate from its body as if abandoned midway through a conjurer's illusion. Its snout is infected. Two trotters rotten.

And flies. Flies arriving as if they have been watching and waiting to hatch as one. Flies laying eggs in the warm gaps in the wounds of the pig; in its hot pockets of flesh. Finding a home there.

He sees himself as an underfed boy in the dirt. He sees the boy rolling over and drinking from the rut because he's not had a drink since Thursday.

He looks up and sees silhouettes in the window. Hears a commotion in the house.

The sound of breaking crashing smashing thudding. Bodies and voices. Men's voices and men's laughter. Her parties.

There's a scream then a shout then broken glass then silence and the summer sun is blazing and the summer sun is burning and the summer sun is beating down on the yard. The flat concrete farmyard.

Beating down on him. It is a hot whip across his back.

The skinny farm cats that they keep loll in the shade. The dogs are distressed and panting.

The sheep and cows are underfed and underweight and ratty-coated. And the slaughtered pigs are rotting.

Hung drawn quartered and gutted. Infected. Their snouts foaming pink; their trotters festering.

And that taste of petrol is in his throat and the taste of desperate thirst is in his throat too. And the sun.

It is blazing. It is burning. The whip hand of it is lashing heat down upon his pale skin.

And the loneliness of solitude is burning its way into Steven Rutter's memory forever.

MACE HAS ONLY been up to the hamlet once before. It was one of his first jobs for the *Mercury*. They'd sent him for a tedious morning up at that grim reservoir with the publicist from the water board and a half-dozen environmentalists and bloggers. It had been some junket to do with future plans for the water that they wished to communicate to the community. It was a nothing story. They hadn't even laid on any food or booze for them the tight bastards.

He had been in no hurry to return to that tiny hamlet down the hill from that black foreboding body of water. Town was remote but – bloody hell. This village was something else. The way it cowered up there. The wind whipping reservoir fret down on the remote hamlet. It wasn't even a village. It was a hamlet. Coming from the city that wide open body of water had scared him. The sheaves of flattened reeds like giant breaded harvest loaves on the shoreline. The wind whispering through the whin. The creamy foam that gathered and bobbed in the shallow inlets. The smattering of clotted duck-down that floated on the surface like the aftermath of a killing – all had seemed like portents of doom to him that first day.

He parks up in the hamlet and waits. He turns on the heater and waits a long time. He sits shivering in his car and then he remembers where he was this time last year. London. A Christmas lunch at the Oxo Tower. Some bars. Some drinks. Powder. A cab up west. More drinks. More powder; too much bloody powder. Then later stumbling through a doorway and down some steps. Below street-level. Under the pavements. Shadows and arches. Men. Dark corners and the stench of amyl. More doorways more stairs. More men. Flesh colliding in wordless exchanges. Insatiable Christmas appetites.

Later still: another man. A mini-cab.

A smudge of street lights.

An unfamiliar tattered curtain pierced by morning sun.

Strange welts and nausea. The usual landslide of regret and

self-loathing.

He sees three policemen coming down the track that leads back into the hamlet. The snow is falling thick again and Mace is only in his shirt trousers and shoes. An old tweed jacket. He winds down the car window and they seem surprised by his appearance. Suspicious. Only when he says that Dennis Grogan is his editor does one of the policeman says oh yes I know you and then asks him what he wants. What he needs to make him go away.

Information says Mace. In this job information is all he ever needs.

The policeman looks at him. Mace steps out of the car. The snow settles on their heads. The snow settles on everything. The hamlet is silent. It is almost beautiful.

LARRY LISTER OBE – still Loveable Larry to those who have grown up under his twinkling gaze and if his agent is to be believed just half a calendar year away from a knighthood (arise Sir Larry is now his whispered morning mirror mantra) – leaves the very shopping centre that he and an actor from *Emmerdale* – or was it a member of Black Lace? – opened some thirty years ago and stops in at Costa where they make up his usual to go: a simple white coffee. No frothy milk no sugar – now you know I'm sweet enough ladies he winks at the all-female staff – no added flavours or syrups or *eye-talian* fanciness; just good old cheap coffee the way he's always had it. He pays with a fiver and tells them to keep the change and as he walks away through the shopping centre while blowing on his hot drink people nod and wave and call out his name. Hi he replies to one and all. Keep smiling – and *be lucky*.

He stops to sign one two and then three autographs before exiting and climbing into his E-Type Jaguar with coffee in hand. He's fat since he gave up the cross-channel sponsored swims and he has to squeeze himself in.

Larry Lister waits until he is out on the ring road before he draws on his e-cigarette. Sweet-cherry flavour. He gave up years back when the ban came in. It's political correctness gone more than a little mad he told anyone who would listen at the time. It's political correctness gone barmy is that.

His fox-red hair heavily lacquered into place from a fire-extinguisher-sized can of Elnett and vaping away with his replica cigarette jammed between his pudgy fingers Larry Lister turns on the stereo and a CD is already playing at near-full volume. It is *God Bless Tiny Tim* by his old pal; released in 1968 on Reprise it not only features his hit 'Tip-Toe Thru the Tulips with Me' but also a rather rousing and tender version of 'I Got You Babe'. Much better than the original. Larry Lister turns it up and points the Jag north. Good old Tim he thinks as he heads up to the Dales. One of the boys was Timmy.

He drives on up there with the windows open the engine purring and Tim shrilling I got you babe over disjointed ukulele chords. As he leaves the city and drives through the suburbs people spot him and wave. Even moving at speed he senses his name being spoken: *Larry Lister* like an echo right through his life. He sees it formed by the lips of strangers and he waves back and gives them the thumbs up. Shouts *be lucky*.

God's own country – that's what it is up here he thinks. The Yorkshire Dales. Bloody beautiful. Nothing like this down south. You can keep the Cotswolds. On weekends visiting old pals down there – Fluff and Ray and Kenny– he never felt right. The Cotswolds was like a theme park for the rich but here up in the valley true remoteness and wild landscape still exist. You can still lose yourself and really that is all he has ever wanted.

He drives down back roads and lanes climbing high up the valley side until the old pine plantation appears and he's turning into the darkened tunnel of trees and down to his bolt-hole – a lone woodsman's cottage – bought in the mid eighties when his stock was at its highest. Back when he was Saturday-night primetime and was making three grand for one-hour PAs – supermarket openings and nightclub turns and the switching-on of Christmas lights in ailing northern industrial towns. Some weeks he'd cram ten in. Insist on cash. Thirty thousand for smiling and smoking – yes the eighties had been kind to him. He had the Lady to thank for all that luck. Good old Maggie.

He hears the gravel beneath the tyres. He had it put down especially because gravel announces unexpected arrivals.

Larry Lister parks up and has a piss in the trees – one of life's little pleasure he has always thought – and then enters the house. Inside it is musty and the curtains are drawn. Just how he likes it. A shower and a brandy and his robe help welcome in the weekend. Afterwards he unlocks the loft hatch and slides the ladder down. Climbs up. Closes it behind him.

IN HIS HEAD he had a brother. For a while at least.

For a while a twin. His brother was so real he went with him everywhere.

They were the Rutters. The Farm Boys. Everyone would love the Farm Boys.

Mike was his pretend brother's name. Mike was a good name Mike was a strong name Mike was a normal guy's name.

Mike and Ste. Two peas.

One day they would have their own TV show. That's what he reckoned. They'd simply call it Farm Boys.

Funny things would happen to them on their programme. Slapstick stuff. The wheels would fall off their car. Pianos would fall from windows and just miss them. One would accidentally-on-purpose custard-pie the other one in the face. Simple innocent fun. No nastiness just two loveable brothers making people laugh. Kids and adults alike. They'd film it on the farm but their mother wouldn't be in it. That would not happen. On their TV show she would not exist.

And they'd be famous would the Farm Boys.

They'd come down from the dale and everyone would recognise them. They'd want to talk to them and touch them and buy them milkshakes and get their autographs.

Those two? they would say in the towns and the cities and in the newspapers. Really great guys. Grew up on a farm. Pig men. Humble. There's nothing about farming that those two don't know.

And now look at them on the telly in the papers with girls on each arm and new sports cars and swimming pools and fancy clothes and foreign holidays.

Separately they just weren't funny. Separately it didn't work. People weren't interested in Steve Rutter by himself. By himself he could not tell jokes; the only laughter he heard was not with him but at him.

Then his mother caught him at it one day. Talking out loud. She asked him who he was gobbing on with and when he said his twin brother she looked at him like he was mad and told him he was tapped and then she cracked him one. Knocked him out stone cold and not for the first time. He slept where he fell on the farmyard floor and when he woke it was getting dark and his neck ached and his jaw ached and everything was black and white for two or three days and he never talked to his twin brother again. Not out loud anyway.

But he was there. He walked with him then and sometimes even now when the loneliness opened up deep inside him like the great whirling bell-mouth drain-plug of the reservoir's floor he would put in an appearance. Even now he walked with him.

WHAT IS LEFT of the Rutter place now sits high up on the valley flank just below the moors and the scars. It has no name except the Rutter Place. No map knows it.

Its steep front slopes slip down to the hamlet.

Beyond it – behind it – past the back fence that marks the end of the ownership of the family land there are only open moors and the reservoir that they called a bold feat of engineering: the biggest manmade body of water in the north. Six years it took to construct and another one to fill it up. An entire year of running water.

Rutter remembers the day they brought out the bunting and held a party on the shoreline. They bussed people in from villages right across the Dales and persuaded them to enjoy themselves by plying them with cold hot-dogs and warm fizzy orange juice. Photographs were taken for the press. A local news crew came down and footage was filmed with a junior reporter given the short straw. Her voice blowing away in the wind and a semicircle of blank-faced Dales families in cagoules behind her appearing as part of a montage on that night's national news.

In the weeks that followed its opening the water board gave educational tours around the circumference and fed the visitors with statistics they didn't care to hear. How the reservoir held 100 million litres and how dual turbines helped generate and store electricity. How a wide variety of aquatic- and plant-life would be supported for years to come.

They were told of conduits and runnels and channels and hidden aquaducts. There were proud corporate boasts of intricate systems. Advanced engineering technologies. The future.

And Rutter remembered photos of the plug hole: a bellmouth overflow with a radius of forty feet installed in the base to drain the entire reservoir. He remembered a black hole of nothingness; a watery abyss. It fascinated him it scared him it excited him. He recognised it as something he felt lay within him.

Now no buses go to the reservoir at all. The dream of a vibrant waterway was just that. Frost and rain have eaten away at the road and the nearest train station is twenty-five miles away. There are no shops no cafes no visitor centre.

No ice-cream vans no toilets. No news crews.

Just a giant pit of water and the moorlands around it. A sad little jetty at one end where a few neglected algae-stained row-boats are tied up. The wind slapping with violence and the foaming furious spray adding to the daily rainfall for the tiny upper-Dales hamlet downhill in the shadows had created a meteorological anomaly that saw sleet in spring time and hail in summer.

There are however more rainbows here than anywhere else in the country. The villagers were told that as a trade-off for the disruption of the reservoir: you'll get good rainbows round here.

RUTTER GOES OUT back. He digs into a sack and throws the dogs some kibble then says halt your whining.

He walks past the pig shed. He walks past the barns and looks down the slopes to the glorified turning area they call the Square.

A dozen houses cling close to the Square and behind it there is another row of houses accessed by ginnells at either end then a dozen or so more each with bigger gardens. Beyond the hamlet are larger farmsteads.

He scans to the right past the last of the houses in the hamlet and along to Muncy's place. Squat and lavish. Gaudy. The bricks not fitting in with the landscape like his. Typical Muncy that.

Because Muncy's a money man Muncy's a big-mouth Muncy's a big shot. He buys a new four-wheel-drive every two years and thinks he's gentry. He has bought up half the top end of the dale over the years. He's got the farm and he's got grazing fields and woodlands and that part of the moor-top that doesn't belong to the water board that's mainly boglands.

The Coast-to-Coast path runs through Muncy's farm and when her nerves hold his sour-faced wife serves sandwiches and flapjacks out of a hatch and in the summer they open up the meadow out back that rolls down to the top set of falls. It's nothing but a sloping field covered in cow scat but come May it'll be dotted with the coloured canvas of walkers and cyclists passing through.

Muncy has put in a toilet block. There is talk of picnic tables and a bunkhouse. Madness thinks Rutter.

And now Muncy has a Merc in the garage too and quad bikes and twice a year he gets cover for the farm and takes foreign holidays. Comes back all smug and leathery.

You should expand your horizon get some sunshine *sunshine* he'd said once and Rutter could have lamped him right there and then. Just put his front teeth down the back of his throat.

But he doesn't need to do that. Because he knows things about Muncy that no one else knows. He can lord it all he likes over him and he can sit on all the boards and be in all the secret clubs and wax his cars every bloody Sunday but there are things that Rutter knows. There is a shared history. And while Muncy has the house and the car and the holidays and the tan what he doesn't have any more is a daughter and though it wasn't planned that way – thinks Rutter as he walks – it's just the way it is.

And then he is thinking back again. Back to the past that he has been frequently inhabiting and those endless nights in the X amongst the exhibitionists. Those that liked to put on a bit of a show for the men. Men like him.

When that happened – when they took seats together somewhere in the centre – the men would circulate like vultures. Sighing and moaning and tugging in the half light. In these moments everyone was equal. The darkness was the leveller. The taxi drivers and the sissies and the Muslims and the mackintosh men: all were hungry for the same things. Release and escape.

He considered the silence and the atmosphere as churchlike. Almost holy. Hallowed. After a week on the fells he liked to sit there indoors with the colours from the screen lighting his face and those of the other men who watched in mute rapt wonder.

Because aside from the two screening rooms there were also two private lounges in the X. One was billed as the Couples' Room. In both they showed films on a loop and there were sofas and tissues and bins.

The films were the old kind from years earlier. The seventies and eighties mainly. Sixties even. Real old stuff. Vintage classics. None of the new glossy Californian crap that Rutter found noisy and vulgar and lacking edge.

He liked the stuff from Germany. He liked the stuff from Sweden.

Britain too.

The Danes made some good ones.

Because the X only screened hardcore. Hairy fannies. Muck arcing across the screen.

The normal stuff – a bit of tit a bit of arse – you could see in the mags in any newsagent. The mags were boring the mags were soft.

The mags got used up and chucked out down country lanes where they belonged. The American stuff Rutter didn't like. Too many tans and fake tits.

No. The women up on the screens at the Odeon X – they were his girls. Each and every of them. In time he knew all their names he knew their works he knew every inch of their bodies and back home up at the farm they occupied his thoughts. They rode with him on the tractor or helped him muck out. They fixed fences with him; they slept with him ate with him. They colluded against his mother with him.

Each Saturday afternoon for months he sat under the cover of darkness as day became night and he slipped into a trancelike state in the manmade state of permanent gloaming.

Marilyn Caramel. Gloria Scoops. Bambi Bigheart.

Boarding School. Bottoms Up! Door-to-Door Salesman. He knew every inch of them.

Mitzi Brown. Cathy Dee. Diane Drinkwater.

French Lessons. Girl-Guide Temptation. Jolly Hockey-Sticks.

Every title.

Non-Stop Spunker. Private Agent. A Taste of Cunny.

He loved the blueys. He loved his girls unreservedly and without discrimination. Age colour shape; it didn't matter. He prided himself on not harbouring favourites.

Sometimes in the X he unhooked his overalls and lazily masturbated. He slowly spread it out over a whole afternoon. Sometimes he sat back and let others do it for him.

He learned things there in the soft light of the Odeon X. Because he was only just twenty and had no one to guide him. He had no brothers no friends no father. All he knew was learned from his mother's parties and from farm animals in the farmyard doing what it is that beasts do to one another.

He loved them then and loves them now as distant memories; faded faces from those early days before things got so involved and life became this big dark cloak that hung upon his shoulders.

HE'S UP EARLY. Christmas Eve and his head is throbbing. He used to be able to sleep through hangovers but not any more. Back when he was a student and in those early days in London Roddy Mace could roll out of a stranger's bed after two or three hours sleep and still be at his desk on time. Coffee and a croissant and cigarettes all day long. Now the hangovers wake him up at dawn and slowly destroy his day. Kill all hope.

Cripple his good intentions.

He's closer to thirty than twenty but already hangovers feel like punishment. Like the best days of consequence-free drinking are behind him. It's something to do with the beer up here. That's his theory. It's stronger stuff. Locally brewed for iron-bellied farmers. It slips down and stays there and in the morning it feels like trepanning.

Mace showers and then rings round for updates on the girl. Calls the local police station. Calls the press office at the North Yorkshire head branch. Calls a pal who works on production at the BBC. *Look North.* He puts an egg on to boil and makes coffee and then drinks it looking at the softly falling snow.

It's too quiet. In an upstairs flat down a side street that's just off the main square in a small market town the silence is unnerving after years living amongst the screaming sirens and hissing bus doors and helicopter blades and street screams of south London.

After the city he had wanted to live on a houseboat. Had the notion but there were no canals round here. The industrial age of cotton mills and coalfields hadn't reached up to the Dales – the landscape was too uneven and it was miles from any city. Sheep and slate-mining was all it had been good for. He turns the radio on. Slade's Christmas song. Sod off.

He hits shuffle on his iPod. Iggy.

Sweet sixteen in leather boots.

Better but this is night-time music. Drug music. Something for the city.

Pretty faces beautiful faces. Body and soul I give to you.

He scrolls through for some folk music. He hated folk until he moved north. Despised it. But then an oil painter that he knew did him a mix CD and now he is hooked on the old dark weird stuff. Comus. Pentangle. Mr Fox. Young Tradition. Bands who made music preoccupied with brutal death and rural misery. It reminded him of the metal bands he had

liked when he was a teenage skateboarder only these artists
sung about crimes and hunting and bloodshed and cruelty
and adultery often without even using instruments. Here
in the Dales this type of music made sense. In the context
of the open moors and the remote farms it chimed with the
landscape. What his friends in the bars and clubs of London
would make of it he does not know. Doesn't care. He is here
they are there. And life rolls on pay-cheque to pay-cheque.
Drink to drink.

He finishes his breakfast and then he checks in with
his editor Grogan. He shares what scant information he's
managed to scrape together: no sign of the girl. The chances
of a runaway are unlikely. Slim. General prospects grim. There
is talk of an accident. Talk of an abduction. Just talk though.
Speculation. They say a dog is missing too says Grogan.
Muncy is trying to call the shots with the cops he says. There
has been heavy snow in the night and there's not a single
footprint to be found up top.

You're still going up there? asks his boss.

I am says Mace. In a minute.

Get some quotes. Get anything. Something is unravelling
here. I can feel it.

Yes says Mace. Me too.

They hang up.

He heaves his suitcase down from the wardrobe. He scoops
up t-shirts and trousers and underwear and throws them in.
He remembers the bottle of whisky that Grogan gave him
and is surprised to find it is down a third since yesterday. He
puts that in the case too. He'll need it to get through a family
Christmas. He cannot face hearing about how he gave up a
perfectly good job and a perfectly good flat and a perfectly
good fictional girlfriend in London; he cannot face this
because he cannot explain it.

The flat is a mess. Papers everywhere. Old copies of the

Mercury and his manuscript scattered and crumpled. Coffee cups. Washing in the sink. The accoutrements of a bachelor's existence. He checks the time. It'll have to wait.

He puts on layers and turns off the boiling egg – no time – and pours the rest of his coffee into a travel cup and then leaves the flat. Takes his iPod with him and plugs it into the car stereo. Gets the heaters blowing. It takes Mace ten minutes to scrape the ice off the windscreen and ten more to get out of his parking bay and round the market square where the road is a slick sheet of black ice.

Out of town it is slow going. Fresh snow crumps and creaks beneath his tyres as the road winds and climbs. There are no edges to be seen; everything is rounded. The cornices of houses and the tops of stone walls – the snow has softened the landscape. Opiated almost thinks Mace. He sips his coffee and feels it chip away at his hangover. The phone lines sag under the weight of all that white and he enjoys the muffled silence.

He passes hamlets of houses that cling close to the road with holly wreaths hanging from their front doors. He sees flashes of other people's lives.

Mace checks the time and decides to make this a fleeting visit. A five-minute sniff-around then send the notes and quotes to Grogan. Then – the train station. Christmas. Family. Annual obligations.

He turns the heater up. Turns the music up.

NOT LONG AFTER his mother took ill Muncy had cornered Rutter outside of the Laidlaws' post office and tried to talk to him about the farm. Suggested he could be doing more with the family land. A place like that he said. All that space. All that potential. You've got how many acres up there?

Rutter had shrugged and grunted and not made eye contact. Muncy's aftershave stung his sinuses.

Prime grazing. You could make a tidy packet Steve. You

rattling around in all that space. There's barn conversions to consider. Holiday homes. Think about it. Or if you're not interested I could make you an offer myself.

I'm not bothered about that Rutter had said.

Then Muncy went on about market gardens and crop rotation; blethered about the price of British lamb and government subsidies; blethered on about grants for fixing up the roof and the outbuildings. Rutter couldn't wait to get away so told Muncy he wasn't interested in no government interfering. Told him right out he couldn't give too hoots for walkers and cyclists because they're mad the lot of them out there in the rain like that.

He told Muncy the Rutter place would stay just as it was; told him to mind his own beeswax. He never mentioned the clause though. The clause that bound him to the place until he was fifty even if he wanted to sell it. It was his mother's doing. She had got it written into the deeds in the event of ill health or incapacitation or her passing. It was her last laugh. A cruel curse bestowed upon him. Her idea of a joke. Payback for his existence. Black Tits' revenge.

In her prime Aggie Rutter was feared Aggie Rutter was unpredictable Aggie Rutter had a tongue on her. She was known to lash out. They made sure she never heard the jokes about her making cheese under those dirty dugs and the half-dozen teeth in her head. And still the dalesmen came and when they put the reservoir in she had a few of that lot too.

Sometimes she had made him watch. The barefoot boy. Her Steven. Some of the men liked it that way. They asked her special. Liked an audience. Two thrills for the price of one up at the Rutter place.

Watch and learn lad she said. Aint no different from cows in the field and you'll need to know your way around a woman soon enough.

Young Rutter didn't want to watch but she'd beat him if he didn't. If he flinched or turned away. Said she'd slap his mouth right off his face.

And so he had watched them with their trousers round their ankles and their knees creaking in the autumn chill. Tugging away at themselves and pawing at Aggie Rutter and twisting themselves into strange contortions and awkward configurations. Grunting huffing and puffing some of them even crying as they hunched over his mother's big white rear that was raised high like a hog at a trough.

Her wrinkled socks gathered round swollen ankles.

All those men. One on a hay bale or two in the quarry. One at each end and another one watching. In the woods in the moors in the cabin of a bright yellow digger.

The old man's long gone they said. Just her and the lad and hogs running wild.

It's nowt to look at but it can suck a golf ball through a hosepipe and it'll never run out of puff. It can go all day they said.

Just follow the smell of the pig shit they said.

Yours for a pike or a wool-knot pullover they said. Yours for a bundle of kindling.

FOLK CRIMES. STORIES in the soil. Skeletons.

This is what James Brindle thinks about as he winds his way up the valley: the things they put beneath the sod. Secrets of dark deeds and bloodspill. Folk crimes and the crimes of folk bound into mute mythologies. The history of the land.

He counts the bars on gates as he drives past them then counts the number of cottages and farm houses that he can see up the hillsides. He seeks order in the numbers and in that order he hopes to find silence and sometimes he briefly finds it. But it is never enough.

The tales these hills and moors could tell he thinks. Every dale a crime scene. Every squat stone home or ancient disused quarry now overgrown. Maybe not today or last year or the year before that but sometime.

You read about Richmond and Ripon. Grassington and Skipton. You read about them in the magazines and saw them on *Countryfile*. You heard about Appleby and Leyburn and Hawes but what about the gaps between – the forgotten hinterlands up the hills and down the dells.

Christmas coming. Brindle asks himself again whether it is because he is the best or if it is for this reason. Is the festive season the reason why they have sent him in? Because they know he has no wife to disappoint. No kids to upset. Because Brindle is the only one pathetic enough to have no one miss him when everyone else is tucking into their turkey. And because they – *they* – know he is ambitious enough not to say no.

And *they* know that *he* knows how this will look if he cracks it and cracks it quick.

He's a DS now. Detective Sergeant.

DS. In Cold Storage they joke it stands for dark shit.

Deceitful suspects. Dead stories. Drowned – what?

He doesn't remember and he doesn't care because he won't stay DS for long.

The road carves a path and the countryside makes him feel uneasy. He tries to count falling snowflakes but it makes him feel dizzy.

He looks at the mileometer he looks at the speedometer he looks at the petrol gauge.

He looks at the mileometer again and calculates how many miles he has driven – sixty-three and most of that on back roads – then he takes the six and three and does calculations with them. Adds them. Multiplies them. Plays around. Seeks patterns. Imposes order.

Facts. Facts are Jim Brindle's religion. Facts are what he worships. Facts and science and numbers. Evidence and motives. Statements and sentences. Order.

And in that order he seeks peace and silence and resolution though it is rarely there. There are things that he has witnessed that can never be unseen. Sounds he has heard. Scents he has smelled.

He remains a stone-turner though. They know it – those upstairs who sent him out here. They know he's cold-blooded and hard-faced and pragmatic despite the traumas of past cases.

He counts the cat's eyes as his headlights pick them out. The sides of the roads are thick with drifts now. The dry-stone walls are disappearing. When he hits upon a number that feels right he plays around with it for a while. Doubles it triples multiplies it by itself then breaks it down to its components.

Other men – other detectives – they get irrational about cases. They unlearn their schooling and put themselves in the position of the victim or the victim's family when it's the mind of those who've done the crimes where you need to be. Never forget the victims: sure. But become the killer. Ask how and when and where and who. The why rarely matters. Only the end results. He's a DS now but not for long. DS. It stands for: derelict spaces. Daughters screaming. Deafening silences.

Soon he'll be move up. DI.

Stands for: decapitated invalids.

Dirty incest.

Dead inside.

The lean of the road pulls his car to the left but then it levels out and Brindle checks his satnav and it tells him he is in the middle of nowhere and that makes his intestines flex for a moment so he starts counting and breathing counting and breathing.

THEY KEPT MORE pigs back when he was young. Breeders for pork and back bacon; breeders for the butcher's blade. A hundred or more of them jostling in the sheds.

His father was long gone. Unknown to Steven Rutter. He was never even there in the first place and Aggie Rutter never expressed regret. She had no time for anything but surviving.

His father was just one more greasy prick at one of her soirees; she was raising the boy herself and made sure it never happened again.

Some joked his father was the reason those pigs were so portly: because whoever *he* was was inside them. Ground up and chewed up and shat out. Bone dust in pellets now.

The farm was hers anyway. Rutter was her name. It was family land and then when she was gone it would be his land. But not until he was fifty. A decade's time. Until then she still controlled him. Still owned him.

They had sheep then too. They kept them for the milk which was a rarity then. But sheep's milk sells if you know those that want it and for a while Rutter's sheep milk went to a man who drove up from Skipton once a week to pick up churn-loads. She sold the wool on when she could too and then when the sheep had birthed their lambs and were good for nothing else come summer she slit their aging throats and sold them on for their mutton.

Tough meat the Rutter meat. Pale grey and gristle-thick. Great hocks and fists of it.

Many gave it a wide berth when it appeared in the butcher's window. They said it took a day's stewing just to rinse the stink out of it.

The farm is a sagging shape on the landscape now. A place of fallen slates and rotten timber. Crooked skeletons of corrugated outbuildings like half-rotted corpses rising from the soil. The ghosts of buildings; the sad remains of a smallholding. The histories of past inhabitants hidden until forgotten.

Rutter still calls it a farm but it hasn't been that way for a long time. Not since the old times. Now he just has the half-dozen dogs and some hens and a few stunted apple trees and even they seem only to produce every three years or so. Hunting and poaching and logging and lurking fills his time. Life does not flourish here.

Rutter hangs his work shirt on the back of the door by the dog lead. Dumps his pack in the kitchen. He stokes the embers of the fire and folds some more kindling in and then goes upstairs to the bedroom. He opens the front of his trousers and lays back on the sunken greasy mattress.

Outside the dogs are whining in their pen but Rutter is lying back and thinking of smoke shadows celebrities videos envelopes photographs wide eye broken fingernails skin hair and sweat and he is thinking of that lonely concrete chamber. Dirt and ice. A slowing pulse.

When he is finished he throws the mucky rag onto the fire where it crackles and hisses and he looks out the window down the valley.

The snow falls. The flakes are bigger now. They fall in broken diagonal cords and when they hit the window he can see the individual shape of each. The sky presses down. Though it feels like the day has barely begun it will soon be dark.

LOVEABLE LARRY LISTER unlocks the cabinet and looks at the archive within. It's all there – the best moments of his life captured on celluloid. The career highlights. Collectively they present a potted history of British light entertainment. His eyes scan the fading labels of the tapes. There's *Uncle Larry's Party* which ran for twelve years and the *Uncle Larry's Party Xmas Specials* – including Christmas Day 1981 right after a speech by Her Maj when 21 million people tuned in; the only show to compete with Eric and Ernie. There's not one but two *This is Your Life* episodes and guest slots on *Around with Alliss* and *Bullseye* and *Harty* and *Celebrity It's a Knockout.* Another features grainy highlights from various *Melody Maker Poll Winner* ceremonies throughout the sixties. There are a dozen Royal Variety Performance appearances including five hosting and a full archive of black-and-white episodes of *Get Down and Groove* (Lister's catchphrase: who's feeling groovy tonight kids?) that the corporation managed not to throw away (there were rumours that the reels that made up the first two series had been used as landfill and were currently embedded somewhere deep beneath the M4) and a few of its shortlived follow-up *Get Up and Groove.* There's the acclaimed interview with the Lady – apparently the first time she had ever been to a theme park. There is footage of him being gunged by Edmonds and serenaded by Bassey.

He crouches down to the locked cabinet below the neat shelving and opens it. There are more tapes here. These ones are untitled but colour-coded with felt-tip streaks. Red. Blue. Yellow. Green. He remembers what each represents. One is both red and blue. Another is blue and green. Purple. Black.

One day he would like to transfer the tapes to disc or maybe even digital but he doesn't know how to and it would be a risk not worth taking. There is only one person who he could ask about that and Mr Hood has not been in touch for a long while. And the last time – over three years ago now – it was via the vile Mr Skelton when he delivered his share of the club's dividends with a message from Hood: the network is down. Dismantled. The building has been sold. The parties no more. Those days are over. We'll be in touch – maybe.

Just like that an era ended.

Later Loveable Larry gave a big chunk of his silent share in the building and his stake in their specialist-entertainment business to one of the kid's charities; it only seemed right. It was about balance. Take – and give. Always strive for balance. Always keep smiling. And be lucky.

Follow those rules and the bastards will never get you he liked to tell close friends and associates though of course he knew that luck had nothing to do with it. Being top dog was what it was about. And you did that by keeping every fucker at arm's length.

There is something comforting about the old VCR player. The click and whir of the cumbersome cassettes. The graininess of the footage. The way you can speed it up and slow it down. Pause a scene. Freeze it. Frame it. It's nostalgia really as the cassettes are relics that have already been replaced first by DVDs and then digital technology but in his old age it's something he finds himself unapologetically revelling in rather frequently. Nostalgia. The closest he can get to all that now is the old untitled films that no biographer has ever written about and whose existence and creation are known to a very small number of men. Watching and rewatching. Remembering and reliving. He has been involved in hundreds and hundreds of hours of broadcast television and radio yet he considers these tapes as featuring some of his greatest production work. His secret side-career. The dark private yin to his indefatigable grinning public yang.

He does not have a room like this in the flat in Bayswater at or the cottage in Kirkcudbright or the maisonette in Horsforth or the static home in Withernsea. Only here.

He selects a tape. A red and black. The heaviest there is. He's in the mood; he has been doing a lot of tiring smiling this week.

He inserts it and sits back on the old sofa given to him by – who was it? One of the chat show presenters. It might have been Frank; it certainly wasn't Selina. She had hated him. She had besmirched him at the corporation and look what happened to her career.

Larry Lister loosens his gown and presses play. He still has his trainers on.

He has them sent over from New York. Sent over from the head office. Box-fresh. He has a contact there.

The film begins and he's back there. Back in that room. Back in the past. The glory days. Down below the X.

The screams of the girl on the film are muffled. It is as if time has worn them down. Yet still she screams. Up here she will always be screaming.

HE IS JUST out of his teens and still green. This particular Saturday it is busy. Seats creak and men cough as one film finishes and another starts and no one moves from their seat. It's a real old one this time. Black and white and hairstyles that say 1950s. It's an antique. Sometimes they do that at the X – throw an old one into the loop. Seeing people at it like that back then is strange. Thinking of them as old people or dead people now is strange too.

There's a sissy sitting along the row from him. A brute in stockings and heels with his cock out. He couldn't even be bothered to have a shave. He is a stocky man and his cock is small. Like a wild mushroom thinks Rutter.

He looks back to where the monochrome image flickers on the screen. There is a woman with a mouthful of man. His head out of shot. Music plays. The music seems as if it was added at a later date. It sounds like music made by an automatic setting on a toy keyboard.

He is losing himself again when there is a ripple of murmurs around the room. He turns around and sees a couple walking down the aisle and taking seats. He turns back and watches the screen but he can feel the atmosphere of the room change so he shifts around in his seat and sees that the woman now has her legs up and open and splayed and her fingers are working at herself down there.

The vultures begin to gather and the man with her watches them watching her.

Soon there is a circle of bodies around them with their necks craning and their arms moving.

She is big is the woman. Her thick white thighs spill over her stocking tops. Half her hand is up there. Stuffing herself like that. Wearing herself.

The men shift and move.

The taxi drivers and the sissies and the Muslims. The truckers and the farmers and the poofters. One two or three dressed up. Eye masks and frilly knickers. Rutter is in his work-wear. Boiler suit and rigger boots. Beanie hat.

Some of the men are touching and sucking each other as they watch the couple.

He slowly stands and moves down the aisle to get a closer look.

He puts his hand into his trousers but then the woman stops and the man stops and they rearrange themselves then stand and slowly walk out of the cinema and into the Couples' Room. Some men follow but others stay and keep on doing whatever it is they are doing to one another. Groping and groaning in the monochrome gloom.

He follows the couple. Follows the men.

The room is small the room is dark the room is thick and heavy from the central heating. It is stale and cloying like a windowless room that has just been vacated after a long boring meeting.

The woman is down on her knees sucking the man now and the vultures circle again. They organise themselves now.

There is a film on the small screen. Really it is just a TV. It is showing a different film to the one in the main screening room. It is harder. The sound is turned low.

He gets it out. He joins them. Gets into it.

It's just like in the films is this he thinks.

She's Aunt Judy she's Schoolgirl Sally.

She's Mitzi she's Cathy she's Bambi.

He positions himself and thinks wow. What a gobbler.
He is part of it now. He is entranced.
Entrenched.

Yes.

The woman takes her mouth and puts it on one of the men.
He gasps and groans and Rutter moves in closer. The circle
tightens.

Yes.

He looks at the men. Their faces are taut with concentration.
He looks down.

She's a big woman she's a fat woman she's a thirsty hungry
dirty woman.

There are no words spoken – just a circle of men and hairy
hanging bellies. They take turns to lean over and clinically fondle
her big breasts and pinch her dark nipples as if they are checking
the ripeness of fruit to be harvested and they awkwardly touch
her hair as she works her way around the circle.

Yes.

He feels ten million miles away from the pig farm.

The woman works her way around the circle. From one
man to the next. Gulping and slurping and moaning. Yes.
The occasional clearing of a throat or whispered word of
encouragement can be heard but mainly there is only the sound
of a mouth and the TV turned down low. The shifting of feet.
Yes. Shoe-soles on the old carpet. Yes. The internal workings of
bodies.

She moves to a skinny man in expensive-looking stockings
and heels. A wig. The full sissy get-up. They are all watching as
she works at him and he leans his head back and swallows and
grunts. His Adam's apple pulsing in his thin neck.

He has his trousers down around his ankles now. They gather
around his boots there in the half-light.

Then she's nearly at him – her wet mouth is nearly on him
– he is next. Yes. Next. He is next. Yes. Her mouth. And he is

waiting. Yes.

She turns to him and then she pauses for a moment. She looks up through thick mascara and she puts the back of her hand to her nose.

She coughs and frowns and then she moves on to the next man.

He is confused. Here wait he says. Wait a minute.

Her eyes shoot sideways. A shake of the head. No.

No.

Then her mouth already full with the next one. Eyes wide with it. Breathing heavily through flared nostrils.

I think you need to clean it mate says a man. Her man. You need to wash it first he says.

You heard him says another from across the circle. I can smell you from here.

Yeah grunts the sissy next to him. You soap it he says. You show respect.

The woman removes the other man from her mouth and looks at him then they're all looking at him they're all looking at him and it is silent even the TV is silent because on it a woman is doing exactly what they are doing only on the TV no one is staring at him and no one is saying probably you should leave fella probably you should go back through there and he looks at each of them and sees that they are urging him to leave and on the TV screen they're still at it – they haven't stopped and he is flushing red with rage and going limp and pulling up his trousers and leaving the room and feeling like a corked cider bottle three months after appling time.

ON HIS WAY back down Mace pulls over into a passing place and calls Grogan again.

Dennis. It's Roddy.

Roddy. What time it is?

Half past late. I'm sorry for calling.

Where are you?

Mace looks out of the window. Sees silent snow still falling. Fat flakes forming and landing and laying.

I don't know.

Are you alright?

I'm fine Dennis. I'm somewhere on the West Kellerhope Road.

Muncy's girl?

Yes. I've been up to have a sniff around.

Any news?

They've not found her if that's what you mean.

How is it looking?

A couple of our local finest have been up at the reservoir but there's nothing doing. You know what they're like. Pottering about like a bunch of old women. They've put the word out to the train and bus stations and rung round all her friends. If you ask me I think they'd rather be down the pub.

Do you think she's a runaway?

Who knows? says Mace. I have a feeling though.

What about Muncy?

Do you know him?

Yeah says Dennis Grogan. Everyone knows Ray Muncy.

How would you describe him?

Slick. But insecure with it too. What about the search? What do you know?

They're talking about widening it. Getting a full party out.

Tonight?

In the morning.

It'll be no bloody good in the morning says Grogan. Christ almighty. They'll have to chip her out of the ice if she stops out there another night.

That's what I thought.

Can you get up there tomorrow?

Where?

Up in the hamlet. Or on the moors. We could do with someone watching the search.

It's Christmas.

It's journalism Roddy. It doesn't stop. I thought you knew that.

Mace sighed.

Do you have plans? says Grogan.

I *did* have plans. I'm meant to be getting the train up to my parents'.

What time?

In the afternoon.

Then you have the morning free.

I suppose.

You're our staff writer.

I know.

There's no one else I can ask. Any freelancer would tell me to get fucked.

Mace sighs.

Remember what you said at the interview Roddy? That you'd do whatever was required.

I remember.

Believe it or not I had fifty-odd CVs for your position. Interviewed ten poor sods too. All of them prepared to move up here to the back of beyond because that's how tough the job market is. You were the diamond amongst them. Fifty fuckers ready to work for my tin-pot publication – that's how tough it is out there in journalism.

OK Dennis. I get your point. I'll stick around tomorrow. I'll head up there early and then get something written. Then get the train.

Good lad. I knew you were a pro – from the very first minute I set eyes on you.

Flattery says Mace. I'm a sucker for it every time.

There is a moment's silence before Roddy Mace realises

that Dennis Grogan has already hung up.

AT THE POLICE station down the town the first thing they see is a small trim man immaculate in his shirt and tie and winter coat. A briefcase in hand. World War I haircut; neat but of another era entirely. On a teenager it might be ersatz and fashionable but on a man whose age is difficult to distinguish it looks archaic. Antiquated.

They see a strawberry birthmark covering half his cheek and jaw. It is mottled and tough-looking like flesh stripped by heat or acid or a hot iron and now dried tight and dappled and the colour of cheap warm claret.

Their eyes lock onto the mark of Jim Brindle and they see a wide-o wanker who thinks he's better than them.

He sees: a parochial shit-hole unpainted since the early eighties. A museum for failed police procedures.

After terse introductions Brindle is briefed. He is shown the notes by a lowly PC. Jeff Temple. Name age description last sighting. A bit of background. A map of the area surrounding the girl's house is spread out on a table in a back room. He is not happy. The map shows that within a two-mile radius there is a reservoir and woodlands. There are marshlands and bogs.

Where's your superior? asks Brindle and then looks at his notepad. Where's Roy Pinder?

He's out says Temple.

Get him here Brindle says then taps the map with his pen. What are these?

He is told: scars.

Scars?

Like quarries. But wooded.

What are they for?

He doesn't get an answer. Gets a shrug instead.

Brindle expected this. It is always this way. He has not been sent to get along with them – he has been sent to do the job that they are incapable of. So it's his way now.

He looks at the map again. He sees crags and boulders. Gulleys and streams.

The terrain on the map is bad enough but it does not show the two feet of snow that has fallen. It does not register temperature. It does not record sound. It does not show blood.

He asks: you've scoured all this? Got the locals on board?

He gets another shrug.

We've checked around the reservoir.

The first twenty-four hours says Brindle. I suppose you know that is when cases are made – or fail.

The PC nods. He is young. His accent local. He has the face of a fat man but not the build. One day he will be bald.

How long since she was seen?

I don't know. I'm guessing it's something like thirty-six hours.

Don't guess snaps Brindle. Tell me.

Thirty-six hours. Hang on. No.

Come on. Make your mind up.

Maybe more. Forty-eight?

Then you're fucked aren't you.

Not necessarily—

Yes necessarily says Brindle. Thirty-six hours plus subzero temperatures multiplied by moorlands equals you being fucked. And you're telling me *not necessarily*.

Brindle continues: frankly everything from this point onwards is just damage-limitation in respect of my reputation. My department.

Are you saying the girl is—?

I'm saying that you lot are fucked and the best you can hope for is that she's being gang-banged in a brutalist tower-block squat as we speak. If you're lucky she'll turn up bandy-legged and bleeding at the local cop-shop by new year. That's the best outcome. But I doubt it.

How can you be certain? says the PC.

Experience says Brindle.

But without a body—

Without a body you're left standing around scratching your heads wondering what the Christmas-day film is and I'll be doing all the work as usual. What about the father?

They call him Ray Muncy.

Any previous?

Ray? No. He's loaded is Ray. A good lad.

Know him do you? says Brindle.

Of course says PC Temple. Everyone knows Ray. He's a dalesman. He's valley blood.

Well enough to be struck off his Christmas-card list when you arrest him?

Arrest Ray? says the constable.

If it came to it.

You think Ray's done something to her?

Highly possible.

But you've got no evidence protests the PC. You've not even met him.

I've got statistics.

Statistics?

Brindle rolls his eyes.

Come on son this is basic stuff. More often than not victims know their killer. Sometimes they're related. Father–daughter usually. This is basic stuff.

You don't know that she's been killed.

And you don't know that she hasn't been.

The PC looks at Brindle. Brindle looks at the map and shakes his head.

Are you lot from the city always like this? says the PC.

Yes says Brindle. Yes we are. Especially me.

RAY MUNCY INTERCEPTS Roy Pinder as he returns to the

station carrying a polystyrene tray of chips and curry sauce. It is steaming in the cold still air.

Well? says Muncy.

Pinder pauses on the station steps and turns to face him.

Well what Ray?

Any news?

Roy Pinder spears a chip on a wooden fork that seems impossibly small in his chubby fingers and slowly puts it in his mouth. It is too hot so he shifts it around for a moment then chews.

My men are on it.

Something's not right here.

And my men are on it.

Maybe you need more of an incentive.

Incentive? says Pinder.

Yes.

Pinder smiles. He spears another chip and points it at Muncy. As he does a drop of curry sauce falls to the snow between them.

Are you trying to bribe me Ray?

No. That's not the word for it.

What is then?

I need you to find Melanie. That's all. You need to step things up. Because from here it looks like you're doing fuck-all.

We're out looking. My best men are up on those moors now.

It's not good enough. I need assurances.

Pinder forks two more chips into his mouth. He smiles through the mush as he chews.

Assurances Ray?

Yes.

Well lucky for you they're bringing someone in. Sending someone up. Some slick cunt. The top boy apparently.

He stirs the chips around in the curry sauce. With his fork he slops it over them and then scoops another one up.

A moment passes before Ray Muncy speaks.

Do you see much of your old friend Roy?

What friend is that then?

You know which one.

I don't believe I do Raymond.

Your famous friend.

A shadow flickers across Pinder's eyes. The fork returns to the tray. He rests it on the lip. He moves down a step closer to Muncy.

Who would that be then?

You know who.

Tell me.

The one they're going to give a knighthood to.

Pinder studies Muncy's face then but he doesn't speak.

Muncy lowers his voice.

Come on he says. You know I've always been good at keeping secrets.

Is this some sort of threat Raymond? Bribes first then threats is it now?

He's retired isn't he? says Muncy. Larry Lister I mean. You don't see him on the telly now do you? Different era I suppose. All those secrets though. So many stories.

Roy Pinder's eyes harden.

It's a shame about your Melanie he says.

Ray Muncy stares back.

Do you know something about where she's at?

Roy Pinder says nothing. He stirs the chips in the sauce a second time. Drowns them in it. He chews one slowly and deliberately noisy.

Because I swear if you do I'll bring the whole fucking thing down.

Pinder swallows then speaks.

As I recall you've said that before. And look where that got you.

Where?

Here says Roy Pinder. Right here. Your lass missing and begging me for my help.

He looks up and then down the street then he leans in and whispers at Muncy.

You'll do well to remember who runs this valley before you start shooting your mouth.

I've got nothing to lose says Ray Muncy. If Lister falls then you fall too.

Pinder points his fork at him.

If I fall everyone falls.

AND LATER THE same night after the humiliation of the X he is drunk in a pub – a quiet pub a dead pub a pub where hope goes to curl up and die – on the edge of the city. It's one of the old ones without the whistles and bells of a branded chain. Just a smoky shell of a place where defeated drinkers slump hunched against emphysemic walls and not even a daily bleaching can clean the floors. Rutter is alone and the safety and comfort of the Odeon X is over it is gone and now alcohol is in him for the first time. The alcohol is whisky and it is in him and it nips at his gullet but he is doing what it is that real men do.

He is drinking and he is glad he has no sense of taste because this way the drink goes down easier.

One tumbler then another. A double then another.

The alcohol warms his stomach. The alcohol heats up his throat and neck; the neck of a wrung chicken his mother once said. Neck like an empty ball sac she said.

He drains his glass and stares into it for a moment and then he stands and moves sideways. He is dizzy on the drink. He clatters into an empty table and somebody shouts wahey – aye

aye sailor and he fumbles in his pockets and he drops some money and then he leaves.

He walks without any thought for direction and he gets lost and then barrels around the streets and at some point someone tries to trip him up – a group of young men in short-sleeve shirts are laughing and jeering – and there are women stumbling and squatting and pissing in back alleys and then he turns a corner and then another corner and he walks down an alley and he finds he is back in the car park and he sees his car but as he heads towards it he sees a woman by her car with her keys in her hand and she's big and he thinks maybe it is the fuckbucket from the X who spurned him or maybe it isn't but the ground is all angles and his legs are running away with him and then he is on her and over her and in her and –

And later he will remember little except the sound of the struggle and the raincoat she was wearing. And her shoes. He will also remember her red shoes.

Then everything is just a series of photographs forever out of reach. Of butting and biting. Of snarling and spitting. The sound of heels being dragged twitching over stone to a cold silent place.

Then a gently slapping sound like a clock ticking and a scarf slipping around her mouth to keep her gagged. Gently almost. Her scarf not his. A fancy perfumed thing pulled back tight like the reins on a gelding. Reining her in breaking her in. Bull and heifer. Steed and mare.

He thinks: mud moors trees wind dogs water flesh touch soil men oil blood mother gravel drains bones pigs stones.

And afterwards he will take it home with him. The scarf and the body.

Limp in the back. Shoes placed neatly on top of her. He will drive drunk through the night out of the city and back to the pigs in their pen in the dark of the dale.

But not before he has been seen; not before he has been

watched and recorded and noted and documented.

If the hills have eyes then so does the city.

THERE'S NO CORDON. He expected a cordon but of course there is no reason for one. No body. No crime scene.

No cordon.

But there are plenty of police up in the hamlet. Their vans and cars line the turning circle and block the road. Roddy Mace parks up and drains the rest of the coffee that's now gone cold. Kills the music.

He sees Elaine Stonehouse. One of the PCs and another pub regular. He gives her a wave. She nods back and stamps her feet to keep warm.

Mace walks over.

Season's greetings Elaine. Nippy out today.

Hello Roddy. Got your newshound sniff on have you?

Dennis Grogan wanted me to check in on the latest he says. Any developments?

Elaine Stonehouse shakes her head.

Nothing you can tell me? he asks.

Are you doing a piece then?

Mace turns the collar of his winter coat up and squints up the hillside.

Maybe he says. Maybe.

What I mean is am I speaking on or off the record here?

Any way you want it Elaine. I'm just doing some fact-gathering. It's Christmas so there'll be nothing going to print anyway.

Good. Because I don't want my name in the paper and there's nothing to tell anyway.

Behind Elaine Stonehouse more officers are quietly kitting themselves out in walking gear. Flak jackets and sticks. There are dogs too. Not all of the men are police though. Some are familiar local faces. Men who help out with Mountain Rescue.

Chasms and quarries and clefts and fissures and bogs and moors are their terrain; all as dangerous as a razor-edged arête in this weather.

There's always something to tell says Mace. That's the first rule of journalism Elaine. Even when nothing has happened there's a story there: missing girl found doing Christmas shopping in Leeds – moorland search-party called off – PC Stonehouse gets the drinks in for the first time in her life. Something like that.

I think it's going to be a bit more than that actually.

You do?

You never said whether I am speaking on or off the record.

How about off the record then says Roddy Mace.

Elaine Stonehouse looks over her shoulder and then checks the radio that is in her breast pocket.

Off the record I'd say something has happened to Melanie Muncy. Something not good. We've turned up nothing that suggests she's run away. Her wallets and keys and money are at home and her phone's been found. Dropped or dumped. She only went out for a walk with the dog. We've checked the cameras at the train and bus stations – and the service stations. Nothing.

Boyfriend?

Not that we know of.

Doesn't mean there isn't one.

Of course. But her friends know nothing about one.

Again – it doesn't mean—

I *know* Roddy.

Christmas he says. It can be an emotional time.

Yes.

A time for rows. Stresses and strains.

Don't I know it.

What about her family?

We're looking at them. The mother's going spare. June

Muncy. Lost it they reckon.

I heard she had a few screws loose anyway says Mace.

I wouldn't like to say.

And the father?

Ray. Hard to say. He's a strange fish.

I heard that too.

He seems oddly calm. Confident that we'll find her.

And you're not?

Elaine Stonehouse shrugs. Raises her eyebrows.

So if she hasn't decided to head south for the bright lights of the big city –

Then something may have happened says Elaine.

Like what?

I'm not into speculating. That's your job. Mace ponders for a moment.

I see myself more as a wordsmith weaving webs of fact and poetry he says. A documenter of the epoch.

You're a pretentious bastard you are.

Mace looks at the hamlet. At the few houses creeping up the hill that is cast in perpetual shadow and the uneven mix of the old wind-chiselled cottages interrupted by the occasional new-build cast in a lighter tone of stone.

By this place's standards yes I'd say I was.

They fall silent for a moment.

Anyone in mind? asks Mace.

There are always names.

Like who?

Like Mr Piss Off and Mrs Mind Your Own Business says Elaine Stonehouse. I'm sure you'll be the first to find out when we know something substantial Roddy. Something printable.

Mace raises his hands. Palms out.

I'm just doing my job Elaine.

And I'm just doing mine. Or trying to. Anyway shouldn't you be at home stuffing something?

Very good. And that's it? That's the local plod's grand plan?

She looks around again and then lowers her voice.

Look – between you and me they've sent someone up.

Someone up? From London you mean?

I don't know. Maybe not London. But someone.

Who?

I don't know.

Can you find out?

Wait a minute.

Stonehouse turns and goes over to one of her colleagues. One of the dog-handlers. They talk for a moment and then Mace sees them both glance over at him. He stamps his feet. Crumps the snow until Stonehouse returns.

Some detective by the name of Brindle.

Brindle says Mace. Jim Brindle?

She shrugs.

Do you know him?

I've heard of him says Mace. Bit of a mad fucker apparently but he's done some big cases. The biggest in the north – murders and worse.

What's worse than murder?

Plenty. They say he's up-and-coming. There's a lot of stories about Brindle.

Like what?

Mace shrugs.

You know – just anecdotes. He's young too.

Just what the valley needs. Another cocky baby-faced prick.

He's not devilishly young like me says Mace. And not half as handsome either.

He looks up at the sky. Elaine Stonehouse follows his gaze.

Looks like more snow she says. A lot more snow.

Can I quote you on that?

No you bloody can't.

THE ROOM IS cramped and still smells of smoke years after the ban. Even now the furniture and carpet holds the stale scent. Clings to it. It is a bygone odour thinks Brindle; one day nothing will smell like this.

He opens the window and looks out across the market square then turns back to the room. It is cramped and dated. Not quaint and period but tired and neglected. Tourists hoping for a taste of Yorkshire past here would find only a sagging mattress and anaglypta. A carpet that looks like a migraine. Curtains a burnt orange colour and a dark stain splashed across the hem of one of them.

A formica surface runs the length of the room with a folded plastic chair propped next to it.

With one finger Brindle opens the drawer. The Bible is a cheap Reader's Digest edition. *Condensed from the original version* it promises.

An unduly large flat-screen TV fastened to a bracket that is bolted onto the wall is the one concession to the modern age. It has had to be tilted and angled to fit in the corner of the room.

Brindle has already met Roy Pinder. Pinder is the man who runs the town's tiny police outfit. Brindle thinks that Roy Pinder is a fucking idiot. Brindle knows that Roy Pinder is a fucking idiot.

And Brindle knows that Pinder feels the same about him too.

Brindle and Pinder he thinks. Sounds like – what?

A figure-skating duo. A type of wallpaper. A recipe for disaster.

The pub is called The Magnet and he can already guess the type of people it attracts.

It's early but already he can hear noise coming up through the creaking floorboards. The clinking of glasses being washed down below. The vibration of a deep raised voice. Traces of that thick accent. Laughter. Somewhere down the crooked hallway a door slams.

Brindle lifts his suitcase onto the bed and slowly unzips his case. Sees everything laid out. Folded and neat but not neat enough. He begins the long controlled process of finding a correct home for everything. He counts woodchips he counts carpet-swirls he counts the seconds in between each breath as he holds it there like a cool soothing cloud of vapour in the centre of himself.

SHEPHERD'S PIE IS all Larry Lister ever eats in his upper-valley bolt-hole. Maybe the occasional Fray Bentos from a tin for a treat.

Christmas alone: *so what*. He has a freezer full of ready meals and a microwave and chocolate and a bottle of brandy and plenty to smoke. Plenty to watch. He could stay for weeks if he wanted to – and in the past he has done just that. Gone to ground. The first time was a year or two after he had his accountant buy the place. The first allegations had just been made and though they had managed to keep it all out of the papers he didn't feel like showing his face for a while. All that smiling made his jaw ache.

In his absence – he considers it an exile – he had lost out on a telethon job. It was for one of the high-number channels but still. It was work; he was wanted and when he finally returned to London it was only after spending two days on a sun-bed. Told everyone he had been in the Caribbean. St Lucia: bloody beautiful.

When the meal is cooked he plates it and then heads up to the attic. He still feels a little exhilarated and anxious after the film. The ending never fails to surprise him. It never loses the capacity to make his heart race.

He selects another tape from the archive. Not one from his special collection – a normal one. He chooses at random and puts it into the VHS.

These tapes he will get transferred to disc as soon he can. Better still he could make a call and have someone from the corporation do it. A ripe young intern.

He presses play and sits down to eat some of his shepherd's pie. He stands and then takes a salt shaker from his pocket and taps it over his plate and then sits again.

The video contains a collection of some of his guest appearances – a compilation that he recalls *was* put together by a ripe young intern many years ago. The tape spans the ages; it traces the evolution of television from the monochrome innocence of the swinging sixties' earliest days (Cathy and Rosko and Cilla and Diddy) through the vibrant technicoloured seventies (Tarrant and Tarby and Cliff and the Cornflake) and onto the anarchic eighties (Noel and Wrighty and Rod and Timmy) then the glossy nineties.

The nineties was when things really changed. That was when the new breed came in. They all seemed to be called Jamie and Robbie and Kat and Zoe. Maggie's kids had grown but they didn't have her sense. No. This lot came from the other camp – the politically correct lefty loons. Stage-school shitheads most of them. Poofters the rest. Cunts the lot of them. He knew for a fact that on more than one occasion they'd tried to have him ousted but he was still a draw even then and it seemed the public's (bless them) opinion still counted for something. They couldn't dump old Uncle Larry. Hell no. There would have been an uproar. There would have been petitions. There would have been editorials in the one or two papers whose editors he had fat files on. He would have made sure of that.

The first clip is of him on *The Good Old Days*. Live from the City Varieties in Leeds. A top show was *The Good Old Days*. A right laugh. He sees himself in a green suit that he has no recollection of ever owning but which dates the clip to around 1979. He's gatecrashed a magician's slot and is walking about the stage like a chicken. Mugging for the camera. The magician is cracking up. Nearly pissing himself he is. But there's fear in the little fucker's eyes too. Fear of being upstaged. A Lovely Larry Lister speciality is that. Get in there. Throw a few proverbial firecrackers. Give the stage manager hell. Leap onto the lap of an old dear in the front row then do one out the back door. Engine still running.

The nineties was when they all started to steal his livewire format and he started spending more and more time back up north. He had reconnected with Mr Hood then. Rekindled something that went way back to the dancehalls and youth clubs. Different days; different ways of doing things. A powerful figure even then was Hood. But unlike him he was not one for the limelight. No Hood was a back-room guy. A behind-the-scenes string-puller. A doer – and feared too. Many a man had fallen at the feet of Hood without him having to raise a fist. Fear was his tool and he wielded it well. He'd seen the same thing in Ronnie and Reggie when he joined them for wild nights a decade or so later at one of their supper clubs; the three of them sat there with a dolly bird each in their laps and cigars jammed between their teeth. Of course Ronnie preferred the other but everyone has their peccadilloes and proclivities.

On the tape the magician is bundling Larry into a box. They're improvising the old sword-spearing routine. But they're stretching it out with jokes and banter and all the while Larry still has a cigarette in his mouth and he is laid back now blowing smoke rings right up as the magician sticks the swords in and the audience are loving it – bloody loving it – because it's good entertainment it's harmless and it's primetime and it's what they deserve it's what they want and there was no health-and-safety shit back then and as the last sword goes in Larry turns and winks to the camera and he finds himself repeating the line now through a mouthful of lukewarm mince and mashed potato alongside his old self and the studio audience: keep smiling and *be lucky*.

He had looked out for him had Hood. Been good to him. When he saw that Larry's career was flagging he reached out and invited him on board as a silent partner and to make use of his showbiz and charity connections. In turn he took full advantage of the speciality services that Mr Hood was able to facilitate. Went a bit mad on it for a while actually.

There is a noise from the VHS player – a whirring and a clicking – and then the image on the screen jams. It is held there flickering – an audience shot – faces forever young frozen in time. His braying paying public. Larry puts down his plate and stands. He thumps the top of the video player and time begins again.

BRINDLE PARKS UP and walks around the hamlet. He stops and looks. He walks past every house and then he takes the back tracks. The ancient lanes that cut through fields and lead up hills and disappear into sunken holloways. He stops again and stands on stiles and checks the angles. There is a breeze and he feels the cold under his layers. The sky is like television static. The disorder of nature is unsettling. He wants to be at home sitting in the dark drinking tea.

He looks up the slopes and down the valley and he keeps looking back at the Muncy place.

When his feet have gone numb he heads up there.

He goes alone. They suggested that a uniformed officer goes with him – someone local; someone who Ray knows – but Brindle says no. No one local. That's the last thing he needs.

When he answers it is obvious to Brindle that Ray Muncy has already been told someone is coming up. Someone from the city. A detective. Him.

He ushers Brindle in and the detective is surprised to see that Muncy's house is a gaudy new-build complete with mock pillars and ostentatious fittings. It is as if it has been transported brick by brick from the footballers'-wives corridors of Essex or Cheshire all the way to the edge of this obscure cleft in the earth. It is a residence that appears at odds with the old stone farmhouses and sheep folds and cottages that define the area. Transplanted is the word that springs to his mind. Tasteless is another. A tasteless transplanted money trap.

It is also in disarray. There are clothes scattered about and damp towels and plates with half-eaten meals on them. The superficial mess puts Brindle on edge. He wants to realign everything. He wants to wipe every surface. Impose order. Sterilise.

Muncy leads him through to the spacious living room. On the walls hang a number of framed inspirational slogans bellowing motivational platitudes like FAILURE IS A LESSON – LEARN FROM IT and THERE IS NO 'I' IN TEAM BUT THERE IS A ME and A MAN SHOULD NEVER NEGLECT HIS FAMILY FOR BUSINESS – WALT DISNEY. The slogans are printed in a childlike rainbow-coloured font. Comic Sans notes Brindle.

Drink?

Brindle reaches into his inside pocket.

I'd appreciate it if you could pop this into a cup of hot water.

What is it? asks Muncy.

Earl Grey.

We've got Earl Grey.

This one's a particular herbal infusion says Brindle.

Muncy looks at the bag in his hand as if it were a tiny dead bird or a court summons.

Herbal infusion?

Some Earl Grey triggers my asthma says Brindle.

When he has left the room the detective looks out of the window and then at the photos of Melanie Muncy. Melanie on a beach as a child. Melanie on a horse. Melanie on Ray's shoulders in what he can see is the back garden of this house.

The view from the living-room window is stunning. From this elevation he can see down the full funnelled length of the valley to where it broadens out to the flatter land where the town nestles two or three miles away. The dale is a white tunnel now that is patchworked by the lines of the old stone walls and the road that snakes downhill. Ray Muncy returns with Brindle's tea.

What department are you with?

Brindle hesitates. He wants to tell the truth. The department of darkness. Cold Storage: home of maimings and murders. Mad shit. The stuff that will send your head west if you let it. Babies buried alive and prostitutes used like lab rats. Torture chambers in mini-cab-office back rooms. Limbs and organs scattered one hundred miles all the way across from the East Riding up to Pendle. Snuff films and worse.

Missing persons he says.

Good says Muncy. They say you're one of the best.

I will do everything I can to find your daughter.

Where are you staying?

I stayed last night at a pub in town.

Which one?

In the square.

The Magnet?

Yes said Brindle. That's the one.

Bull Mason's place. Have you met Roy Pinder? He's top boy up here.

Not any more thinks Brindle. Instead he says: yes – briefly.

Muncy's face strains at this. Brindle struggles to interpret the meaning.

Are you going to help with the search party?

No says the detective.

No? Why not?

My job is not to organise a search party. That's down to the officers on the ground – those that know the land. Roy Pinder. To search you of course need to be meticulous but ultimately I think that it also involves a certain amount of luck. The needle in the haystack.

Now wait a minute—

Please don't be offended Mr Muncy. My role is to gather information and piece it together. I use facts rather than luck. Why search for something before you know it is even there? My skills are more logistic and forensic. Of course the groundwork is important but I like to step back from the microscope and see the wider picture so to speak.

There's no reason for her running off says Muncy. That I do know. No explanation for her going off and not coming back. And I know what you're thinking. You're thinking about me aren't you? I'm not stupid. You're looking at me. You're wondering.

Brindle blows on his tea. Muncy has left the bag in.

My job is to look at everything he says.

I bet you've done your homework though haven't you? I know the statistics: how often it is that there's a family member involved.

Involved in what?

Now it is Muncy who is hesitating.

You know. Wrongdoings. Disappearances. Murders.

Well we don't even know that any wrong has been done Mr Muncy. Out of respect to you and your wife murder is not a word I would think of using at this stage. And also because it is unfounded.

Good says Muncy leaning forward. And I'll tell you now son: I've got nothing to hide. Plenty have but not me. Ask around. They all know me in the valley. I've got my enemies yes but haven't we all?

I don't know says Brindle. Have we?

All men have enemies.

Brindle looks at the wall above Muncy's head. Sees another framed slogan. SHORT-TERM THINKING IS A CRIME.

I'm not sure that's entirely true says the detective.

Judge me by the enemies I have made. Roosevelt said that. I bet you've picked up a few in your game.

Game?

The crime game.

These enemies says Brindle.

I've misled you says Muncy backtracking. I'm talking about business stuff here. Minor things. Nothing to do with this. Nothing to do with my Melanie. I'm nervous that's all. Not slept. Tongues wag around here that's all. There's them with their secrets but I like to be upfront.

What business is it that you're in Mr Muncy?

I started out years back with an MOT garage. Ran that for years down in town. Or the edge of anyway. You wouldn't think there was brass round here but there is. There is. Provide a unique service that folk will always want to use – that's the key. Specialisation. So then I opened up a petrol station next door. Fuel: that's where the real money is. People will always need fuel. I've invested in a few other projects since. I part-own a couple of cafes. A property investment in the city. And we've got the campsite out the back. That brings in buttons but it gives June something to do. Is this relevant?

Everything is relevant. Any business partners?

No.

Brindle sips his tea and then adjusts the knot on his tie. Says:

So you think she had no cause to run away?

Muncy shrugs.

No. Of course not.

Brindle takes out his notepad and thumbs through it.

And she goes to boarding school in –

Ripon.

Oh yes. Slater's Girls School. Would you describe your relationship with your daughter as a good one?

Very good.

And with Melanie's mother?

Me or Melanie?

Either. Both.

Fine says Muncy. Melanie's at school now so things have changed of course. She boards in term time. She has changed.

Melanie or your wife?

Muncy ponders the question.

Well both I suppose.

Is Mrs Muncy here?

She's resting. All of this has taken its toll.

I gather your wife was unwell already?

June is sensitive that's all. She has a fragile disposition. Look – no offence – is this the best you can come up with lad? I've already gone through this with some of the boys.

The boys?

Yes says Muncy. Pinder sent some of his gorillas up for a gentle grilling but I thought you were here to actually do something.

Brindle looks at the picture frame on the mantelpiece. ADMIT YOUR MISTAKES AND THEN MOVE ON. He thumbs through his pad again.

And what about people in the valley he says.

What about them?

Get on well with them do you? Your neighbours.

Most of them are sheep.

Brindle raises an eyebrow.

Sheep?

Yes says Muncy. You know: like the animal.

Right says Brindle. How?

Most of them have been here all their lives. They just follow what their fathers did – and their fathers before them. Me – I like to strive for more. I've travelled as well you know. South America. The Far East. Florida three times.

Are there any people around here who strike you as suspicious Mr Muncy? Odd I mean.

Muncy snorts. Muncy laughs without smiling.

We're all odd up here Detective. I would have thought they'd have warned you of that much.

Steven Rutter. Do you know him?

Of course I bloody do.

His name has been mentioned.

In respect to what?

In respect to this Mr Muncy. This investigation. Your daughter.

Muncy stands and smoothes down his hair. He pats it nervously.

Do you need more tea?

No says Brindle. How would you describe him?

Rutter? Shy. Keeps to himself which is just as well as he's not big on hygiene. He's a valley boy isn't he. He's part of the scenery if you know where to look. Odd as a cod and twice as smelly. But harmless.

How can you be sure?

I can't says Muncy. No more than I can say you're harmless. But I will say this: I've known the lad a lot longer than I've known you and he's never bothered me personally. I'd not exactly invite him in for tea or encourage him to join the Rotary but his business is his business just as mine is mine. Do you actually think he's got something to do with this?

I think that everyone within a hundred-mile radius has to do with this until I've eliminated them says Brindle. Now can I see Melanie's room?

You're too late. They've already been in there too. The local lot.

They have?

Yes. Of course. June let them in; I'd rather have none of them coming anywhere near me.

Why? asks Brindle.

Muncy just shrugs and turns away.

You can't trust any of them. Especially Roy Pinder. Watch him.

Have they touched anything? says Brindle.

I wouldn't know. The place is a pig-sty.

I'd like to take a look. Muncy's jaw tightens. He stands up and Brindle follows him. The staircase is curved. Above it there is a window to increase the natural light in the hallway. Muncy notices Brindle glance at it.

It gets dark otherwise he says. The girl's room is a typical mess of clothes and posters. A suitcase on the floor with more clothes spilling out of it. A dresser with a mirror and make-up and photos. A teenage space.

Brindle looks at one of the framed pictures.

Who's the lad?

Muncy shrugs.

Some pop star. She's outgrown that stuff now.

How do you mean?

She left for school a girl and has come back a young woman. Even since the summer. She's less impressed by anything. Harder to get on with.

I thought you said you had a great relationship.

We do says Muncy. You know what teenage girls are like though.

Brindle doesn't reply. Decides to let Muncy speak.

Do you have kids Detective?

No.

Are you married?

No.

Not married?

No.

Any plans to get married?

No says Brindle.

You're not into the idea?

No.

Churchill said his greatest achievement was persuading someone to marry him.

Brindle looks around the room.

Then again says Muncy. Churchill was no looker was he?

Brindle notices something on the floor. He squats. It is an inhaler.

Is your daughter asthmatic?

Mildly.

And her inhaler is here.

It looks like it.

The detective opens drawers and carefully begins to rifle through them.

He stops and looks at Ray Muncy.

You don't mind do you?

Muncy turns away and looks out the window. Looks down the valley.

Do what do you have to do.

Brindle continues. He methodically looks through boxes and make-up bags and flicks through notepads. He shakes magazines and opens wardrobe doors. Upturns shoes. He crouches and looks in a suitcase which lies splayed open. It contents strewn.

His hand closes on something. He stands.

Is your daughter sexually active Mr Muncy?

Muncy turns back to face him.

What?

I'm sorry but I have to ask.

She's fifteen for Christ's sake.

Yes says Brindle.

Fifteen.

A lot of girls are active at that age.

Not my Melanie.

You'd be surprised.

Muncy's face darkens. He turns to Brindle.

Now listen.

Brindle looks at him impassively.

I don't like your questions.

I have to ask them says the detective. They are necessary. I'm sorry.

And I don't like your tone either.

Muncy's voice is raised now. He is frowning. His brow is pushing down on his eyes. His jaw tight again.

Brindle blinks.

So. Is she?

What?

Boys Mr Muncy. Men. Women. Is your daughter sexually active?

What difference does it make?

Brindle opens his hand. He is holding a pregnancy-testing kit.

Potentially a huge difference.

THE CAR SLIDES sideways across the road and begins to fishtail. Mace squeezes the brakes and they lock and only by turning the wheel into the spin does he prevent the car from crashing into a wall. Three times this happens on the three-mile journey down from the hamlet. It takes him forty-five minutes. He parks the car and runs through the snow dragging his suitcase behind him but when he gets into the station it is silent. Dead. There is snow on the line and snow on the platform but there are no people. He looks up and down the tracks. Snow even hangs from the power lines. Everything is blanketed. There has been no activity but snowfall here.

He walks back through to the tiny entrance hall to the ticket office. Its shutters are down. He looks up at the screen. The message ***ALL SERVICES CANCELLED*** runs sideways across it. Mace stands and watches for a longer time than is necessary then he turns and leaves the station.

RUTTER AT TEN.

As a growing boy in the corner. In the playground.

Five or six boys are sitting on the wall. Village boys and farm boys singing a song.

Your dirty mother. She likes to have a fiddle. She done it with the milkman with you in the middle.

It is directed at him it is sung at him it is jeered at him. Sneered with venom.

At him in the corner; him in his rags. By the boys on the wall the five or six of them. Big boys rough boys dirty tough boys.

Village boys. Farm boys.

They sing another verse.

Your dirty mother. She likes to have a fiddle. She done it with the coalman with you in the middle.

Sneered and jeered and while making wanker signs with their hands.

Your dirty mother. She likes to have a fiddle. She done it with a black man with you in the middle.

Now he is standing and now he is rising and now he is walking over.

Rutter is walking over to the boys. The boys singing the song. The sneerers and the jeerers. No sense to that song but. No. No sense at all but. A nonsense song is that.

There are five or six boys sitting on the wall. If one of those boys should accidentally fall.

Your dirty mother. She likes it back scuttle.

Rutter is tightening and Rutter is coiling and Rutter is breathing. He is walking over to them. His arms hanging down like sledgehammers. Hands feeling like steel heads. Making him walk funny.

He is breathing and he is walking over to them and he is walking up to the biggest one. The thickest one. The biggest baddest bastard one.

And cracking him one.

And the big boy – the bad boy bastard stinking tough boy – falls.

Falls from the wall.

Smacks his head. The sound of it. Humpty bloody Dumpty diddums thinks Rutter.

But he gets back up does the big boy. He stands back up. He straightens and touches a fingertip to his scalp and he smiles.

Because he's a big boy bred to wrestle animals all day long.

Then it's him that's getting stomped. Then it's Rutter that's getting hoofed then it's Rutter on the ground. It's him in the corner again and it wasn't meant to be like this.

It is him in the middle. It is boots and fists and dirt and gravel. Footprints and bruises. It is digs and jabs and kicks and punches.

She done it with a black man.

A no-sense song that but. A nonsense song but.

He is in the corner and he is by the wall he is in a ball and it wasn't meant to be like this. It wasn't meant to be like this at all.

BRINDLE DECIDES TO climb the hill to the Rutter place in the fading light.

Beneath the snow the path is rutted and uneven and for a short while it sinks into the hillside as black hawthorn bushes spring up on either side as if to trap him.

Once a woman told him – told James Brindle – that he had

weak lips.

Weak lips. Her exact words.

He was in a nightclub. He was still drinking then; still functioning socially then – and it was loud so he thought he had misheard and asked her to repeat herself. She did. He had not misheard. *Weak lips.*

Ever since then he had wondered what that meant. To have weak lips. Even now years later every mirror was a reminder of this one cruel comment; one comment against a thousand others about his vibrant birthmark He considered what it said about him as a man and how all the success at work – the awards and the promotions and the killers brought to justice – could never change this and that perhaps it all somehow linked up with the well of loneliness that he felt inside. That his weak lips were at the centre of it all. That and the birthmark and the counting and the touching of surfaces and the powerful aversion to dirt and the feelings of bubbles coursing through his bloodstream and snakes squirming in his arms and the rest of it.

He pauses to look back on himself. He looks down at the village and the way the houses cling to the road and then he looks over the other side to Muncy's house and his land out back running down to the river and trees. Then he turns to the Rutter farm up the hill and heads towards it.

AS HE LEAVES the cinema a hand gently touches his arm. Fingers curl around his elbow and seem to grip a nerve there. There is a shooting pain up his arm. There is a cold voice in his ear.

You need to come with me.

He goes to turn round but the hand presses the small of his back. Guides him.

Just keep walking. Through that door on the right. No fucking about.

He tries to stop but the hand is forceful.

They get to the door and the man opens it.

In he says.

He is young and afraid and the man is very thin. His cheekbones are prominent and the skin on his face seems drawn tight. In the low light it has a waxy sheen and there is something about his mouth. His top lip is crooked as if had once been split all the way up to the nose and then stitched wrong. Stitched up too tight.

His hair is combed back. It is crisp with wet-look gel. He is wearing a shirt and tie. He is wearing spectacles.

What's this about but? he says. What's going on?

Mr Hood wants to see you.

Who is Mr Hood?

Not someone you want to say no to.

He stands aside and ushers him through the doorway. They enter the darkness at the top of a flight of stairs. Again the hand is at his back – urging and pushing with a lightness that he finds unnerving.

They go down the stairs and turn right then down more steps. They are at the back door of the cinema. They are in the bowels of the cinema.

Not there says the man. He nods to the ground.

There.

He looks confused but the man squats down and touches a mat that is laid there. He feels around and then pulls at a metal ring and lifts the rug. A hatch opens.

He nods to the space that has opened up and says: in.

He looks down and then steps onto a ladder. The man follows and closes the hatch above them. They go deeper into the heart of the buildings. They pass through a series of low-ceilinged arched cellar rooms. Some are full of junk – old carpets and chairs stacked up and damp newspapers and bottles and rat traps and plastic crates – and others are empty.

They turn a corner and he sees a large screen and he sees men sitting around it drinking and watching a film. Smokes hangs heavy in the air. The film is silent and black-and-white but not old. It is CCTV footage.

He sees a struggle. He sees a man on a woman he sees a man in a woman he sees a man going through a woman. At it. Dismantling her. Wild.

He sees the shape of himself. Rutter.

Him. Rutter. Possessed.

It is of the car park outside – the car park of the X – and it is like a strange dream.

He looks to the man now and the man smiles and says cameras young man. We had them sent over from America special. They call them eyes in the sky. Capture anything.

He looks back to the screen and sees the way in which the woman is stumbling and falling and the way you can only really see her legs sticking out from behind a car in the dark and how his legs are bending and folding into hers.

The men are watching in silence.

Then the footage suddenly ends and the lights come on. The men – seven or eight or nine of them; men with suits and wallets and wives and pictures of children back on their office desks – put down their drinks and begin applauding. The thin man is looking at him sideways. He sees that as the lights come on the lenses of the man's spectacles darken. The thin man says come on and leads him to stand in front of the screen.

Gentlemen he says. The star of the show.

In the low light he sees that some of the men are in work suits and one or two are in black ties and dinner jackets. Others are more casually dressed. They are of differing ages. A couple seem very old to him.

Get the lad a drink for fuck's sake says one of the other men.

He doesn't want one.

I'll have his then.

I see he's dressed for the occasion says another voice. More laughter.

He looks at the men's faces. He thinks he recognises two of them. They seem familiar. Just as he is trying to place them one of the men says Christ – it's fucking Steve Rutter.

He squints. He places the face. It is Wendell Smith. One of the valley men. The owner of a chicken-packing plant.

Wendell says Rutter.

The thin man turns to him.

No first names here.

Wendell Smith speaks again.

He lives up by Muncy's place.

This causes interest amongst the men.

Rutter looks at the thin man and sees that his glasses have darkened further and then he looks at the men again. One of them is wearing a large brightly coloured baseball cap.. He thinks perhaps that he is off the television but he does not have a television so he cannot be certain.

I'm Mr Skelton says the thin man. And that as you know is Mr Smith. Now that we're all friends maybe you can tell us what you did with her?

With who?

The men drink and smoke and shift in their seats. They watch with interest.

You can speak openly son. You're amongst like-minded people.

He says nothing.

Skelton nods to the screen. A guaranteed life sentence that. Guaranteed. Isn't that right your honour?

One of the men smiles and nods.

The thin man – Skelton – tips his head towards the young man and says to the others: imagine what they'd do to someone like him in prison gentlemen.

The men smile and laugh and rearrange themselves again.

It only takes one phonecall says Skelton. You could be anywhere in the world and all it would take is one phonecall to have done to you what you did to her. Mr Hood's not happy about this.

Who's Mr Hood?

One of the men interjects. A fat man in a tuxedo.

Who is this joker Skelton?

Skelton ignores both questions.

Now. Answer carefully and honestly: what did you do with the woman?

He swallows and shifts his weight from one foot to the other.

Dumped her.

We'd gathered that. Where?

What does it matter?

If her body was found and traced back to here it would matter says Skelton. It would matter a great deal. One more time. Where did you dump her?

He sniffs then scratches at his patchwork stubble.

The pig pen.

There is silence for a moment and then Skelton says the pig pen?

Aye. The hogs ate her.

The man in the baseball cap leans forward in his seat and removes his cigarette from his mouth and says with a big smile: the hogs ate her.

He nods.

And that works does it?

Aye. A half-dozen hogs and a few hours and they're all gone. Every last bit of them – all except the teeth.

The man in the baseball cap smiles again. The men are smiling back at him.

He's right you know says Wendell Smith. The lad's a farmer. And his mother. Centuries old that lot. As old as the soil itself.

You wouldn't think he was capable would you? says the man

116

in the baseball cap. Who else son? How many others have you put in this pig pen of yours?

None.

He's lying says one of the men. You can tell.

Tell us the truth now lad and we'll look after you says the man in the baseball cap who he now sees has a level of authority over the others. Lie and you won't see the morning.

None.

Mr Skelton says the baseball cap. Please remove one of the young man's eyeballs.

Skelton grabs him and moves in with a clenched fist with one thumb sticking out.

Wait he says. Wait.

Skelton stops.

There might have been one before.

One what?

One lass a while back. A bit ago. Just some lass. Will you tell the authorities?

The man in the cap starts laughing at him and the other men start laughing and then they are all laughing. All except Skelton.

Son says the man in the cap. We are the authorities.

CHICKENS ANNOUNCE BRINDLE'S arrival into the yard.

Brindle sees a place defined by absence. The barns are missing panels and reduced to rotten skeletons. A tractor sits slumped without a windscreen and a front wheel leaning to one side like an old man who has keeled over. There are empty oil drums and grain buckets and spools of frayed rotting rope. He sees another piece of farmyard machinery. It is a digger of some sort but all its parts have rusted and the paintwork is chipped and there is a film of algae on the inside of the open window. Everything once mechanical now seems rusted and locked and beyond purpose.

He pauses by the chicken coop and sees sad thin birds who

have pecked at each other's feathers in agitation. He sees no sign of cultivation or growth. Nothing harvested or stored.

Brindle turns a corner and suddenly dogs are barking at him. He sees them only as small dark braying shapes. He pauses and then moves closer. Terriers scrabble at chicken wire to get at him from inside their pen. Brindle crouches and they bark louder and fight each other in the melee.

The back door swings open and a form fills the doorway. Brindle stands up slowly.

Who's that out there?

Mr Rutter? he says.

I said who's that out there?

It's the police Mr Rutter.

Get away from my dogs you shithouse.

Brindle walks towards him. Brindle moves towards the light.

I'm a detective. James Brindle.

The coppers have already been. I've already answered all your questions.

Brindle steps into the elongated rectangle of light spilling from the house. Sees a small man in the doorway. A weasel.

Not my questions he says. Can I come in?

Have you got a warrant?

I don't need a warrant for a chat. Warrants are for searches.

They've already been in. You're not searching my house.

I know says Brindle. I just want a chat.

About what?

You know what.

Brindle faces him now. Rutter looks shrivelled and lined. All sinew. A dirt-marked creature of the landscape. He is holding a poker in his hand. He is staring at the birthmark on Brindle's face.

Can I come in? It's cold out here.

No says Rutter.

As he stares the detective stares back.

Melanie Muncy. How well do you know her?

I don't.

You don't know her at all?

Rutter shrugs.

Only I've just come from her father's and he says you've been here as long as these hills.

So?

So. They're just down the hill from you. Melanie grew up here in sight of this house.

Rutter shrugs.

Aye.

And you're still saying you don't know her?

I'm not saying I don't know who she is. I'm saying I don't know her. There's a difference.

You're right Mr Rutter. There is a difference.

Well then.

Brindle turns to face the dark farmyard. Puts his back to Rutter. Shoves his hands deep in his overcoat pockets.

Live here alone do you?

Rutter grunts an affirmative. Brindle turns back and fixes him with a stare. He studies his face and notices that there is red raw grazing on his right wrist then without blinking he says where have you put Melanie's body Mr Rutter?

The question throws him.

Rutter leans on the door jamb.

I've not done anything. Ask Roy Pinder.

I don't know Roy Pinder. I don't care about Roy Pinder. I don't give a fuck about Roy Pinder – or you. Only the girl. I know that you are involved in her disappearance. We might as well admit it now and then we can progress.

I'll admit to nowt.

You know I don't need witnesses – only evidence.

I know you need to arrest us first.

Arrest you? says Brindle. Good heavens no. I believe I just intimated that you were involved. That you are withholding information.

Rutter's eyes flicker. He cannot make sense of the odd-looking detective on his doorstep. Brindle is not like any policeman he has ever met before.

There are so many opportunities up here aren't there continues Brindle. So much space. So much soil.

Rutter shrugs.

I mean it'd be easily done though wouldn't it continues Brindle. Getting rid of a body. A young girl. Only small. Lost in all this space. All that soil. Those moors. I bet nobody knows up here better than you do they Mr Rutter? You're probably a handy person to know.

They look at each other.

How long have you lived up here?

You know how long says Rutter. Or you would if you'd done your job.

Seen some changes I bet says Brindle turning away again.

He is acting the part now. He knows other detectives are better at this side of things but he continues anyway: the world never stands still does it he says. These wind turbines must be annoying.

You get used to them.

Much else changed?

Rutter shrugs again. Looks from the sky to the ground and then at Brindle's shoulder.

You must have seen *some* changes says Brindle. To the landscape and farming I mean. What about the famed waterway? How did that affect things for the farm? The reservoir I mean.

Rutter looks away.

It didn't. I never go up there.

Brindles feels an itch in his nose coming on. He removes

a handkerchief and then sneezes into it. Once and then twice. He carefully folds it and then puts it back into his coat pocket. He hopes that he is not getting a cold.

For a moment it looks like he is going to sneeze again but then it passes. He turns his back again and looks over to where the dogs are penned.

I think I might have a dig around he says. That's what I do you see Mr Rutter. Dig around. I'm known for it. I'm good at it. Bloody good at it. I'm like those terriers of yours: once I get a hold of something I don't let go. I lock on. I bite down. It's a weakness in a way – a character flaw – because once that happens no one can pull me off. You'd have to kill me to end the process. But it helps get the job done.

Brindle steps out of the rectangle of light and into the darkness. Into the darkness of the yard. Into the cold dark blue space of it.

Merry Christmas Mr Rutter. I'll be in touch.

BRINDLE ONLY MAKES it down the hill from the hamlet before the road becomes impassable. The drifts deepen and swallow the stone walls. There are no straight lines in the landscape; no vertical or horizontal. Only cambers and curves and smooth fresh slopes. His chest feels constricted as he scans the landscape for grids or patterns or parallels or anything that offers continuity but he sees nothing but nature's chaos.

At the bottom of Back Haslet Road the few cars that are still out have been abandoned at odd angles at the roadside or around the perimeter of the market square.

Christmas Eve and Brindle is stuck. Trapped. The town has him. Fucksake.

He goes back to his room in the Magnet. He walks through the bar and up the back stairs. Along the stale creaking corridor. Enters his room.

He calls the train station only to be told by an automated

message that all trains have been cancelled. He gets numbers for the nearest taxi firms – there are two – but neither is operating. No point they say. The third one is thirty miles away and won't risk it.

The snow has shut down the dale. For a moment he considers calling for a cop car to come get him but dismisses the idea. That would look terrible. And besides – that may not make it through either. He is going nowhere.

Brindle unlaces his boots and takes his socks off. They are wet. He takes his tie off. He puts his socks on the radiator and turns on the TV to drown out the noises coming through the floor from the pub below. It will only increase over the coming hours.

He can smell the fresh cigarette smoke. He could do the landlord for that if he wanted to – but then what?

There are five channels on the television and every programme is Christmas-related. He washes his hands and face and then pats them dry. He combs his hair.

He looks in the mirror and sees the tightly drawn mask of his face. The weak lips and the dark red defect – thinks: short for defective. Defective detective. Defective man.

Mirrors he thinks. Always mirrors and masks and memories.

He turns away and from his suitcase he takes out a clean tea-towel and spreads it on the bed and then opens one of his cartons of cold rice and vegetables and places them on the towel. He takes a plastic fork from a cellophane wrapper and pulls the one chair in the room over to the side of the bed and then awkwardly leans forward to eat the rice and vegetables. As he does he reads his way through one of the many box-files that are stacked by his bed.

There is no kettle in the room so he takes fresh socks from the drawer and puts his tie and jacket back on. In the bathroom he combs his hair again and brushes his teeth and counts bathroom tiles and then closes the door behind him. He walks down the hallway and the bright swirling patterns of the worn carpet make him feel dizzy. He smells chip fat and aftershave cutting through the cigarette smoke as he walks down the narrow stairs.

3

SHE IS PROPPED up like a puppet that has been put aside between performances. A puppet with its strings cut. Slumped inanimate.

She is staring at him and she has brown eyes and she is dead.

The scream is in his ears still. He can hear it. Piercing and girlish. Way over the top that was he thinks. A right fuss she made over a few thumps.

He may have used his feet too. Then again he may not.

In some small and unexpected way he is both surprised and disappointed; she was meant to be a country girl this Melanie Muncy. Rural stock. He thought it would be stronger than this. Tougher than this. Sturdier than this. Hardier than this.

He only gave it a few thumps. A slap.

A couple of kicks. A boot or two.

A little slice. A nick.

She should consider herself lucky in a way. He had had a rifle and a machete and a paring knife and he had been polite enough to use none of them. Man enough. Gentleman enough. With his own hands he had dispatched her. He had shown love.

Dead though. No pulse no warmth no blinking eyes.

Dead and always dead now.

She is something else now.

Somewhere else now.

All his now.

THE HUM OF the wind turbines cuts through the air as the

blades spin elongated circles of shadows across the hillside. Their shapes wheel across frosted rock and brittle heather. Darken the snow.

The fire is not lit. Rutter is in the crepuscular light of a mid afternoon in winter.

He is straight he is still he is staring ahead at the wall.

He is staring at the dancing windmill shadows entranced. And remembering.

Remembering the other girl. That first girl.

He is allowing himself to recall her. To raise her up. Revisit her. She had not been much younger than him.

Late teens the pair of them. Must have only been a year or two in it.

It was a long time ago now. Two decades or more ago now. A long long time. Before the X. Before the car park and the whisky and the cameras and the cellars. Before all of that.

She was not a hamlet girl not a village girl not a dale girl not this one – no she was just passing through. Stopping down at Muncy's camp site. Not a town girl. No.

It was summer. High summer. A hot August. Scorching it was.

The girl. She was doing the Coast to Coast walk carrying her tent roll-mat and sleeping bag on her back. Tins of beans pots and pans and a map in a plastic case around her neck. All of that. Fetching up on a different site every night. Mad that lot said his mother.

Here was where she chose to rest up for an extra day before heading off to meet her boyfriend. So the papers said. Him leaving her alone like that. This lad. Leaving her up in the hills to fend for herself. It wasn't right.

She could do better. Young Rutter knew this. He saw a nice girl a polite girl a clean girl. A bit of a scruff maybe but not a dirty cumslut. Not a dirty spunkjar. He saw an outdoors girl a sunny girl a free girl.

Marriage material maybe. Yes. A keeper this one. Maybe.

What was he thinking letting her camp out like that? The boyfriend.

If she had been Rutter's he would never let her go. He wouldn't let her out of his sight. No. Too many weirdos out there.

No. Not this one. This one was a keeper.

A nice girl a polite girl a clean girl like that. A rarity.

It wasn't right. There were dangerous people about. Even around here.

Nice girls need protecting.

She was out walking. Just a little leg-stretch up top past the hamlet. A gander round the locale.

He met her coming down the Corpse Road and into the gorge. He had been fishing. He was green himself then. Green as a winter sprout. He'd not even started shaving. Not properly. Once a month maybe.

He met her hopping great boulders along the rusted river where the steep gorge-sides ran right up to the sky.

Oh hello she said. You gave me a shock then.

It's a lovely day and so beautiful here she said.

So wild and unspoilt she said.

He said nothing because there was nothing to say to that.

I'm so lucky to be camping by this river.

He cleared his throat. Held his rod in his hand.

At Muncy's are you? he said.

What's that?

The farm.

Oh yes. At the campsite. I've got it all to myself. And thank God for that shower block. Any luck?

She nodded towards his rod.

With the fishing.

He looked at her feet. She was wearing plimsolls.

My boots she said reading his mind. They're drying out.

She looked at his feet. He was wearing rigger boots.

I could do with some of those.

She could smell him from where she stood: sweat and farmyard effluence. Stale tobacco.

Are there many fish in this river?

He looked down at the water.

Yeah.

What kind of fish?

A few trout.

He sniffed and cleared his throat and then said they say there's grayling but I've not seen any of them.

The girl pushed a strand of her hair behind an ear. The ear was bright and translucent. He could see sunlight through it. She was wearing a button badge too. It said: *Madchester*. It said: *Rave On!*

I've been eating noodles all week.

Eh? he said.

Oh I was just saying I've been on the old walker's diet all week. Super Noodles.

What's them then?

Super Noodles?

Yes.

Well you boil them in the pan said the girl. They're the eastern spaghetti. They're pretty boring.

She smiled and cleared her throat then she looked away.

He wondered if perhaps this one was a filthy cuntslop after all. A lot of them were these hippy girls. Not wife material. No. He'd not allow that type of behaviour. No. Never knowing what she was up to when his back was turned. Men knocking at the back door all day long. Work men delivery men old men dirty men. No no no. Not that. Not that never. Not that again.

What was she really doing by the river on these boulders anyway? No one ever came down here but him. The path ended a half-mile back then after that it was a scramble and a clamber to the best pools. No one knew about it. It was Rutter's land.

She was lurking and looking that's what she was doing. Looking for a man. She must have been. She was looking for a local lad. Looking for fun.

Looking for him.

He had read the stories in the magazines that people dumped down the back lanes around town. He salvaged them. He saved them and he collected them and he pieced them back together like wet flesh-coloured jigsaw puzzles.

Horny girls in the country. Randy girls in the bars. Yes. Rolls in the hay and romps in the heather. Or like dogs by the river.

Yes. He had read the stories about these girls who dropped their drawers at the first sight of a man.

Well she said and swatted a fly away. One landed on his cheek but he didn't seem to notice or care.

He moved towards her this boy. He moved across the rocks. He hopped from his boulder to her boulder and his tackle bag rattled.

The girl went to brush the lock of hair behind her ear again but it was already there. Her translucent ear was a delicate shell glowing in the sunlight.

Well she said again. I should get back. Back to the noodles she said then gave a forced little laugh.

I could get you a fish he said. He heard himself stammering.

For your tea like.

That's really kind said the girl. But there's no need.

It's no bother.

They were standing on a boulder at the bottom of the gorge by the rust-coloured river. Up close the smell of him was stronger. Toxic almost. She wanted to gag. She had smelled tramps on the tube in London and she had worked for a week in a shelter for the homeless in Leeds helping men who pissed themselves and sweated out Special Brew and never ever showered. This smell was just as bad. This smell was *worse*.

That's fine. But hey it was nice talking to you.

She turned to leave and then a hand settled on her shoulder.

No one will see us.

See us. Sorry?

His hand was still on her shoulder but she was facing him now. Now was the time. His time. Yes. He had been waiting and now he was going to make this happen. Yes. Time to make the move. He had read the stories he had read the magazines. Those flesh jigsaws. He knew what happened next.

He leaned in to kiss her. His breath was foul and the river was fetid. There were flies everywhere. She could not disguise her feelings. She recoiled. Wincing.

He knew her game. Wasn't this what they always did? Cat-and-mouse they call it. Well OK then. He would be the cat and that was fine.

There was a pool below them. The water was slowly gliding through it then running down to a lower level where it made a music of sorts – like broken glass being poured onto cold concrete.

Sorry she said. I think perhaps you've got—

His tongue. He stuck the tip of it out and closed his eyes and leaned in again.

Stop she said but he dropped his fishing rod and his tackle bag and his other hand was around the back of her head now. His fingers were in her hair now and he had her clamped.

She pushed at his chest with her hand and said don't wait please stop but he knew that when they said don't and wait and please and stop they meant the exact opposite. Do. Now. Come on. Don't stop.

He went in harder and she tried to knee him in the groin;

she tried to remember everything she had been taught everything she had been warned about if ever a man tried to attack her but he sidestepped and though he saw this coming he was still wrong-footed. He stumbled. He stumbled and they teetered and then they fell together. They fell from the boulder to the rocks below. Pure accident. It was six feet or more. He still had a hold of her and their heads clashed as they landed and he heard something crack and give within her. She was beneath him. She had cushioned his fall. He was winded. She was hurt. They were both hurt.

The girl tried to speak but her breath was trapped in her throat and then he was at her shirt ripping at it yanking at it buttons popping material tearing and she was not wearing a bra.

She was unable to move.

Silent. Blinking. Choking in the shadow of the boulder the foul river silently gliding by a halo of flies around his head. Fetid and foul.

Then he was thinking: fish flesh boulders flies eyes films maggots hooks gills scales slime blood button badges pins spikes rave on.

Then he was becoming a man a real man a powerful man and the secret seed was planted in the soil of his silent dark centre.

MACE SEES HIM across the bar and knows who he is straight away. He doesn't need telling. The blood-red birthmark is a giveaway.

His stiff posture makes him look like he's been dipped in varnish and his white shirt and tie – are those *croupier's armbands* lifting his cuff from his wrist? – and fighter-pilot short-back-and-sides with oiled parting confirm it. He doesn't look like a detective but neither does he look like someone who might otherwise be in the Magnet. Mace had heard

Brindle was an oddity but he didn't know he was such a freakishly formal-looking one.

The detective is at a table in the corner. A cup and saucer sit in front of him. Spoon on the side. Notepad. Mace looks again and sees that he is drinking what looks like tea. Christmas Eve and the fucker is drinking tea and staring at the evening punters as they fill themselves with beer and spirits and smoke.

Mace takes a drink from his pint. He cuts through bodies and trades acknowledgements and greetings. Brindle looks up. Looks at him. Through him. Mace nods at Brindle. Raises his glass. The policeman stares back. Blinks.

Merry Christmas to you says Mace.

Yes says Brindle not moving. And you.

Mace thinks he see the flicker of a frown pass over the detective's face but then it is gone and something far more unnerving is in its place: a blankness. Nothing is being revealed.

So says the journalist. Seems the trains are cancelled and the roads are fucked.

Brindle sighs and then clicks the end of his pen and places it on the table. Touches it once.

I'm stuck says Mace. Can't get back to my parents' now. Not tonight anyway. Though that might not be such a bad thing.

He suddenly feels silly and exposed and flushed with the beer. Unduly scrutinised. He hears himself saying can I buy you a pint?

No says Brindle. But thank you.

That stare thinks Mace. Like someone trapped under ice. The look of a man who has seen too much.

Sure? It's a once-in-a-lifetime chance.

I don't drink.

Wow.

What?

A policeman who doesn't drink says Mace. A rarity. Especially a detective.

Brindle adjusts himself slightly in his seat and presses his back against the chair. He holds his hands in his lap.

How do you know I'm a policeman?

Elite-murder says Mace then lowering his voice adds: Cold Storage. Am I right?

Brindle says nothing.

I bet you've seen some right grim cases says Mace. I read about a few of them. Even reported on one or two up here. The body parts in the suitcases. The microwaved babies. Gangland torture. Lively Leeds. And then before that – beautiful Bradford wasn't it? The red-light. Street-walkers and their sad little punters. Lasses hacked and torn on industrial estates. In crack dens. And you went into all that straight at the deep end – straight from a degree. Criminal Psychology. I am right aren't I?

Brindle stares back.

Go on he says.

Four years up in Durham on a scholarship continues Mace. A First I believe. A rapid rise. Fast-track and all that. Stayed out of the politics of it all I imagine. Best way. Made yourself trustworthy and reliable. Sidestepped the snide remarks about being the college boy. Old-school detective work aided by modern thinking; the best of both worlds. And then of course the notorious Cold Storage – more secretive than Opus Dei and a nickname invested with double meaning. Triple meaning. Cold bodies and icy cops. Only ever spoken of in hushed tones. A near-mythological place. They say it takes a certain type to work Cold Storage yet here they are sending you up here in the middle of a bloody snowstorm on Christmas bloody Eve the bastards. It's almost as if they want to punish you for being—

For being what?

Too good.

Brindle gently moves his cup of steaming tea a half-turn on its saucer then clears his throat. He looks up. Squints.

Journalist he says. Delusions of literary grandeur but neither the dedication nor basic talent to actually do anything about it. Has a degree and the debt that goes with it. Has forgotten most of the useless information he learned about French poetry and classical drama and the godforsaken Russians. Drinks too much; drinks his bitterness away most nights in fact. Promises himself abstinence at an unseen point in a distant future; promises himself it every sorry morning. Lungs like a spent fireplace. Still in his twenties and thinks he has seen everything. Thinks he knows everything. It doesn't feel like the rot has set in just yet but it has – oh it has. Good enough at his job but then again it's not exactly hard work up here in the hills where sheep-rustling stories and cake-bakes hog the front pages. Spent some time in the capital. Sure. The wild years. Got up to all sorts. Thought he was being rock 'n' roll by embracing Blakean excess; thought he was being a modern bohemian but he was just doing what millions of others have done before him: pissing his life away. Found out that the road of excess leads to the palace of a Balham bedsit. Said he was there for the culture but that soon faded; said he was there to make his name make his fortune make his bones as they say but that soon faded. They were proud of him back home but – Christ almighty – that soon faded too. Considers himself anti-capitalist but does nothing about it; considers himself a freedom fighter but feels trapped. A liberal in rhetoric only; a humanitarian who does nothing for humans. Might like narcotics and the seedier side of life. Certainly he's experimented in that area. But then everyone of his generation has and isn't it boring to think just how much they have experimented yet have singularly failed to gain any further insight into the human condition from these hedonistic pursuits? I wonder what state he'll be in by the time he hits forty?

Jim Brindle fixes Roddy Mace with another of his grey stares.

Am I right?

AFTERWARDS HE PUT the body of the girl whose name he did not know into the river. Wedged it under an overhang. Weighted it and wedged it. Deep. Submerged it and left it. Sunk it. Dumped it.

Underwater so the flies wouldn't get to it.

When he went back that night it was bloated from the river water but otherwise the girl looked like she was just holding her breath.

It was warm. A balmy July night. Beautiful. He unhooked the button badge pinned to her chest – *Rave On!* – and pocketed it.

The sound of water over rock seemed louder in the half-light.

He fished the body out and took it home. It took two hours to walk one mile.

It was heavy and dripping.

He was tired and stumbling.

Halfway home he undressed it and touched it and then dressed it again.

On the way he saw a barn owl explode from a branch like white fireworks. Its magnesium feathers shimmered in his torch-beam and its wing-tips were chromelike. Its eyes like lasers. Talons stowed.

And then later after cups of tea in the darkness of the kitchen as his mother slept upstairs he went to Muncy's campsite in the early hours and took down the girl's tent. He quietly collected the poles and pegs and folded the canvas and took it all to the farm where he burnt it all out back.

Shoes.

Clothes.

Sleeping bag.

Noodles.

The tent poles he hammered flat and later still he used them to trim the rotting edges of the chicken-coop gangplank.

After the fire was gone he put the ash in the ash pit and that was that.

The tinned food Rutter kept for him and his mother.

And the girl went in with the pigs. By dawn she was digested. By midday fertiliser.

There had been a small mention in the *Valley Mercury* a week or so later. Local not national. STUDENT MISSING ON COAST-TO-COAST. They had presumed that she had moved on. That she was already walking to the next site. They suspected the boyfriend. They always do. They searched the route between the two sites. The boyfriend had an alibi. They found nothing.

What remained of the bones he bleached and scattered in the scars up top. One or two thrown in each. Offerings to the soil. Traces of their brief time together.

He had only ever wanted someone to gently touch him.

THE COLD HELPS. Winter is in his favour because the frozen ground and the icy air and the compacted snow have slowed the process. But it has been days and now the body is discharging though its exit points. There is fluid leaking from the Muncy girl. Leaking and running and foaming. Rutter feels it – viscous and gluey.

Even in the most remote storm drain – the one that is gated off and way beyond the last bleak shore of the reservoir – even here in this frozen mausoleum in which he has hidden her the process cannot be prevented. It can only be slowed to a snail's pace.

Her coat and trousers and blouse and sweatshirt help hold her together but underneath the body is already rotting.

She is a darkening red now and the skin is papery thin. It reveals a complex map of blue veins that appear to have risen to the surface in their hardening. Patches of it are blackening into blood-clotted lesions like small countries on a map of the world.

When he pulls the girl's trousers down things are worse. When he tugs them down he sees that the body of the girl has soiled itself and the underwear is full of matter. Discharge.

And things are receding already. Even with the cold the girl is receding from view. The flesh is withdrawing from her narrow frame. Her gums fingertips eyelids and lips are all shortening; yet the torso seems an oversized trunk that is bloated and distended. He has seen it happen to enough pigs and sheep to know that the ballooning is part of the process.

When Rutter looks in the mouth the teeth appear lengthened too. He puts his fingers in and feels the tongue: black and sponge-like. He pulls at the teeth and feels them wobble in her jaw. He pats her hair. It is dirty and matted and brittle.

There are no maggots though. Not in winter.

No. Not yet.

He thinks again. Remembers. Remembers that same feeling rising. How he only ever wanted to feel the touch of another.

IT'S A GOOD job your reputation precedes you otherwise I might be offended.

Brindle closes his notepad and looks up at Mace.

Mace pulls out a chair and sits. He puts his fresh pint on the table but the table is unsteady and some of it slops out. A small puddle forms on the table and then runs over the edge. Brindle winces. Drips hit the carpet.

So you're stuck here too then.

Yes says Brindle.

Christmas Eve and you're stuck in the Magnet.

He nods.

That has been established.

Haven't you got somewhere you're meant to be?

Of course says Brindle.

A wife waiting for you I mean.

No. No wife.

Across the pub a group of teenagers enter and furtively look around. Brindle notes they're underage. At the bar there is a group of men with their feet planted and their arms cocked at right angles. Their chests puffed as pints are upended and drained. Big men. Farm men.

What about your family? says Mace. Mine are going to be gutted I'm not there in the morning to try on another ill-fitting sweater and express excitement when I open my Lynx bathroom pack. All that fake bonhomie just feels so fucking hypocritical. Don't you think?

Brindle does not answer for a moment. Then Brindle says:

You should be grateful. Some people have nothing. Have no one.

Mace sips his beer. He feels wrong-footed; he feels wrong-headed.

You really guessed all that stuff by looking at me?

Brindle pours more hot water from the teapot into his cup and then reaches into his jacket and pulls out an Earl Grey bag and drops it in.

Across the room someone put some coins into the jukebox and it kicks into life. ABBA. When Brindle says nothing Mace raises his voice over the music and says I'm Roddy Mace by the way. And despite what you might have heard I fucking hate ABBA.

I know who you are. And – no – I didn't guess all that. I already know about you.

You know about me?

Yes says Brindle.

He dunks and dips his tea bag. Across the room a party popper is pulled and both men flinch. Thin twists of coloured paper float down then settle on the head of a bald man who has his back turned. He brushes it away and then carries on drinking.

So you think she's dead then?

You're a reporter says Brindle. I'm hardly going to tell you that.

I know she is anyway. Or I'm fairly certain. No one survives the moors in this weather.

It's a small town continues Brindle. My job is to find out about people here. All the people. Sift through the information that is already there and piece things together.

Information?

Crime is a jigsaw. Information is the pieces. We are all of us being continually documented. You find what pieces you can then you join them together and see the big picture. As a journalist you will know this already. Or you should.

Well yes says Mace. Of course. We all leave a trail.

So I know about your time on the tabloids. The London years. Your odd decision to take a career back-step by relocating to here. It's all documented.

Should I be flattered? Or scared? Are you always this – what's the word?

Thorough? says Brindle.

Invasive.

Both men fall silent. Mace sips his beer and Brindle his tea. The detective puts down his cup.

This place says Mace. Don't be too confident. It's full of secrets.

Why did you do it? asks Brindle. Move here to Yorkshire. It's archived in the media trade-press. Your move away from tabloid-land I mean.

Mace takes another sip.

I didn't think anyone had noticed.

Someone always notices.

Mace shrugs.

The things you have to do to get ahead didn't interest me. I've always wanted to be a writer and that's not writing. Working on a tabloid. It's just not creatively satisfying. It wasn't writing.

The music on the jukebox changes. It's another Christmas song. They are all Christmas songs now. 'Little Drummer Boy' then 'White Christmas' and now 'Fairytale of New York'. A drunk couple do their own rendition. They take the male and female parts and emphasise the swearing. Brindle watches them for a moment and then turns to Mace.

And that's the only reason – it wasn't creatively satisfying?

Mace nods but he is unsure.

It's different here he says. There are other things going on. Things beneath the surface. There's a community.

What are you running away from?

His voices rises in pitch.

I'm not running away from anything he says. He frowns and then adds: you've not said if you think Melanie Muncy has been killed.

You've not said why you left London and came to this backwater.

Why should I? I'm not under questioning. I only came over to say hello.

Hello says Brindle.

He picks up his cup.

Are you like this with everyone?

Brindle doesn't reply.

It's true what they say then says Mace.

I don't know what they say says Brindle.

139

Aren't you interested in what people say about you?

No.

No?

No says Brindle.

Mace shakes his head.

So you're stuck here for Christmas Day then.

Brindle looks bored. Impassive. His interest waning.

Unless I get airlifted out he says. Yes. It looks like that.

You're staying upstairs.

Yes.

They're doing a roast says Mace.

What?

A turkey dinner. For Christmas. All the trimmings. Looks like I'll probably be here too.

The jukebox-volume seems to rise a notch. Brindle finds himself forced to raise his register with it.

I don't eat turkey.

Me neither. It's barely digestible. Who do you think did it?

Did what?

The girl. Melanie.

I didn't say I thought anyone had done it says Brindle.

Mace leans in. He is trying to be discreet.

I could help you if you like.

Help me?

If you like says Mace.

I'm fine says Brindle. I like to work alone. And anyway you're not even from here. And I need to go and make some calls.

I've been here long enough to get established though says Mace. Especially working on the *Mercury*. It's only a local rag but it's what they read. It outsells *The Times* or the *Guardian* a hundred to one round here and it's opened plenty of doors for me. Got me in all the meetings that matter.

That's what you think.

Maybe but that lot over there at the bar – they're all from the Dales. They're born and bred. They know everything about everyone. More than any copper from the city ever could. Trust me: there's things you get to know about only if you live here.

The volume of the pub has increased to a level that is making conversation difficult and some younger men appear to be involved in some sort of organised drinking game that involves a lot of grunting and back-slapping. They are upending glasses and then putting them on their heads. They have weathered faces and big boots.

Mace finishes the rest of his beer and emits a small belch. He leans back in his chair and runs his hand through his hair. He pulls it back so that it's left standing in tufts.

Alright he says. Let me say two words to you and I'll then leave you to it. There's beer to be drunk and Christmas to be commiserated and I'd be an even greater failure as a regional hack if I didn't even at least attempt to get in on this.

Brindle raises his eyebrows.

Two words says Mace.

Go on.

Steven fucking Rutter.

RUTTER AT THIRTEEN.

A summer's evening in the copse up top.

Way down below his mother is shouting.

She's shouting. But she's miles away.

Get them pigs slopped out she bellows. Get them grunters fed. Fetch the logs and kindling in. Then get on off up to bed.

Bed he thinks. It only bloody seven.

He's a pig-man now. It means he is an expert in something now. It means he is a farmer now. He has a purpose. He nurtures these beasts and he knows things the other boys don't know and he can bond with animals and he can read the habits of animals and know the ways of animals.

He knows responsibility. He knows pigs.

Big pigs angry pigs aggressive pigs. Hungry pigs. They eat through anything. Slops and carcasses. Offal and bones. They'd eat all day if they could – and do.

Strong jaws strong teeth strong stomachs – these beasts can make almost anything disappear. Barely a trace.

They eat through anything.

Yes. Slops and carcasses offal and bones. He knows this. He notices this. Twelve hours is all it takes to process anything once living. Digest it.

And like a sow he has noticed his mother getting bigger. Getting fatter. Getting porkier. A big fat pig hog she is. One day he notices her distended belly bulging through the gaps of the house coat she wears over her great flopping namesakes in the summer. Her dirty dugs fuller than ever. Waddling about.

The men had stopped coming around and then just a couple or three weeks later he had heard howling and moaning and heaving from her bedroom and he put his ear to it and then his shoulder and he pushed but there was something weighted up against it and it was her but the door opened an inch or two or three and he saw there something small and wet blossoming from inside her. A brown thing hanging out. Halfway to the floor. A mewling thing. Life.

Feeling the door shift she screamed at him. She told him to piss off and get out and look after those animals and then get yourself disappeared. So he did. He did that. Disappeared himself up the dale.

When he came back from the reservoir hours later he heard something crying and then he didn't hear something crying and that night late when he was meant to be sleeping he looked out the window and saw his mother limping out towards the pig pen with a bucket and a torch and for the next seven days he had to do all the chores himself. The feeding the slopping the cleaning and the cooking. For a week she was bedbound and then she was back on her feet again.

Her belly went south and her tits went south and everything went south but the men started coming back round again.

She never mentioned what he had seen and he never mentioned what he had seen and they never mentioned what they had seen.

It was as if it had never happened. That night.

It was as if it had never existed. That night.

Through anything those pigs can eat. Slops and carcasses. Offal and bones. Everything but the teeth.

LATE-AFTERNOON WINTER SUN is shining down and Rutter has his eyes closed and is feeling its warming rays on his face when the chair is wheeled into the anteroom that the care-home staff call a conservatory.

He is exhausted. He has not slept; has not changed from his snow clothes. He sees first her feet then the thin airless tyres and then her mottled veiny legs emerge through the doorway. Rolls of fat sitting on her slippers. Belly pork he thinks. Like belly pork.

Mother.

The nurse winces and draws back. It is the smell of him. It fills the room. It is overpowering.

It is the fug of old wood-smoke and sweat and layer upon layer of clothing congealing into one mass; the smell of dried urine and soil and semen and moss and mildew and rotting teeth and bleeding gums. It is the smell of rotten human flesh and putrefying skin and death gases and decomposition clinging to a physical form. It is Steve Rutter.

The nurse. She is new here. She has not encountered Steve Rutter before. Not experienced him. When her manager sent her to fetch Aggie Rutter it was with a word of forewarning:

her son's a character mind. That was all: a character.

And now she is reeling.

Rutter thinks his mother fills her wheelchair like too much jelly fills an overflowing mould. It is as if her skeletal framework has been removed and she has been poured in. She has no centre and her mouth is twisted into a wet grimace. There is dried saliva crusted around the edge of it. Her eyes are wet and glassy. They roam the room before settling on her son.

A ventilation tube runs into her nose. At the other end is a breathing apparatus. Her hands are folded in her lap like two dead birds.

Those breasts that made her famous are now two sad empty deflated balloons from a party long since over.

Here we are says the nurse but speaking involves breathing and she does not want to stay in the room a moment longer. The smell is from beyond the realm of normality. It is sad – sorrowful even – but it scares her too.

Twice in one day says the nurse.

Rutter says what?

Your brother. He was here earlier.

Rutter fixes his eyes on her and the way he stares unnerves her. Makes her feel naked. She wheels the chair to the space beside him and locks on the brakes before retreating.

He closes his eyes and feels the sun on his face again. The conservatory door opens out onto a small patch of patio where many bird-feeders have been hung.

All he can hear is the sound of his mother's breathing aided by the ventilator. It is a taut wheeze. An automated rasp. Robotic almost.

Rutter finally opens his eyes. He glances at his mother. She has hairs growing from her chin. Thick black hairs. They are on her upper lip too. A bubble of spittle has formed at her mouth. It is her breath made physical and for a moment it is as if time has stood still and he watches the bubble expand

144

so that the sun catches it and he sees spectral colours in it and everything is silent for a moment and then his mother wheezes and the bubble bursts and flecks her impassive face with her own milky spittle.

Aggie Rutter's eyes stare back at him and Rutter is sickening for something and anxious and his throat feels like it is tightening. Suddenly it is hot in the room. Too hot. The heat is a cloak hung over him.

He looks at her. His mother is a pathetic mound of hairy sagging flesh who is only staying alive to spite him. Of this much he is now certain. Spite keeps her heart beating. She may be imprisoned by her useless body but he is imprisoned by the whole stupid world. By the farm. The only world he knows. It was she who said he had to stay until he was pushing fifty before he could sell up. Another decade yet. Ten years trapped. The real world slipping further away.

He knows she knows this. The way she drools – it is directed at him. Each suspended string is mocking him.

Rutter's breathing is tight and quick where his mother's is measured and aided. Automated.

The other thing that angers Rutter: each day she spends here takes money from the future sale of the farm. Yes. His property. His farm – his land. His legacy. Each day alive is a roof tile taken.

He closes his eyes again. Takes a breath. Feels the sun.

Brother thinks Rutter. What bloody brother?

RUTTER'S TRUCK IS a VW Caddy pick-up bought second-hand twelve years since. It is open-backed and red-rusted. The front-left wing has been replaced by a fibreglass panel sprayed black and there are holes in two of the wheel arches. Inside the small cabin the passenger seat and floor are a mess of mud and sweet wrappers drinks cans and carrier bags and branches and cigarette dimps and broken lighters. A tangle of wire and string and rope and sheep-skull and oily rags and a boiler suit and an old pair of gumboots and torn gloves and some damp newspapers and a rancid yoghurt pot and spilled dog biscuits and dog hair and dried dog scat. The open back has more junk on it. Logs branches kindling an empty oil drum a funnel a spanner a wrench more rope more string more wire a spare tyre and all held down under a tarpaulin by straps.

The windows do not open. They are jammed shut from dents and prangs in both doors. Inside the stale smell is strong. Just as a discarded jar on a town tip cultivates life so too this airless space is rife with white mould and green mildew.

The snow has laid and the snow has flattened and the snow has iced. Driving back from the care home the road is a rink and the truck is a figure skater warming up. It slides from side to side following the tilt and dip of the road. Twice Rutter hits the verge. Once he scrapes a wall and the wall comes off worse as the truck leaves red flakes of paint in its wake.

The gritters don't come this far up.

The light snowfall is turning to a total whiteout by the time he reaches town.

Town is dead.

Town is dead quiet.

Town is dead quiet like a morgue.

He parks up he gets out he walks across the square and the snow creaks beneath his boots.

He passes Barry Harbottle coming the other way.

Now then Rutter.

Rutter nods in recognition.

What about this snow.

What about it? says Rutter.

It's coming down thick but.

Aye well. It's winter.

Harbottle is the coal man Harbottle is a drinker Harbottle

is a father of many. Rutter has known Harbottle most of his life. He has never liked Harbottle but circumstance and the passing of time binds them in some way. They call each other by their surnames as if still back in the playground.

How's that farm of yours?

Fine.

What you doing for Christmas then?

Rutter shrugs.

It's for the kiddies isn't it says Harbottle

I suppose.

Harbottle stamps the snow from his boots.

Aye. The kiddies love Christmas. As for me I can take it or leave it.

Yeah says Rutter squinting across the square. He wants to get out of the cold. He does not want to talk to Harbottle. He does not like Harbottle. He doesn't care a fig for Harbottle.

Stand you a Christmas drink if you like.

Rutter toes the ground.

Nah he says.

A quick one. One for the festive season.

Rutter squints through the falling snow again.

Come on Rutter it's taters out here. Buy you a nip.

Rutter toes the ground again then turns his collar up and clears his throat.

I'll be seeing you he says.

Suit yourself.

Rutter jams his hands in his pockets and leaves Harbottle staring at his back as the snow falls thicker and he walks across the square. His feet softly crumping the virgin white.

DID I HEAR you say Rutter?

Mace is on sailor's legs and the man has him cornered by the Magnet's fruit machine. He is standing too close to him and a drop of his beer flies out and lands on Mace's cheek. He wipes it away with the back of his hand but the man doesn't seem to notice.

Maybe says Mace. Why?

You were talking to that bloke before.

Yes.

Who is he?

Some copper.

The man's neck is fat with ripples of flesh. It sits on the buttoned collar of the checked shirt that he has washed especially for Christmas. He's large but with an unusually small and lipless mouth closing in on itself. Like a cat's anus thinks Mace. His features seem lost in the vastness of his face and there is an intensity to his eyes. Mace has seen him around town but has always given him a wide berth.

Is he here about Ray Muncy's girl?

Yeah says Mace. Why?

You want to look into that Rutter one. He's not what he seems. Tell the copper.

Thanks I will.

But don't tell him I said so.

I won't. Sorry – what's your name pal?

Everyone just calls me K2.

K2?

Yeah.

So why do they call you that?

He looks at Mace as if he is stupid.

Because of my size.

Right. I'm Roddy Mace.

The man – K2 – stares back. Mace feels cornered.

I know who you are. You're the writer. That's why I'm telling you about Rutter. You can put it in the paper. Only don't say you heard it from me.

You know him do you?

Rutter? Of course I do.

A friend of yours? asks Mace.

Is he hell. That smelly bastard'd gag a maggot on a shit-truck. But Ray Muncy is.

A friend?

He's been good to me has Ray. I've done bits and pieces of work for him over the years. I know what they say about him but he looks after his own does Ray.

Like what type of work?

Like anything says K2. Lifting and that. Building work. Anything going.

Right.

And it's fucking terrible what has happened with his Melanie. I've been up on the moors helping them look for her. We all have.

His small eyes look around the pub for a moment.

Waste of time looking up there though if you ask me.

Why's that then? asks Mace.

You want to look at Rutter. Have a dig. There's more to that one than meets the eye.

Like what?

Can't say. But it runs deep and wide.

What does?

Rutter's business. I'm thirsty.

Are you? says Mace before taking the hint. Oh right. Pint? And a whisky.

When Mace returns with the drinks K2 takes the whisky from him and downs it in one gulp and then takes the beer from him.

Go on says Mace. Tell me what you know.

K2 downs half of his pint and then belches.

Well he says. For starters there was that other girl what went missing wasn't there.

4

THE VALLEY IS white and the hamlet is jammed with police cars and vans when Rutter returns.

He sees that the road in is blocked. Blocked by cars with flashing lights around which stand police in luminous jackets. Some are talking in low voices. Others are stamping their feet and rubbing their hands together.

Rutter pulls over on the verge and gets out. He leaves the engine running and exhaust fumes mottle the snow. Policemen are stood around with some of the villagers. The muffled sound of barking dogs comes from the back of a van. A young policeman walks over to him.

Sir he says.

Rutter grunts.

Where are you planning on going?

Where do you think I'm going?

I don't know. That's why I'm asking.

Up the hill.

I need to take your name then.

I've already spoken to you lot once.

I still need your name.

Rutter.

The policeman turns away. There is a small burst of noise and then he talks into his radio.

Turn off your engine and wait here he says. Rutter walks back to his truck and kills the engine. He leaves the keys dangling.

The policeman walks over to one of his colleagues. It is the one who came to Rutter's house; the one he went on the search with. Muncy's pal. Jeff Temple. He approaches.

I need to speak to you Steven he says to Rutter.

You already have.

I need to speak to you again.

The dogs need feeding but.

I'll be up to see you in ten minutes then.

Why?

I'll be up to see you.

Not found the lass then.

We're still conducting enquiries.

Rutter runs a finger along his jaw line. Follows the weft of his bristles.

Expect she'll be on the National Express to London by now.

That's as maybe says Temple. We're checking all the stations again.

Rutter shrugs then hawks mucus from the back of his throat.

You'd be minded to he says.

You seem to know a lot about it.

Another policeman walks over. It is Johnny Mason. The landlord Bull Mason's twin brother.

I've got this Jeff.

No – you're alright says Temple. It's in hand.

As I said – I've got this. Me and Steve go back.

A moment passes between the officers and Temple looks from Mason to Rutter and lingers a moment longer and then he says OK then and leaves.

Johnny Mason checks his radio and then moves in close. He looks at Rutter. Studies him. Shoves his hands in the armpits of his gilet.

Not like you Steve.

What's not?

To do anything that you might get caught for.

I've not.

Johnny Mason steps closer. He is right in Rutter's face now.

His voice is low and measured.

I'm worried Steve he says.

What for?

I'm worried about you.

Why but?

You know why.

I've not done owt says Rutter.

You've done plenty.

Rutter tries to pull his eyes away from Johnny Mason's but he can't seem to.

You and I know of families in this valley says the policemen. Strong families. Tight-knit families. It'd be a shame if some fucking loser who's not a part of this decided to open his mouth and destroy those families.

Rutter says nothing.

There are secrets says Johnny Mason. There are livelihoods to think about. Endeavours to maintain. Don't forget your obligations Steve. Don't forget your position.

I've not done owt. I don't even know what you're on about.

Play dumb but we all know you carry secrets Steve and that makes your position precarious. And if you happened to have done something stupid.

I haven't.

We know what you're capable of.

Aye says Rutter. Well.

I wonder what he'd say if he got a phone call on Christmas Day?

Who?

I doubt you've forgotten.

You mean Mr Hood.

Johnny Mason looks around and then hisses:

Don't say his name you fucking stinking scut-hole. Try saying his name again round here and see what happens.

Johnny Mason steps back. He takes a packet of mints from

his pocket and pops one into his mouth.

Either way the thin man will be getting a call.

There's no need to do that says Rutter.

It's happening. It's already happened. And you'd be wise to have a tidy-up.

How do you mean?

Use your head. Get up there and sort that place out. I'll come up in a bit. Jeff Temple and that lot aren't from the valley but. I'm sure Roy'll do what he can as well. And keep your fucking mouth shut or you'll have Mr Skelton up here with his pliers and blowtorch. Now fuck off.

IT CAME FROM a man.

Just some man. Any man.

Another country man passing through his mother's bedroom.

He must have taken pity on the lad because as he sloped out the back door looking sheepish one day he gave him a pig off the back of his truck. Gave young Steve his first grunter. Just like that. Free of charge.

It was a little thing. A grunting thing.

A stinking thing.

That's a special pig said the man swinging it to him by its back heels. From strong stock. A rare breed that they call a large black. None will grow bigger.

He handed it to the boy who was now a teenager dotted with spots and sprouting hairs.

It was only eight inches long; hard to believe it could grow to be big.

It's a nipper now but just you wait he said as if reading Rutter's mind. Feed it right and you'll have a giant on your hands. Vicious buggers too the large black. Aggressive like. I reckon this breed got some wild boar in it way back when. Things got muddled. You'll not need a guard dog with one of them about the place.

What do I feed it? he asked.

Anything. Feed it anything. They're not fussy. Just feed it often and feed it well. I bought the semen that made that one. I inseminated the mother myself. It's one of the oldest breeds in England is that.

The man stopped and smiled at this then he said aye better than any bloody guard dog then he climbed in his truck and he left and the boy thought how it was the nicest thing anyone had ever done for him.

The pig ate constantly. Its appetite had no limit. It grew and it grew quickly.

It ate and it roamed and it followed him around. And still it grew.

His mother liked to prod it and cajole it. Kick it and whip it. Boot it and prod it. Always at it.

It'll help train it up tough she said. Keep it on edge. They like it that way. They've got to know their place.

Soon the large black was dominating all the other creatures on the farm. The cats and dogs gave it a wide berth. The wandering fell-sheep stayed well away. The chickens ran strutting and clucking at the sound of it.

It ate the slops and peelings. It ate worms and bark and shoots and flowers. It ate chicken carcases and mouldy bread and shoes. It ate rats from the rat traps and baby birds that fell from their nests. It ate dead piglets.

And it grew to weigh 600 pounds.

Six hundred pounds of wobbling black flesh with long lop ears framing its fat jowelly face and great teeth that jutted from its lower jaw.

The pig had free run up top and when any vehicle drove up the farm track it wheeled and bucked and screeched a warning shot across the dale.

Only when he scratched behind its ears and fed it scraps and whispered to it was the pig calmed. The rest of the time it ate and screeched and tormented every living creature who crossed its path.

It would snap and trample. Snarl and rip. Yes. The pig was the teenager's only friend.

Once one of his mother's men – a grubby mean-eyed man with a caliper on one leg – gave Steve a clump. A hard open-handed slap for no good reason other than he didn't like the snot that was dripping from his nose. As he reeled and howled the pig charged the mean-eyed man and knocked him flat on his back in the straw and piss. It tore through his calf muscle on his good leg like a knife through butter; like it was nothing. Lacerated him. The man screamed. Rutter laughed and kept laughing.

There was potential in the pig and there was money in the pig so his mother decided to seed the pig – she wouldn't let him name it; said that was sentimental – out to serve and stud.

One day two men came to take it away. They hog-tied it and muzzled it and Rutter protested until he got a belt from his mother but then they returned a day or two later. This began to happen often. Then when the pig was off the back of the truck the men would go indoors for a while. They'd stay with Black Tits a while and Rutter would take the hog out back to give it an apple and a scratch behind those flapping ears.

And it went on. The pig coming and going and spreading its genes all over the north of England.

And then one day the two men came again and tied the pig again only this time when it came back it was vacuum-packed in plastic in a hundred pieces. Porcine parts piled high.

His only pal. In parts now. In pieces now.

There you go said one of the men to his mother as he slapped one of the packages down on the kitchen side. No part wasted.

You've got the brains for brawn he said.

Then we've shoulder steaks and rib racks.

Over here's what you call the hand for cubing.

These here are sides and blades for curing and hanging.

The loin for back bacon or roasting or chops.
The belly's for rolling or roasting or skinning.
Trotters for jellying or the braising of shanks.
And then there's a bucket of blood for black pudding and
your offal for stews and stocks.

The man still had his apron on. His hands were unwashed
and there was blood beneath his fingernails and some of it was
matted in the brief streak of his knuckle-hair. He looked pleased
with himself.

It was past it said his mother when she saw her son's face
crumpling. Old. That hog was eating us into poverty. Now help
get this lot inside then make yourself scarce. These boys need
paying.

THE BARKING OF the dogs sets the chickens off when the
men arrive at his door.

There's Jeff Temple and Johnny Mason and the one who
stopped him before. The young one who looks barely old
enough to shave. They all stand there looking at one another.

Just need to ask you a few questions Steven says Temple.

I've not got the fire on.

That can wait.

It's cold but.

That can wait says Temple. Where've you been?

When?

Just now. Where are you returning from?

Town.

Which town?

Which town?

Yes. I'm asking you which town.

Which town do you think?

I've been through this with him Jeff says Johnny Mason.

What were you doing in town on Christmas Eve?

Rutter digs into his scalp with his fingers and twists at a

matted hair-lick.

Shopping.

Busy was it? says Temple.

Rutter shrugs.

So where is it then?

Town?

Your shopping Steve.

I left it too late.

What were you after?

Christmas stuff.

You mean presents?

Rutter says nothing.

Who were you getting presents for? asks Temple.

None of your business.

It was for your Mam wasn't it? says Mason. That's what you told me out there.

Where's your Mam at? says Temple.

Aggie Rutter took bad a few years back says Mason. Everyone round here knows that.

Are you expecting anyone for Christmas? asks Temple.

Rutter shrugs.

Answer the sergeant says the young officer. Yes or no?

Maybe.

Yes or no?

Yeah.

Who?

Rutter rubs his nose.

My cousin.

Your cousin.

Aye.

Where's she coming from?

He says Rutter.

Where's he coming from?

From London. For Christmas. That's why I was in town.

Getting some bits for us.

When's he due?

Hours back.

Is that right?

Yes says Rutter.

He's not lying Jeff says Mason. I heard them talking on the phone before.

Temple turns and looks at Mason for a moment.

Is that right. What's he called – your cousin?

Michael.

Michael Rutter?

No.

Michael who then?

Michael Smith.

Whereabouts in London is he from?

Why? says Rutter. What's he got to do with this?

I never said he'd done anything Steven.

We should get going says Mason.

Whereabouts in London is he from Steven?

Again Rutter scratches at his scalp. He looks from Temple to the younger policeman to Johnny Mason. Johnny and Bull Mason he thinks. A nastier pair of cunts you couldn't meet.

Wembley he says.

Wembley?

Aye.

And this could be verified could it?

How should I know. You're the copper.

He exists says Mason. We know that much – I've checked it out. Come on – let's leave this one to his sprouts.

What does he do for a living? says Temple.

Rutter shrugs.

So where is he then? Hiding in the bloody kitchen cupboard?

I don't know says Rutter. Reckoned he was setting off

first thing.

Mason leaves the room for a moment. Temple persists.

How's he getting here? he asks.

Driving.

Driving.

Aye says Rutter. Likely the snow stopped him.

Temple shakes his head.

What is that gloop anyway he says nodding towards the table where stew sits steaming in a pot.

Call it slumgullion.

Mason returns. His hand is on his radio.

Right he says. That's enough for now – we need to get going. We've been called back.

Call it what Temple says to Rutter.

Call it slumgullion.

What the fuck's slumgullion?

Rutter shrugs.

Meat and that.

You mean stew.

If you like.

Well what type of meat?

Rutter pauses.

Animal.

It looks like dog shit.

THE DOGS ARE barking their alarm call again and when Rutter looks outside a figure steps from the shadows. The police only left five minutes earlier.

Hello Mr Rutter.

The formal address gives him away: it is Skelton.

It's you says Rutter.

Yes. It's me.

Skelton steps forward and Rutter sees him properly. He sees the healed split upper lip and the spectacles. The thin skin of his bloodless face. He looks older. He has aged.

The coppers have just been says Rutter then immediately wishes he hadn't.

I know says Skelton. I know that.

You're lucky they didn't see you.

Luck has nothing to do with it. We're one step ahead of them.

How do you mean?

You're forgetting who Mr Hood's friends are.

Rutter looks at him.

He asked me to check in on you.

Why but?

You know why.

Rutter rubs his nose again. Leaves a slug trail across the back of his hand.

Why couldn't he come himself?

Skelton scoffs.

What – Mr Hood? Come *here*?

Why does he want you to check in on me though? says Rutter.

He wondered if perhaps you might have seen our mutual acquaintance.

What acquaintance?

Our mutual friend. The one who does a lot of work for charities.

Eh?

Skelton looks at Rutter and tries to establish whether he is deliberately playing dumb.

Off the television.

You mean Lar—

Skelton raises a hand palm up. Halts him. Halts Rutter.

Don't say his name. Don't do that.

Why would I have seen him?

Our friend has been quite complacent of late. He's been

doing things. Extra-curricular work. Taking risks. He has been doing things he shouldn't have been doing. People have been talking and now those voices are of an increased volume. Recently he has not been seen and Mr Hood is concerned. You see there have been further allegations and our friend has gone to ground. Were he to surface we would want to know about it. They say he has a place near here.

I've not seen him says Rutter. I don't know anything about a place near here.

Skelton sniffs.

As tight-lipped as ever. That's good.

Skelton hesitates then says: and of course what with all this other business going on. Mr Muncy's girl. How is Ray? Such a shame. Any sign of her?

Skelton looks at Rutter in such a way that he does not know how to answer. Does not need to answer.

Such a shame. Still it'll be his downfall will that gob of his. But we can trust you can't we?

Unsure Rutter nods.

And this girl. It would be a shame if the police were to find out anything else about it. Mr Hood does worry about these things. He hates to think of trails being left.

Again Skelton looks at him. A wordless exchange passes between them.

We're all only ever seconds away from death says Skelton.

Yes says Rutter.

Good says Skelton. Good. Knowing that makes you feel so alive doesn't it?

RUTTER'S THERE. HE is in Brindle's head all night long. Scratching at his skull.

Brindle is processing. It is what he does. He is composting thoughts down until new ideas push through the murky morass of disjointed facts and theories.

The noise of the pub below keeps him awake. As he expected there is a lock-in. There is whooping and jeering and the same Slade song being played over and over. An occasional smashed glass followed by a cheer.

He runs through a mental list.

There is always the possibility of a boyfriend or boyfriends. Teenage girls have secrets.

Or the father. Ray Muncy. He's right in it. Right in there.

There is the sound of more laughter and singing from downstairs. It is coming up through the floor and snow is falling outside to add a fresh layer to the square.

He turns over in his bed. The sheets are stiff. Too stiff. Stale-stiff. Starched-stiff.

And still he keeps coming back to Rutter and the facts that are stacking up around him. He fits the profile. He hears the reporter's words.

Steven fucking Rutter.

There's the dog to consider too. They all reckoned she loved that dog. Loved the bones of it they said.

He hears voices outside – of people spilling from the pub and slipping and sliding across the square. There is a snowball fight. Screaming. Bottles being drained and dropped. Men grabbing other men in headlocks. One has his top off and is rolling on the ground while others kick snow over him.

One thing Brindle has learnt: people never just vanish. He knows the statistics. One in thirty million people might fall into a crack in the earth. People disappear all the time but there is always a trail or a witness or an accomplice or a remnant of a conscience. Rarely nothing. There is always an answer to every question eventually. Something always comes up.

Usually a body.

And that's what missing.

Her body.

Find the body – find it – her – then trace it back to Rutter. Because she's dead already.

The thought hits him squarely: she's dead already so everything else now is just a process of walking backwards in the snow. Retracing the footsteps.

Brindle turns the bedside light on. The bulb is so weak it barely makes a difference.

He hears church bells. It is midnight. It is Christmas Day.

Then over them – cutting through them – he hears the same fucking Slade song again.

HE HAS BEEN summoned back. Back to that cathedral of humiliation and fear. To the Odeon X where a parallel world was unfolding in the semi-darkness.

Many months have passed and it is dreek out on the evening that he returns. It is slewing it. Rain lashes the windscreen of the truck all the way from the valley. He is anxious.

He shows his membership card and waits as cars slosh past on the City Road. He hears the clicking heels of a passing hen party who look and point and laugh and then pass leaving trails of cigarette smoke hanging behind them.

It's a different girl doing the door now and they've got a new drinks machine in the lobby. The girl is pale and bored and bloodless-looking and the machine makes frothy coffee. There are free condoms scattered about in little baskets. They are fruit-flavoured. Some of them are ribbed.

The girl looks up and says no admission.

What? he says then: oh. He turns to leave.

No says the girl. You don't have to pay. Management have marked it up.

Marked it up?

Just go in will you she says.

Inside the cinema is the same. The same cheap air-freshener that catches in the throat and the same worn seats. If anything it has got dirtier. There are dried stains on the walls and floor and the toilets have not been touched by detergent for many months.

It doesn't bother him though. They are beyond him. He doesn't care. Surfaces are just a type of skin.

Inside Screen One there are no women today no couples today only men today.

The midweek late-night hardcore.

They are desperate men they are lonely men they are unemployed men. Deficient deviant depraved men.

Some in knickers.

Some disabled.

He takes a seat. Presses himself down low. A Danish film dubbed in German is playing. The dialogue is out of sync but it does not matter. Nothing in here matters.

On the screen a doctor and a nurse are in an office. They are talking and their conversation quickly become more animated. Then they stop talking and the nurse strips off. She has large sagging breasts. The camera zooms in on the doctor's inane face as he leers at her. When it pans out again the nurse is on her knees and she is sucking the doctor. He is large and he is still leering.

After a while the nurse stands and turns around and lifts her tunic and the doctor does her from behind while she makes a phone call. The film is grainy and keeps speeding up and then slowing down. It creates an accidentally comical effect.

After a while the doctor withdraws and finishes noisily on her arse and again the camera frames his face. This time he is gurning. Then a pregnant women enters and after a long boring conversation in German they – her and the first woman – both suck the doctor off together then he does the pregnant woman while the nurse sucks on her tits.

Watching the film he is not even hard.

Two sissies walk down the aisle and take a place in his row. Both have stout hairy unshaven legs and are wearing tight silk knickers. One is swarthy with a moustache and wearing thick glasses and the other has a thinning comb-over that fails to hide his visible crescent of flaky scalp.

They sit a few seats along from him. They watch the film for a while then they start playing first with themselves then each other.

He watches the screen and wonders if there will be any couples in tonight. He would like a floor show. He wants to see a woman. He wants to try the back room again. He has washed himself this time and the sissies are making him feel sick. The sissies are nothing like women. And it is different now. Management have marked him up whatever that means. He's a non-paying guest. Invite-only.

He wants a woman. Young old fat thin doesn't really matter. He has waited long enough.

The sissies are watching him watch the film. They stand and move into the two seats beside him. The one with the moustache sits to his immediate right.

He turns his head to one side and the man smiles in what he takes to be an attempt at flirtatiousness but is actually grim and pathetic. He has no front teeth.

A hand hovers over his crotch. Lets itself rest there like a bird after flight. Gently presses there. He moves it away. The sissy waits a minute and then slides from his seat and it flips up and then he is on his knees in front of him. He shuffles round to face him and licks his lips. Again he reaches for his zip. He snatches at it. Hungry.

He stands and his seat also flips up and then he knees the sissy in the face and the sissy falls backwards. Goes down. Perhaps his cheekbone is fractured. Perhaps it is not. His friend with the comb-over next to him jumps up and says hey in a deep rough voice and his penis is sticking out of the side of his women's underwear and it is erect. It is abnormally large. One testicle hangs out the side of his knickers below it and for a brief *moment the film reflects in the thick lenses of his spectacles.*

The one on the floor growls a threat and his friend stoops to help him up and then he goes to say something but Rutter has already turned and left

He walks up the aisle and through the lobby.

A hand grabs him at the elbow and pulls him to one side. It is the thin man. It is Skelton. His lip twisted. Hair slicked. He guides him towards the door. To the stairs. To the cellar.

To Hood.

HE HAD TRIED travel. Brindle. Holidays. A few years back when he felt he still needed to make the effort. He'd take a week and just go. All-inclusive – alone.

Two phrases that do not belong together.

Once he went to Turkey then a few months later to a resort in Mexico. The Caribbean side. The Yucatán Peninsula. His Chief Supe told him to go. Forced him to take time off. Sort your head out he said. Go and drink cocktails from a pineapple and get your junk sucked he said. It'll do you good.

So he paid for an upgrade and they gave him the honeymoon suite with a fridge and tea-making facilities and air-con and an empty hot-tub on the balcony whose plug hole periodically gusted a faint smell of excrement. The hotel was populated by loud obese Americans and he regretted it immediately.

Jet lag and the heat made him sluggish so he closed the curtains and sat in the dark and watched soap operas in Spanish. He ventured out only to gorge himself at the breakfast buffet then waddled back upstairs to his room with the pool-side view. He hated the sun. He was an Englishman. And a northerner at that. It didn't feel natural to be out there. It tightened his skin so each day he waited until it had set before going back. To the dining room where the tea didn't taste right and the vegetarian option was a wet omelette that looked like the by-product of something surgical.

Once a day a maid came to empty his bin and refresh the mini-bar and leave a towel twisted into the shape of a swan until he tipped her and told her that she did not need to do his room for the rest of the week. She did not argue.

He has not been abroad since. He has not had more than two continuous days off since.

When he wakens on Christmas morning the room is freezing and Brindle doesn't know where he is and Brindle is scared for a moment and then he remembers where he is and he isn't scared any more – only very alone. There is a block of ice in his chest where his heart should be.

THE DOOR CREAKS open. The top hinge needs fixing. A screw has fallen out.

As he steps inside he feels that something is different. He shuts the door and the room rises and moves and reconfigures itself. Small new details confuse his line of vision. His understanding of the space. The dust motes on the window sill and the burns on the hearth rug from amber embers of years gone by and small drifts of ancient ash and the blistered varnish of the table and the tufts of sponge stuffing from the armchair appear to rise as one and move. The room ripples and flickers and oscillates and hums in a low malevolent register. Flies. Ten or fifty or one hundred thousand of them move and rearrange themselves then settle on the bare bulb settle on the horse brasses. They settle on the mullion lip settle on the poker handle on the curtain rail on the mug rim. They settle on the deflated half-plucked dead chickens in the corner. Their necks twisted. The pimpled white skin exposed. Rutter is out of grain and they have been dying off in batches; the weakest ones becoming victims to those with some fight left in them as they turned on each other. Rutter found five more yesterday. He brought them in intending to gut and boil or bake them but he can't seem to do the necessary actions in the right order to make that happen. It seems too complicated a process. So now they are piled in the corner like dirty clothes. Bones and beaks held together by pitted skin and dried-out sinew.

Then the room is still again. It settles. It is playing a trick on him. It is toying with him. Testing his senses. Rutter takes a step forward and the mad dance begins again. More movement. More flies. And all the while that noise – that hum – the sound of death; a symphonic rendering of decay and decomposition deterioration and dissolution and the death–life–death cycle wheeling forward forever feeding upon itself.

He steps back and closes the door behind him and decides not to use that room any more.

THE FIRST THING he sees down beneath the arches that night is two bodies on top of each on the floor. They are on a rug. They are writhing. No bras but their pants still on. Small tits. Barely any at all. The two girls are going at it while men mill around with drinks in their hands. The girls do not seem very enthusiastic but then a man bends over and gives one of them a kick and says go on girl put some elbow grease into it and then he nudges one of the other men and says elbow grease and they laugh and the other one says I'll wear her like a glove later then she'll know about it.

Rutter recognises something about the first man but cannot place his face. Then he remembers: he is a newsreader on the local radio station. Rutter hears his voice every day. He is the flamboyant face of the station. In years to come he will move to London and smooth away his Yorkshire accent and rise up to become a correspondent – rumours will abound at the corporation about his suspiciously quick career-trajectory – before becoming a widely respected news reader who specialises in interviews with heavyweight politicians. But that was all to come.

Again there are other men down there. Eight in all. Some are seated and others are standing watching.

A halo of smoke hangs in the air and in the corner Larry Lister is watching and smoking a cheroot. His red hair is combed over to disguise the crescent of still-visible scalp below. He beckons Rutter.

Go and see him says Skelton.

Rutter walks over.

The pigman he says. Enjoying the floor show son?

It's alright.

It's alright mimics Lister. Well I think it's boring.

Larry Lister is wearing a silk shirt that is unbuttoned to halfway down his hairless chest.. The shirt is straining against his stomach and his nipples are big – like a woman's thinks Rutter. Larry Lister is also wearing sunglasses.

Does Mr Hood want to see me?

Mr Hood isn't here.

I thought he wanted to see me.

Mr Hood doesn't see people son. I want to see you. Have you not been given a drink?

I don't drink.

Don't drink? Cigar then?

No says Rutter.

Christ man says Lister is there anything you do? Oh yes – I remember what you're into: one of the last taboos. Sure why not?

Stuck for something to say Rutter says I've seen you on the telly.

They say it adds seven pounds says Lister. What do you think?

About what?

Lister shakes his head.

Never mind. My colleague Mr Hood asked me to ask you what you are doing tomorrow night.

Tomorrow night?

Yes.

I don't know says Rutter.

Well I'll tell you what you're doing: you're coming here at 2am and you're doing as you are told like a good lad. It's a special night is tomorrow. It's film night.

Film night?

Yes. Film night.

But it's a cinema.

Clever boy.

There's films on every night.

Not like this one.

Which one?

Tomorrow's film will be special.

Rutter looks at Lister.

Special cast says the TV presenter. Gripping finale. Invite-only.

Famous people?

I'll be here. Aren't I famous enough for you son? Anyway you're not invited.

But you said—

I said you're coming here at 2am. We'll get you a room. Film night will be over so you just make sure you're here when you're meant to be. Bring your truck and keep your mouth shut. There's work will need doing. You're on clear-up.

THE PHONE IS ringing. It seems always to be ringing. It is an aural drill boring holes into his hangover. He ignores it.

Mace is on the sofa with his trousers snaked around his ankles. His penis is pasted to his belly.

The room is freezing. He pulls the blanket over himself and remembers beer and remembers whisky and remembers something that was blue and came in a thimble-sized glass and he thinks about trying not to be sick. The phone stops ringing. He unpeels himself.

He looks around and sees signs of a disturbance; the aftermath of other people being here. He can't remember who or why his trousers are down. There is a bitter taste in the back of his throat. It feels retched and wretched.

It is – he thinks – just like the London days all over again.

Then his mobile rings. Mace reaches over to the coffee table for it. He knocks over an empty beer can. Curled cigarette butts fall from it like the clippings from a horse's hoof. There is a dribble of ashen residue. An acrid wet nicotine smell.

It is his mother.

He cannot face Christmas cheer – not now not even at arm's length. No. Not now. Not yet. Not even from a distance of a hundred-odd miles. He will call her later when his tongue works and he feels a little less like he wants to cry or die or both.

Roddy Mace looks around for water for something to drink for anything wet. There is nothing. The tap seems impossibly far away. He pulls the blanket over his head and thinks of cold water and what it feels like when it is swallowed – like mercury he thinks – and then he tries to go back to sleep but his mind is awake. It is doing its best to recreate the night. To piece it together. His head is a kettle boiled dry.

He remembers Brindle. He remembers feeling odd in his presence. Strange. Almost – not *mesmerised* – but drunker than he knew he was at that early stage in the evening. It was his eyes. Fucking freaky. It was Brindle's entire demeanour. The way he sat up straight and sipped his tea – tea in the Magnet on Christmas Eve for fuck's sake – as if every movement was trained or considered and he didn't care what anyone thought as all around him a town full of people got sloppy. And there in the corner he sat neat and buttoned-down with a haircut to match. Just looking. A stranger in a strange place emanating negative vibrations.

There was something about him that made it hard

to look away. Maybe it was the birthmark like a target inviting ridicule. That blood-red thing. Mace remembers an overwhelmingly compulsion to reach out and touch it. To put his tongue out and—

The phone vibrates and then beeps in his hand. A text. MERRY CHRISTMAS LOVE FROM MUM AND DEAD.

Mace remembers K2. The big lummox with the wet lips and the spittle flying. He remembers him telling him something significant.

Mace reaches down for his trousers and rifles through the pockets. Coins fall out. A lighter. A depressingly old condom. He tries the other pocket and pulls out half a beer mat. Written on it are the words: OTHER GIRL – 20 YRS AGO – CAMPSITE – 'THE NETWORK'. MASON / PINDER / RUTTER. THE SECRETS OF CONNECTED MEN. ARCHIVES?

He lies back and thinks about how Brindle never blinks – maybe that's what makes him seem so weird – and then the phone vibrates again. It is Dennis Grogan texting this time.

Fucksake.

POLICE RAID 2NIGHT. STEVE RUTTER'S. SECRET. SORRY NEED U THERE. BIG STORY.

And then immediately afterwards:

STICK TO BRINDLE LIKE GLUE (MERRY XMAS ETC ETC)

What he wonders is it with old people and capitals.

And why the *fuck* is he having to work on Christmas Day when they – the paper – are already responsible for him missing the festivities as it is. And therefore are responsible for this hangover. In a way. Not that he could face the family now. But still. It's the principle.

Mace texts back – TRIPLE OVERTIME? – and then he sits up and finds there are cigarettes still left in a packet on the table. He lights one and when he inhales it feels like a thousand tiny shards of glass filling his lungs and he knows that at some point in the next few minutes he will need to go and be sick. He drops the cigarette into the can and then pulls the blanket over his head. He thinks about fresh water slipping down his throat like mercury from a broken thermometer and pooling in his stomach. Cold and fresh and beautiful. Then he rolls over and is sick on the carpet that was laid several years before he was born.

THEY PUT HIM in a nearby hotel room and he had never been in a hotel room and it made him nervous so he sat in a chair in the corner in the dark and when they were ready Mr Skelton called the room and said we're ready and then he hung up and within three minutes he had his truck by the back door of the X and leaving the engine still running he knocked and Skelton let him in and then they went through the hatch to the cellars and they went into a room in the far corner and there was nobody down there and the air was warm and there was plastic sheeting on the floor and a tripod and cables and empty bottles and full ashtrays and a pile of clothes – a dress with sequins – and a pair of large Nike sneakers with a strange stain on them and a table with various alien-looking implements or toys or tools on it – strange clear plastic and Perspex cocklike things that didn't compute – and Skelton pointed into the corner and Rutter didn't flinch at what he saw and Skelton noticed this and then he said do it exactly the way we told you and he looked at Skelton and said now? and Skelton said yes now – get it out of here tonight and by morning I want it gone and then he grunted. Make Mr Hood happy said Skelton. Make Mr Lister happy.

VALERIE PINDER GROANS and then shoves the broad back of her husband as it rises with the slow breathing of his deep sleep. Up and down. Like a hog she thinks. A fat hog. She shoves again.

Roy.

He does not respond.

Roy. Phone.

He had come in late stinking of booze and acting strangely. Her sister had been round helping her peel vegetables and do the last batch of mince pies and he had been rude to her. Said something cutting about her weight like he was one to talk about that. She had left under a storm cloud. Another Christmas Day of tension sat in front of them like a great polished black marble gravestone.

The phone is ringing. She shoved him again. Hard this time. He jerks awake.

Answer your fucking phone.

He scrambles out of bed and takes his phone from the pocket of a pair of rumpled trousers that were kicked off in darkness.

Hello?

She is awake now. She listens to him listening. She long ago stopped believing that these phone calls and mysterious nocturnal disappearances were entirely work-related; long ago gave up believing that her husband Roy Pinder was the hardest-working man on the force. The man who held it all together. She has always known that he was involved in *things* but aren't they all round here? She also knew that it was nothing as simple or straightforward as another woman and that comforted her in some strange small way. She never once suspected an affair.

The light from the phone lit up his face and made him look sallow and demonic. It lit up the corner of the room in cold blue.

Pinder grunted into the phone then said yes and then yes again and then it's Christmas everything shuts down at Christmas and then he paused for a while and said yes of course of course I do.

She noted he had that voice that was reserved only for these late-night unexpected calls – a tone of reticence and reverence and was it possibly even fear?

He spoke again. He said tell him he won't be a problem then there was another long pause before he said OK I'll handle it and then rung off.

Who was it? she asked when he climbed back under the duvet.

No one – work stuff. Don't worry about it.

Are you in trouble?

No.

There was a long pause. The room was silent as they lay back-to-back both of them awake. Eyes staring into the dawn darkness.

One day your secrets will get the better of you Roy she said but he didn't reply.

BLUE.

She is turning. She is turning blue.

Down in that drain. She is turning blue now.

In that open-mouthed grave she is hardening and stiffening.

The girl is turning blue before him. She is hardening she is stiffening.

Her blood is clotting and her blood is coagulating and her blood is blackening. And the flies are laying.

He wants to take her home. Wants to light a fire and place her before it and wrap her in blankets and then massage her cold hard muscles.

Blue does not suit her blue is not her colour because he prefers her as she was. Blue makes her more of an *it* and he does not want an *it* he wants a *she* a *her* a girl.

She should stay the colour she was he thinks. She should stay with him.

Stay here. With him. Up top.

Him and her. Me and you. Together forever.

Because he loves the girl. He knows this. He feels it. And he feels that the girl loves him. They should be together forever; this much is obvious to him.

Together. Forever.

She likes it here. He can tell. Things are easier this way. For the both of them. This way there are no arguments no disagreements no backchat. No disappointment. They have gone beyond conversation – beyond small talk – beyond all the awkwardness of the early stages of a relationship. He has freed her from everyday living; he has given her that power; no worries. No. No bills to pay. No. No parents no rules no nothing.

Just him and her. Yes. No homework. No.

No stupid boys and bitchy friends. No.

It's a gift really. The gift of not living.

The gift of nothingness now.

A gift from him.

Steven Rutter.

5

HE IS OUTSIDE the Magnet when Bull Mason pulls down the front door's deadbolts and opens up. It is just after 11am.

Now then he nods.

Roddy Mace shivers and nods back.

Merry Christmas says Bull Mason.

Is it?

You're keen says the landlord. I'm surprised you're back so soon. I would have thought you'd still be mullered.

I think I am. Are you still doing the Christmas dinners Bull?

We are indeed. It'll be a while yet mind but come in.

Mace follows the landlord into his pub. The smell of it takes him straight back to the night before. To the pints and whiskies and the blue stuff in plastic tubes and the singing and someone putting him in a headlock and a snowball fight and a table of drinks being upended and laughter and two girls clawing at each other's faces and pulling at each other's hair until some of it came out in clumps and then later making lots of late-night phone calls to men whose numbers he has saved in his phone but whose faces he can't remember. Men in London men in the city. Maybe a premium chat-line too. He'll find out when his bill arrives. And he remembers meeting Brindle.

Did I do anything stupid last night? Mace asks the landlord as he pulls him a pint.

How should I know?

You know everything. You're at the heart of this town. I've always thought the landlord holds as much power as the parish priest. More in a way. You heed the confessions and see the sins of your flock up close. You carry the secrets and you deliver us from evil by way of redemption in a glass.

What are you blathering on about now?

Mace shrugs.

I don't know. I'm still a bit pissed.

From what I remember – and I might have enjoyed a couple of pale Dales ales myself – you were only being your usual arsehole self.

Anything specific?

Nothing out of the norm.

What about the copper?

The copper?

Your guest. Brindle.

That nebby cunt? He'll solve fuck-all that one. Mark my words.

I wouldn't be so sure says Mace.

I would. His prying will get him nowhere but trouble. He's already had words with Roy. I'd give him a wide berth if I were you. People will talk.

Roy Pinder?

Yeah. He's already upset a few of the boys.

But the missing girl –

He'll find nothing. And you're best off out of it too if you ask me.

How did he handle the Magnet on Christmas Eve?

Bull Mason shrugs.

Ask him yourself – he's booked in for dinner too. Only the vegetables he said.

What do you mean?

Vegetarian isn't he. He just wants greens and spuds. Weirdo.

He only drinks tea as well says Mace.

Yeah grunts Mason. Tight bastard. He should piss off back to the city and leave us lot alone. Likely that girl's run away and that's all there is too it. I'd be doing the same if I had to live with Ray bloody Muncy.

Mace takes his pint to a table and watches as bodies file into the pub over the next hour. Most are in a similar state to Mace. Crumpled. They are all men. Most of them seeking brief respite from the chaos of a Christmas morning at home while a few are bachelor farm-hands here for the lunch before heading back to their cows and sheep.

The roads outside are still thick with drifts and all vehicles left overnight are now covered in a fresh layer of snow. Those in the pub have come on foot and will leave on foot.

At midday the door to the upstairs rooms opens and Brindle enters. He takes his same table in the corner. Back at the bar ordering his second pint Mace gives a wave of the hand and Brindle nods. The journalist notes that the detective is in the same shirt and tie again but the shirt is clean. He must have brought spares. Even on Christmas Day – even in the pub – he is dressed formally. His hair too is oiled and parted.

Brindle comes to the bar and orders a pot of hot water. He removes a tea bag from his pocket pays with a ten-pound note and then stacks the change in a neat column in front of him. He moulds it into place with long lean fingers.

Merry Christmas detective says Mace.

Yes says Brindle. And to you.

On the hard stuff again I see.

Brindle looks at him quizzically and then sees that he is attempting a joke.

Hair of a very large dog says Mace. You sure I can't tempt you?

I'm fairly certain I told you last night I don't drink says Brindle. And I'm working.

On Christmas Day?

Yes.

Well that makes two of us then.

Really.

Yes really.

What's that then?

Brindle gestures towards Mace's pint.

Fortification says Mace. My editor's got me on the case. On Christmas fucking Day. Can you believe that?

The case?

The raid.

Brindle frowns.

What raid?

Mace looks over his shoulder then leans in.

Come on.

Brindle stares back.

You know. The raid on Rutter's tonight.

Brindle stiffens.

What are you talking about?

I'm talking about you and your lot getting a warrant to raid Steve Rutter's farm tonight says Mace. Only these things take twenty-four hours don't they and it's Christmas bloody Day so now you're left snowed-in – town-trapped until that warrant is signed and emailed or scanned and faxed or whatever it is you need to do in order to give the nod to the local plod – half of whom were in here last night getting steaming and the rest who will be sat at home with heartburn and the Queen's speech barely even aware of the magnitude of the story they're a part of whether they like it or not. That's what I'm talking about.

Brindle takes a sip of tea.

How do you know about this? he says.

I told you – this place is full of secrets but not all of them stay that way. I offered to help you last night. I thought two heads might be better than one.

Yes. And I declined.

So I decided to pursue my own line of enquiry.

Brindle can smell the young reporter. He can smell the sweat and the sleep on him again.

Look – I'm a journalist says Mace. A pretty good one. And despite the grumbling I love my job just as much as you love yours. No. Maybe love is the wrong word. Tied to it. That's what it is: I'm tied to it. It's in me – writing is a part of who I am so I'm not just going to sit back and let this story happen right under my nose without getting involved. This is *my* story as much as it is *your* case and the way I see it now is the Muncy girl is still out there and you've yet to uncover a single trace of her nor have you made an arrest and here we are sitting in the pub about to have a Christmas dinner of Bull Mason's tough turkey for me and a plate of dry sprouts for you on what should be our one guaranteed day of the year off. And there's still so much more truth to be uncovered.

What do you mean by that?

I mean there's more to this than meets the eye. Of course there is.

Like what?

Mace takes another drink and shakes his head.

Come on says Brindle. If you know something.

You're the detective *detective*. Your reputation precedes you.

It is illegal to withhold information that pertains to an existing case says Brindle.

I don't know specifics yet. Secrets. Things unseen and unsaid. Some of the men around here have known each other for years. But I'm still an outsider too. That's why I offered to help you.

I don't need your help.

Sounds like you do says Mace.

I really don't says Brindle.

You think I'm just a provincial hack says Mace as the anger rises in his voice. Just some young pisshead. And maybe you're right. But I'm not an idiot. And I can write. Maybe I'm just biding time up here in the Dales and taking a breather from life. Sweating the city out of my system and taking a career detox if you like. But you forget that unlike a lot of people around here I have experience beyond these dales. I've worked stories – big stories – for a national newspaper. I've seen and heard plenty. And the people round here – you might see them as woolly-backed inbreds but they've been alright to me. Most of them have welcomed me well enough. You know why? Because I've made the effort to integrate and ingratiate. To win their trust. And to do that you have to mix with them. And that's the difference between you and me you see. You're happy to sit in the corner bad-vibing everyone but I get involved. I get to know people – even the dodgy fuckers. I stand my round and go to their kid's christening when I'm invited or help dig them out of a ditch when they've driven off the road half-cut on a Friday night. Community – it's about community. Don't underestimate it. I might look like a sad-sack underachieving writer but I've won the trust of people around here and because of that it's me that's one step ahead of you on this.

Brindle sniffs and stirs his tea.

What do you want he says. A medal?

RAY MUNCY LURCHES into the pub. He is drunk. At first they do not hear him over the chatter and the jukebox but the atmosphere of the room slowly begins to change and Roddy Mace sees heads turning towards the door where Ray Muncy is whirling around and shouting – Mace thinks he hears him growl where's Roy Pinder? – and though some people are laughing at him and assuming that he is just another town lad who started on the sherry at breakfast time some say things like he's off his head and fucksake get him out of here. But then Ray Muncy crosses the pub towards the bar and he starts shouting you – *you* know what I'm talking about and Mace nudges Brindle and they see Bull Mason standing behind the bar looking stern-faced and Muncy makes it through the bodies and he is pointing his finger at Mason and saying you – you lot think you run this bloody place and then someone says he bloody does run this place you spanner – his name is above the door and there is more laughter but it is muted and then Johnny Mason comes up behind Ray Muncy and clamps a hand on his shoulder and says come on Ray it's a bit early for all this maybe it's time to go and Muncy spins round and says and *you* – just because you wear the badge doesn't mean you're not rotten either – the whole lot of you are rotten and Johnny says come on Ray and goes to turn Muncy around but Muncy shirks him and says you're doing fuck all about my girl because it's me and then he says this bit again – *because it's me* – and he spins around and sees eyes on him and he looks at them all then straightens his rumpled shirt and he walks out of the pub. When he has left the people in the room seem to breathe a collective sigh of relief. Glasses are raised again and there are mutterings of nutter and wanker and the poor bloke's shot it. Mace sees a look pass between Bull Mason and his brother Johnny. Brindle sees it too.

THEIR PLATES SIT barely touched. Mace's slices of turkey and lumpy gravy and Brindle's half-eaten boiled carrots and cabbage and roast potatoes and mashed turnip have a cold congealed sheen to them.

I'm coming with you says Mace. Later I mean. I'd like to come with you.

Brindles stands to leave.

No you're not. You can't.

He says this mater-of-factly.

I'd like to come with you on the raid says Mace. You might need me to translate.

Well you can't. It's not procedure.

Fuck procedure it's Christmas Day.

You're drunk. And you're a liability.

I'm not drunk. And even if I am – *so what*. Whatever works.

I don't need you.

Let me ask you something says Mace.

Brindle sighs and busies himself adjusting his cufflinks.

Are you a glass-half-full or -half-empty type person?

He considers the question. Considers his answer.

I'm neither says Brindle.

You've got to be one or the other.

I'd need to see the glass.

Mace smiles.

You'd need to see the glass?

Yes. I'd need to see it before I could make a judgement.

You've got to be one or the other.

No I don't he says. I don't have to be anything.

Brindle turns and leaves. He leaves the bar and goes to his room.

HE HEARS THE ENGINE and then the boy is already in the yard before Rutter sees him. The boy is young. Twelve or thirteen. He is sitting on what looks like a new quad bike and he is revving the engine. He is not wearing a helmet.

Rutter picks up his rifle and opens the back door.

What do you want?

Are you Rutter?

What do you want?

Steve Rutter? My dad sent us.

Who's your dad?

Bull Mason. From the pub. He's got a message for you.

Why couldn't he come himself?

Dunno says the boy. That's what I asked but he said I had to tell you and only you. He wouldn't use the phone and he wouldn't write it down.

What is it then?

He said to tell you to expect visitors tonight.

Who?

Dunno.

What else did he say?

He didn't say nowt else. Just to tell you that.

Rutter stands for a moment thinking about the message.

What time tonight?

I don't know. Do you like my bike?

Rutter lowers his gun and then points it vaguely in the direction of the road back down the valley.

Off you go then.

Where's my Christmas box?

What Christmas box?

My Dad said you'd see me right and if you didn't he'd have something to say about it.

Rutter says wait here then and he turns and goes into the house. In the living room he looks around for a moment and then he walks to the corner and picks up a handful of porn magazines and then he goes outside and says here you go and hands them to the boy then he goes back inside and closes the door and leaves the boy looking at them on his bike. The engine still going. Ticking over.

THE TYRES FLATTEN the virgin snow as they drive in quiet convoy through the hamlet and up the hill. There's no way of sneaking up on the Rutter farm. There can be no element of surprise.

The extra half-dozen officers have been pulled away from their dinners and their families and briefed at the station. Brindle tells them that Rutter is their man. He does not mention anything else. It is something he has learned: always keep things back. Even from your colleagues. Never reveal your hand until the final play.

They are instructed to carefully and methodically sweep the house for any trace of evidence. He emphasises these words: *carefully* he says. *Methodically*. For anything at all.

They park up and walk in silence and once at the farm they surround the house at its corners. Two officers are dispatched to check the outbuildings.

Roy Pinder is there too – reluctantly. He is doing his very best not to be seen taking any orders directly from Jim Brindle in front of his men.

Brindle bangs on the door and when there is no answer he gives the nod and one of the officers takes the breaching ram and slams it into the lock and the door gives easily. Half the rotten framework falls away with it.

They pile in shouting. They shout police they shout his name – they shout Steven Rutter – and then Mace follows. Not one of the officers has mentioned his being there.

The smell hits them first. The stench of decay.

Jesus.

It always smells like this says Jeff Temple.

They are in darkness and stumbling into one another until someone finds a switch and they sweep through the rooms but the house is empty. There is no sign of him. No Rutter. No. Not here. Rutter is not here. No.

Brindle goes from room to room expecting to see – what? Rutter. Melanie Muncy. Clothing. Weapons. Stains. Belongings. Anything to link him. He moves through the house feeling neither careful nor methodical but increasingly hopeless and sick and dizzy and only just capable of maintaining control. He wants to moan. He wants to scream.

There are dirty dishes and a filthy mattress and a layer of dust on everything and there are dead flies and smelly clothes and holes worn through the lino and porn magazines and broken televisions and dog shit and hens' eggs laid weeks ago sitting on window sills and shelves and a bicycle frame and dead chickens and empty toilet rolls and stumps of burnt-out candles and horse brasses and pen knives and a green loaf of bread and strips torn from the wallpaper and more dead flies – thousands of dead flies – and rust-coloured water running down one wall and a sack of potatoes spilled across the living-room floor and three pram wheels and mushrooms growing in the corner of one room and a rocking chair that's missing a runner and matted tissues and a peacock feather and a copper bed-warmer hanging from one wall and a button badge with *Madchester: Rave On!* written on it and old red and blue and clear apothecary bottles and a blackened fireplace and Brindle has his men and women sift through it all – they sift through the bins and the matter and the ashes – Pinder too – but hours later all they have is the evidence of a sad and lonely life gone sour and samples to send to the lab – so many samples – and though the smell makes them nauseous and the damp mildewed interior of the farmhouse makes their breath tight they have no Steven Rutter and no sign of the missing teenage girl and none of her belongings and while the police stand around wondering what to do next and look to Roy Pinder for advice Brindle paces the yard outside kicking at the dirty piles of snow and cursing those chickens still living that cluck at him with menace.

It is then that Rutter returns on foot. He has come down a back way from up the hill. Through a gap in the back fence and into the farmyard. Before him his dogs strain on their leads.

He sees Brindle and then Brindle sees him and then Rutter sees police filing out from his back door. He shines a torch at the detective.

Where've you been Steven? asks Brindle.

You get fucked you.

Where've you been?

You'll find nothing in there. I already told you.

Where have you been at this time of night?

I'll have you done for this. There's rules. I'll sue.

Brindle steps towards Rutter who lowers his torch.

It's Christmas night says the detective. I'll not ask again: why are you out wandering?

Why do you think says Rutter. I've been walking the dogs. They don't care that it's Christmas night and neither do I.

Brindle takes a breath.

Where've you put her Steven?

By now other officers have left the house and are watching the conversation. Mace too.

Who?

You know who.

I don't know who.

You know who. The girl.

What girl?

Don't play silly – Brindle catches himself again. Melanie Muncy he says.

I told you. I've not put her nowhere.

They stand for a moment looking at each other in the darkness. Across the yard an officer's radio crackles with static.

I know it's you says the detective.

You know what's me?

I know you killed her.

You better not have made a mess in there says Rutter.

Brindle laughs. He laughs at this. It is a hollow noise that erupts from his chest. A joyless sound that sounds like a stifled choke. Like food dislodged. It is the first time anyone has see him laugh. This cold detective sent in from the city to ruin all their Christmases actually laughs and it is an unnerving sight.

He turns and looks behind him. He sees Mace standing there awkwardly fumbling with a cigarette and thinks he shouldn't be here and he sees Roy Pinder sneering and urging him to fail and he feels things slipping beyond his control.

Brindle turns back.

A pig couldn't make a bigger mess than that place already is he says.

Well you would know says Rutter. Am I being arrested?

Brindle jams his hands in his overcoat pockets and kicks at the snow. An attempt to regain composure.

You better not have broken owt neither says Rutter as he feels the balance of power shifting. I'll get compo for this.

Over my dead body you will says Brindle.

Mace is smoking his cigarette. He inhales. Watches.

Brindle hears Pinder say something and then a muttering runs through the officers. The detective steps towards Rutter and the dogs strain and snarl at him.

I'm going to get you says Brindle. I'll prove it and I'll have you – and I'll crucify you.

Rutter snorts phlegm down the back of his throat and then turns his head and spits.

It is going to happen says Brindle. I am going to have you for this. Best pack your bags and be ready.

Rutter hawks more phlegm. He looks at the officers in the shadows. He looks at Roy Pinder for a moment and then over to the barn.

What is it? says Brindle. What are you looking at?

I need a piss.

So piss then.

Rutter walks over to the barn. He undoes his trousers and drops them and his underpants down around his ankles. He pisses noisily into the barn. His sagging bare arse as white as the snow.

The policemen roar with laughter at this but Brindle knows that it is aimed as much at him as it is Rutter. They are still laughing when he turns and walks slowly to the car.

Mace hangs back for a moment and he hears that Pinder

say Christ what a useless bloody plum-faced freak but when Mace hears the engine start and sees the brake lights go off he throws his cigarette and dashes across the farm yard and climbs into the front seat.

Well that went well he says.

Brindle turns to him. Stares right at him. Through him. He holds his gaze. Mace thinks he can see sparks flashing in his eyes.

Get out he says.

What says Mace.

Get out of my car.

Why?

Brindle leans over him and opens the passenger door. Shoves him.

Get the fuck out of my car.

PINDER SENDS HIS officers home. Tells them to go to their wives and husbands and girlfriends and boyfriends and kids to make amends while they still can. Fill yourselves with booze and turkey he says and then bill that prick Brindle for your overtime. Then he hangs back. He waits until the officers have left then he beckons Rutter out to the derelict barn. As they walk in he can hear something skittering away. The sound of claws on wet concrete.

You got the message then he says.

What message? says Rutter.

What have you done with her?

With who?

Look – don't fuck me about. You know who. The girl.

Muncy's girl?

Yes Muncy's girl.

Pinder and Rutter can barely see each other in the dark.

I thought we'd just been through all this with that cunt Brindle?

I'm not Brindle says Roy Pinder. You can talk to me.

What for?

Look – I know all about it. I had a phone call in the early hours.

Rutter shrugs.

From Mr Skelton says Pinder.

Rutter pauses.

Who's he then?

You know who.

I don't think I do.

I get it – you talk to your pigs but you don't talk to *the* pigs. Forget the uniform. This goes beyond all this. You're not talking to a copper now Steve. You're talking to someone in – here Pinder lowers his voice and chooses his words carefully – someone inside. Remember?

Rutter reaches into his pocket for a rolled cigarette and then lights it. In the spark of the lighter Pinder sees Rutter's eyes. Black and beady with the roaring flame of the lighter reflected in them.

Larry Lister says Pinder.

Rutter says nothing but in the dark his left eye twitches.

We think he might talk says Pinder. We think he's lost it.

This is what-do-you-call-it is this says Rutter. This is police harassment.

You'll keep your mouth shut then says Pinder.

About what?

About everything.

HE IS AT the corner table again but his tie is off and his top two buttons undone. Even from across the bar by the door Mace can see he is in a state. That something about the detective has changed. There are empty glasses in front of him. Shot glasses. Four of them.

He walks over.

What the fuck?

Brindle looks up. His dark eyes are glassy. Wet. His head rolls up.

What do you mean what the fuck?

What was that all about? says Mace. Making me beg a lift back in a bloody cop car?

Brindle's neck is loose in a measured posture of disdain. His eyes red.

They're your mates not mine.

Well it was fucking embarrassing. They were joking about making me walk back through the drifts and that fat prick Roy Pinder is no mate of mine – especially now. He's crooked is Pinder. Owns houses all over. On his wage? Come off it.

I thought you were mates with everyone round here spits Brindle.

Mace cuts him off and points at the glasses.

I thought you didn't drink.

It's Christmas. Everyone drinks at Christmas don't they?

The Magnet is full again. It is late again. The day has been chased away by whisky and brandy and many of the men have red faces and new jumpers and are joined by their wives and girlfriends now. Some of the men are still wearing their paper cracker hats from their family lunches while others have been here all day. They are in high spirits. The jukebox is turned up to full volume and is playing Christmas songs again and the fireplace is roaring.

You're forgetting that I'm an outsider from the city too says Mace.

Oh yeah. The Clark Kent of the countryside out to win a Pulitzer by riding my coat tails.

Hardly says Mace. I've helped you out.

Helped me out? Helped me out? Behave. You're bloody useless son.

I'm useless? You're the one who just raided a house and

turned up precisely nothing. You embarrassed yourself up there man. I thought you were meant to be the best there was. Golden balls. The enigmatic Jimmy Brindle from the top-secret new-breed Cold Storage lot. Christ almighty. It doesn't bode well for the Yorkshire force does it if you're the best there is. No wonder Pinder's still up there laughing his cock off.

Brindle looks at Mace and shakes his head.

I'm being lectured by some provincial pisshead with a pen who thinks he knows me. I'll tell you something. You don't know jack shit. You've got a long way to go before you're on my level. A long way.

Your level?

Indeed he slurs. A higher plane of processing.

I know as much as you do says Mace. I know Steve Rutter is your man. That hasn't changed. But this runs deep. I'd bet good money Rutter is involved in all sorts. That he's not in on this alone. Are you really going to blow this now?

I'll blow nothing. It's Christmas Day and I want to enjoy myself.

Brindle – enjoying himself? laughs Mace and then he says: they all came up together you know.

Who did?

The men who run this place.

What men?

The men who run this place.

This cruddy pub?

No. The town. The valley. Haven't you seen that connection yet?

Mace looks around to check that no one can hear him.

The fact that Steve Rutter and Ray Muncy and Roy Pinder and for that matter Bull Mason and his brother Johnny and others too – they all came up together. There are certain men now in positions of power who went to school together. They are of the same age and they move as a pack. That lot have stayed friends and help each other get a leg up. But some of them did their own thing. Ray Muncy is one of them. Some of them – Steve Rutter – were never a part of that network of people in the first place; for whatever reason they were rejected by those guys since the first day of school. Rutter because he was a gimp probably. They were the victims of those guys. My boss Dennis Grogan told me all about it. Warned me to tread carefully with anything I write but fuck them. I could name you others too. They drink together they holiday together go into business together. Swap wives – all of that. They're like some weird backwater mafia but without the cool clothes and sunglasses. Do you know Benny Bennett?

Brindle shakes his head.

Look him up. He controls the council funds. He makes sure money only flows to those who he wants it to flow to. There's a committee for appearance's sake but it all comes down to him. There's a simple reason the pot-holes round here never get fixed yet he drives a BMW. And there's a reason Bull Mason pulls in four times more than any other pub round here.

Which is?

Because that is the way it has been decided says Mace. Because he's on the inside. I don't know the specifics. It's all just beneath the surface. Bull's alright but I wouldn't trust him to feed my cat. Then there's Wendell Smith and the Farley brothers. These are people you should be looking into if you want the full story. They're all the same age too. They might not look like they have money or influence but they do. In their own ways they do. They've been doing what they want round here for years. Decades. They police themselves that lot. They're their own law. That's why the crime rate – the visible crime rate anyway – is nonexistent. Any thieves or burglars round here find themselves waking up in a quarry with broken legs and shattered fingers. Junkies? Forget it. They've been intimidated away. But I'd bet there's plenty of other stuff going on too.

Like what?

That's your job detective. But I can still help you. You and I both know that there is—

You know nothing.

Mace shrugs.

You're killing the case but that's your problem. Justice is your concern not mine. Either way I'll have my story. Jesus. I need a drink.

He returns with a pint and two whiskies and a new packet of cigarettes.

So with all that in mind says Mace: what now?

Brindle looks at him like he is insane.

What do you mean what now?

What's your next move?

None of your bloody business.

Come on says Mace. You can drop the front now. I've seen behind your armour detective. Your vulnerability. Seen your failings.

They fall silent for a minute until Mace speaks again.

You must have a plan though.

Brindle points at his glass.

More of that.

What about Rutter though?

Brindle stares at Mace. Stares at him for an uncomfortably long time; stares so long without speaking that Mace wonders if he is even seeing him.

Don't you have somewhere you need to be? he says finally. I mean isn't there anyone waiting for you? There must be a way out of this town tonight.

Mace sips his drink then places it on the table.

No and no and no he says. Anyway. Isn't there anyone waiting for *you*? You can't be a detective every single minute of every waking hour.

Brindle does not respond. Instead he drinks his whisky. He downs it and winces then he stands and says: Rutter first then Pinder. If he's crooked I'll bury him. I'll bury all of them. This entire town if needs be.

IT WAS EASY not to think of them as people. Now they were something else; they were spent forms broken things damaged goods. These people he was sent for were the bruised apples in the barrel. The broken biscuits. They were the gristle that clogs the butcher's drain. The discarded by-products of specialist tastes.

The work was irregular. Months could pass with nothing and he would begin to think that perhaps he had imagined it all but then two jobs would come in a week apart. A message sent up from the city.

They called it clean-up. He was the clean-up man. He had no choice.

Between the parties and the pigs was his time. That was his payment: the total freedom of a few hours alone with whatever was left to him.

He never saw Mr Hood and he never saw any of their films. To see the films you had to be a part of it all. You had to be invited in. He was just there to do a job for Skelton – just like the women who took the tickets at the X or the women who cleaned up the spunk from the toilet floor or whoever it was who procured the party guests and amateur film stars in the first place. He suspected Skelton; it certainly wasn't Lister.

He knew he wielded no wider power. He knew that was why he was not in that network. Because he had no sway in politics or law or town planning or property or investment or the media so he was simply not worth corrupting. He was wild he was feral he was a hillbilly. He was the pig man and all that mattered was that the bruised apples were ghosted away; never to be found or used or consumed again.

THEY DRINK UNTIL it is closing time and after Bull Mason has locked the doors and dimmed half the lights he carries on serving.

At one point Brindle says am I safe here? but Mace does not hear him and Brindle is not even sure if he said it out loud so he stands and sways and staggers into the wood-panelling wall of the pub and mutters something about Rutter. He knocks a picture frame askance and then looks around the pub as if seeing it for the first time. Bull Mason looks over from the bar.

Mace stands.

Whoah there he says. You're banjaxed Miss Marple.

I'm DS James Brindle he says reeling to one side.

Mace is unsteady too but he catches the detective by the arm before he upends the table and all its empties. Mason looks over again and catches Mace's eye this time. He nods to the door leading upstairs. Mace understands the message.

Come on then he says. Christmas is over. I'll help you up.

Brindle scowls at him and says get your hands off me but is still in danger of falling so Mace gets one arm around him and guides him to the door. They barrel through it and then navigate the stairs. At the landing halfway up they pause and Brindle turns to look at Mace. Their faces are close. Brindle's eyes are like the pebbles of glass that wash up on beaches; pieces shaped by the violent shifting of the shale. Mace can smell the detective's breath. He is looking at his birthmark. It is right in front of him and appears even redder as if full of blood. Brindle says nothing so Mace hoists him up the rest of the stairs and along the hallway. They get to Brindle's room.

Keys says Mace. His arm is still around the detective.

Brindle turns to him. His head rolls on his neck.

What?

I need your keys.

Their faces are close again. The birthmark is there again.

Fuck it says Mace and puts his hand into Brindle's trouser pockets. He roots around and brushes against something. It retracts and stiffens. Doesn't give. It is hard. Surprisingly hard. He moves his hand and finds the keys but then he touches it again. Closes his fingers around it.

Brindle looks at him with wet red eyes. They are both breathing deeply. Mace is staring at the birthmark. It appears engorged. It is as if it is pulsing. Mace takes out the keys and fumbles with them. He finally gets them into the lock. Opens the door. Brindle stumbles in. The door swings on its hinges. Mace pauses for a moment and looks up and down the hallway and then follows him in.

PART II
SPRING

6

WEIGHTED AND WAITING hung from rusted chains once sinking the trunk of the girl stands bound and suspended ten feet down in drain water now melting. She rises with the temperature her chainlinks bending quietly jack-knifing her bloated browning body angelically ascending. Tiny ice bubbles encased for the winter return to the ether as the reservoir water inches upwards rising clandestinely through conduits and culverts. Rainfall and ice-melt raise the meniscus of this great black basin as currents plumb and push it in all directions until the moor-top can no longer contain it and the frosted channels bob with diminishing blocks and bergs slowly dispersing disintegrating evaporating.

Ice is never ice forever. Once it was water and in time it becomes water again. And life begins again. Here in the cracks and clefts of this concrete fissure underground aquatic insect larvae hatch and flourish. Fomented in the dampness of this man-made cave they unfold unfurl and stretch anew.

Stoneflies mayflies caddisflies danceflies dragonflies.

The waters rise and rise until the body of the girl gently rests against the underside of the drain's grill like a death-row prisoner pressed up tight in a plea for mercy. Then the waters fall and fall and she floats suspended tied and tangled and trussed.

Only now do the mites and gnats and flies arrive.

Bluebottles greenbottles blowflies fruitflies hoverflies.

These cold-blooded creatures come in stages to feed and lay and hatch. Word of the spring-feast spreads.

Rove beetles skin beetles clown beetles. Clothes moths heather bees and roaming wasps. Spiders to prey on the flies.

And so the process begins again. Decomposition accelerates. The body hovers; a host to life of another kind. Its flesh and its organs and its cavities and skin and fluids busy with activity. This once-person is now a rich protein source for the subspecies that gnaw and suck and fester there.

She floats below the moor under the red waterlogged soil. The girl. Weeks have passed here. All she has known is darkness and ice and the echo of the bogland breeze whistling into this lonely mausoleum. The sky shifting the snows drifting. But now the snow has gone and the ice has melted. And as the first shaft of sun passes over and through and into this space even in death there is change and growth and movement.

It is spring.

WHEN THEY COME early in the morning – and perhaps deep down Larry Lister always knew they would come and that yes perhaps half of the thrill of it all was the never-knowing; the sheer fucking thrill of getting away with it – it is not because of the business interests and the silent shareholdings in the old cinema or the parties or links to Mr Hood or Mr Skelton and their implication in disappearances and snuffed-out lives and subsequent disposals or the vast collection of celluloid relics – the torture tapes – and the photo albums and the very *very* niche DVDs he's had brought in from Vietnam and Laos but an allegation from way back when. The early eighties. Just the one. By a girl – now a woman with a husband and a life and kids of her own – who he has no recollection of ever meeting. Which isn't to say her allegation is bullshit. In fact it sounds convincingly accurate; not just her description of the brand of cigarettes he smoked during the 'session of prolonged inappropriate touching' (a quick internet search would reveal those; a detail that would never stand up in court) or aspects of the interior of his on-location

Winnebago (a Minnie Winnie Premier with Californian-sunrise upholstering and walnut chevron design – he later bought it for his own use with cash from the corporation and left it in the grounds of a church in the Pennines where he was made an honorary warden in the late eighties) but her description of the three small brown moles on the underside of his cock-shaft which configure to form what the 'victim' describes as a triangle shape that she saw close up all those years ago.

Other than remarking that the girl is clearly one of those particularly fixated fans who has crossed a boundary and blurred fantasy with reality and ill-judged fact with fiction (don't worry he tells the arresting officers – it has happened several times before lads; that's the power of television) no comment is the mantra he reverts to during the initial questioning.

No comment repeated one hundred times or more until his solicitor arrives at which point Lovely Larry Lister beams back at his questioners and says with no small amount of confidence: now how about we all go for a nice big drink once this nonsense is over with? No hard feelings eh?

THE NEWSPAPER IS spread across his desk. There is a picture of a man with red cheeks and wide wild eyes and a beaming smile. The headline says LARRY LISTER: DOWNFALL OF TV FAVE. And then beneath that it says SORDID SEX ALLEGATIONS OF THE MAN THEY CALLED 'UNCLE'.

Brindle looks out of the window across the sterile landscape whose car parks and always-empty bus stands and cultivated roundabouts and endless internal reflections are more familiar to him than the inside of his own flat.

Ask him what colour his curtains are and he would struggle to provide an answer; ask him what the slogan bolted in metal onto fake marble beside the park's – they actually call it a park – entrance half a mile away is and without missing a beat he will tell you: *Innovation. Opportunity. Enterprise.* One of those empty mantras gleefully unveiled by some long-forgotten perma-grinning mayor years ago under New Labour. His department moved in only two years ago. Before that it did not exist. In many ways it still does not officially exist. And that is its strength.

The view of this surrounding space – quadrangles of grass; silent roads; twinkling windows – is soporific. All that glass and chrome and tarmac creates a false impression of the world: one of straight lines and right angles and mirrors reflecting one another in an endless visual echo that can feel either inspiring or imprisoning depending upon the viewer. So much so that Brindle now finds himself daydreaming of uneven carthorse tracks slick with algae and the smooth flagstones of an old market square. His winter week in the country.

He closes the paper and leans back in his ergonomically customised chair.

He closes his eyes and considers the chaos of nature; the way boulders have been scattered across valleys by icebergs tens of thousands of years ago. He thinks of houses built into hillsides that are slowly being reclaimed by nature – one fallen roof-slate or minuscule moss-spore at a time. He thinks of dead bracken and thick black mud and soft downy feathers that have fallen from way up in the sky and the sweet smell of pig shit being sprayed from a solitary muck-spreader whose engine sputters down the valley.

He thinks of the valley. He thinks of town. He thinks of the hamlet.

He thinks of the fixed faces of men.

He thinks of the matrix of secrets – shocking and sordid and still buried – and his own failings. He thinks he can smell spring. He can sense it and he can taste it.

AT THIRTEEN AT fourteen at fifteen. A boy becoming a
young man and that young man learning to meld and mingle
to sink into the scenery; to become a trunk a static entity able
to modulate his movements with his surroundings. To make
himself barely recognisable to the naked eye.

Outside of school and his farm chores all he does is hunt and
poach now. Lurk and linger. Walk the hills unheard.

His legs carry him for miles in all directions until he knows
every ancient pass and every cart track. He turns himself into a
human statue or a scarecrow and there he stands unmoving as
he watches the sky. Other times he climbs trees to sit and listen
to the birdsong and the breeze. He scales crags and boulders
or lowers himself down ravines. He explores dead forests and
methane-stinking moor bogs. He goes to the places few other
people go.

He masters the art of stillness and silence of merging and
blending and sinking.

There is a girl. A classmate whose freckles made him feel
dizzy. She is not the prettiest girl or the most popular girl or the
cleverest but she is the nicest girl because once she let him hold
her hand. For a few fleeting moments one break-time when no
one is looking he makes a connection.

She is a farm girl too. She is clumsy and grubby. She does
not wear make-up or have friends and she has joined late from
another school and perhaps this is why she lets him talk to her.
She likes animals and she has dirt under her fingernails too and
once she tells him that peacocks are her favourite birds because
their feathers are so beautiful that they are almost unreal and to
look at them is like looking at the sea from the top of a great cliff
on a beautiful clear sunny day.

He has only ever seen a peacock in the books that he has
thumbed his way through at school when he should be learning

mathematical formulas and silly poems and facts about oxbow lakes and dead kings from a long time ago but he never forgets the look in her eyes as she says this. He has never seen the sea either.

On one occasion he is out wandering. He leaves the old stone houses of the hamlet behind him and he crosses the dale. Down and across and then up. It is summer. It is humid. It has been raining for two days but the rain has stopped and now the air is close. The air is clammy and the air is tightly tuned. More rainfall will come.

The young man walks.

He walks without direction purpose or intent. He is simply moving. An hour passes and he is two valleys over and then he is moving down a hill and through a densely wooded area. There is a stream running through it. He stops and stoops and drinks and it tastes beautiful. These woods are not like the woods around the hamlet or the copses up the top end of the dale. These woods have been tended to. Maintained. Through the marshy area a boardwalk has been laid and on top of the wooden boards there is chicken wire to stop people slipping and where the path has eroded it has been fixed with flagstones. There are signs to explain which plants and animals can be found in this dell. It is a nature reserve of some sort. There is nothing like this in his valley. Only sky and scree.

The wood broadens out and takes him downhill and then he is leaving the trees behind and he is in a broad pasture full of buttercups with a track running through the centre of it and other tracks leading off to either side to large houses nestled in amongst trees.

Here there is space and sunlight and the houses are large and many look new and come with their own land and their own driveways and their own landscaped gardens featuring ponds and summerhouses and polytunnels. They have actual lawns. These lawns are tended. Neat. The sunlight reflects off the large *gleaming cars in their large driveways.*

He is three or four or five miles from home but he is in another world.

Then he is by a big house and there is a screeching sound. The house is large. The house is huge. Even bigger than Muncy's pile. It has a gravel forecourt and a curved driveway and outbuildings and a walled garden. There is a big wooden electronically controlled double gate out front and it is open.

The screeching is coming from around the side of the house. He hears it again. A piercing noise. An urgent cawing. He takes some steps up the driveway and peers round the side of the house. He walks on aware of his feet crunching on the gravel. Around the side of the house he sees a large beautiful peacock. A few metres away perched on the corner part of the garage roof there is another one.

He thinks of the girl and the look in her eyes and it makes his stomach flip.

He recognises that the peacock on the ground is a male; this much he knows. The one on the garage is female.

They are the most beautiful creatures he has ever seen especially the male whose long graceful neck fades from bottle green into cobalt blue and a thousand other shades in between. When the light catches it it seems like its feathers are shimmering like a new type of fire.

He immediately knows what he needs to do.

He walks towards them and the female – the peahen – screeches again. It is less stunning but he still wants to get closer to observe it.

Though its neck has shades of blue in it too the bulk of its body is a dullish brown – charmless and flat like ditchwater. It is plumper also. Perhaps it is pregnant.

Both birds have crests atop their heads. A row of ornate feathers that spread out into delicate blue fans at the tips.

He treads carefully towards the male. He stops then squats to the bird's level. It walks from side to side and then suddenly without warning it fans out its tail feathers into their full plumage.

He gasps. He actually hears himself draw a tangible intake of breath that he holds in his centre.

A wall of eyes stares back at him.

The plumage is breathtaking. Literally breathtaking.

The eyes are blue in the centre but it is the shade of green that encircles them to create a mock iris that he is dazzled by. It is electric. It is iridescent.

How he wonders can such a colour be possible? How can nature create something so utterly beyond anything he has ever seen?

The colour seems so at odds with the grey Yorkshire stone walls and the grey Yorkshire stone skies of the dales.

He has to have one of those feathers. Just one for the girl to hang from her curtain rail so that the sun can catch it in the morning.

He needs one of those feathers.

Hunched he walks towards it but before he can get close the peacock closes its plumage and without grace flies up to the garage roof to join its mate.

Its train of tail feathers hangs over the edge and he is amazed that such an impressive fan can fold away so neatly.

The two peacocks survey him with suspicion from the garage roof as he first pulls gently at the plastic drainpipe to test its security and then begins to shin his way up it. He has had a lifetime of climbing up trees – fifty sixty seventy feet up sometimes. The drainpipe will be easy. One hand over the other.

For one feather.

Just to treasure. To study and touch.

To give to the girl to make her love him.

The birds strut across the garage roof when first the young man's head and then his torso appear beside them. One of the peacocks is within reach. The stunning male. He slowly stretches out an arm and counts to three then he grabs it and he feels feathers in his hands and he holds on tight and he yanks but as he does the whole section of guttering and drainpipe comes away with a splintering crack.

He tumbles backwards pulling the bird with him. It screeches. Both birds do. He holds on tight. With his free hand he snatches at blue sky.

The dark form of the bird blocking out the sunlight before him – above him – is the last thing he sees before blackness. Blackness closing in and then nothing but silence.

When he comes round the sun is a lot lower in the sky and he is surrounded by black piping and feathers. Lengths and shards of shattered plastic are scattered about and small pieces of gravel are embedded in his back and arms and face; his neck and head are pounding.

There is something beside him. It is the male peacock. It is crooked and it is trying to stand but its feathers are jutting out at odd angles and it keeps keeling over. It can no longer tuck its plumage away and its eyes are wide with despair. It seems broken somehow.

There is a low hum in his ears. The young man feels cold and nauseous and numb. He slowly sits upright. He can barely move his neck and his vision is blurring then focusing. Blurring then focusing. His jaw hangs loose. His jaw is in agony.

He stands and the earth tilts. He takes a moment to regain his balance and then breathes deeply. He brings a hand to his lower lip and touches blood. He licks it with his tongue but it is tasteless so he brings a bloody finger to his nose and smells it. There is nothing.

The bird is still flopping about on the ground in a heap. The other peacock is nowhere to be seen. He goes to it and it screeches for a moment and he looks at it for a moment then it falls silent as he stamps on its neck and he stamps and stamps

and then when it has stopped moving he pulls out feathers – one
two three – entire handfuls of feathers – until he hears a car
crunching its way up the pitted track of the house. He turns to
leave and cuts across a side lawn and climbs over a fence with
his jaw aching his head aching and the entire world black and
white except for the feathers in his hand that capture the white
sun as he runs and runs.

RUTTER WORKS HIS way through the melee muttering to
himself.

Crowds line the streets all the way along to the market
square where there are stalls selling locally produced foods.
Pies from Wharfedale and great slabs of Kit Calvert's
famous cheese from Wensleydale. Milk from shorthorns up
in Weardale. Beer in casks from a new micro-brewery in
Leyburn; apple juice pressed in the Wolds. There is chocolate
that has come from a chocolatiers in Skipton. Biscuits and
cakes and parkin from the valley. Lamb chops and pork cuts
and spicy cured sausages too. Appleton beef Angus beef all
types of beef. Poultry and game from an estate near York.
Sweets drinks hot dogs candy floss.

Winter would not give up the ghost. It clung on as long as
it could. It clung and it clawed and clutched before it finally
relinquished its grip on the landscape.

And now it is the feast of winter's end. Town is busy. It
is the day of the Long Sword dance. The snowdrops have
sprouted and the daffodils will soon be unfolding. Spring is
in the post. It is a time for looking forward – for preparations
and reparations; for rebirth and growth.

The Long Sword is a town tradition and one of the only
remarkable things about the place that has been recorded in
books about folklore and tradition. Even Rutter heads east
down the dale for it.

He pauses this morning at a stall and picks up a vacuum-packed herb-fed free-range chicken. He looks at it plucked and pimpled. He brings it to his face for a closer look then prods the meat beneath the plastic then throws it down. He walks away with his hands jammed into his overall pockets.

Later there will be a street play telling the history of the Mummers in the valley. They'll start at the Golden Bough then work their way through town to the centre of the market square banging their drums and shaking their bells in The Magnet where Bull Mason will lay on a cold-meat feast.

Rutter passes through the crowd. He edges his way between bodies. He feels exposed. Too visible.

He sees familiar faces; the faces of farmers and their families and delivery men and labourers. Men he went to school with. He sees Wendell Smith he sees Andy Champion he sees Den Paget. He sees John Wade out with his wife. Ben Bennett and his girlfriend too. Knocked up again. He passes the Farleys – Duncan and Dan. The pair of them flushed and half-cut.

He sees fat Roy Pinder and his even fatter wife but he keeps his head down. He steps on and off the pavement and is already regretting coming into town today. He only came to pick up some bits but all these bodies and voices and jostling puts him on edge. He cannot share their excitement. They are like children on days like this; the years slip away and they become hysterical over a few sweets some daft costumes and stupid dancing.

Tapped he thinks.

Mad he thinks.

Mad – the lot of them.

HE GAVE HER one of those feathers. The girl with the freckles. He was off school for a week with head pains and vomiting and his sense of smell never came back but when he returned he had three feathers for her but by now she had made some friends;

she had been accepted into a circle of boys and girls who smoked
together at lunchtime round the back of that substation building
near the top yard and when he approached her with the feathers
she laughed and said er thanks and then he just stood there for
a moment turning the colour of a plum while everyone tried to
stifle their laughs so he turned and left and as he walked away
he heard them screaming with laughter and saying things like
freak and fucking dickhead and dirty pig-fucker needs a wash
and when he looked over his shoulder he saw one of the lads
whipping the feathers against the chain-link fence until the fine
coloured barbs tore away from the main spine and hung in the
air for a moment catching the sunlight along with the smoke
from the cigarettes that they passed round as if in some ancient
ritual. The pieces of feather floated down into the dust and
became part of the dust; became part of the architecture of his
failings.

THE LONG SWORD dance has started by the time he has
looped round the other side of the square. The crowd is not
moving and Rutter has to push through it. Voices tut as necks
crane to get a view of the seven men skipping in a circle; the
first reel of the year.

Unable to move in any direction Rutter stops and watches.
He has no choice.

They dance to the sound of a fiddle played by the eighth
man. They wear matching clothes of white shirt-sleeves white
trousers with piping and thick clogs and they hold their cold
metal swords by hilt and tip.

The dancers move in unison. They weave and they reel and
they duck and slot their swords into configurations. Over the
shoulder and under the arm; round the back and through the
legs to form interlocking latticed shapes. The fiddler speeds
up and the men follow picking up their pace. There is a brisk
skip in their steps now. A hand-clap starts up from the crowd.

The dancers reel in an even tighter circle with their faces more concentrated as blades cross and clatter. Feet shuffling and stamping. The clapping increases and the crowd closes in even tighter around Rutter.

The sun is out and the breeze brings in a warm front. Rutter starts to sweat in his many layers. Winter is finally in retreat. It is being danced away and cast out.

The fiddler's bow is bouncing off his strings as the dance fans out now. Each man holds on to the tip of his neighbour's blade then they swoop in tight again and three of the men duck down and let go and make a half-turn then come up to create a new shape with their blunted blades. One man shouts and the blades come unstuck and then the dancers are marching a quick-step in the same direction – like bloody show ponies thinks Rutter. The clapping from the crowd is getting louder and his shirt collar suddenly feels tight like it is closing in around his neck. There are bodies squashing against him; the bodies of people clapping and laughing and grinning but then when they push up against *him* their faces change. They scowl. He has to get out. He has to leave.

He pushes back through the crowd the way he came but after a few moments a hand closes on his shoulder. It clamps on with strong fingers curling around his scapula and pressing down hard. Rutter flinches. Rutter thinks of broken bones and a lolling neck and open wounds and flies laying eggs. Rutter thinks of a cold kiss on lips turning blue. The firm feel of them.

It is a man with a beard. Rutter turns and shirks. He tries to free himself from the grip but it holds. Tightens. Rutter turns and sees a man with thick hair over his ears and a heavy beard flecked with grey at the chin.

Steve says the man.

It's Muncy. It's bloody Ray bloody Muncy. The man's barely recognisable to him.

The vice grip loosens then turns into an arm flung around

his shoulder as the crook of his arm bends around Rutter's neck and the Long Sword dance crowd closes in around them again. The clapping is getting faster and louder as the fiddler's elbow jerks and thrusts.

Rutter sees a change in his neighbour. He sees burst capillaries and ageing. He sees that something has snapped deep inside.

You look different.

I am different Steve. I am different.

Muncy smiles as he says this but it is a non-smile. An unsmile. A lie on his face.

Rutter wonders why Muncy has his arm around him. He has never done that before. He can see Muncy's fillings. He wants to not see his fillings. He wants to not have Muncy's arm around him.

The dance is reaching a frenzied pace now. Rutter can hear it in the fiddle player and the clogs on the flagstones and the way the crowd is clapping faster and louder still.

Not seen you since the snow says Muncy. Not since Melanie. Strange isn't it? How someone can just disappear like that. No one can know what it feels like until it happens to them. It keeps me awake at night the thought of her. June's in bits. You've no doubt heard. Gone to pieces.

Rutter shakes his head.

Oh yeah I forgot you're Steve Rutter the village idiot keeps himself to himself and never asks questions. Stuck up that farm. Tied to that farm for life aren't you. You and your secrets.

Muncy finally loosens his grip and Rutter steals a glance at him. His eyes are glazed. Different. Something has changed inside Muncy forever.

Rutter shakes his head.

But I thought your mother had made it so says Muncy. Old Aggie's final cruel trick. Keeping you tied to our little hamlet till when?

Rutter turns away again and mumbles but he is trapped by bodies. The dancers are red-faced dervishes whirling in the May sunshine.

What's that? says Muncy.

Till I'm fifty says Rutter.

Say again? says Muncy.

Till I'm fifty.

Oh aye that's right says Muncy. Until you turn fifty. Must be a hard one to take that but Steve. Knowing that wreck of a house is yours and all them outbuildings too – I mean the land alone'll be worth a sum that someone like you can't comprehend. And then to find out from the solicitor how she wrote it into the paperwork that whatever happens to her you have to stay until you're *fifty* before you're allowed it. Jesus man. That's a betrayal is that.

Rutter says nothing so Muncy continues. There is venom in his words now.

Stuck up on the dark side of the dale like that he continues. Them turbines whirring away all day and all night and the rest of the world around you changing and you not being able to leave for years and years. No wife no kids no company. Just some stupid pigs and some half-bald chickens. That's not farming; that's desperation. No escape and knowing that if you left you'd have nowt. Legally nothing. The farm the land the buildings the stock – all that would revert to the government. They would take it all. Just sitting there waiting for time to pass waiting until you turn fifty. Must be a decade or more by my reckoning. That's a life sentence is that.

Rutter shrugs and makes to turn away but Muncy has him in his grip again.

You've got to ask yourself why she would want to do that to her own son. Keep him tied up in red tape like that. It's like she never wanted you to have a life Steve. It's like she's laughing at you. Mocking you Steve. It's enough to turn you funny is that. But still I'd swap my life for yours in a heartbeat if I thought it would bring our Melanie back.

Something flashes in his eyes. Across them. Like a shadow at the back of his mind.

Just to see her face says Ray Muncy. The police had you down as a suspect you know.

The police had you down as a suspect as well says Rutter. I heard them say so.

They raided you though.

They turned up he says.

Muncy is pressed in close to Rutter and all Rutter can think about is getting away. Turning and walking then running through the crowds and out of town. Up the valley and through the hamlet and across the hill. Maybe he'd keep going. Past the farm out the back and up to the top. Across the moors to the deep dark water to memories of the way the silver moon played across its surface last winter and how thin frosted fractals of ice formed on the stiffened sand of the shore.

The dance reaches a climax as the men shout and thrust six swords together to create a hexagram while the seventh pierces it and holds it high. The crowd cheers and whistles.

Muncy still has the same desperate smile playing about his mouth. The broken look in his eyes. Around them the crowd loosens and relaxes and breathes a collective sigh.

Funny how they never got you on anything.

How do you mean? says Rutter.

Well they say that that Brindle is the best.

So?

It's almost like you knew they were coming.

Rutter looks away but Muncy's face is in his. It is inescapable. Muncy's grip and the push of the crowd holds them together. He grimaces beneath his beard; his eyes are desperate and his eyes are deranged as they search his mind for an answer.

Our Melanie –

They are face-to-face now their eyes black as something tightens in Muncy.

If ever I find out –

Muncy cannot finish the sentence; doesn't need to. His hand grips harder still but this time Rutter doesn't shirk or flinch and doesn't even blink. Muncy's eyes search Rutter's now but he sees that they are black and they are still and they offer nothing in response.

MACE SEES RAY Muncy lurking behind a rack of faded birthday cards in the newsagent's. Mace is buying his morning cigarettes and escaping the thrust and pull of the Long Sword dance crowds. His head is thumping to the beat of a distant bodhrán.

Muncy looks nervy. Wild. He corners Mace on the way out.

You're the writer lad aren't you?

Yes he replies. Roddy Mace. And you're Ray Muncy.

He extends a hand but Muncy ignores it.

You've been helping that copper Brindle look for our Melanie.

Yes says Mace. He makes sure to choose his words carefully. I covered the initial story. You know I was really sorry that—

Have you heard about Larry Lister?

What? says Mace slightly thrown by the question. What about him?

They've got him.

Who has? What do you mean?

He's been done this morning. Sex stuff. An underage lass. Maybe loads of them. Boys maybe. I don't know.

The TV presenter?

Of course the TV presenter says Muncy. Yes. Lovely Larry. *Uncle Larry's Party* and all of that shite.

Bloody hell says Mace. Then again it's no great surprise though is it?

How's that?

The guy's a creep. Anyone can see that. There's been rumours for years.

Yet no one did anything about it.

Yes says Mace. It would seem that way.

He used to come up here a lot you know. Uncle Larry. I used to see him about.

Where? Town?

Oh aye. Friend of Roy Pinder's.

Really?

Yeah. Two creeps together.

You're not a friend of Roy's then? says Mace. Didn't you two go to school together?

If you're asking then you probably know that we did. And no we're not mates. Roy Pinder has his own friends and his own ways of doing things.

How do you mean exactly Mr Muncy?

Use your noggin lad. Everyone knows Pinder runs things round here. He doesn't run Ray Muncy though. Heck no. None of them do. Why do you think I moved all the way up to the top of the valley? To get away from him and his lot. Bull Mason and their friends in the city. Because they can't bend me that lot. No way. Pressuring me to do all sorts of things.

Would you care to explain what exactly?

No I would not says Muncy. That's best left unsaid for now; I've still got businesses to run. But you should look into Pinder and Larry Lister. Thick as thieves those two.

He turns to leave.

Larry Lister he says again. A whisper this time. He's a filthy sod. Pinder too. You investigate that.. Find it out and bring them all down. This town can burn for all I care.

You might be surprised says Mace but you're not the only

person who thinks that.

BRINDLE LURKS. BODIES press against him.

Here's up here again. Town.

He can't leave it. The valley.

The valley has haunted him. The town has got him. The hamlet too.

They ribbed him about it when he first left Cold Storage and came up here when the case was first called. They stuck a picture of Edward Woodward burning in the giant wicker effigy on his monitor.

And now winter has birthed spring and many weeks have passed and there's still no body and no evidence and no leads. Set it aside they said. Leave it be. There's fatter files in Cold Storage. New cases coming in. You don't even know she's dead. Put her down as a runaway and come back to it later with a clear head.

But this is Brindle and he has silently relived the disastrous raid of Christmas Day time and time again. He has tortured himself with the shame. All those officers dragged out at night on their one assured day off. The turning-over of Rutter's house and being outwitted. That's how he felt. Outsmarted by an unhygienic imbecile.

He had got drunk. He had shamed himself. He had nearly broken himself.

They had seen a difference at work. Supe Alan Tate had said he was losing focus Supe Alan Tate had recommended counselling. Said Brindle was only human and all humans needed help from time to time. Cognitive behavioural therapy he said. It's a way of rooting out the causes of anxiety. Of righting wrongs and moving on. Nothing to be ashamed of he had said. A lot of the detectives had it – especially here in Cold Storage. Brindle had said he would think about it.

No need Tate had said. He was already booked in.

All part of the twenty-first century policing package he had said.

So he had *had* to come back: to right this wrong. There was no question. It's like a different world up here today. He barely recognises the small country town now that it is no longer covered in the stifling blanket of silent white.

With the residents out in the sunshine after months of winter darkness and the music and the dancing and the hog roasts he could almost grow to like the place on a day like this. Almost – were it not for the folk crimes. The stories and secrets buried in the soil.

He would find her. He would not give up. He told himself he was doing it for the girl and doing it for the family but deep down he knew that more than anything he was doing it for himself.

THE SCREWS ARE practically queuing up to get a look at him. They don't know how to react. On the one hand he's suspected of committing the worst of the worst crimes but on the other he's Lovely Larry Lister. Larry Lister – here and in their care.

He's as much a part of their childhoods – all their childhoods because Lister has not been off the idiot-box for fifty years – as bicycles and scabby knees. And so it confuses them now seeing him sitting in his cell and wearing the same fat trainers they've seen a thousand times on television (the only difference now is the necessary removal of his laces).

Surely not Larry? No. Not Larry. It must be a mistake.

He's under protection yes but Lovely Larry Lister seems in good spirits. None of this suicide-watch nonsense that they usually employ on the beast wing. No. He has a grin and a nod of the head and a wave of the hand for everyone. Keep smiling he says to the screws – even to those who aren't – and *be lucky*.

Some of the younger POs forget protocol and have their

pictures taken with him on their phones. They open up his cell door and stand next to him against the dull taupe gloss wall. They want to put their arms around the big man but do not dare to because how would that look – befriending a (if the charges are to be believed – and amongst the screws they are always believed until proven otherwise) sexual predator? They exchange small talk though. Small talk and banter is fine. They quiz him. They ask him about television and who is the most famous person he has met and the millions he has raised for charity and how many houses he owns and how many birds he's shagged and *Christ who does your hair?* and is he comfortable. How is he set for smokes and Mars bars?

None of them asks if he did any of the things that the newspapers have been drip-feeding out to the public on a near-daily basis. Each more extreme than the last and a growing gallery of faces of those new victims coming forward to make statements.

Because to hear an admission of guilt from Lovely Larry Lister would be like having a small part of their own childhood destroyed; hearing Lovely Larry Lister confess to those crimes would be an abuse of the trust they had placed in the man who has been with *all* of them for *all* of their lives.

Perhaps Larry Lister knows this. Perhaps this is why he continues to wear the mask he always wears. That of smiling wisecracking joshing punning Lovely Larry Lister: son of Yorkshire and lynchpin of light entertainment. King of television.

MACE IS SIPPING bitter instant coffee and watching the live broadcast of Larry Lister being released on bail. Everyone in the office of the *Valley Mercury* is watching.

He comes out not under a dull military-grey blanket thrown shamefully over his head in the scrum nor by a side door two hours before the morning press have assembled but walking purposefully out the front door where he pauses at the top of the old granite steps and forces a smile that inadvertently twists into a smug sneer. He is wearing what appears to be a freshly tailored Harris tweed three-piece suit beneath which he sports a Hawaiian shirt and down below a garishly luminous pair of Nike trainers and matching baseball cap worn askance at a jaunty angle. Mace sees the stringers and paps swarm him: *Larry Larry. Over here Larry.*

The face of light entertainment – the man who *is* the history of British television – raises his hands in a gesture of supplication. He smiles. Appeals for calm.

Out of the melee of flashbulbs and elbows comes a voice louder than the rest – the recognisable bellow of one of the *Yorkshire Evening Post*'s most ardent stringers.

Larry – what do you say to the accusations that you're a sexual predator?

Having clearly had plenty of time to prepare for this scenario Lovely Larry Lister removes his electronic cigarette from his pocket and draws on it before exhaling a thick fug of synthetic cherry smoke into the lenses of the assembled throng and with a big beaming smile as if he is anchoring the opening night of *Get Down and Groove* back in sixty-three he winks at the assembled throng of hacks snappers coppers supporters fans jeerers protesters amateur bloggers autograph-hunters iPhone-wavers and rubber-neckers and says: keep smiling people keep smiling – and *be lucky.*

And then as Lister pushes through the crowd Mace hears a smaller voice – one that is thick flat and defiantly Yorkshire – picked up by the BBC's boom mic as the big man himself passes by.

You're going to need all the fucking luck in the world pal.

And back to the studio.

BRINDLE HAS BEEN back up to the hamlet – how many

times? Many. Every weekend plus numerous midweek visits. In any free time he has made his excuses from Cold Storage – from his other cases – and put on his walking boots and filled his rucksack and made entire days of it.

He has got to know the higher slopes of the valley. He has a feel for them now. The bogs and marshes and turbines and copses and tumbledown dwellings long since abandoned. Rutter's turf. He has inhaled the sharp clear air. He has slowly filled his lungs with it and mapped the area in his mind and found to his surprise that he likes the solitude of the open spaces and the breeze in his face. The broad landscape of the upper valley and the moor-tops fit his personality. He now understands why people might choose to live here.

He has walked the path along the gill that leads out of the Muncy's campsite and followed it all the way down into town then followed it back up again. He has circumvented the reservoir and found it bleak and functional and ugly; a kind of nowhere space over which the darkest clouds seems to gather. A foreboding puddle.

And he has become obsessed with Rutter. He knows this. He knows this is what it will take. What it always takes. So he has infiltrated Rutter's terrain and made a record of it all: the drab details about how he buys his food from the same market stalls and the supermarket in town and his petrol from the same station. How he has no known mobile. No internet account. How he seems to go nowhere but down the dale or up top with his dogs. The moors the woods the quarries. Trapping and hunting mainly. How he doesn't take a drink – or at least not in pubs. How there is no trail of battered women or overdue child-support or outstanding warrants. How there's a clean driving licence and no passport.

His father is unknown and his mother in a home.

There is so little from his past that is recorded it is as if Rutter does not exist.

The others though – Bull Mason and Roy Pinder and that circle of men that Roddy Mace suggested he looked into – their lives are documented and have been revealed in long arduous hours of fact-finding. Slowly he is piecing together a picture of each; tracking connections and figuring out anomalies.

As for the pigman's mother – machines do most of her body's work now. Brain damage from a stroke they said and the fall that came with it. They're counting down the days.

Brindle has even sneaked up to Rutter's truck after dark and taken a reading off the petrol gauge and mileometer. He returned two days later to find that the next reading tallied with Brindle's tracking of him. There were no nocturnal or uncharted journeys that he knew of.

Rutter's life of routine and solitude is mundane and moribund and the recognition of elements of his own life in this pathetic individual only infuriates Brindle even more.

Brindle cuts across the market square and down the side street where the sound of Steve Rutter's footsteps still echo and then turns the corner straight into –

Mace.

JARS. JARS ARE placed around the room. On the floor and on shelves and on windowsills. Some with lids some without. The stench. It's strong. Like sour vinegar – only worse. Sharper. The jars are of differing sizes filled to varying levels and containing graded shades of urine ranging from burnt toffee through to near clear. Jam jars honey pots pickle jars chutney jars bell jars.

There's the odd tin can too.

Rutter's toilet does not function. First the cistern broke and then the bowl got cracked and leaked on the floor and soaked through the floorboards. Rotted them. He does not remember how this happened. He does not remember many things now.

Small details – like how he got the cut above his eye or when he last ate or why more chickens were found decapitated when there was no sign of a disturbance in the coop or what happened to one of the dogs to leave it bleeding in the yard or when his birthday is or why he got a note in the post that said CARELESS TALK COSTS TONGUES and a clearly recent photograph of Rutter on an identifiable part the moors taken from a distance.

So now he goes in jars. Sometimes he goes in the sink but mainly he goes in jars. He leaves them in the airless room. Soon he will empty them he tells himself. Soon. There is just so much to do about the place and he can't seem to –

Day becomes night becomes day and the hearth holds winter's white ashes. Soon he will need to go logging. He will need to get his bow saw and his axe and his splitter and his mallet and fetch some firewood. Soon. He has seen some nice fallen silver-birch trunks; if only he could remember where they were.

Amongst the jars the mattress sits grey and greasy and the curtains are permanently drawn. Tangled knots of clothes that have been kicked off are on the floor but the room holds little else. He wears the same things all the time. Vest t-shirt shirt jumper padded work shirt. They are matting together. One day they will be one laminated garment glued by sweat and soil. A plaid second skin.

He sleeps in the front room in a chair placed by the blackened fireplace and he thinks about the dead girl almost constantly. Sometimes Rutter talks to her. Tells her what he is thinking in a muttered running commentary. He talks about the few fumbled moments they shared he talks about the weather he talks about how they'd never find her and how just because they were separated didn't mean they were *apart*. They still had the memories and the good times. Always. Those could never be taken away from them whatever happened.

Not by Pinder or Skelton or Brindle or his mother or Hood or anyone.

Once he used to talk to his mother this way. Many months after she had gone he spoke out loud to her. Sometimes he laughed and cursed and scoffed and other times he told her about his day and down in the hamlet people would hear him and say it's Steve Rutter what do you expect he's always been that way.

But now he talks to the girl out loud when he is out poaching or logging or in the yard staring at the great cinema screen of a sky onto which speeding clouds are projected.

In an increasingly frantic mumbled tone he talks about the weather and the animals. He talks about their time together and their future together and he tells her how he never meant for it to be this way.

One day I'll make it up to you he says. You'll see how I'll make it better. I'll bring you up from down there I'll bring you back I'll dry you off. I'll get a fire going a nice big one to warm you up and dry you out and make you feel better. And if you don't want to stay here that's OK because one day soon I'll be able to leave and I'll sell the farm and we'll leave in the middle of the night and never come back.

The sentences run into one another and it sounds like Rutter is speaking in his own unique rural argot. Like he is speaking in tongues. A whispered cant.

He has to check himself and make sure he never speaks her name in case it becomes too familiar in his mouth; in case he accidentally utters it in town or down in the hamlet.

Only at night in the dark in his chair does he dare to whisper it:

Melanie.

Melanie.

Because one day it will be his fiftieth birthday and on that day he will leave the farm forever. He will sell up and he will fill his suitcase with the money he has stashed and he will turn the chickens loose and he will set the dogs free and he will drive away and he will fetch her and they will be reunited.

Hours he can sit watching the first sunbeams of spring illuminate the glass receptacles that fill his floor.

7

FIRST THEY COLLIDE awkwardly and then they peel themselves away.

Christ says Mace then: hello.

He sees that Brindle is wearing a shirt and tie as he was at Christmas only this time the shirt has short sleeves. No croupier's armbands this time. Every hair is oiled in place and the birthmark is gleaming. But this time the detective has walking boots on his feet.

Brindle shifts his weight from one foot to another. His face is fixed.

I've not seen you since Christmas. Since—

Brindle cuts Mace off.

Yes.

You're back says Mace. Well obviously.

They've got me on a number of other cases. High-profile. The workload is…

His voice trails away.

Mace sees Brindle's jaw tighten. He sees him clench and then relax one of his fists.

She's not high-profile any more? The girl.

Brindle says nothing.

You left a bit suddenly.

I had work says Brindle. There were reports to write. I had to be back in Cold Storage.

Right says Mace. And did you get a bollocking?

For what?

For raiding Rutter's like that.

I'm actually very busy says Brindle stepping sideways. I need to get going. And then as an afterthought he adds: nice to see you.

Brian Laidlaw said he'd seen you about.

About.

Yeah says Mace. Skulking around the hamlet dressed as a yomper.

What's a yomper?

A hill-walker. A day-tripper. A tourist.

I'm not a tourist. Tourists go places on holiday – this is not a holiday.

Mace nods to the walking boots.

I see you've been having a wander anyway.

Brindle looks embarrassed. Says nothing.

I'd been thinking about you actually says the journalist. This story—

Look Roddy says Brindle again. I really need to get going.

He moves to walk away.

Mace speaks to the detective's back.

I've been doing some research. I think I've unearthed a few things that might interest you. A lot of things actually. Stuff that goes way beyond this town. Beyond this valley.

Brindle pauses and turns and they look at one another. Something passes between them.

I'm sorry says Brindle. I really do have an appointment.

He turns and leaves. Mace calls after him.

There are things you need to know he says.

A GIRL BRINGS them their drinks and stands for a moment as if waiting for them to say something but when they both look at her and say nothing she turns and goes back to stand behind the counter. She picks up a paperback book and resumes reading it. Brindle sees that it is Faulkner. *As I Lay Dying*. He notices these things.

I tried to call you says Mace.

What? says Brindle. He lines up the salt and pepper shakers

and then adjusts his tie. He is pretending to be distracted. Mace thinks he is trying too hard. He is a bad actor.

I tried to call you.

I didn't know.

I left messages.

I didn't know.

I spoke to one of your colleagues.

I've been busy.

I heard him ask if you were free and then I heard you say who is it and when they said it's some reporter called Roddy Mace I heard you say no.

Brindle looks pained.

Who was it? Who did you speak to?

That's not the point. You're a terrible liar.

Brindle takes out a teabag from his pocket and drops it into the cup of hot water. He says nothing. He is squinting. The sun is on his face. His birthmark appears grainy and illuminated.

This Cold Storage place of yours is hard to track down says Mace. It's as if it doesn't even exist.

That's partly deliberate says Brindle.

Most people I called on the force had never even heard of you lot.

Again – deliberate. Secrecy is our MO.

You've been avoiding me though.

Brindle sighs. Says nothing.

Look don't fucking flatter yourself says Mace. Please. I'll save you the trouble of wondering: I was calling you about Melanie Muncy – nothing else.

I'm not used to drinking Brindle says so quietly he is not sure whether he has spoken at all.

The cafe is empty except for the girl. She does not look up from her book. Brindle gnaws at his bottom lip. Presses his palms to his thighs.

Why did you want to talk to me about her? asks the detective.

Because I've been on it all this time – that's why. The case. And I've found out important things. Big things. Jesus. You are so fucking unreachable I nearly called the local cops at one point.

Why didn't you?

You've met Roy Pinder haven't you?

Brindle moves the salt and pepper shakers and then stirs his tea.

Brindle frowns and looks down at his tea. Stirs his tea. Sips his tea. The cafe door opens and a group of six people walk into the cafe. Tourists. Two more follow behind them. Eight in total. Brindle counts them. Eight eights are sixty-four he thinks. A good number is sixty-four. You can do things with sixty-four like how six and four is ten and six times four is twenty-four and that makes thirty-four which is fine. Thirty-four is fine. But three times four is twelve and three plus four is seven and add them together and what do you have? Nineteen. Nineteen is not good. Nineteen can never be good because nineteen cannot be tamed because one multiplied by nine is still nine and one *plus* nine is ten – add those together and then what do you have? Still nineteen. Still nineteen. Nineteen going nowhere.

Mace continues.

I still think that it's true what they say: that you're the best there is. Just like I'm the best there is. Or could be if I could just catch the right fucking break. I can write – I know that. No one else on that local jizz-rag of paper is as obsessed with the written word as I am just as none of your lot are as obsessed by murder cases as you are.

Brindle says nothing.

Admit it says Mace. It drives you mad this job. Because it's more than a job. It's part of who you are – a huge part. I feel it too. My great novel may have stalled and I may be a drunken fucking idiot who never gets round to doing the washing up but this isn't forever. I'm still young. And I've seen how *you* live. Your tics and anxieties and weird ways.

Nineteen thinks Brindle. Fucking one and fucking nine and fucking one times nine and—

Oh he says. Have you now.

I've seen enough says Mace. It tears you half-mad being close to all these corpses all the time but I know you're scarred by it and scared too because this is all you can do. Know *how* to do.

Scared?

Yes. Scared.

Of what?

Mace picks his cup up and looks Brindle in the eyes.

You're scared that if you ever gave it up you'd go completely mad.

Brindle says nothing so Mace continues.

You're scared because you know you're only ever one step away from the people you pursue.

A moment passes. Anyway. Listen. We need to talk about Larry Lister says Mace.

Lister? Why?

Because says Mace choosing his words carefully. Because there may be a link.

You said you've been trying to track me down for months though?

Yes.

But that story has just broken. Lister has only just been bailed.

Yes.

So what is it that you want to talk about? What does he have to do with all this?

Their cups sit empty before them. The cafe is busy now and it is Brindle who quietly asks the question this time.

Larry Lister says Mace. Lovely Larry. Uncle.

What about him?

He has links to the valley.

Go on.

Ray Muncy told me that Lister and Roy Pinder are associates.

Associates?

Friends.

Raymond Muncy's a damaged man says Brindle.

Aren't we all? I mean isn't that what's going on here?

Maybe. Maybe not. Perhaps they sent him that way. Perhaps he's actually the sanest out of the lot of them.

Seems like Lister knows every bent councillor in the country the amount of awards he's been given and clubs he's an honorary member of says Brindle.

Yes says Mace. But it's Pinder we're talking about here. Roy Pinder who did little to help your initial investigation into Steve Rutter. Pinder who it could be said put obstacles in your way. Roy Pinder who practically runs the town.

Brindle raises his eyebrows. Urges Mace to continue.

And Larry Lister: career sexual abuser. He's been at it for years.

So it would seem. But I don't get why Pinder would want to stop me nailing Rutter. Or what bearing his friendship with Larry Lister has on this.

Well neither do I says Mace but maybe you need reminding that in the middle of all these shitehawks – Lister and Pinder and Rutter – are victims and a girl that's still missing. The daughter of a local man – Ray Muncy – in fact; a man who is most definitely not a part of Pinder's clique.

You think Lister and Pinder and Rutter are linked?

It's possible. And there's more.

There is?

Steven Rutter says Mace.

Yes.

This girl might not be the first.

Brindle looks around. He considers Mace. He stands.

Come on – let's go for a walk.

They leave the cafe and turn right down an alley and then down steps. They cut through a snicket and onto the Old Hardraw Road and then down to a back lane that leads behind the last row of houses. Cherry Tree Lane. Beyond that are paddocks.

Right says Brindle. What are you saying?

I tried to tell you at Christmas but you were such an arrogant bastard that I kept it to myself.

Kept what?

That someone told me about another girl that had gone missing – years back.

Girls go missing all the time.

Not from round here.

From where *specifically*? says Brindle.

The upper valley. The hamlet. The last sighting was at Muncy's campsite. I've looked into it all and Rutter was there then too – just up the hill. He was young but not too young to do something like this.

Like what?

They walk down the lane side-stepping dried-up dog shit and litter.

Mace shrugs.

Well why the hell didn't anyone tell me this? says Brindle.

Why would they? You didn't exactly endear yourself to the locals.

But this is police business.

And this is their business. And never the twain shall meet. This runs deep.

How do you know all this? About the other girl I mean.

Because I'm a journalist says Mace. Because it's my business – just as it is meant to be yours.

They walk in silence.

One more thing says Mace. Larry Lister.

Yeah?

He bought a property.

So?

Years back.

And?

And it's in the valley.

Brindle stops. He looks at Mace. The red mark on his cheek appears to be pulsating with a heartbeat of its own.

I need to know everything you know.

I imagine you do says Mace.

Will you—?

Brindle coughs. Clears his throat. He looks around and then he looks at Mace. Swallows.

What? says Mace.

Will you help me?

ONLY WHEN THE rain falls does the symphony of the windmills abate.

The spring rain falls. First as a fine drizzle then in a torrent. The air tightens and turns sepia then thunder growls and the rain falls harder. Drops hit the ground like nails from a nail gun. They scoop out tiny divots.

It spatters it disturbs it rearranges. It pools then runs then it pools some more.

Dubs of dirty water gather in the farm yard and diesel and petrol that was spilled long ago and held in the grit now rises to the surface to create a film across the puddles.

He slaughters the occasional remaining undernourished chicken. He boils them up until they fall apart then he scoops up the wet mess with bread. Then he boils it the next day and the day after until the bones are reduced down to a thin watery stock with an oil-slick surface. He drinks it down. It is his sole sustenance.

The dogs are agitated. Neglected. With ribs showing and ears down they whine in unison.

And it keeps coming. The rain. Like bullets from the sky. Machine-gun deluges. It rattles the asbestos roof of the wood store and teems down through the barn. Where there are cracked roof slates the water seeps into the house and streaks the nicotine walls a darker shade. The puddles spread and join together to turn the farmyard into a blackened morass. He watches from the window smoking. Hears it come rattling down the dale like sheets of metal stacked up one behind the other.

There is lightning. He feels it first charging the air around him then he sees the flash: a brief white shuttering of the sky. He sees an upper stretch of the stream swelling into a river already. Down in the hamlet the puddles are turning into a pond that will inch its way up to sand-bagged doorsteps if the rain continues.

Then comes the thunder. A greedy sky-gulp of it.

He thinks of rain on the reservoir. The sound it makes and the way it hits the surface. He thinks of the rising water and the engineering that went into making it technically impossible for the reservoir to overflow.

He thinks of –

The storm drains.

He thinks of –

The portals. He thinks of –

He pictures the reservoir rising rushing surging gushing. Underwater underground. Unseen. Through tunnels and runnels and channels and fissures. Running and spurting and flowing and flushing. Down the hidden concrete conduits through the earth and out the storm-drain exit points. He sees streams swelling into rivers that flow down the flanks and into the valley. Down the dale.

Panic –

He sees the face of the girl rising to the surface as her body is battered by nature's flotsam. He sees the branches and bones and algae and plastic and all that has been held in the reservoir's freezing murky depths encircling her. He sees the water pushing past her bobbing trunk and through the locked grate; her swollen face pressed up against it her mouth gaping her lungs full and weighted her hands bound her flesh loose and puffy from a season suspended in water.

Panic as the flood-warning siren groans into life. A long moan down the funnel of the valley.

Panic because floods bring people bring trouble bring logjams and cracked pipes and blocked drains and news crews. Obstructions. Floods bring sandbags and council men and engineers and surveyors and TV crews. Intrusions. Even here. Especially here. Up top in the rain-battered rural outback.

Panic –

As he sees her half-dressed and rising like an underwater angel.

Panic as he sees tomorrow today: the men in their luminous coats and waders trudging through new streams and slipping over rock-falls as they climb the dale to the storm drains whose grates need lifting unblocking unclogging disentangling.

He sees: a work crew of men with hard hats and torches and draining rods. He hears voices and the crackle of walkie-talkies. He sees them splinter off as some of them are given the short straw of checking the furthest drains. Miles away they are. Over the ridge and around the water and down the other side.

And he sees keys. He sees keys in hands.

He sees padlocks and puzzled looks.

Tomorrow today.

And down the valley – down the dale just past the hamlet

– the flood-warning siren wails like a clarion call announcing the end of the world.

I'VE PUT IT all together says Mace.

They are in his flat. Mace has brought the detective here and now he clears space on the sofa for Brindle to sit. He moves clothes and newspapers. An empty pizza box that rattles with stale crusts. The detective brushes the sofa with his hand and then picks something off the upholstery.

Don't worry says Mace. You won't catch anything.

That remains to be seen.

It's all here says Mace as he holds up a file. Or what little I've been able to find anyway.

Which is?

That Rutter's a weasel. He's gone unnoticed for years.

Mace tells Brindle what he has heard. About the backpacker and the campsite. About twenty years ago. About the close proximity of Rutter. About her vanishing without trace. Brindle listens without saying anything. He takes in the information and then he says where are you getting all this information?

A source. Various sources.

Who?

Some guy.

And you trust this source?

No I don't trust him. I don't even know him. Drunken information imparted in a pub can only ever be a starting point. I work too you know.

Right says Brindle.

Are you aware of microfiche?

Of course. I'm also aware of disco music and fondue parties. All are relics.

Maybe to you but here in the hills we still use the tried-and-tested methods says Mace. Not all of us are blessed with fancy multi-million-pound new-build premises and all the technology that goes with it. I've been sifting. I've been sifting for fucking hours and hours actually. Doing what you do: digging and rooting.

Brindle takes out his laptop and turns it on. He finally – reluctantly – sits and then taps at the keys. Taps for five minutes.

There's nothing online about any of this. Did you get a name – of the other girl I mean?

Mace sits. He puts the file down on the coffee table in front of them and ignores the detective's question. He is relishing having the upper hand. The extra insight.

OK so in the new year I called a journalistic contact at the *Yorkshire Post* in Leeds he continues. I didn't tell him what it was about only that I was working on something minor. Something boring. He invited me in for a day. They've got the archives there you see – all the pre-internet stuff is on microfilm. Microfiche.

I know. I know all of this.

Right. So. It goes back decades. There is reams of the stuff. You could spend months going through all the stories and still never find it.

But says the detective. I sense there is a but.

I only had a rough date to go on. Twenty years ago. Summertime he said. *But* by lunchtime time I had found it. A two-inch press cutting.

Mace opens the file and rifles through papers to pull out a photocopied story. He hands it to the detective.

Look he says.

STUDENT CAMPER MISSING

Police are conducting enquiries in the search for a student who has been reported missing on the Coast-to-Coast walk.

Margaret Faulks, 19, had last been
seen walking in the heart of the
North Yorkshire Dales where she
was due to meet her boyfriend, Ian
Rogerson, also 19.

Faulks, a second-year medical
student at Keele and a keen walker,
had completed approximately half of
the 192-mile walk by herself and was
last seen leaving a campsite in one of
the most remote parts of the famous
route, which attracts hundreds of
walkers per year. Rogerson raised
the alarm after Faulks failed to meet
him. Police have now expanded their
search up to the open moorlands.

Rutter says Mace. His stink is all over this. Don't you think?
Brindle re-reads it.

Possibly. Do we even know Rutter was around then?

I've checked it all out. He's never left the place. He will have
been about the girl's age then too. Maybe a year or two older.
A desperate farm boy. Horny. Barely socialised.

What else? says Brindle. What else do we know?

We? You mean *I*.

What else do you know?

I know he and his mother Aggie Rutter were questioned
as part of the routine enquiries – as was everyone around the
area. And I know the search was discontinued due to the lack
of any substantial evidence or leads. Case unsolved. She was
never found. One for your predecessors no doubt. How long
has Cold Storage been operational?

Brindle ignores the question.

The boyfriend he says looking at the paper. Rogerson?

The boyfriend was questioned but had a watertight alibi says Mace. She simply vanished. A healthy happy girl with bright prospects and no known enemies – gone. No debts no drugs; none of that. No baggage. Just gone. Over.

He finds a map of the Coast-to-Coast route and hands it to Brindle.

He has marked the area of her last sighting. Muncy's campsite. He has also marked Rutter's house and highlighted the abandoned overgrown quarries and the reservoir and a gorge with a river running through it. He follows the Coast-to-Coast pathways with his finger; he traces west then east then west again.

And then there's this.

Mace produces a chit from the campsite – a simple raffle ticket. On it written in shaky faded biro is FAULKS. PITCH 17. 1 NIGHT. £3.

And on the reverse there is an ink stamp.

It says KELLERHOPE CAMPING.

From Muncy's says Brindle.

Mace hands him a glossy but faded leaflet. A brochure. It is for the site.

The front shows pictures of a field and a farm by a river. Happy campers sitting around. Tents and bikes and gas bottles.

Brindle opens it and phrases jump out at him:

A lively lovely working farm.

Long established stopover on the Coast-to-Coast.

The heart of the Dales.

Unspoilt and beautiful views.

Walkers and cyclists welcome.

Basic amenities. Barbecues allowed.

Family-run.

Contact June Muncy.

So says Brindle.

So says Mace. So we have confirmation that a girl went

missing from right under Steven Rutter's nose. So I did more digging. I put in more calls. Tracked down the boyfriend.

Really?

Brindle is surprised.

Yes really. It's what we trained journalists do. He wasn't hard to find. He's married now. Has two kids. Lives in Kent. Travels a lot for his job. He likes sailing on a weekend. He brews real ale was a contestant on *Who Wants To Be Millionaire?* Apparently he won thirty-two grand – not bad. Anyway I spoke to him and he confirmed what I suspected: she vanished into thin air. He suspected foul play but was helpless to do anything. He was just a kid with no say. He reckons the local dibble fucked it up. Inept fucking hillbillies was the phrase I believe he used. He had nightmares for months. Years. Her family hired a private detective but got nowhere. Hired another one – same thing. Nothing. Gone. Ghosted. He says he still fears her returning. He says that's what scares him the most – not that she might be dead but that she might return. That's weird isn't it?

It's a natural reaction says Brindle. Does your editor know about this?

Grogan? No.

Why not?

Mace pauses. He runs a hand over his stubble.

I don't know he says. I guess I didn't want anyone else but you and me to get their hands on it.

Why not?

Because the hills have eyes and the walls have ears and careless talk costs lives. Now we just need to prove Rutter did both. And then—

And then I think what you're saying is that you want to play the hero.

Maybe says Mace. Maybe it's that. Or maybe it's more.

Brindle shakes his head.

There are no heroes in this business. Only resolutions. No one wins when there are dead girls being unearthed. Of course I'll need to speak to Muncy again. And there's the whole Lister thing.

Mace stands and takes a cigarette from a box on top of his television then lights it.

Muncy – why?

Because he's the girl's father says Brindle. And he told you about the connection between Pinder and Lovely Larry. And because I think she was pregnant.

Melanie?

Maybe. I found a pregnancy-testing kit.

Mace inhales and holds it then exhales. He taps ash into an empty beer can and then places it on the coffee table.

Then I'll come with you.

The detective waves the smoke away.

It's not procedure he says. I can't.

Can't or won't?

Both says Brindle.

So – what? You're going to take this away from me?

When the detective doesn't reply Mace speaks quietly.

You asked for my help.

Brindle stands.

And I'm grateful for it says the detective.

Brindle holds the file. Flaps it.

I'll need this.

Fuck you Brindle.

BIBLICAL RAIN FALLS as he slips and struggles through mud. He takes no torch. His feet know the way. He wears his mother's old long waxed mac. The one with the cape on the shoulders. It is the only outer layer he has that is waterproof.

On her it came down to her shins and even now it still carries her stains. The faint scent of her. Even now. Three or four years down the line – or however long it has been. He has never been good with time.

And still he is soaked within minutes as the long grass swipes across his jeans and sticks them to him; soaks his skin soaks his underwear soaks through his boots.

All around him he hears the sound of running water. Water finding a way – a way across the earth and down the hills and through the soil. Water dampening down the bracken; water settling and sitting on the bog. Bubbling there. Water carving up the landscape – always sculpting and remoulding the shape of things. Creating gullies and grooves and gorges as it gouges soil and lifts stones and sets them a mile down the dale. Water at work – always.

Water muting the turn of the turbines for once. Silenced by the sputter of rain.

Water waiting for him ahead too. Up the hill and down the hole.

She has been with him in every waking moment since he put her down there just before Christmas gone; sometimes in dreams and often in nightmares. Trapped between two worlds she has hung suspended.

Certainly she has haunted his heart.

Once twice three times that first night he had stopped to lay in the frozen heather with her. He heard her body creak and groan and crack and snap beneath him as he held her one last time then one last time more. Hugging the bundled tarp sheet. He couldn't let go. Hours it had taken him. Hours of sweat and tension and muscle-strain.

He had been lucky. He knew that there was a risk of getting caught and then what? Then everything – decades of secrets – would unravel.

He enters the storm drain again. He descends the steps in the murky darkness. The floor once dry is now knee-deep in water and the dislodged flotsam of flood water bobs on its surface: pieces of wood and a plastic bottle. A tangle of wire lurking beneath.

He has a bag with his bits in. Tools and a torch. Crowbar. Extra rope.

He leaves the bag by the entrance where the water has not yet reached.

He turns on the torch and treads carefully over the uneven floor. The water is tinged umber and carmine from the peat and as he walks through it it slaps against the tunnel wall.

From somewhere deep below he can hear the run and rumble of underground channels and above him the slow drip of droplets running down mineral deposits before falling to the overflow. She is close.

If it keeps raining this heavily the water will rise up the steps and out the entrance in only a matter of hours. He has to do this and he has to do this now. He has to do this tonight.

Because floods bring people. Floods bring the authorities and men sniffing about with rods and head torches and blueprints and –

He goes deeper into the hillside and takes the right turn of the reservoir's run-off into utter darkness. The torch between his teeth.

He comes to a dead end and the drain grill underfoot. The water is rising up through it. Bubbling. She is down there. She is below him.

He needs to smoke. He has a craving for it greater than any he has ever known. He takes out a tailor-made and wedges the torch into his armpit while he lights his cigarette with a shaking hand. He inhales deeply. He holds it there. Lets it calm him. He smokes some more until water drips from the stalactite ceiling and extinguishes the cigarette for him.

He pauses then stoops with the torch and retrieves the wet butt-end and puts it into his pocket.

Rutter bends to the grill. It is hidden beneath the murk

and swirl. And beneath that an abyss. He rolls up his sleeves but they don't go far enough and the water is too deep as he reaches down to feel with his fingers. It is very cold. Straight away his jacket is soaked.

His fingers find the grill and then walk their way to the top-knot of the rope he tied on. He remembers which side the hinge is on.

This will not be easy. All that water to pull against and the breeze block he added to weigh it down.

He bends his knees and curls his fingers around the metal bars of the grill and he lifts. It gives a little.

He walks back to the entrance and he takes the crowbar from his bag and then he wades back through the water and round the corner and reaches down again. Past his elbows and up to his shoulders. He slots the bevelled end into a gap and then he jemmies it. He pulls and hefts and manages to open the grill but only by inches. The weight of the load that hangs from it is too much.

He lets the grill fall back into place and then he stands. His back aches. He splashes back to the entrance of the portal and feels around in the water. His hands settle on something solid. Another breeze block. He hefts it up onto his shoulder and then carries it around the dank corridor to the grill. He takes the crowbar and bends and jemmies again. He levers the grill and then slides the breeze block into the gap to wedge it open.

All underwater. Everything done by touch.

He catches his breath and then crouches so that the water soaks his trousers and waist and he gets one shoulder under the grill and he slowly rises. It gives. It opens. With his free hand he hooks the crowbar around the rope and pulls it to him to alleviate some of the strain.

His knees are bent and his thighs are burning screaming straining. The metal is digging into his shoulder. He takes a deep breath and pushes some more and the grill levers open and then in one quick moment he tosses the crowbar away into the water and grabs the rope with both hands. As he does the weight of the parcel pulls him forward and his back spasms and one foot steps over nothingness.

For a split second he teeters. One foot hovers over the abyss and he is on the brink of giving himself to it but he manages to shift his centre of gravity and stumbles splashing backwards into the tunnel away from the deep dark chasm of the vertical drain. With him comes his quarry.

Would it be so bad he wonders to have joined her in this wet underworld?

He moans and yanks at the rope. He hears his voice; hears his own desperate cry. The rope slides through his hands and it burns his palms – strips the skin right off – but he tightens his grip and pulls and pulls. And it burns.

He pulls hand over hand for eight nine ten feet of rope that snakes slack on the surface of the dirty drain water behind him then he feels the metal of chains in his red raw hands and he knows he is near the bottom.

He leans against the wet stone of the tunnel wall and gives it one final pull and with a splash and another moan that comes deep from within him the bound parcel of tarpaulin and rope and chain and breeze block and dead girl comes rising up from the deep.

He uses its partial buoyancy to his advantage and drags the body of the girl through the water to the steps. He flops down in the moonlight. Soaking gasping wheezing and sobbing. He can't catch his breath and his hands are screaming.

He waits a minute. He waits two minutes.

Then he stands. He moves the parcel around so that it lies across the widest step. He squelches as he moves. The concrete is grey. The concrete is dry. The concrete is a mortuary slab.

He slowly begins to untie the rope. Rutter unwraps the parcel. He turns it over as chains clink and dirty water runs out from it.

He is aware of the feeling of water on his skin. The stillness of the air. The silence.

Then he is untying and lifting and hefting and dislodging.

Rolling and clanking and unwrapping and reeling.

When the ties are undone he jerks the tarp sheet out like a magician doing the tablecloth trick and it unravels and then she is there.

She is there. The girl.

She is an abstract bloated thing. A recondite form face-up.

The girl has doubled in size and lost her shape. She seems so pale and rounded now.

In his hurry to rid himself of her he had forgotten he had packed her naked; her clothes bundled down by her feet with the breeze block.

Dead when she was dangled down the empty drain the girl's epiglottis was closed but when the recent storms came the waters rose and must have forced their way in through her orifices to fill the girl so that her body is now a yellow barrel with translucent skin and a roadmap of hardened veins sitting below the surface. The fat-tissues in her body have coagulated into hardened soaplike clots in places. Within her there are pockets of trapped gas.

Rather than halt it the cold waters have merely slowed the process of decomposition. Her small breasts are only partially there. One of them has half rotted away to leave a concave brown mush and the sallow skin of her torso is smeared with dirt and blood and darkened lesions. Her lower half remains hidden.

The dead girl's arms have ballooned to oversized proportions so that she now appears grossly overweight. She is a grim caricature of a human now; an inflation.

Her face. She has no lips no ears no eyelids. Her visage is a slick wax mask and a dark brown patch covers one side of it like a wet blistered birthmark. Part of one cheek has rotted away to make her mouth a twisted grimace that reveals blue gums black tongue and loose teeth.

He sees his hand reaching out and he touches a front tooth and it inverts. He touches it again and it falls into what remains of the girl's mouth. Down into her. He flinches backwards.

Her hair. It is barely there. What is left of it hangs from the back of her crown. It is darker than he remembers and resembles the matter found in a bath's plughole or at the bottom of a blocked U-bend.

Her eyes. It is the girl's eyes that are the hardest part to look at. Her sockets are empty now they still stare at him. They stare but they do not see. They look at him from one thousand years away. As if she is trapped beneath an Arctic plain.

He is struggling. He is struggling to recognise the girl as she once was; a living breathing entity capable of independent thoughts and actions. Capable of breath and laughter and dreams.

Now she exists only in another dimension called death.

IN A FUGUE-LIKE state he sits and he looks and he reaches for the body of the girl but then he turns and leaves the storm drain and he stands in the rain and he smokes another cigarette and he smokes it down to the nub and the rain falls gently and it sounds like music.

He realises that any notion of moving the body now is completely impractical. Bloody stupid that is. Suicidal.

His mind has become so muddled of late. So muddled.

It is still night but it won't be night forever and she won't be here forever and he won't be him forever.

They are out there he thinks. Her family. The police. People in houses; people in villages and towns and cities.

He turns back to the gaping dark entrance and the concrete

corridor of this mausoleum he has created.

It scares and excites him to think of the things he is still yet capable of. The things he has done in his life and the things he may yet do.

So he finds himself returning to her; finds himself squatting. The soles of his boots squeaking on the concrete. The rain outside. The black moors.

And Rutter.

8

UP THE DALE. Along the road. He thinks about folk crimes. Stories in the soil. Skeletons.

He winds his way up the valley and thinks about the things they put beneath the sod. The mute mythologies. The history of the land.

He counts the bars on gates as he drives past them then counts the number of cottages and farm houses that he can see up the hillsides. He plays around with the figures in his head. He adds and subtracts and divides and multiplies to make new numbers.

Numbers wheel by the window.

Brindle climbs the valley and turns into the hamlet. The sky pressing down. The clouds hurrying by. He parks up.

Folk crimes. Stories of the soil. Names of the living and names of the dead. Steven Rutter and Melanie Muncy and Aggie Rutter and Margaret Faulks and Ray Muncy and Ian Rogerson and Roy Pinder and Roddy Mace and June Muncy and Bull Mason and Johnny Mason – names he never knew three months ago. And in there somewhere Larry Lister. Of course Larry Lister. Of course.

He walks up the drive and knocks on the door and waits then knocks again and then a man answers. A wild-looking man – as wild as Rutter in his own way – with thick out-grown hair and a thick beard. Wet lips and grey hooded eyes. The eyes of the medicated.

Mr Muncy?

He says it as a question even though he knows it is him.

A grunt of confirmation greets him.

It's DS Brindle he says and it comes out as a question again

– as if he himself is not sure. James Brindle? The detective. We spoke about your daughter.

The man stares back. Slack-jawed and hostile. Holding the door. Almost clinging to it.

Yes. Of course it is.

Something changes in Muncy's eyes when he says this; something awakens within him. It is the brief re-ignition of hope and in this moment Brindle knows that this is going to be painful. And he knows that Muncy is not his man. He didn't do it.

This man did not murder his own thinks Brindle. He knows this. Is sure of it. Less than a second is all it takes. Ray Muncy says:

Have you found her?

His pale face is expectant.

No says Brindle. No I'm afraid not.

Muncy's face slackens. It visibly drops as hope slides away.

He lets go of the door that has been supporting him and it slowly begins to close.

Can I…?

Muncy stares at the carpet. Brindle reaches out and gently stops the door from closing with his fingertips. He speaks quietly.

Can I come in Mr Muncy? I just have a few questions.

The words when they come are a torrent. A garbled deluge.

She's dead isn't she?

Well we can't be—

I've tried to hold out hope says Muncy. June hasn't. June gave in months back – she's not got that kind of disposition. Never has had. But not me. No. Not me. I've always believed she's out there. That's the important thing isn't it? To know that she's coming back. One day – doesn't matter when. Just that she's coming back to us. The reason why didn't matter so long as she was coming back. Hope. Hope was what would deliver her back to us Mr –?

Brindle.

– but it's exhausting. Hope drains you. And seeing you here now – and I remember you of course I do what with that red thing on your face – seeing you here now with that look about you I know it was a stupid thing to cling to. I feel a bloody idiot for thinking she was ever coming back. Naive. She is dead isn't she Mr – what was it again?

Brindle. DS Brindle. I'm afraid I can't answer that question Mr Muncy. But there have been sufficient developments to convince me that perhaps now is the time to begin preparing for the possibility that your daughter may have been murdered.

Muncy's face drops further.

What developments? says Muncy. What are you on about? Have you got someone like?

No. Not as such. If I could come in for a moment I'd like to run through a few questions. There are certain points from the initial investigation that I would like to clarify including your alibi.

Muncy's mouth tightens.

Is that what this is about – you lot sticking me under your microscope again? While you're looking at me the cunt who killed my Melanie is out there. You lot never change.

I assure you I will be as quick as I can says Brindle. I'm sorry for the intrusion.

A week you lot were up here in the snow and then you packed up and shipped out and I've barely had a peep since winter. Do you know how many times I've called up to try to find what's been going on and now you turn up banging on about murder and wanting to check my alibi?

I want to talk to you about something you mentioned to a friend of mine.

What friend are you on about?

Roddy Mace. The journalist. You told him that Roy Pinder has links to Larry Lister.

Muncy's face changes again.

Lister?

Yes.

Oh says Muncy. Oh yes. I know all about them. There's things I've heard you wouldn't believe. Not in a million years. The papers haven't reported the half of it. That dirty fucker.

And I also wanted to talk to you about the other girl.

What other girl?

This isn't the first disappearance round here is it?

You're not making sense.

The student Mr Muncy. The girl who was last seen on your campsite and who has never been seen since.

Muncy looks at Brindle. He studies his face.

I remember her.

Good says Brindle.

Do you think…?

Yes says Brindle. Yes I do.

THERE ARE NO visible signs of a disturbance. The scene officer will later correctly remark that whoever did this had come in through the door – that the victim knew his killer. He invited them in. Nor are there any obvious signs of a struggle or fight. There are no tables or chairs upturned or pinhead dots of blood on skirting boards; no bruises in the shape of fingers or defensive knife wounds on the victim's palms. There is nothing broken or smashed or disturbed.

He is sitting in his armchair when they find him in his Horsforth maisonette. Framed photos of himself on the walls; a wardrobe full of old stage wear. Stale smoke still hanging above him like a miasmic shroud.

It is his solicitor who finds him. In a rare showing of non-legalese speak he tells one reporter that the way Larry Lister was sitting in the chair with his unlaced trainers planted on the carpet was just like when he used to deliver his straight-to-camera opening monologue on *Uncle Larry's Party* before adding that he had thought his client was sleeping or – slightly more disturbing – playing a trick on him.

When repeated banging on the windows failed to rouse him the solicitor had called the police. There is he explains no one else who has a key to the property.

The police arrive about thirty seconds before the first journalist does. Clearly someone on the inside has been leaking information to the media.

Only when they try to move the body and his slack mouth falls open do the officers discover the cause of death: Lovely Larry Lister's tongue has been removed. The complete lack of blood and Lister's calm pose and blank – almost tranquil – face are baffling to one and all.

And only when the police pathologist strips him bare on the mortuary slab hours later do they find the king of light entertainment's missing tongue – that instrument which has been the making of him and in many ways also the breaking of him – inserted partway up his puckered anus. A smattering of fine grey hairs surrounds it.

MACE SEES BRINDLE'S car parked up. He is out of breath. His car is in for its MOT so he has hailed a taxi from town. It dropped him on the main road and he ran all the way down into the hamlet with his lungs on fire while promising himself he'll give up smoking soon.

Mace knows he's in there. At Muncy's. Using what he gave him. All that information. All that work. Brindle claiming Mace's research as his own; Brindle stealing Mace's thunder.

He takes the knife from his pocket and walks down to the detective's car. He plunges the blade into a tyre. It's stupid and it is immature but as the stale air hisses from the slit in the black rubber it still feels good. The air it emits smells like rotten fish guts.

RUTTER UNWINDS THE lower half of the twisted tarpaulin.

Full length she lies with her thighs as decomposed as her torso. Mottled and transparent and waxed and unreal. His eyes move down. Taking it all in.

There is something down there. His eyes see before his brain computes. His mind scrambles. Hurries to process.

There is something pushing out. Out of her. Something rounded and real and alien and horrific. Something unknown.

His mind races to take it in.

A trick of the light. It must be. Maybe the shadows are –

He leans in. Squints.

Maybe it is –

No. It is not a trick of the light.

Something is protruding from her.

He looks and looks again.

Rutter makes out the suggestion of tiny features – eye sockets and the remains of a nose peeping out – and he reels backwards. He presses himself against the portal wall. He is hyperventilating. Vomit splashes the back of his throat. He is gagging yet still he looks.

Down there. A tiny alien thing. Pushing out her stretched dead slit.

Abdominal gases must have forced it. In putrefaction the gases have put pressure on her uterus and that secret that grew within her.

Decomposition pushed it. Laboured it.

Part-delivered it.

After death came a fleeting life.

A stillborn.

Still born.

Not newborn but *old*born.

Deadborn.

A coffin birth.

He turns and runs into the night. He runs gasping.

IT WAS WINTER when she fell.

Right there in the yard between the hen hut and the pig pen. He saw her from his window.

Black ice. Dusk. Horizontal. Her head. Two buckets of feed flung high as her feet went from beneath her.

He hadn't moved. One bucket rolled in a crescent shape spilling seed as it went. It made a slow searing sound that he found thrilling. The sound of cold metal on colder ice. Then it stopped.

She had laid still with the toes of her boots pointing skywards. Her breasts and belly spread flat beneath her coat.

It is her fault he thought as he looked on. All of this. All of this is her fault. Everything that has happened to him and all the things he has had done to him and all the things he has done to others – her fault.

Just knowing you're the combination of all those men's filthy muck mixed up and carried for nine months and moulded and born into the shape of you. Just knowing that will destroy a man.

Often he thinks about what it would it be like to have never existed. To have never known the pains of the world. To have not experienced loneliness and desire and disgust and fear. To have never felt hatred for the only relative he has ever known.

Ten minutes passed. The white sky softening and darkening. The spilled buckets.

Perhaps this is it he thought. Perhaps it's over perhaps it's finished perhaps I'm free.

Ten more minutes passed before he stepped away from the window and went downstairs. Put on his padded shirt and beanie. Picked up his tobacco pouch and truck keys. Money.

He left by the back door. Went to lock up and then decided not to lock up because he didn't need to lock up. He walked out into the yard.

Careful of that ice now –

His mother laid out. Just yards away.

He turned and quietly walked round the side of the house to the truck. He climbed in the truck. He started it. Revved the engine and noticed that it needed tuning.

He pulled out and the crunch of rubber on frost-covered ice was satisfying.

Down the track. Squeezing the brakes.

The tyres skidding and the rear end fishtailing. Through the hamlet now. Turning left. Avoiding town and instead going down the dale. Heading east to the city; the only place he could think of that could provide an alibi. That could provide a place to be both seen and unseen.

His mother up there on ice.

Heart slowing to near nothingness.

HIS FIRST MANIC thought keeps returning: is it mine?

A baby he thinks. Don't be stupid.

He doesn't know much about all that stuff – the hows and wherefores – but he knows enough. Dead girls can't conceive no more than dead cows can.

It cannot be. The unborn thing. Can it? No. Surely not.

No. Dead girls don't breed.

No. Do they?

So how did –

A family.

Could she –

No.

Could she –

He sits amongst the soaked young shoots of the emerging heather. He takes deep breaths. Darkness surrounds him and darkness swallows him and darkness consumes him. Darkness destroys just like he destroyed the girl.

Is that thing my doing? he wonders. Maybe it is.

No.

Stupid bloody stupid. Don't be so –

Of course it isn't.

Well if it's not mine then whose?

RUTTER. IT HAS to be Rutter. The tyre has been neatly stabbed with one-inch wounds through the rubber. The car is leaning at the front left corner.

Who else in the hamlet would –

It has to be Rutter.

Brindle opens the boot and pulls up the carpet and Brindle lifts the spare from the wheel well. He rolls up his sleeves and unfolds the jack and sets about changing the tyre. Dirt and grease and gravel. The new tyre looks odd. Its rims seem too thin. Brindle has nothing to wipe his hands on. Other people would have dusters or newspapers or carrier bags or anything but his car is immaculate. There is only bottled water and mints. Air-freshener. The satnav. A roll of pound coins for parking meters.

The grease is in the creases of his skin and under his nails. The sight of the dirt quickens his breath. Shortens it to a tight ball in his throat. He starts quietly counting out sequences of numbers and is surprised to hear them adopt a childlike sing-song melody.

Sometimes he wishes he could pay someone else to live his life for him.

Brindle gets back in the car and looks at his hands and Brindle takes some long slow deep breaths and then puts a mint in his mouth and his hands on the wheel to stop them shaking.

He wishes the world was different and he was different and everything was different; he wishes there was a place in the world into which he could fit. He wishes he was ignorant because he has heard that it is blissful.

And that is when he hears the noise of another car. Looks in the rear-view mirror. Sees a truck speeding by. Up the hill. Out of the hamlet. Away.

It's him.

Rutter.

RODDY MACE IS in the off-licence buying four cans of Stella and four bottles of lager when he hears the news over the radio.

Both he and the female shop assistant stop to listen.

TV presenter Larry Lister has been found dead in his home in West Yorkshire. The entertainer was recently released on bail and was facing charges relating to the sexual abuse of minors. Police had been taking statements from several dozen men and women who claimed to have been a victim of the popular light entertainer over the past four decades and were building a case which has been described as disturbing and extensive. Seventy-nine-year-old Lister first appeared on television over fifty years ago and was awarded an Order of the British Empire in 1999. The cause of his death is currently unknown.

Bloody hell says Mace. That fucker.

The assistant shakes her head.

I always said he was a bit odd. But he raised a lot of money for charity.

You better give me a half-bottle of vodka says Mace.

She hands over the bottle and he pays.

I met him once you know she says.

Mace is distracted.

Did you? he says. Where was that then?

Here. It was right here. He was buying his cigarettes. I distinctly remember he paid with a tenner but let me keep his change.

Did you see a lot of him?

Yes. He was often about. We had what's-his-name from *Emmerdale* once but you don't get many celebrities round here.

Why says Mace. Why was he often about?

He knew some of the boys I think. He was friendly with them like. Roy Pinder was with him.

Pinder?

Oh yes. Good friends those two. Thick as thieves.

Really?

Yes. He spent a lot of time up at Lovely Larry's house did Roy.

Which house?

The one here.

In the valley.

Yes. In the valley.

Where's that then?

Well that's the thing isn't it. Folk reckoned he had a bolt-hole in the area but no one knew where exactly. It was a secret like. A place to get away from the media and that London lot.

And no one at all knew where this house was.

The woman shrugs.

Roy used to visit him. Take him his messages and that. His bits and pieces. Some said they'd been in business together years back. I expect that'll all come out now.

What type of business?

She shrugs.

I don't know. You'd have to ask Roy that. But I wouldn't advise that.

Why not?

She shrugs again then sniffs.

I've never had a problem with Roy she says. He's helped me out.

You lot talk about him like he's untouchable says Mace. But I'm telling you now – he's not. Defending him is the same as defending Lister as far as I'm concerned.

Mace turns to leave the shop. His cans and bottles clanking. Wait says the woman.

Mace stops and turns. She lowers her voice.

Roy wasn't the only one who knew where the house was.

HE EMPTIED HALF a tank driving off his indecision and uncertainty before he found himself on the edge of the city that night.

He drove through hamlets and villages. The street lights getting closer. Then he cruised down slip roads and around roundabouts. Passed people. Then he saw it. The Odeon X. It had been a long time since. He needed to go there to be documented. Recorded.

What's on he asked the girl who took his money and handed him his laminated card. She was reading a glossy magazine with an orange woman on the cover. Bored she jerked a thumb at a print-out tacked to the wall.

> Films for January:
> Slut Puppies Get the Bone
> Extreme Homeless Hussies
> Four Hours of Fuck-Hungry MILFs
> Who's Your Mama
> Den of Depravity

The titles sounded different. Harsher than the vintage flasher-mac romps and schoolgirl farces that he liked and remembered in the early nineties. Films that fitted the times. But now the internet had happened and porn had exploded in all directions. The Odeon X was just trying to keep up with a new millennium.

What's showing now? he asked. Again she didn't look at him. She ignored him.

I said what's on now he said again and this time she looked up at him and held his gaze for a moment then said does it even matter? and went back to her book. And he thought: she's right. Does it even matter.

He walked down the hallway. Screen One on the left. The smaller Screen Two and the tiny Couples Room on the right. Just as it always was. He went into Screen One and let his eyes adjust to the light. There were a half-dozen heads scattered around the room. Their faces illuminated. Each exiled in their own internal fantasies.

The film was more modern-looking. It had been made using different techniques too. Different technologies. No longer was the image on the screen grainy and full of awkwardly edited jump-cuts. Now cameras were handheld and the scenes crisp and ultra-sharp around the edges to create their own strange digital unreality.

And the women. All the women were lithe and all the women were tanned and all the women were shaved. Bald snatches and the hair on their heads straight. No. There were no big hairy bushes or perms this time. Times had moved on. They wore thongs and neon heels now. Their full breasts barely moved on their chests. There were no moustaches or hairy chests on the thrusting grunting men either. The men were hairless and gym-hardened. Tattooed. As determined in their work as ploughmen.

The scenes took place in empty night clubs and sports cars and alleyways and gymnasiums. Places repurposed.

The woman on the screen was older and taking two men at once. She had blonde hair. She had them both in her mouth at the same time. There was a lot of saliva.

He watched the scene until its completion. The next one featured an older black woman with a white man wearing a baseball cap and a faded Celtic band inked around one arm. They had sex on the sofa in an empty flat. He could not tell what their nationality was as no word was uttered between them.

They had mechanical sex in different positions for ten fifteen twenty long minutes.

He drifted off. He slept for a while.

When he came round he was cold and shivering a little and on the screen a woman with small breasts and black hair was forcing a dildo up a woman who was on all fours in a park on a nice sunny day. Only when the women receiving it turned around did he realise it was not a woman but a man with a ponytail and a penis.

He yawned. Felt a craving for a cigarette.

He tried to focus his thoughts on these singular acts of humiliation and not let his mind wander back to the farm. He was OK here. He was a part of this. The X was a part of him. He was a cog in its machinery; that had been proven. He had proven himself amongst feared men. He was OK. Everything would be different now that she had fallen to the ice and the frost. His mother. He told himself that this was not an end but a beginning.

IT CANNOT BE seen from any road.

He has the taxi drop him half a mile away and at first he thinks perhaps he has been given misinformation or written down the wrong directions but he follows a pitted track on foot into a large plantation of pines. It is dark and still in there; a green cathedral. There is a density to the silence. A deadness. Off the track the ground is a carpet of brown needles and rotted stumps and tangled roots and fallen trunks and patches of moss.

The media is already going to town on Lovely Larry. Many journalists and editors have been waiting for a long time for this moment; entire careers have passed while carrying around dirt on Lister. They certainly have plenty to draw on: the allegations and his illustrious half-century career; his awards and charity work and outlandish appearance. And the rumours of much much darker secrets that were only ever shared over hushed pints in the back snugs of off-Fleet Street pubs for years. Rumours of friendships with the high and mighty and untouchable in the media and politics and the church. People you do not accuse in print unless you've had a small army of lawyers go through it all first.

They still have to be careful what they print now – especially a regional rag as small as the *Mercury*. Not for nothing is Lister also known around Chancery Lane as Litigation Larry.

But what the national inkies do not know about – and therefore the one thing that Roddy Mace has over them all – is the existence of Lovely Larry's Dales getaway. The place he has managed to keep quiet from everyone except a few town locals who for reasons unknown were complicit in the secrecy of its existence.

The house is tucked away in one corner in a clearing. It was here long before the trees which have been uniformly planted around it as if to deliberately enclose and imprison the building. To pull it away from the outside world. Mace thinks of *Grimm's Fairy Tales*. Of *Hansel and Gretel*. Gingerbread houses and TV presenters.

It sits three long miles out of town down the valley road and then up narrowing back tracks; a dead-end location with half of the house cast in permanent semi-darkness.

He has explored further leads and got nowhere. His local sources have seized up. He tried ringing Roy Pinder on the way up with an official press enquiry – do you have a comment about Larry Lister owning property in the valley – but was told: on the record? You fuck off you little faggot.

His exact words.

Mace said what about off the record then Roy? and Pinder hung up.

THE CURTAINS ARE drawn but there is a car out front on the gravel driveway. A nippy sports car. A newish-looking blue MG. Mace looks through the tinted windows and sees CD cases spread across the passenger seat: Tiny Tim and Noel Coward. Slade and Bucks Fizz. The good stuff. Noddy and Jay and Cheryl and the gang. Otherwise there is nothing of note in the car.

He takes a photograph of the registration plate and then knocks on the front door. The knocker is a brass fox whose tail he lifts. He knocks and counts to ten and then he knocks again. No one answers. Mace walks to the front windows and then past them around the side of the house where there is a garage – locked – and then around the back. There is a small side window. Mace cups his hands to his eyes and looks inside. He sees a hallway of sorts. He sees a wooden banister. A framed photo of the Queen at her coronation. A coat stand with one coat and a baseball cap hanging from it. He cranes his neck the other way. He sees an open door into what looks like an empty kitchen. He sees a shabby brown rug.

He cranes his neck further and sees a photo of Larry Lister sitting on the fake jewel-encrusted throne he used to have on *Larry's Party*. In it he is surrounded by smiling children. He is wearing a green shirt and a purple tie and a hat that holds a can of coke on top of it and from which protrudes a long curly coloured drinking straw. Larry is sucking on it. He has his thumbs up.

His eyes are crossed.

HE KEEPS HIS distance. All the way down into town Brindle lets the distance between them increase. The twists and turns of the road help keep him hidden from view and two three four times Rutter disappears from sight but there is nowhere for him to turn except into fields between here and the city.

Brindle can almost smell him.

As he takes the Hareton Lane route into town he sees a figure ahead of him. An ambling man with a can in one hand and a carrier bag in the other. Without turning around the man steps out into the road.

Brindle brakes. The tyres squeak. He winds down the window.

Get in.

Mace turns and sees the car and looks confused for a moment.

Why?

I'm following Rutter.

So?

So get in.

Why?

Look says Brindle. I'm sorry. For what I said. But get in.

Mace shrugs and then climbs in the passenger side.

Have you heard then?

About what?

Lister says Mace.

That he's been bailed?

That's he's brown bread.

Dead?

Yes.

When did you hear this? asks Brindle.

On the radio in the shop.

What happened?

They don't know.

Suicide?

They don't know.

They sit in silence for a moment and then Mace says alright fuck it I might as well tell you the best bit seeing as you've already stolen everything from me anyway: he had a place round here.

Mace lets the words sink in and then he continues.

Lister he says. A house. And Roy Pinder was a regular visitor. Apparently the two were in business together. Or had been.

What business?

You tell me. Nothing good I'd bet.

They skirt town and take the main road further down the dale.

I've seen it says Mace. I've been there.

Where?

Lister's bolt-hole.

They round a bend and a hundred metres ahead they see Rutter's truck trundling at a steady forty.

Neither the detective nor the reporter say anything. Mace swigs from his can of beer.

Brindle calls Cold Storage. Mace swigs from his can again.

Is it true about Larry Lister? says Brindle into his phone. What do you know? Yeah – that's what they said on the radio. But what do *we* know? Well find out then. No – don't talk to him. Why? Because he can't be trusted. Find out directly and then call me. Don't speak to anyone in between. And I need you to look into his finances too. I need you to find out what properties he owned. Well how should I know? Just find out will you? And be bloody discreet about it.

He hangs up: for fuck's sake.

He'll have killed himself so he doesn't have to face up to what he's done says Mace. All those girls. Those kids. That's what will have happened. He'll have taken the chickenshit route so that his secrets go to the grave with him.

We don't know that. We don't know that for certain.

They drive through tiny Dales villages whose names are unfamiliar. Today they look hostile and unwelcoming; closed off to the world.

The road crosses the river once twice three times and Brindle steals glances down at gravel banks and shallow

267

stretches where the water runs and bubbles white with foam and where young trout bolt through shallow runs like electrical surges. Mace plays the ring pull on his can.

Who do you think the father is? he asks.

Which father?

The father of the girl's kid.

We don't know that says Brindle. All I found was a pregnancy-testing kit in her drawer. It doesn't mean anything.

The road runs alongside the river and they see the slow flow of the deepening waters and the occasional lone angler fishing corner pools where the water circles beneath the overhang of willows that drape tenderly across the silent flow. Minutes pass as Mace drinks more beer and Brindle clears his throat and counts trees and then white lines and then cat's eyes until his eyes feel strained and ache in their sockets and he feels sick.

All we ever see of Rutter is around the hamlet or in town or up on the moors says Brindle.

Yeah.

So this might be significant.

What might? asks Mace.

This. Him leaving the valley.

Mace looks at him with scepticism.

I have a hunch says Brindle.

I thought you didn't believe in hunches?

I'm varying my methods these days.

They pass pine-lined caravan parks and woodlands planted high up on the hillsides two or three or four decades ago and after fifteen or twenty minutes the dale flattens and widens and the roadside gets busier with houses. The river disappears from view but Rutter's truck is still in sight.

Brindle hangs back. He lets other cars get between them.

You fixed your tyre then?

Brindle looks at Mace. Back to the road. Then at Mace again.

I knew it was you.

No you didn't.

Then there are golf courses and care homes and they are in the suburbs of a town but they bypass it and soon they are turning onto a slip road and then they are on the motorway heading south and Brindle has to take extra care to keep Rutter in sight but it's not hard as Rutter's truck seems incapable of doing more than fifty miles an hour. He lets the gaps between them open up. He grips the wheel and his knuckles crack and he tries not to count the motorway lampposts that arch overhead like giant herons poised over perch-filled ponds.

Mace's can is empty. It sits in his lap between his thighs now.

Why have you brought me?

Because I owe you.

Too fucking right you do says Mace. I'm the only ally you've got round here. They all hate you up in town. At the station too – there more than anywhere. They despise you.

Brindle checks his rear-view mirror and then shrugs.

Doesn't it bother you? asks Mace.

What – being hated?

Yes. By your peers.

Who says they hate me?

Everyone.

They're not my peers says Brindle.

Your colleagues then.

They're not my colleagues either. They're just policemen and women who I'll probably never see again. Roy Pinder is knee-deep in shit; when I'm done with him he won't be a concern. His days are limited. The countdown has started.

But their abiding impression of you is that you're a cunt says Mace.

So?

Mace looks at the policeman and laughs.

Brindle looks at him sideways and then back to the road and Mace detects the faintest of smiles.

Maybe I am.

Oh you are. You definitely are. But it clearly doesn't keep you awake at night.

Brindles feels for his tie-knot. He touches it lightly. Straightens it.

A million things keep me awake at night he says. But what people think of me is not one of them.

THE NIGHT THAT his mother fell on the ice he stayed in the X for hours. He watched the rest of Four Hours of Fuck-Hungry MILFs *then he had a coffee and a cigarette and then he went into Screen Two and he watched* Den of Depravity *as around him old men masturbated. Some in stockings some not. One of them was clearly drunk and commentating both on the film and what was going on around him.*

When the film finished the other men left but he stayed in his seat and waited for a few minutes and then he watched Den of Depravity *again.*

At some point he must have fallen asleep because he was woken by someone tapping him on the shoulder. He saw the twisted healed lip as Skelton loomed over him.

He slowly stood and then followed him through the door and down into the subterranean labyrinth beneath the cinema. No words were exchanged; they didn't need to be. He was taken to a room at the back that he had not been in before. It had a strong metal door on it and was like a very large prison cell but with a rug and a rail with some clothes hanging on it. Dinner jacket and several bow ties. A picture of Princess Diana torn from a magazine was tacked to the painted brick wall.

Sit down said Skelton. Wait here.

After a few minutes Larry Lister arrived.

Well well he said. So you're the young pig man.
He stood.

Yes.

Have we met? says Lister.

Yes.

Larry Lister did not appear as friendly as he did on
television. He looked different without his manic smile.

I've been up your way said Lister. The valley. Pretty wild
up there. Nice place. Nice place to escape to. Here: how's that
mutual acquaintance of ours?

Who? said Rutter.

You know. Your friend and ours. The cock of the midden.
Raymond Muncy.

Muncy?

Lister looked to Skelton and then back to Rutter.

This boy's a fucking simpleton.

Answer him said Skelton.

Rutter sniffed and looked confused.

I didn't know you lot was mates with Muncy.

We're not.

When Rutter said nothing Larry Lister continued.

Just the opposite. It seems Mr Muncy is a moralist. It seems
he prefers to do his own thing. The lone wolf and all of that.

Rutter stared back.

He was welcomed in and he tried a taste but then he turned
his back. Embarrassed the fuck out of Roy Pinder did that. And
now he carries our secrets around with him and we can't be
having that. Fuck no. Especially me with my reputation. Not
now. No. Do you understand?

I think so said Rutter.

You understand nothing son said Lister. But lucky for you Mr
Hood says you've been doing valuable work for us.

He shrugged.

He says you like to have your way with leftovers said Lister.

Is that right?

Again he did not say anything. He looked at the carpet by the door.

You don't need to be shy son. We all have our peccadilloes. That's what this place is all about. You should know that. Have you got nowt to say for yourself?

He shook his head.

Good said Lister. I like that. Discreet. Muncy's got a big mouth but not you. Have a cigarette son.

He pulled a pack from his pocket and offered him one. He shook his head again.

Go on – take one.

Again he shook his head but then Lister said take one in a voice that he couldn't refuse and then he said how's your mother? and that threw him because he didn't think Lovely Larry Lister knew anything about him or his mother or the farm or the pigs. Lister continued: we've got to look after our mothers because it was them that brought us into the world and without them we'd be nothing. And you always look after your own.

When he said this he stared at him. As he searched his face he wondered whether Lister and Skelton and Hood knew what had just happened up at the farm. But could they really know that already? Had Pinder put somebody on him?

You live close by said Lister. Ray Muncy has a daughter doesn't he?

Aye.

Know her do you?

Rutter shrugged.

Seen her.

Often?

She's off at school somewhere.

She comes back though?

Again Rutter shrugged.

Lister looked at Skelton.

It's like blood out of a stone is this. But you know who she is?
Yes.

Good said Lister. Mr Hood says he knows you'll not let us down.

Larry Lister made an elaborate show of lighting a cigarette with a match and then puffing on it for a moment.

Stick with us son and you'll get everything you want in life just like I did. You wouldn't want to make any enemies here.

Not like that flash cunt Muncy said Skelton.

No said Lister. Not like him.

Because cunts like that need taxing.

Lister put his hands into his tracksuit trousers and studied him. After a few moments of this he pulled a handful of badges from his pocket. He jiggled them in his hand and selected one.

Here you are. There's a good lad.

He reached over and pinned it to his padded plaid work shirt.

We'll be in touch said Skelton. Might be next week. Might be next year. But we'll be in touch.

Rutter looked down at the badge. Everything you want in life said Lovely Larry Lister. It's all for the taking.

He turned and left.

IT WASN'T SUICIDE.

Brindle puts away his phone.

What? says Mace.

Lister. It wasn't suicide. I've had the call.

No?

No.

Then what?

A tongue up the arsehole.

A tongue up the arsehole? What does that mean – is that cop slang?

They found him with his tongue cut out and shoved up his arse.

What the fuck says Mace.

It's true.

They both fall silent.

Are you joking? says Mace.

Have you ever heard me joking?

Can you even die from – Obviously. In his house. It's symbolic.

Symbolic?

Of course. Symbolic *and* practical: cut out someone's tongue and they can't speak. Mexican gangs do it so that their victims can never spill the secrets of others. It's a trust thing. A fear thing.

It's a medieval thing says Mace. No – it's biblical. That's Old Testament stuff: *the tongue is a restless evil full of deadly poison.*

I didn't have you down as an altar boy says Brindle.

I'm not. But I've got a good memory.

Mace drinks more vodka from his bottle.

Seems apt he says. People always said he talked out of his arse.

I knew you were going to say that says Brindle.

And I knew you were going to say that says Mace.

HE STAYED UNTIL two in the morning. When he stepped out onto the street the cold hit him instantly. From a takeaway lit so brightly it hurt his eyes he bought some chips and a can of fizzy orange juice and he ate the chips and drank the juice in his truck and then wished he had bought a hot drink instead.

He had to de-ice the windscreen. He kept the engine running for a long time. The syrupy remains of the orange drink began to freeze on the dashboard. Smoke mingled with his breath and this corner of the city was silent.

He drove for the rest of the night. On and off the motorway. Then onto a dual carriageway. He pulled over to buy petrol with his bank card and he kept his receipt and he made sure he was seen on the CCTV cameras and then he drove on down country lanes with the heater blasting warm air and he drove through towns and villages he had never been to.

He found himself driving slowly around suburban estates where the houses and the gardens and the cars all looked the same. Neat and clean and trimmed and uniform. He lost himself within their streets and cul-de-sacs and felt like the last living man on the planet.

He drove down unknown dales and darkened valleys. Across moors.

He fixed his eyes to the road and let instinct guide him.

He followed the first streaks of the rising sun back home. The light of day seemed to say that it was alright to return now; that the night and the cold and the ice had conspired to do that which he had been unable to: to silence his mother. That it had ended. That it was over. That she was over.

It was still early when he drove up the dale and turned into the hamlet. A needle-sharp hoar frost clung to the fences and the dry-stone walls and the roof slates. It shone.

Only the light in the Laidlaws' place was on. Brian and Sheila at the post office.

He took the track up to the farm in first gear. His wheels spun on the crushed ice powder. He considered turning back and driving off and never returning. Just leaving.

He didn't want to see her heaped and frozen because that would start a process that he had no interest in.

He pulled up on to the verge around the side of the house and smoked a cigarette before getting out and taking some deep breaths and then he walked around to the back of the house to see –

Nothing. A space where she had been.

She wasn't there.

His mother was not there.

He looked to the house: no sign of lights or movement

from within.

He scratched his head. He took off his beanie and scratched his damp matted scalp. Then the cockerel started crowing.

Sherrup you he said.

He felt for his tobacco pouch in his breast pocket and instead touched the button badge. On it was Lister's grinning face framed by a star shape and then beneath it the phrase Keep smiling – and be lucky.

It was the postman who had found her.

Rare was the day when he made it up the track of ice and frost in his van at that time of the year but that morning was one of them.

She had ordered a new housecoat from the catalogue. It had needed signing for.

It was still dark when he saw her form laid out in the yard. He mistook her for a woodpile but something drew him closer.

He felt her wrist and she still had a pulse – just. He had banged on the house door but when no one answered he covered her with his coat and a half-dozen empty mail bags and then he ran slipping and sliding down the hill to Brian and Sheila Laidlaw's post office.

Might be she's been out there all night said the postman.

They called it in and then he and Brian ran back up to the farm to cover her slumped form in more blankets.

The ambulance took an hour and twenty minutes. She had a severely fractured skull and hypothermia.

The trauma of the blow when her head hit the farmyard floor had caused an aneurysm then later that day – in her hospital bed – she experienced a series of small strokes. She would never speak again. Pneumonia followed then a collapsed lung. Each was enough to kill anyone.

Yet somehow her heart kept beating. Intensive care was her home for three weeks then she spent four months on a ward. After that she was moved to the hospice for the incapacitated the

infirm and the terminal. Round-the-clock care for everything.
Soon his future inheritance would run out though and there
would only be the house to his name. He received letters from an
accountant wishing to discuss financial matters but he binned
them. After a while the letters stopped coming.

BRINDLE'S PHONE RINGS again. He answers it saying
nothing. He only nods. He says nothing for a long time. Yes
he says and then he says it again. Yes. OK good. And you're
sure Lister's prints are on it? The property can be traced to
him? When? OK good. That adds up. Now look at his money.
See what incomes he had. Where it came from – and what
for. Talk to the team who are working his catalogue of cases
– they'll have a head-start on this. Be sure to tell them it's for
Cold Storage. Mention Tate. Mention me if you have to. Just
get those accounts. I need you to look into something else too.
Yeah. Roy Pinder. *Pinder* he says again. He's a copper. Don't
worry about it – he's a nobody. No – not one of us. Find out
any investments he has too. Incomes. Check his accounts. You
know the drill. Yes. Thanks. As soon as you can. He hangs up
and turns to Mace.

The dominoes he says. They are set to fall.

9

THEY JOURNEY DOWN the motorway for many miles. A drunk Mace and an agitated Brindle. There is flat arable land either side of them. It is turning into a clear bright day.

More familiar sights pass by. The army garrison. The service station in whose lorry park Brindle and a team had once staked out a dawn death-fight between two rival gypsy families. They had waited until their suspect – a man known only as Yarm Kenny – had been beaten unconscious then cuffed his shattered wrists and arrested him on an unrelated manslaughter charge. It was easier that way.

They see disused quarries. They see a gatehouse and the high boundary walls of an ailing country estate. Brindle watches the white line and the speed limit.

Long minutes pass and then the motorway presents options and Rutter takes one and Brindle follows.

Still they keep a discreet distance from Rutter. Brindle is back in more familiar territory now. Up in the Dales there is too much space and silence. Things are left to fester unnoticed. At least in the city the rot is visible for all to see. Eyeballs watch from doorways and everything sits on the surface; everyone a potential witness.

You were right about Lister's house in the valley says Brindle. His retreat.

I know says Mace. I told you.

Cold Storage are tipping off those already working on his cases as we speak.

Mace reaches into his jacket for his bottle of vodka. He uncaps it and takes a swig then offers it to Brindle who shakes his head but then a moment later reaches out and grabs it and takes a gulp. He winces. Mace smiles.

So you could probably thank me at this point he says but then Brindle's phone rings again. He answers and listens.

You're sure about this? he says to the caller. What are they called? And you're sure? OK. He hangs up.

Who is that you keep talking to? asks Mace.

One of the best there is says Brindle. We have our link.

Which is?

Lister was down on the board of a company. He was on many actually – about a dozen so it seems – but only one of them pays Roy Pinder a quarterly income. Blue Kingdom.

Blue Kingdom? Who are they?

Some company who are listed as having owned properties in the city – a club a pool hall a cinema – but not much else. A front probably. They have also traded under the name Cellar Entertainment but there are no tax records. They're fake. Or a cover for something that I will bet involves Lovely Larry Lister.

Involved says Mace. Past tense.

Suddenly without indication Rutter pulls over. They are deep in the city now. They are on a side street whose name Brindle is unaware of. He keeps driving so as not to get spotted. A hundred yards down the road he turns around in the forecourt of an MOT garage and then heads back towards Rutter.

What's he up to? says Mace.

They park up at a distance.

Rutter climbs out of his car and is on the pavement. He is looking up. Squinting and craning. Looking at a large stone building. Something that was perhaps once a bank or housed an accountancy firm or was maybe even a small theatre. The ornate original features of the frontage are still in place but it is in need of external work.

The incongruity of Rutter in the city strikes Brindle. Seeing his suspect like this – amongst the visual clutter. Dwarfed by billboards and buildings. Diminished by architecture and trailing Dales mud on cracked pavements. It doesn't sit right.

But there is something else about him – something he can't at first identify. Then it clicks. He is dressed differently. Rutter has changed his clothes for the first time since Brindle has been watching him. The first time in what must be weeks. He has swapped his filthy torn tartan blue padded work shirt for a slightly less filthy slightly less torn red tartan one. Nor is he wearing his woollen beanie hat. The trousers may be the same as he always wears and the gumboots definitely are but from here across the road he nevertheless looks slightly less malodorous. It is as if he has made an effort for this visit.

Mace seems to think the same thing.

He's dressed differently he says.

Yes.

What do you think he's up to?

I don't know says Brindle. I don't know.

They watch. They see Rutter squint and crane again then scratch his head. They watch as Rutter turns to face the road and looks up and down it. Then they see him turning back to the building one more time. He appears puzzled. . They see Rutter walk up the stone steps to the wooden door and try it. It is locked. He walks down the steps and then Rutter quickly walks back to his car and starts the engine and leaves.

A minute later Mace and Brindle stand before it.

Neglect and the Yorkshire weather have combined with the city smog to blacken its facade. Perhaps it was originally a bank or an accountancy firm or a chartered surveyors built 150 years or more ago with profits from the industrial boom but now it is a shell. There is a sign bolted to the building but it is too high for them to read.

That sign says Brindle. Can you see what it says?

No. Wait a minute.

Mace steps back and takes a photo of it on his phone and

then when the picture is saved he zooms in on it. He studies the sign. It is cheap and plastic and at the top of it there is Islamic writing printed in blue on white and then beneath that it says:

ABU MADINA MOSQUE

Beneath that is a phone number. He shows the picture to Brindle.

Not what you would call opulent says the reporter. Not like these new-money new-builds with their fancy minarets.

Brindle studies the building again.

It's derelict he says.

Now I see why they made you a detective says Mace.

I'll need to send someone in.

Brindle's phone rings. He answers. Says nothing. Mace studies his face. Still he says nothing. Then he hangs up.

THEY DO NOT follow Rutter.

Instead Brindle turns the car around and heads back out of the city to the motorway to take them the forty miles back to Cold Storage.

Where are we going now? says Mace but Brindle does not reply so Mace says great wonderful it's not like I don't have anything to do anyway.

It is still light but the moon is already out. It sits high and large in a pinkening spring evening sky.

They turn into what looks like an industrial estate. They drive deep into it and skirt a roundabout. The roads are empty and they see no one. Brindle drives into a maze of squat buildings. He parks up beside one whose exterior gives nothing away. Close up it looks more like a base from where exhausts are distributed or where catalogues are printed or frozen curries are made.

Where are we? says Mace.

We're here says Brindle.

I thought so.

They enter through glass doors and Brindle produces a card which he scans to open a turnstile which closes behind him. He walks around to a side gate and swipes his card and then gestures for Mace to follow him.

They pass through more doors and then up a flight of stairs.

Is this where you work? says Mace. Is this where they put you?

This is an issue of trust replies Brindle.

You poor bastards. Stuck out here in the middle of nowhere.

Bindle says: you're one to talk.

Give me sheep shit and a nice upper-valley ale any day says Mace. This place is dead. It's like a retail graveyard. A chrome nightmare.

Brindle strides down corridors and when they reach it there is no one in the open-plan office of the upper floor.

Where is everyone? says Mace.

The other detectives actually have lives to lead says Brindle. Wives to placate and children to feed.

He fills a coffee pot from a water cooler and then turns on the percolator. He fits a fresh sachet of coffee. From a cupboard he takes out an Earl Grey tea bag for himself.

You need coffee he says.

Fine says Mace. So this is Cold Storage then. I can see how it got its name. Full of stiffs I bet. Why are we here?

To find out about that building.

Couldn't we do that online from anywhere?

I need to show my face from time to time.

But there's no one here to see it.

Even better says Brindle.

So who did you call before?

A colleague. A contact.

You said they were in Cold Storage says Mace.

I said they were from Cold Storage. *With* Cold Storage.

You're fucking weird man.

Welcome to modern policing said Brindle. I hope you appreciate the river of shit that could flood my life for bringing a drunk journalist in here.

That's quite poetic. Anyway I'm not –

What – a journalist?

Drunk. Prick.

While Mace pours the coffee for himself and the tea for the detective Brindle goes online. He researches the Abu Madina Mosque. He looks up past sales and ownership of deeds.

Mace brings the drinks. He pulls over a chair and sits next to him. He hands over the tea. He looks at Brindle's work station. He sees neatness and order and hygiene. A system. A sterile environment.

Is your desk always this tidy?

The detective ignores him.

It's not a mosque then says Brindle.

What do you mean?

It's going to *become* a mosque. But it's not one now. The signage out front is the first step. It was acquired by a Muslim conglomerate. It is one of many.

Right. Yes. I thought that.

Brindle looks at him blankly.

Really? You never said.

What's the link to Rutter though? says Mace. He doesn't seem like your typical Muslim. Or property owner. Or human.

Brindle takes a sip and flinches at the heat.

He is not connected to the mosque he says.

But him just being there surely connects him.

He is connected to the building – yes. But only to what it once was. We know its future but not its past. Didn't you see him approach the building with surprise – with trepidation?

I thought he looked almost hopeful says Mace. Or confused. But that's a permanent state for Steve Rutter.

He expected something else. Or hoped for something else. Like what?

Brindle picks up his desk phone and makes a call. He waits. He puts it on speakerphone and sits back with his tea. It rings for a long time before a young lady answers.

Hello?

I need to check out prior ownership of a building says Brindle.

I'd be happy to sir. The office is closed for the day so if you'd like to call back—

It's Abu Madina Mosque on City Road.

As I said the office is closed for the day so if you'd like to—

I wouldn't says Brindle.

Well sir I'm afraid—

Brindle interrupts her.

You should be.

Excuse me?

And it's not sir – it's DS. Detective Sergeant James Brindle. And this is urgent police business.

Urgent?

Yes. Murderously so.

Mace smirks and shakes his head.

Failure to assist in enquiries can be treated as obstruction says Brindle.

Oh says the young lady then she sighs.

I know for a fact that this will take you about sixty seconds even if you only have half a functioning brain.

The woman sighs again and mutters something which Mace thinks is wanker and he stifles another laugh.

I'm meant to be going home she says.

We'd all like to be going home says Brindle. So. The building currently registered as the Abu Madina Mosque on

City Road. I need to know what it was – and who owned it. Let's say over the past five decades.

He waits a moment. There is no reply

Got that?

Yes says the woman. It'll take longer than a minute though.

Call me back in ten then.

He ends the call and sips his tea.

You have such a nice telephone manner says Mace. Warm. Ever thought of joining the Samaritans?

Ten minutes later the phone rings. Brindle doesn't put it on speakerphone this time. He listens and writes words down on a notepad.

He says thank you – you have been very helpful. Make sure you have a nice evening and then he puts the phone down again.

Bingo he says.

AND THEN SKELTON stopped calling upon him. No messages ever reached him and weeks and then months went by with no mother to mither him and no nocturnal assignments. No envelopes of cash coming in.

His mother existed in name and flesh and heartbeat only. She was a monthly direct debit now. The shadows of the farm grew longer and life began to ebb from it.

Only one message reached him. Typed and posted: stay away. So he did and he tried not to think about the films and parties and Pinder and Lister and Hood and all those other men with their secrets and their suits and their cigars and the things he had seen and the things they had made him do. He stayed away until the need to return was overwhelming because back at the farm he floundered. He stopped washing and eating and tending to the animals. The roaming dogs hunted the hillsides and the penned pigs soon began to starve.

These pigs that had dined on tragedy now scratched furiously at the dirt for a missed acorn or a worm or anything and then when the weakest fell the others gorged on it. They tore away the richest flanks and then devoured the rest of it. It sustained them but not for long. Two days later they were squealing for attention again. They butted their shoulders and brows against the pen sides. They ran in circles and like desperate concentration-camp prisoners they tried to make an escape. They scratched and gnawed at wood and they tried to dig. Bestial moans cut through the night but he was deaf to them. He was adrift. Each emaciated hog that starved and fell then fed the rest of the dwindling drove. Over the weeks only the fiercest were left. Five then four then three then two and finally like the snake that consumes itself the pigs were reduced to nothing but one. The food cycle had shrunk down to an irrefutable singular then that final animal slowly faded until one day he went out and saw nothing but one dead rotting pig and a pen full of excrement and teeth and bones. The food cycle had become a circle. A zero.

That same day he got the call from Skelton instructing him with one last job – and not just a clean-up operation this time. Right down the line from Mr Hood himself. Non-negotiable.

He felt no need to ask why Muncy – why his girl? because he knew what Muncy was like and he knew he had a big mouth and he knew that some secrets didn't stay buried forever. But he did say to Skelton: I don't have the pigs any more.

So find another way said Skelton.

What way?

Any way. You owe us.

Owe you?

We had a call a few weeks back. From the police.

Why?

Something about you being in the cinema the night your mother died.

She didn't die.

Skelton said nothing to this. He heard his breathing down

286

the line.

What did you say?

There was talk of checking our records. Our security.

Is that why the cinema closed?

That has nothing to do with the cinema being closed. It's just business.

Does Ray Muncy have anything to do with the cinema closing? Or Larry Lister? Is it something to do with him?

Again Skelton did not respond.

Hello? he said. Hello?

SKELTON HAD TOLD him to do it and he had done it and now he needs just one last time with her. One last visit. Because Steven Rutter is barely sleeping now; Steven Rutter is barely eating now. All his thoughts are occupied with her. The trace of her – what is left of her – still up there in the great space of the moors.

Like the pigs before them the dogs are starving now too. With jutting ribs and forlorn eyes they only appear to come alive to fight over the scraps that he throws into the pen – if he remembers to.

Unfed the chickens have contracted an infection. They are no longer laying. Those that are still alive are turning upon one another in frustration and starvation and madness. They fight and peck. The carcasses of the weaker ones litter the floor of the coop; those that live pluck and pull at the feathers of the fallen. They nip at their white elastic skin.

He has become fully nocturnalised now.

In the darkness he passes the windmills. He feels their slicing of the air and hears the malignant sounds they make. That torturous canticle.

He drags his feet across moss and heather and bog.

And then he is there and he is lifting again and pulling again and crowbarring again.

He is prepared this time. This time he is prepared. With more tools and a new tarpaulin. He also has gloves and rags and ropes. A facemask and lime.

The goodbye package.

The slaked lime is his final present to her. Calcium hydroxide by its other name. It is used to eliminate odours and deter animals and further bacteria and flies. Easy to get hold of and when doused on her moist flesh the powder will dehydrate and burn away the past. It will slowly sear any remnants. Burn away all record of him and preserve Melanie Muncy forever in myth and memory rather than reality.

The lime will erase all physical trace of a person who went to theme parks and shopping centres and pop concerts and libraries and who sat in cars with boys.

The crackling of the tarpaulin seems deafening as he peels it. His senses accelerate and then she is there looking impossibly small and withered. The bloating has stopped and what flesh that's left has sunken and withdrawn. Tightened. She seems half her previous size and this visible retreat from her physical form suddenly moves Rutter to tears.

He hears a sob and shocks himself.

He climbs into the tarpaulin with the matter that once was a girl and he pulls the sheet around them so that they are encased. Cocooned. Her rotten flesh is squashed beneath him and makes new noises and emits smells that he will never get to experience. Her juices are on him. He is breathing her gases. Their bones are knocking.

In the darkness his fingers find a way to gently touch that hard cranial curve that is protruding from her down below.

And as he does so it is as if his blood is coursing and bubbling through his veins and popping and fizzing in his ears. Near death – tasting it and entering it – he feels more alive than ever.

His hand touches the skull of the girl and wipes away

matter that was once the skin of her scalp. It feels like the remains of soap in a soap dish.

Beams of light and energy seem to be rushing out of the top of his head.

IT'S THAT NAME again says Brindle. Blue Kingdom owned the building beforehand.

Let me write this down says Mace.

Forget about that and just listen says the detective as he stares intently at his computer screen. It seems they had it for over three decades. Ran it as a cinema.

So?

An adult cinema. The Odeon X. A notorious flea-pit. I remember the name says Brindle – vaguely. It has come up before. I certainly remember seeing City Road as a boy in the early eighties.

Eighteen eighties?

Very good. I remember the feel of the place. The dirtiness of it.

It's still bad now says Mace.

It was even worse then. It always had an edge. It felt like the North.

How do you mean?

The true North as it was says Brindle. Before gentrification. Before coffee-shop and cocktail culture turned all the towns the same. Before town centres tried to become European but they couldn't change the weather or the people or the architecture or the mentality.

You don't like Europe?

Europe is fine. Europe works where it is.

You're a Tory?

I don't care for politics.

Brindle drinks more tea and then searches online for the Odeon X. There are dozens of Odeons but only one with the X suffix.

Mace points at the screen.

That's where we need to look.

It is a reference to a search term on the forum of a swingers' website.

When Brindle clicks the necessary link it tells him he needs to register. He takes out his credit card and enters his details in the drop-down boxes and then signs up.

Good luck claiming that one back on expenses says Mace but Brindle does not reply.

We're close says Brindle. Pinder has been getting paid by a company that made money out of sleaze. He's right in there. Him and the late Lovely Larry Lister. And now Rutter is turning up at the very same building. That's no coincidence.

The screen tells them that they need to create a profile in order to proceed.

Brindles hesitates. His hand lingers over the mouse.

Let me says Mace. I'm the writer.

He moves to the keyboard and starts typing. He fills in more drop-down boxes. He deliberates for five seconds then he continues. He clicks a link and they both look at pictures. Pictures of women and pictures of couples. Couples on holiday couples with their faces blurred; couples in tacky sex clothes. And pictures of fat lonely men in cold lonely rooms too. Each is a hopeless window into their respective worlds.

I wonder if all these people really do all the things that they say they do says Mace.

An email comes into Brindle's inbox. Mace clicks a link to confirm their membership and then they are into the members' area of the site. He goes straight to the thread titled *any1remberOdeonX?*

He scrolls through the responses. There are pages and pages of memories and recollections.

The semiliterate scribbling of the perverted pining for the

old days of communal wanking to grainy grot says Mace. It's depressing.

They sit in silence and they read comments from people with names like TurboTommy and HevvyRepeater that lament how home entertainment and the internet have changed the way that users indulge their dubious tastes. Mace can hear Brindle breathing. They read stories about how things were much better in the seventies and eighties and on into the nineties when you could still pay the five-pound entrance fee to the Odeon X and stay all night. There are discussions about the old stag films. The blueys.

They're living in a black-and-white world says Mace. It's like listening to old people talking about rationing. He keeps scrolling down but Brindle stops him.

Wait – look.

> Hi. Did any1 here ever no Neville Hoyle? He went missing in November 1992 and was last seen leaving at the Ode X. Nev was one of the trannys and well known on the scene. Mid 30s worked for British Gas. Police found f-all. Pleaz pleaz get in touch if you rember my Dad. Thanxx.

Brindle writes down the name. Neville Hoyle.

They read on. More recollections. More nostalgia for the days of the rain macs and the contact mags. Lots of talk about glory holes and vintage porn when lasses – so one user writes – looked like lasses and had a bit of meat and hair on them. There are some odd digressions about football. Some racist messages. Then he sees another posting.

> Hi babes. I remember your dad

Neville. He was a pal of mine a good
lad. Always wondered about Nev.
There was a wifey that went missing
round about then an all. Also last
seen at the X. Mebbes worked there
mebbes a proz. Red hair. Agree wiv
u about police being useless tho.
Much talk of cover-ups back then
cos many of them used to cum to
the X for a wank amongst other
things so who nose. Backhanders
LOL. Parties and pornos. Couldn't
make it up. Worth luckin into.
Direct message me for memories of
Nev a top lad.

Brindle taps his pen to his pad then writes down a list of keywords. Finishes his tea.

He shows the pad to Mace.

It is late. The office is dark now. It is lit only by the light from Brindle's monitor. Mace has his elbow on the desk and his head is resting in his hands.

They scan the rest of the thread. They read a few more adverts and look at some pictures of some naked and semi-naked housewives and then Brindle closes the website and leans back.

We still don't know what Rutter has to do with it all says Mace.

With the balls of his hands Brindle rubs his eyes. He rubs them for a long time and then he opens them wide and lengthens his entire face.

It's just a process he says. Each step brings us closer.

It's just a process he says again.

THE DOG IS rooting. It is scratching at the soft soil. The walker calls the dog but the dog is sniffing at the ground. It is a spaniel.

The walker says to his friend: this bloody dog. He just does what he wants.

Probably eating sheep shit says his friend. They do that sometimes. It's like sweets to them.

The owner calls the dog again but it ignores him so he takes off his backpack and walks over to it. The reservoir is in the distance. It is shimmering like a mirage. He leans over to pull it away by its collar and as he does he sees the metal pencil case. He squats down and picks up. He shakes it. It rattles. He opens it up. Inside are coins and bus tickets and a passport photo of a teenage boy and stickers and a bank card and an ID card and some specks of hash and a lighter and the words MELANIE MUNCY LIVES scratched on the inside with a classroom compass.

Melanie Muncy he says. Isn't that Ray Muncy's daughter?

His friend shrugs.

Who's Ray Muncy?

His garage does my car.

What about him?

Melanie Muncy was the one who disappeared.

Disappeared? Where?

Fucking here by the looks of it.

A SERIAL KILLER. Is that what we're looking at here?

What?

Brindle is distracted. He is searching the database of open missing-persons cases. Mace is stretched out across two chairs beside him.

That Steven Rutter may conceivably be linked with a number of missing persons cases says Mace. Possibly murders. So he's a possible serial killer. Is that what you're saying?

I never said anything about a serial killer.

It is fully dark outside now. Only Brindle's desk lamp is on. Beside Mace is a pile of box-files that he has been instructed to sift through. Brindle meanwhile is staring intently at his monitor screen. The cool light from it has cast his birthmark in a muted blue hue.

I don't like the term serial killer says Brindle.

Why not?

It's too American. Too sensationalist.

What do you mean?

People get excited about multiple murderers says Brindle. They make films about them and they have fan clubs and women want to marry them. They get elevated to higher echelons in the criminal worlds and become almost mythical characters – they become part of the folklore. And that's wrong. Leave that to the Americans.

It's probably inevitable though says Mace. Humans like stories. We like demons.

You would say that – you're a journalist.

Is that what you call them?

Brindle turns to Mace.

What?

Multiple murderers? Is that what you call them?

Yes. If you like.

But it's the same thing as serial killer.

What says Brindle again. No. Serial killers are the subjects of late-night made-for-TV movies. They are the people who amateur criminologists discuss; they are the people who appear on t-shirts and mugs and album sleeves by Scandinavian heavy-metal bands; serial killers are bogeymen who revel in this newfound status that is afforded them. Multiple murderers meanwhile are pathetic people who do not deserve this attention. Rutter is a pathetic person who needs to be brought to account – delivered to the legal system – and

294

then buried forever.

Buried?

In the system. Where he can do no harm to anyone.

Do you believe in the justice system?

The justice system is a process that's beyond my control says Brindle. My remit is to investigate. My job is to answer the same stock questions: who when and why. I then pass the answers and suspect on. I build the case and then I hand it over. Beyond that is none of my business. I just serve the system.

You see. That to me seems odd. Do you not think that—?

Brindle interrupts him.

Should I be regretting bringing you here?

Why? says Mace.

I'm trying to work he says. I'm practically handing you a story on a plate here – and when I nail these bastards it will be the crime story of the year – yet I don't think you even realise how big this will be.

You're joking aren't you? says Mace. While you were back here licking your wounds it was me – *me* – that found out that Roy Pinder is the link between Rutter and Lister. I got us to here. There would be no case – no story – without me. And correct me if I'm wrong detective but without any witnesses to confirm or corroborate our shared suspicions about Rutter is it not evidence that we should be looking for?

Of course says Brindle. Evidence is crucial.

So we need Melanie Muncy says Mace. His most recent probable victim. We need to know where her body is.

Yes. Of course.

And in a way we've already answered this question ourselves.

Go on says Brindle.

All we ever see of Rutter is around the hamlet or in town. You said it yourself. Or up on the moors.

Yes.

So this might be significant. Those were the other words you used.

Yes.

Rutter never leaves the valley says Mace. Maybe he's too scared or too set-in-his-ways. And he certainly wasn't able to leave the valley the week she disappeared – you and I both know that; the snow kept us all there for Christmas. Snowed in. Plus the hamlet was flooded with police. We know he's stupid and that he could do with bathing in a gallon of the old Blue Stratos but maybe he's not a complete idiot. He was going nowhere with that body.

Go on.

Nowhere but up.

Up?

Uphill from his farm. You searched the house and found nothing. Nothing in the outbuildings either. So uphill was the only way.

Brindle rubs one of his eyes again and then the other. He looks at Mace. Considers him. Brindle's eyes appear red. Sore. They seek sleep.

So Melanie Muncy is still close by Mace continues. Still close to Rutter's I mean. She has to be. He wouldn't risk moving her. Melanie Muncy will have been stashed or hidden or buried as far as he could carry or drag her in the snow. No further. Why bother searching all these other cases when her body is – more than likely – still up there. Find the body and then the rest will follow.

Brindle opens a drawer and pulls out the file that Mace gave him. He unfolds a map of the valley.

THE WALKERS THINK about going to the police station. They think about it for too long a time; so long that they convince themselves that it is not the best plan of action today because that would mean going all the way down to town when they're right in the middle of a two-day forty-mile walk that they've had planned out for months – and it is planned with trig points and OS coordinates and food stops and a visit to the Six Standard Bride stones and even a possible (weather permitting) outdoor swim at a remote tarn – and which is due to culminate in a lot of drinking tomorrow night at a pub that sells the best real ale over in Wensleydale.

After much discussion they reason that going straight to Ray Muncy's place will only add an extra mile or two to their trip because there is a tight schedule to stick to if they want to make it across the boglands in daylight so they turn and walk down into the top of the valley to Muncy's house. They know it. They pass the plantation of pines and the rundown farm and follow the track to the incongruous new-build.

The curtains are drawn when they get there so they ring the doorbell but there is no answer. They ring again and wait but again there is no answer. They don't know what to do. They discuss it for a while and then they decide to post the pencil case through the letter box with a note attached. They take out a pen and paper and explain that they found the pencil on the edge of the moorland past the last farm and that they have the exact coordinates if needed. They leave their names and phone numbers. They post the pencil case and turn around and walk back up the hill. They talk about the missing girl for a while until it starts to rain a little and then the subject changes to something else. The dog runs on ahead.

They don't want to discuss the implications of their findings. They want to discuss anything but that.

HIS PHONE IS ringing again. His desk phone this time. Brindle answers it. He raises a hand to Mace palm out and then he points at the phone in his hand. He mouths the words: Muncy.

He listens for a moment and then he says Mr Muncy I'm going to put you on speaker phone for one moment. Is that OK?

Mace sits up in his chair. He rubs his face.

Brindle pushes the button and Mace hears the gruff tones of Ray Muncy in mid flow. He sounds like he is outdoors. Out of breath. There is a background noise of movement.

– thinks he can push me about well he can fuck right off.

Slow down Mr Muncy please says Brindle. Now what is it you wanted to tell me?

Rutter.

What about him?

He did our Melanie. I'm sure of it now. What are you going to do about it?

Is there something we should know about?

Are you going to arrest him? Because if you don't I swear I'll sort him myself. I heard about Larry Lister on the news as well. Dirty rotten pervert.

Brindle raises an eyebrow at Mace.

Yes he says. I heard all about that.

But do you know about him and Roy Pinder? says Muncy.

I know they were associates – yes.

But do you know *everything*?

Everything?

Do you know about the porn cinema in the city?

This catches Brindle off guard. He looks at Mace. He looks at the phone.

What do you know about that?

The Odeon X? Plenty says Muncy. More than enough; more than I ever wanted to know.

Like what exactly?

The parties. The parties they threw. Horrible parties.

In their cinema?

Not their cinema.

I'm confused Mr Muncy says Brindle. If not theirs then whose?

Lister and Pinder had their parties in the Odeon X after hours. But it wasn't their cinema.

Then whose was it?

Some man who struck the fear of God into the lot of them.

Who was he?

Muncy falls silent. Mace and Brindle can hear his breathing. They can hear the wind wrapping itself around his phone. Mace can hear the moors; the great bleak and barren expanse of them.

All I have is a name he finally says.

Go on.

Hood.

Hood? says Brindle.

Hood says Muncy.

First name?

No.

And these parties – how do you know about them?

I was invited to one once says Ray Muncy. A long time ago.

OK.

I thought it would be – you know. A few drinks. A bit of a floorshow.

A floorshow? says Brindle.

Muncy pauses again. When he speaks his voice is thick. It is weighed down by the words.

Strippers and that. Prossies. A bit of tit. You know: harmless stuff.

And it wasn't?

Brindle looks at Mace.

No. It was so much more. I can't even begin to tell you.

Try says Brindle. Try and tell me.

Muncy's voice softens. Drops a tone.

There was a girl there. She was young.

299

How young?

Young. I didn't want to be a part of it. She looked out of it. Didn't know what day it was.

Go on.

There was a boy too. Also young. They could almost have been brother and sister. And there were cameras.

Where were they from?

I don't know. I mean if I knew that maybe I could have—

Muncy falters.

I think maybe they were from Eastern Europe.

Why do you say that?

Because they looked it. Romanian or something.

Who else was there? asks Brindle.

All of them. They were all there.

Who Mr Muncy? Who?

The lads. All of them. That lot.

Like who?

Like Roy Pinder. Like Johnny Mason. Bull Mason. The Farley brothers. Benny Bennett. Wendell Smith. Others too. Some guy called Skelton. Really creepy. Steve Rutter. And Larry Lister. Lister was there too. They were forcing them.

Forcing who?

The lad and the lass. To do stuff. They were stood round watching as the girl was tied up.

And the cameras?

They were filming it all.

Filming them doing what exactly? says Brindle

Muncy says nothing so Brindle says: then what happened Mr Muncy?

I kept thinking about our Melanie. She was only young. About the same age. I kept thinking about how it was that these kids came to be down there in the basement. In the cellars. What was going through their minds and whether there was anyone out there who would even miss them when they were –

Again he trails off.

Cellars? says Brindle

Beneath the cinema.

Mace mouths the words to Brindle: Cellar Entertainment.

I told them to stop. I told Lister he was a sick bastard and that I wanted no part of it.

Why Larry Lister specifically?

Because he was the one who seemed to be orchestrating it all. And he was the famous one. He was the one using his position. Abusing it.

Then what happened?

I tried to leave.

I sense there's a but here Mr Muncy?

But this Skelton one. He stopped me. Told me no one left during one of the shows. He grabbed me. He was the one who seemed to keep everyone in line like; he didn't seem bothered by anything that was going on. He said once you were in you were in and that was that. He said you didn't turn down their invitations. I told him what they were doing was wrong. Very wrong. Then he made me watch what happened next. Forced me too. I wanted to puke.

And what happened next?

Muncy says nothing.

Watch what Mr Muncy?

When he speaks it is with a whisper that sends a shiver through both the journalist and the detective.

Everything.

Why are you only mentioning this now?

Because of Lister.

What about him?

They said he was in line for a knighthood says Muncy. This was a few months back. I saw him on the telly. There is talk of Her Maj laying her sword on my shoulder he said. Those words. I couldn't stomach the thought. Not him. No way. It's a mockery. I couldn't sleep nights knowing what he'd done. Him in the palace? No way. So I sent a letter.

To who? They all fall silent.

To him of course.

Brindle looks at Mace.

We'd like to come and see you to discuss this further. We'd like to talk to you about what else it is you think you know about Roy Pinder and Larry Lister and Steve Rutter and everything you've been witness to. As soon as possible.

There is no reply.

Mr Muncy? says Brindle. Mr Muncy?

But Ray Muncy has hung up.

10

ITS THREE IN the afternoon or it's eleven in the morning or maybe it's midnight when there's a banging. A thumping at the door. Rutter ignores it but then there is more banging and a rattle of a handle then a voice. A raging voice.

Rutter. *Rutter.*

Muncy. It's Muncy.

Rutter says nothing.

I know you're in there. I saw you come back.

Rutter looks for his rifle but he can't find it so on the way through he grabs a knife from the kitchen and tucks it in the back of his trousers. It runs cold across one buttock and part the way down his sinewy thigh. He opens the door.

Ray Muncy is there in the yard. He has his back to Rutter and is pacing and looking out into the night and when he turns round Rutter sees that Muncy looks wild. He steps into the light. In his neck a vein is pulsing. Rutter thinks of worms.

I've been talking to that copper. The detective.

What for?

About our Melanie. Rutter takes in the man on his doorstep. Sees his hair at all angles and mad roving eyes. Imploring eyes desperate eyes. He sees spittle at the corner of Ray Muncy's mouth and once nice clothes now gone to seed. He sees mud streaks up his expensive chinos. It looks as if something has snapped inside of the man and then been glued back together again but not glued properly.

Might have had a copper up here the other day says Rutter. Asking a few questions.

Was it Brindle?

Don't know says Rutter. Yeah.

I told him everything says Muncy.

What do you mean?

About that night.

What bloody night?

You know what night. In the cellars. The X. The night they forced me to stay there.

Muncy says this with a raised voice. Some of the spittle comes loose. Flecks of it fly. Rutter thinks how odd it is to hear a man normally so confident and arrogant and preoccupied by appearance and status now swearing and raving like this.

Don't know what you're on about says Rutter.

You were there cunt. You were part of it.

No says Rutter. Not me.

Yes you. You and Pinder and Lister and all of the lads. You sick rotten bastards.

Muncy continues.

I told him. I told Pinder that I wanted no part of any of this and that one day it would all come out and now it is and the whole lot is coming down.

Rutter stands with one arm behind the half-open door. Gripping the door. The door holding him up. His fingers curled around the old warped wood.

It's the not-knowing that eats you up like a parasite says Muncy. You can't sleep you can't eat you can't do anything because this thing is eating away. Do you know our June has shaved her head?

Rutter is confused.

What?

Oh aye. She took the scissors to her own hair. Made a right mess. Tried to cut a couple of her fingers off an all. Nearly hacked the fuckers off. You could see bone. They say she's lost the use of two of them.

Well what did she go and do that for?

I told Pinder he'd get his.

Muncy is ranting now.

I told him that time was up for him and Lister and everyone. I told him.

Told him when? says Rutter.

Not long back. I couldn't keep it in. That lot might be able to but I bloody can't.

The cinema's shut now says Rutter. That's all in the past. Larry Lister is dead.

Aye and I wrote him a letter to tell him exactly what I thought of him. But it's not over is it? Not for me it's not. It never was. Not for me. Not for the parents of those kids. Not for the families of them prossies that Hood had snuffed. Not while those vile tapes still exist somewhere in the world. So I told him. Told Pinder. And now it has all become clear.

Rutter scowls.

What do you mean like?

I've been driving myself loopy and it all keeps coming back to the same conclusion. The same thought over and over again. It's all I can think about. You Rutter. *You*. I know it was you. Pinder got scared and Pinder gave the word and now my Melanie is never coming back.

Still leaning against the door Rutter lowers his left hand and reaches round behind his back.

Eh? It's nowt to—

Liar says Muncy. Course it is. Why else would they rope you into their scene? Get you into their club. They never fucking liked you. They used you. Used you to do their dirty work. You were their clean-up man. Pinder used to joke about your pigs but he wasn't joking was he?

I don't know what—

And that got me thinking. But what was in it for Rutter? What was in it for *you*? Not money. I don't reckon it was ever money. And I realised: they let you have exactly what it was you couldn't get out in the real world. Access – that's what.

When the cameras had stopped rolling and those bodies were spent they let you move in on them. And all you had to do in payment was clean up and keep your trap shut. I'm right aren't I?

No says Rutter.

You're a liar you are. A stinking fucking dog-fucking inbred liar.

I'm not but.

It has to be you says Muncy. It can only be you. They found her pencil case out the back of yours man. Yeah. You didn't know that did you? They've had you doing their bidding for them. I know you done something to our Melanie. To pay me back for threatening to blab. That's it isn't it? Because I know all your secrets. Because I told Pinder that one day this would all come out – and now it is.

Then Muncy bellows at Rutter: and that's why Pinder's been covering for you all along.

He leaps forward and shoulder-barges the door which swings opens jarring Rutter's shoulder and jamming his arm against the wall.

What did you do with her?

Rutter howls in pain.

Ayaz you bastard.

Muncy is in the house now and Rutter stumbles as Muncy goes for him with his teeth bared and his eyes wild. His hands grabbing at his face. Ray Muncy is everywhere. He is all over him. Fingers tear at Rutter's cheek and thumbs find his eyeballs. They press. Now Rutter really howls. Muncy is blinding him – fucking blinding him the mad bastard.

Tell us where she is he screams. Who gave the word he screams again. Where is she?

Rutter kicks out but they're both locked in too tight in the hallway. The knife is still down the back of his trousers. He can't reach it and the point of the blade is sticking into his leg.

Piercing it. They scramble and stumble and there's no room so in desperation Rutter knees Muncy in the groin and though he barely connects Muncy releases his grip for a moment and then Rutter does it again. Harder. Muncy doubles over with a concertina face. He is retching he is gasping. Rutter's eyes are burning from the gouging and he sees flashes of colours. Bright flashes. Through the colours Rutter sees the dog lead hanging from the hook on the back of the door. He snatches it and he takes it and he loops it and he tightens it around Muncy's neck. Muncy is still bent double. Rutter pushes down on the back of his head with one hand and jerks the lead up with the other.

The red leather lead is taut. The red leather lead is tight. The red leather lead is true.

Muncy grabs for the makeshift garrotte around his neck but he can't get his fingers beneath it. He cannot get a purchase on it and Muncy is clutching at his throat but Rutter has his knee in his back now. He is pressing down on his spine and bending it. The arm that was jammed behind the door is screaming with pain and he can taste blood in the back of his mouth but he pushes down with renewed effort on the back of Muncy's head and jerks the dog lead harder tighter harder tighter. There is a lot of gasping from the both of them and the sound of their feet shifting on the wooden floorboard in brute movements. A tangled dance.

Struggling and straining.

Lurching and lunging from one wall to the other.

There is frantic shuffling and then Rutter is tightening and Rutter is jerking and Muncy is deflating and Muncy is crumpling beneath him.

He is bent double. His eyes bright with capillaries bursting. Quietly coughing brilliantly gagging silently slipping away

Rutter thinks: rope chains rubber splits scars gouges holes hair ears teeth chew snarl pigs dog rats shit shit blood blood hard heavy iron steel birth mother mess blood bulging. Shit shit Muncy.

He thinks: fucking Pinder fucking Skelton fucking Lister fucking Hood fucking corpses fucking everywhere.

Muncy's legs are giving and he is gurgling and their feet are shifting in smaller movements now but still it takes a long time for Rutter to extinguish him. A long long time.

He leans and whispers into Muncy's ear. His breath a rasp.

Of course it was me you daft sod.

WHAT WOULD YOU do if it was you?

Mace asks the question. They are both tired. They are both exhausted but they are gaining momentum.

If what was me?

What would you do if you killed a girl? Or a bunch of people.

I wouldn't kill a girl says Brindle. I just wouldn't do it.

But if you did says Mace.

I wouldn't. I'm a detective. I'm meant to be one of the good guys.

I'm asking for the purpose of research here – play along. I'm doing your job here. It's role-playing.

I'm capable of doing my job myself.

Brindle is bent over the maps. There is one of the Yorkshire Dales and there are another two of the valley. The first shows old mines and cart tracks and the other is a recent Ordnance Survey map.

Let me rephrase it then says Mace. If you were Steve Rutter and you had killed a young girl – a teenager who was the daughter of your arsehole neighbour – where would you put the body? I mean how would you get rid of it? What in your experience is a typical method?

Brindle speaks without looking up from his map.

There is no typical way but obviously burial is the most

common method of disposal. Obviously.

So let's say he buried it. Buried her.

He would do it on the moors says Brindle as he sweeps a hand across the map. All this space.

He moves from one map to the other.

Of course agrees Mace. That seems like the obvious place. They never found all the bodies of those poor kids up on Saddleworth Moor did they? Some maybe but not all. But in the middle of winter? When the ground is frozen solid and covered in a layer of snow and the place is flooded with dibble? You'd need to burn a day-long fire to soften that soil before you could even get a spade in. And who's going to light a fire on the moor-tops? You might as well have a sign advertising what it is that you're doing.

That's a good point says Brindle. You've actually made a good point there.

From you I'll take that as high praise.

So let's think about it for a moment then. If he didn't bury the body he either stored it somewhere and then got rid of it when the ground had softened – or he used a different method. One that didn't involve digging into rock-solid ground. And if he stored it at the farm we didn't find it. Maybe because—

Mace cuts in.

He was tipped off.

He leans over Brindle and looks at the maps. He adjusts the desk lamp to get a better look.

Brindle runs his fingers across the map again then Brindle coughs and then he shakes his head. Then he laughs. James Brindle starts to laugh. Mace looks at him. It is the first time he has seen the detective laugh. He thinks it is like seeing a cat or a dog laugh.

What is it?

Brindle's laugh fades to a tight uneven smile.

I'm losing it. I must be.

Why?

I'm such an idiot. A blind idiot.

He runs a finger across the map

How do you mean? says Mace.

Weeks I've been working this case. Months. Months of sending myself mad thinking about that hillbilly. I've barely slept you know. And all the while the answer was right under my nose.

What do you mean?

This is the easiest case I've ever worked on. It was me that made it difficult. *Me*.

You're not making sense.

Brindle taps the map.

He dumped her in the reservoir.

How do you know?

He practically fucking told me.

How?

When I first questioned him. I asked him what had changed up round that way during his lifetime. He said not much. I asked him about the reservoir and how it had affected the farm. He said it hadn't. That he never went up there.

He said that?

He said that and I didn't even follow it up.

Brindle shakes his head and then he continues.

He might as well have told me: that's where she is. That's where I put her. Sometimes it's like they want to be caught. When murder is their only achievement for people like Rutter it becomes a milestone event in their lives; becomes a totemic moment. Some invest it with spiritual meaning. Because they have impacted on the world and naturally they want the world to know. *Of course* he has been to the reservoir. Of course he has. He's a bog-man. A moorland clod-hopper. He's a lurker. He's bound to have been up to the reservoir. It's on his doorstep. And that was the signal.

Signal?

Yes. His signal to me. I never took his lead though. Never read the sign nor received the signal.

That's because you came with your city head and attitude says Mace. All you had to do was ask around.

They fall silent then Mace asks: but why Melanie Muncy?

It has to be payback of some sort says Brindle. Pinder or Lister or whoever is really behind all this knew Muncy was the weak link in the chain. He wasn't on the inside like everyone else. They didn't have enough over him. So they struck.

They got Rutter to do it?

Yes.

Why him?

That I don't know. But I would say that our pig man is the stooge in all this. Money or fear or intimidation or blackmail – take your pick.

How will you ever find the girl? There are drifts and undertows. There will be hidden caves and all sorts.

No says Brindle. You're wrong. It's man-made isn't it – the reservoir. A modern construction.

Yes.

So it will likely be stone-lined. All the modern reservoirs around here are. I looked into it. We'll find it eventually. We'll drain it if we have to. Have you seen one of those things emptied?

No says Mace.

I have. It's like looking down into hell.

WHEN ROY PINDER gets home late and glassy-eyed his wife is not there but Skelton is. Skelton is sitting in the living room and Skelton is smoking a cigarette and watching a game show.

Hello Roy.

Pinder starts. Pinder freezes. Pinder immediately knows.

Knows everything changes from now. This moment. The moment that he has visualised for years is here.

How did you get in? Where's Val?

Your wife has gone.

Pinder's knees go slack. He reaches for the sideboard to steady himself.

On the television fifteen or more women are lined up and vying for the attentions of a man who looks like a shaved gorilla. Skelton is watching with a small smirk on his face. The gorilla man is dancing suggestively and the women are dancing along too. The audience are clapping in time.

She's having a lie down somewhere for a bit says Skelton. Don't worry.

Where is she you bastard?

As I said she's having a little sleep and keeping her mouth shut until everything is settled. You knew I was going to pay you a visit didn't you Roy? I mean you must have known Mr Hood would be in touch Roy. Surely you must have known that?

On the TV programme the gorilla man has dismissed some of the women. The lights above their heads have gone out. They are cast in shadow now. The TV presenter has an inane look on his face. His hair is combed in such a way as to look less bald.

Lister says Pinder. Was that your doing?

Skelton slowly turns away from the television programme. He feigns an innocent look. In the dull light he looks particularly cadaverous.

Was what my doing?

He stands.

Now Roy. Forget all that and listen to me.

Pinder steps back.

The pig man says Skelton. Smelly Steve Rutter. Is he going to be a problem for us?

He did what was asked of him says Pinder. Mr Hood shouldn't be concerned.

And what was asked of him?

You know what. Do I have to say it?

Yes says Skelton. Say it.

The girl. Personally I thought—

You thought *what*?

I thought it was a bad idea that says Pinder. That it would only bring trouble to the valley. Unwanted attention. And it has.

Mr Hood doesn't give a shit about your backward valley Roy. You should know that. Mr Hood is a long way away from here. You should know that too.

Why Rutter though? Why get him to do it?

Because there's no one around to miss him.

I've had to run round covering up his tracks says Pinder. He was *this* close to getting rumbled by some cunt they sent up from the city.

Oh you mean James Brindle.

You know about him?

Of course says Skelton. Of course. Mr Hood has been watching Detective Brindle for some time. They say he's tipped for the top. Could go all the way. He's young too. That must feel strange for you Roy.

Strange. Why?

Skelton leans back in his chair. The TV casts a cold glow across his face.

Well. You've been a copper – how long? A lifetime. And here you still are. Policing the same people you grew up with. Stuck in the same arse-end town. Small fish in a small pond.

Pinder tries not to look hurt.

I happen to like it here. And I run things here now. You should remember that.

Skelton stands. Skelton moves closer to Pinder.

You run fuck all. You run what Mr Hood tells you to run. That's why he's chosen you to tie this all up for him. Tie off the loose ends.

There is much cheering coming from the television. The gorilla man has picked a woman. She is orange and now the two of them are walking up a staircase adorned on either side with rows of flashing lights. The lights flash across Skelton's face. The woman wobbles on her high heels. The pair stop to turn and wave and wink at the camera and then they disappear into an unknown future.

What are you on about?

Skelton rubs out his cigarette.

Rutter's time's up.

I thought you said he was trusted?

With lovely Larry a national news story and this Brindle not giving up Rutter is the weak link in the chain. So you've got the job. Rutter goes tonight.

Pinder looks at Skelton.

Tonight? How?

However. Like you said – you run the valley so you've got the job.

Look. I'm a policeman.

Exactly. You're a policeman and you're in on this. And Rutter knows you're in on this. So it won't look odd when you turn up at his house in the middle of the night.

On the television the end credits of the game show are rolling. Behind them the host is gyrating and mugging for the camera. The audience are on their feet loving it.

IT'S THE SAME rope he wrapped her up with. Bound and trussed. Tied and tangled. It's the last of it. It makes sense this way. To symbolically bind the two of them together like that. Father and daughter. Makes Muncy look accountable somehow.

The body of Ray Muncy is heavier than the body of Melanie Muncy and Rutter can only carry him for a minute or two before he needs a rest but at least Muncy's not shat himself in his passing. This is what Rutter tells himself. At least he has not shat.

They're going to need to hide them scissors from June Muncy again he thinks.

It's not far to where he is going. It is the nearest copse to the Muncy place. It'll do. A five-minute walk that takes Rutter a half-hour. His left arm and shoulder ache and his thigh is cut from the blade of his own knife. His fingers feel numb but he tries to ignore the pain. His bag with his bits in is strung to his front.

He turns his head-torch on.

The copse is comprised of pine trees and that's not ideal for his purpose but near to the middle in the densest part he finds a good one with nice thick branches. He puts Muncy up against the tree half-expecting him to wake up at any moment and the fight to start all over again.

Rutter throws the rope over a branch fifteen or twenty feet up and it takes three four five attempts to get it right but he manages it. He loops it and pulls it tight so it's plumb.

Double ties it. Jerks it.

The other end he loops and ties in a slipknot and then he puts it over Ray Muncy's head and then he stands back and pulls on the rope. He loops the rope around his good shoulder and under his armpit and walks backwards with it. He digs his feet into the soil and heaves and hoists. His shoulder screams but he takes a short intake of breath and then another and he jerks at the rope and the dead weight jerks with it. Ray Muncy slowly rises. His feet leave the ground. He is a marionette now just like his daughter was when she was down that drain. Like her he hangs between two worlds; between ground and sky. Animation and decomposition.

Ray Muncy is rising. Look at him thinks Rutter. Daft bastard. Of course it was me you silly sod he says again.

His voice sounds strange. Faraway but yet loud in his ears.

Who's the smug one now eh? he says. Try digging into my life now. You thought I was just some loser but who lost this game? You were right about one thing though Raymondo: I'm the one they call when they want a job done properly. Me – not you. *Me.*

He pulls and heaves until Muncy is hovering in his own space then he ties the rope around the trunk. Double triple quadruple ties it. Muncy hangs with a soppy look on his face. The rope creaking.

Rutter looks around the copse floor. He find a large stone and rolls it twenty feet through the dirt and then sets it below Muncy's slowly turning body then he takes a branch and as he walks backwards he uses it to sweep away any markings or disturbances. It'll remove Muncy's imaginary footprints too he thinks but to hell with it. The world will never catch up with me.

He's about to leave but then he stops. Puts his bag down. Opens it. Takes out his penknife. He walks back to the tree. To the shadow of Muncy's swinging body. He leans in and starts scratching at the trunk.

The blade forms the crudest of calligraphy. It reduces the lines of the letters down to diagonals – like scars in flesh. He digs and drags and levers and scratches. Chips and gouges. He steps backs then leans in and scratches some more. Muncy creaking behind him. Above him. The torch lighting the way. He steps back again. Admires his handiwork. On the trunk it says:

> WAS ME
> I SORRY
> I DID IT

11

MACE STRETCHES OUT across some chairs in an anteroom
and sleeps for a couple of hours. His body is tired but the
coffee fills his dreams with chattering spectres and images of
flesh projected across screens. Voices drill through his sleep.
Accents and faces and noises overlapping. Of policemen.
Of TV presenters. Music. Women with their faces blurred
obscured pixelated. Rubbed out. Dank cellars. Dark corners.
Shadows. Smoke. Wide eyes. Hairless torsos.

There are glimpses of his own past too: nightclubs. Sweat.
Strobe lights. The saunas. Eyes. Fingers. Torsos. Endless nights.
Endless men.

When he wakes it is just beginning to get light.

Brindle is not there so he wanders the open-plan office. He
passes between desks which are empty except for thin laptop
computers and empty plastic cups and phone chargers. There
are whiteboards with notes written on them in blue and green
marker pen that make little sense and there are other informal
areas containing sofas and low coffee tables.

Mace tries doors into cupboards or maybe corridors
or unknown rooms but they are locked so he walks to the
window and looks out across the industrial estate as the sun
begins to rise. Its rays reflect and gleam off the squat metal
buildings. His phone beeps. A message from Brindle.

> I had to leave and you should too
> before the cleaners arrive at 6.30am.
> There is money on my desk for a
> taxi. Prepare your story asap. Don't
> speak to anyone. The exclusive is

yours. I'll be in touch later. Best
wishes, Detective James Brindle.
PS – don't touch anything. There are
cameras.

Mace snorts at the observance of the traditional
grammatical rules usually ignored by others in text messages.
He snorts at Brindle's sign-off too – as if he would not know
who it was messaging him shortly before 6am. And he smiles
at the detective's terse tone. Admonishing him even from a
distance.

He stands for a moment longer watching the sun spread
across the flat dull tarmac and he thinks about Steve Rutter
and Melanie Muncy and Roy Pinder and Larry Lister and how
they all link up. Yet he knows there are so many details still
beyond his reach. Things still obscured and hidden or buried –
perhaps forever.

He thinks about the story – his story – and how of course
it is too big for the *Valley Mercury* and really he is too big a
writer for the paper too and maybe that was what Brindle
had seen in him that first night in the Magnet at Christmas:
unrealised potential. He knows if he handles it correctly he can
still be the one to break the biggest Yorkshire crime story since
the Ripper. He Roddy Mace will have the scoop the exclusive
the definitive account– and even when it goes national which
it will within hours maybe minutes of Rutter's arrest – he will
still have more information than any of the nationals could
dream of; the full back story about other murders and other
victims and the cinema and Rutter's mother and corrupt police
and girls and vice and money and the strange and haunted
geography of the valley and its surrounding villages and
hamlets. And that this could generate work for him for weeks
months or years to come and if he plays it right this could
be the making of him; this could be his ticket back out into

the wider world – back to London maybe – back to national bylines and big features and travel and awards – back to – what exactly? Anxiety excess exhaustion emptiness alienation loveless fumbles in dark nightclubs to the banging pulse of bass drums and mournful mornings waking up sick and sticky in strange rooms in Zones 5 and 6 and the long journey home. The cold empty room. The noise of neighbours never seen heard muffled through damp walls. Abject emptiness.

No thinks Mace. Not that. Not that again. No.

No: a book is where he needs to be. He needs to put it all into a book. Just as he always threatened he would. He could become a proper writer finally. Here was the opportunity. The valley has given him something; that something he was seeking when he left London.

Only now though does he realise that after today things in the valley will never be the same again. When the first edition hits the stands that will be it: his words will bring the world to this murderous outpost. It will be forever tainted by Rutter. By the whole lot of them.

The sunlight stretches right across the forecourt of Cold Storage now. Mace sees movement down there. He sees a blackbird pecking and tearing at something. It stiffens its neck and levers backwards. A worm pulled tight in its beak.

He needs to get his notes in order. That's what he needs to do. He needs to straighten up and get to the office. He needs to dig deeper than he has ever gone; to tell the story of Rutter and the cinema and Lovely Larry Lister and everything. He needs to get back to town. He needs to speak to Dennis Grogan. He needs to tell him to clear the decks and get ready. He needs to end this beginning and begin the ending. There are so many things to consider.

Mace turns to Brindle's desk. He picks up two twenties that are as flat and clean as everything in Brindle's flat clean life.

He calls for a taxi.

ONLY WHEN THEY near the farm does it occur to Roy Pinder that he does not know Skelton's first name. He does not know where he lives or what else he does in his life beyond vice and violence and serving Mr Hood who he knows even less about. How he wonders did it come to this? After all these years he doesn't know anything about him. This disparity – he now realises – is all part of the control game. Maybe he is not even called Skelton. Maybe it is a nickname bestowed upon him because he looks like a skeleton. Hood he knows even less about. Hood is nothing more than a blurred black shape. An absent yet powerful presence. Hood is a feeling that Pinder gets. The feeling is fear.

And only when they near the Rutter farm does he finally regret his twenty-year involvement. The gatherings and the films and the men and the drink and the women and the money and – yes – the kids. Pinder regrets it not because his wife is being held somewhere and indeed may already be dead nor because he is being forced to commit murder or be murdered himself nor because his police career may well be over. Neither is it because some junkies and prostitutes and some tearaway kids who no one cared about anyway were snatched and used and filmed and killed and dumped.

No. He is full of regret because he knows the best days of his life are now behind him. Whatever happens after this will seem boring. Tame. And that will be hard to deal with.

How do you intend on doing this? asks Pinder.

Not me says Skelton. You.

I told you I can't. I can't do this.

Mr Hood says so. It has to be you. And it will be you.

What if I don't?

If you don't we have an associate in Russia. A middleman.

What does that mean?

He sells material to the oligarchs and the war generals. You can imagine how extreme they like it if they're coming to us to get their entertainment.

Pinder looks at Skelton and swallows. He does not say anything.

Your wife will be kept alive for weeks says Skelton drily.

You wouldn't.

I think you know we would.

I thought all that business was over says Pinder. I thought all that ended when the Odeon X closed.

Mr Hood has business interests all over. The X was just one tiny cog. It was a property move that's all.

But why now? Why all this now?

You know why. Because of Larry Lister. Because of Rutter. And because of Brindle. The charges against Lister were going to stick and Muncy was the only one who would have talked. Brindle would have made sure of it. Rutter stopped us getting our hands dirty. That's all.

When Pinder says nothing Skelton continues.

So now you take care of one pig man and I'll worry about the other.

You're going after Brindle?

Mr Hood doesn't like worrying about the possibility of people meddling in his interests.

But if I do Rutter how do I know you're not going to kill me straight afterwards?

You don't says Skelton. You don't know that.

I wouldn't say a word if you just let her go. Let my wife go and then I'll get rid of Rutter.

You'll do it now says Skelton. Today. This morning. Come on Roy: you've had your fun all these years – surely you knew it would come at a price? All those specialist parties Roy. Imagine if the press got hold of some of the photos Mr Hood has in his collection? You balls deep in underage runaways. Well. It wouldn't look good would it?

Pinder swallows again and says: but how will I do it?

321

Skelton sighs.

For fucksake.

He takes a gun from inside his jacket.

BRINDLE SHOWERS AND changes and then returns to Cold Storage. He worries that Mace will still be there; that he will have done something stupid like bought a four-pack and settled in. Turned the office into a rave.

Before he leaves he spends a full ten minutes touching light switches and checking the gas hob and opening and closing blinds and taking sips of water and locking and unlocking the front door. He feels that his rituals take on an even greater importance because today is a big day. The most important yet.

When he finally gets to work Mace has gone.

It is a little after 7am and they are both in their separate offices and at their desks: Brindle preparing the paperwork needed for another search team – frogmen this time – and an arrest warrant and then a list of everything else that might follow. Mace frantically trying to make sense of the reams of notes that he has taken. He makes a list of likely stories that he may need to write. Drip-feeding it out will be the best way – first via the *Mercury* and then maybe a news agency. There is way too much for a local weekly paper to handle. He could place this stuff with every broadsheet and tabloid and website in Britain and beyond.

He thinks of the salient points. Murders. Missing bodies. Pig farmers. Corrupt police. Showbiz. Pornography. And worse.

The thought of it all makes his head spin and knowing that Brindle will see this process through to its dire conclusion and that his role as reporter is to document it all somehow only makes it spin even faster.

Mace wants a drink. He wants to switch off his computer

and leave the office and walk across town and back to his flat to climb under the duvet with a bottle or two and stay there forever. He wants to ignore it all; shirk responsibility. To forget everything. Ditch the story. Kill the opportunity.

Part of him wants to do this. The other part wants to write every detail; to craft sentences that tell of sordid desires and the diabolical acts of men. To dig deep and map it out; to chart Rutter's life just as cartographers once charted this brutal land. Every bump and divot. Every dark corner and undulation. To put it all in order and start to make sense. He is scared of what else he might find.

At 11am in Cold Storage James Brindle walks over to the desk of Chief Superintendent Alan Tate. He has a file under his arm and his hair looks particularly well oiled. His shirt especially white. In the file are photos and maps. There are old case files and newspaper cuttings. There are pictures of Steve Rutter and Melanie Muncy and Margaret Faulks and Aggie Rutter and Larry Lister and Roy Pinder and pictures of the farm and the reservoir and the campsite and town and the Odeon X. There are print-outs from internet forums and ownership deeds and business accounts and files on Lister and reservoir plans and there are warrant forms. There is everything he needs to present the case for the arrest of Steven Rutter. Everything is ordered. It has a narrative now. It makes sense. Things have moved beyond the moors and down to the village and the town and then the city and ultimately all the way into the living rooms of the nation.

They talk for a moment. Tate gestures over to a conference area in the corner. Coffee table and sofas. Modern policing. They sit. Brindle talks. Papers are spread out before them. They wave away anyone who dares to approach them.

At 1.30pm Brindle stands and stretches and Chief Superintendent Alan Tate follows him. Tate clears his throat and then whistles. Heads look up from screens.

Stop what you're doing he says. Stop everything.

THE LIME HAS worked. He can feel it burning his throat and nostrils even from under the double-wrapped tarp.

After hanging Ray Muncy Rutter went home and it was still dark so he relit the fire and he slept in front of it for a couple of hours and then when he awoke he wasn't sure where he was for a few moments then he made some tea and drank the tea and ate some biscuits and some sardines and some nuts and then he made some more tea.

Rutter repacked his bag with more food. He has also packed more rope and a spare jumper and a torch and a paring knife and a machete. Another tarp. Water and his tobacco and his lighter.

It is not yet morning when he turns the dogs out. He opens up their pen and coaxes them into the yard where he has piled what was left of his meat supply from the freezers. The hanks and hocks and sides will defrost slowly. Will feed them for days. They'll feast on the defrosting mound for days and then after that they'll be on their own.

He goes to the chicken coop to turn the chickens out but the few remaining hens are now dead. Slack and lifeless.

Rutter reaches in and pulls them out one by one and then Rutter throws them on the pile of frozen old meat.

He fills a couple of buckets with water and stands them next to the meat pile and then he thinks about burning the house down – just filling it with petrol and throwing a match in and illuminating the night sky – but he doesn't burn the house down and instead he just turns and walks out the back way. Away from the house. Through the yard and past the barn and up the hill and away. He tells himself that he won't look back and he doesn't.

ALAN TATE WANTS to send the whole team but Brindle

persuades him otherwise. He uses what he has as strategic capital. As leverage.

Are you sure about this? Tate asks.

Yes says Brindle though he no longer knows whether he is or not.

It won't be like last time?

No. It won't be like last time.

Alan Tate knows Brindle. He understands him. He knows the need for trust; knows that all those detectives working out of Cold Storage are different. They are the special ones. He knows that Brindle is negotiating the situation around to the way in which he wants to play it. He knows that Brindle is a strategist.

Because it seems like you're unduly fixated he says.

Unduly fixated?

On this Steve Rutter.

I'm always unduly fixated on murderers says Brindle. You know that. I thought that's why I'm here. In this department I mean.

We can't afford another fuck-up. Not after last time.

I won't fuck up.

And what about the girl's family. They live close by don't they?

Yes.

They're going to need to be informed says Tate. We can't just drop this on them. They're going to need to be prepared. We all are. Are you sure these links to the other cases exist.

Yes.

You're not just making leaps?

No says Brindle. I'm not just making leaps. I thought you knew me better than that. Knew my methodology.

I do says Tate. I do. Which is why when you messed up at Christmas –

That was a blip says Brindle. That mistake had to be made

in order to get us to this point today. Sometimes that is the way it works. It's a process. Sometimes when you go down a blind alley you turn left instead of right when you leave it. But you have to go down that blind alley to make that decision. I've trailed Rutter every moment since then. I've watched him and I've fleshed out the profile. The case is much stronger now. So much stronger.

The media will have a field day says Tate. We need to be ready.

I am ready.

We'll need to get our press team prepped.

Of course.

We'll be working for weeks without sleep.

Fine.

Then I'll get the papers signed and we'll bring him in.

Good says Brindle. Good.

BRINDLE CALLS MACE as he is driving in. As he is driving up the valley. Down the dale.

There are fields on either side. Stone walls containing him.

He counts the poles that carry the wires and the pylons that carry the wires and he thinks about folk crimes. Stories in the soil. Skeletons. Girls under water.

He thinks about Yorkshire. About the Dales. The country.

The dark country. The spaces between the places. The black water.

The wind whipping across it.

The sound of lapping.

Flesh peeling off and floating upwards. Fish feeding on it.

Be ready he says when Mace picks up.

Now?

Yes. Does your editor know?

I've told him about Rutter.

Have you told him about Pinder.

No.

Good – wait on that. And don't tell him I'm taking you up there. Not yet.

We're going up there now?

Yes now. Is that a problem?

No – it's just that –

You wanted the story. And if you're going to tell this story you need to commit to it totally – you need to be ready. You need to be there in the moment.

Are you going to arrest him?

Of course says Brindle. But first I need to speak to Ray Muncy.

Why?

Consider it a courtesy call.

Why can't I tell my editor?

Because I'm going to do this my way. This is about trust – remember? Or lack of it anyway. Trusting no one. Not even the people you think you trust.

You did it your way last time.

That's why I especially want to do it my way this time. To rectify.

I'll need a photographer there. I'll need to tell—

You'll need to tell no one. You don't need a photographer. You can get all the photos you need afterwards.

How many officers are you bringing?

None.

None?

Just me.

Just you?

Yes. And you.

They're not sending a full support team with you? asks Mace.

No.

Why?

Because I can't trust anyone at this stage.

Not even Cold Storage?

When Brindle says nothing Mace says you trust me though and Brindle hesitates for a moment.

Against all judgement – yes. It seems that way.

Won't you get in trouble? says Mace. I mean isn't there some sort of protocol to follow here? Warrants and precautionary measures and all of that.

I have the warrants. Anyway – it's me that is meant to worry about protocol not you. Your job is to record and document. Be the eyes and the ears and weave the narrative. Use that literary flair that you say you have.

What if things turn nasty?

Nasty how?

I don't know says Mace.

Why – are you scared?

I don't know.

You should be says Brindle.

Why?

Because the world is a dark and chaotic place that is ruled by disorder and desire and impulse. Because there is no sense to any of it and if you think about it too much you will want to end your life immediately.

Jesus.

Just be ready says Brindle. I'll be there in twenty minutes.

NOW HE IS here. Deep in the earth. Now he is in Acre Dale Scar. Resting up. Rustling the tarp. Its contents soft and acrid. He is feeling the ammonia rather than smelling it. The girl softening within. Becoming fluid. Burning holes in it.

Rutter lies back and Rutter lays the parcel across his chest and holds it. Rutter cradles it. Rutter treasures it.

He has found a hollow up one of the steep bank sides. He is in the shadow of a boulder and he has pulled ferns fronds over to him – over the two of them – so that they are covered. So that they are camouflaged.

The quarry is thick with balsam and ragwort and wild grasses and some of the larger trees have nearly grown to ground level out of the sunken scar and their branches are in full bloom with leaves.

Visibility is limited and his gun is beside him. Anyone climbing up or down will be heard before they are seen. Rutter allows himself a cigarette. Rutter allows himself two cigarettes. His head hurts. He drifts off.

Rutter has no dreams and Rutter has no nightmares and he is glad of the sleep. When he awakens it is later in the day and he stands and stretches and urinates and then he eats some biscuits and drinks some water and then he needs to excrete so he does that too. He turns the parcel away from him so that she doesn't have to see this even though she is dead and has no eyeballs and her flesh is bubbling with the burning effect of the chemicals that he has carefully sprinkled over what is left of her face and torso and especially her fingertips.

When it is fully dark Rutter picks up the bundle and leaves Acre Dale Scar and walks across the open moor.

A BREEZE SWEEPS across the fell side above them. It draws swirling patterns in the grass.

So says Mace in the passenger seat. We're just going to roll up there and knock on Rutter's door?

No.

Because he might see us coming.

Try saying something less obvious says Brindle.

At a passing place the detective parks the car and turns the engine off.

Come on. We'll walk down.

They leave the car and follow the road down into the hamlet. Brindle sneezes and then removes a handkerchief from his pocket and blows his nose.

Hayfever he says.

What are you going to say to Muncy?

He needs to know what's going on. That we're going to search the reservoir. It's right on his doorstep. He needs to know.

What if he does something stupid.

Like what exactly?

Attack Rutter.

I won't tell him about Rutter. I'll talk to Muncy then I'll bring Rutter in. I'll keep them separated. They will never again see one another except in a courtroom.

Are you sure of that? asks the journalist.

Until something has happened you can never be sure says Brindle. So no. But that is my intention. As we speak my boss is putting his full weight behind this. Two dozen detectives have been told to drop their cases and make this a priority. They're being brought on to check every shred of information. We're linking up with the Lister investigation and internal have been briefed about Pinder. Press statements are being prepared. I'm bringing it all down – that I can tell you.

You'll be on the telly says Mace.

No. No I won't. That is one thing I won't be doing.

You'll be a fucking hero.

I very much doubt that either.

The men reach Muncy's long drive.

You need to disappear says Brindle. While I speak to Muncy.

Where to?

I don't know. Give me five minutes.

There's nowhere to go.

There is an infinite number of places to go. Five minutes.

Brindle turns and walks up the driveway. Brindle is about to ring the doorbell when the front door opens. A frail frightened-looking woman peers round it. Her hair is cropped. It is uneven and near bald and Brindle can see small cuts on her scalp. It is alarming. One bandaged hand holds onto the door.

Oh – I thought you were Ray coming back she says.

Brindle is hesitant. Brindle is surprised.

Mrs Muncy?

Have you seen him?

No. But I'd like to speak to him if possible. Are you – are you alright?

He went out but he's not come back she says.

Brindle looks into her eyes and sees that June Muncy has gone somewhere far away.

When did he leave Mrs Muncy?

Before. Have you seen him? He was very angry.

No. But I was hoping to catch him. I'm a policeman you see. A detective.

You can't come in she says. He told me not to let anyone in – ever. I'm not even meant to answer the door.

There is a tremor in her voice. She grips the door with her hand to steady it.

Are you alright Mrs Muncy? Are you hurt?

I just want Ray back. Have you seen him?

Why was he angry?

Her face drops.

I hope he's not started up all that again.

Started up what Mrs Muncy?

All that carry-on.

What carry on?

June Muncy's eyes search Brindle's face.

You'd not heard? Getting into arguments. He's fallen out with most of them in town; reckoned they'd tried to make him do things he didn't want to do. Wouldn't say what. My Ray's his own man. A good man. Treats us well. He's even fallen out with that daft one up the hill now.

Who is that then?

She opens the door wider and with her bandaged stump of her hand points higher up the valley side.

The pig man she says. Aggie Rutter's boy.

Did you know Mrs Rutter well?

She was alright with me was Aggie says June Muncy. People called her all sorts but she brought no trouble to our door.

And what about Steven?

Well they had a row didn't they?

Who did?

My Ray and Steve Rutter. I heard them. Ray said he'd fix the lot of them. He was fuming. It's this place. This valley. People always fighting. Families falling out. And if it's not raining it's snowing and if it's not snowing it's blowing a gale. It's cursed is this place.

Brindle tries to hide his surprise. He raises a hand to halt her. Palm up.

Wait a moment. When was this?

I told him we should move but he's stubborn is Ray. He said we'd lose money on the house if we sold now. He said he grew up here and was going nowhere. Stubborn. He hated him off the telly as well. He wrote and told him so.

Larry Lister?

Called him all sorts of names.

When was this? Brindle asks again.

Reckoned it was the recession.

When did Ray say he was going to fix them Mrs Muncy? When did he write to Larry Lister?

She shakes her head.

Do you know what it was about?

Again she shakes her head.

How long ago? asks Brindle. Before Christmas?

June Muncy stares off into the distance. When the words

come they are vague.

I don't know.

Before Melanie –?

Maybe she says. Maybe.

If I came back could we speak some more?

Will you find my Ray? Will you bring him back with you?

I'll try Mrs Muncy says Brindle. I'll try.

THEY WAIT. THEY wait for hours for a sign of movement. They wait for Rutter to leave the house so that Pinder can lure him onto the moors or into the woods so that he can shoot him even though his hands are trembling but when they see nothing – no curtains being opened and no animals in the yard and definitely no Steve Rutter – Skelton gets annoyed and tells Pinder to get up there and bang on the door and get inside the house and end Rutter and let's get this over with and don't even think of doing a runner or else I'll start by cutting Valerie's tits off with scissors so then Roy Pinder walks up the hill to the Rutter farm and he bangs on Rutter's door and he looks through Rutter's windows and he checks Rutter's outbuildings and then he tries the door again but still there is no sign of Steven Rutter so he walks back to the top of the track and looks down the hill to where Skelton is sitting in the car and he opens his arms and shrugs as if to say what now? and Skelton decides that this is procrastination and this is bullshit and that if you need a job doing properly you have to do it yourself so he gets out of the car and takes out his gun and he shoots Roy Pinder in the face from thirty yards away and the gun sounds like nothing but a man spitting out a shred of tobacco and then he walks up the hill and drags the policeman's body down the track and Roy Pinder's face is like a blooming flower and he hoists him into the boot of his car.

HE WALKS WITH as much purpose as he can muster and

he does not use the torch and instead relies upon his innate understanding of the landscape. He knows which blackened bogs to avoid – perilous even during a dry spell – and where the first of the season's heather burning has taken place and where there are dangerous drops into the foundation pits of dwellings abandoned since tin miners and peat cutters and shepherds lived up here.

Because Rutter is more than someone passing through the landscape. He *is* the landscape. He is the dirt and the roots and the tumbledown walls; he is the sheep skulls and the rabbit warrens and the buried secrets and as he walks he feels as if he is a man on a planet that only he can navigate. That only he understands; a world that others consider barren and inhospitable and alien. A large and lonely place where sound is consumed by a vacuum and the dust and rocks are scentless and the water runs as red as blood.

There's a larger ruined building up ahead. They say it may have been an ancient hunting lodge built back in the 1600s when red deer were the landowners' prized quarry. Others say it was an old farmhouse with barns built on its ends. Or maybe it was a makeshift base for the old quarry teams. A dynamite store perhaps.

They said a feral man had lived here seventy or eighty years or more ago. Certainly it is over fifty years since it was occupied.

Rutter doesn't know about any of that; he is too embedded in the present – too much a part of the landscape – to gain the necessary distance that perspective provides. Like the rocky outcrop or stagnant sump pool or the fallow paddock Rutter simply is.

To him this ruin was a place of solace and shelter from the elements as a child and as he passes by now he has to resist curling himself into one of its stony corners with the foaming remains of the burning girl and going to sleep. Because they would be found here. They would be found and their story would be told in disrespectful detail in newspapers and on television and they wouldn't understand him and he does not want that.

No. He does not want that all. Rutter wants nothing but silence and nothingness. Rutter wants to be a question mark.

Yes. A question mark.

A mystery man.

Yes. The both of them. Yes. The two lost lovers.

Because this is – he thinks – a tale of romance and eternal love.

Yes. Just because she is dead – that has never mattered to him. No. Not at all.

No he says out loud. *No.* Because love endures and love lives on and love conquers and this is a love story.

It has always been about love.

COME ON.

Brindle walks across the turning circle to where Mace is waiting outside the post office. He is leaning against the window and smoking a cigarette.

Have you see this? says Mace jerking a thumb at the window behind him. It's shut.

So?

Shut for good. The Laidlaws must have sold up. Or gone bust. The post office is the last link to civilisation for the hamlet. This is big news.

So tell your editor then says Brindle walking past him.

What's got up your nose?

Come on.

Mace follows behind Brindle.

How did he take the news about the reservoir search?

Mace says this to the back of the detective's head.

He didn't.

Why? says Mace but Brindle does not reply so then he says was he not there?

No.

Well where is he?

I don't know. Dead maybe.

Mace stops.

Hang on – Muncy's dead?

Brindle continues walking so Mace runs to catch him up. They are leaving the hamlet by the old back lane that cuts up through a field towards the copse above the Rutter place. A circuitous route.

I spoke to June Muncy.

What was she like?

A ghost says Brindle. A maimed ghost.

And what did she say?

Brindle stops and turns to Mace. He looks around to check that there is no one nearby even though they are beyond one of the most remote hamlets in the north of England. He lowers his voice.

June Muncy suggested that her husband may have frequented a certain cinema in the city. Or certainly had incurred the wrath of those that did.

Mace whistles in disbelief.

Fucking hell. She told you that?

As good as. And she said that he had rowed with Rutter and was going to fix the lot of them. Her words.

When was this?

Before Christmas and—

Before Melanie says Mace. So they're linked in more ways than one. Not just by here – not just by this piss-hole hamlet.

Yes says Brindle. It would appear that way.

A revenge attack.

Maybe.

By Rutter though?

By Rutter acting on orders.

From who?

From whoever is behind all this.

Pinder?

No. Maybe. Others too though.

Seems like an extreme measure.

When people want their secrets to stay that way they do extreme things says Brindle. Rutter's the stooge here. Rutter's disposable.

Christ says Mace.

The track takes a tight turn and the two men climb over a stile and start the uphill climb.

But what does it all mean? says Mace. I don't understand.

It means Rutter had something over Muncy – or vice versa. Seems like our man Ray had a falling out with the special gentlemen's club who congregated at the Odeon X. He knew too much but they left him alone.

But then they acted.

Yes.

Because he knew all about the place. And maybe he was about to spill the beans?

That's a possibility. A very strong possibility.

Even though it closed says Mace.

Just because the building closed doesn't mean activity ceased. There are allegations against Larry Lister from as recently as six months back. I've seen the statements; he didn't always act alone. One girl described other men being present. Other men watching.

Mace shakes his head. They have come to an old stone building in the corner of the field. It is the tumbledown shepherd's bothy. They pause for a moment to catch their breath.

So should we be worried that Muncy has gone AWOL? says the journalist.

Brindle turns around. They are above the hamlet's tight cowering cluster of houses and the whole of the valley is stretched out beneath them and snaking off to their left like a giant drained riverbed.

The amount of enemies he has and given the state he has left his wife in I'd say we should be says Brindle. Something has happened. You'll see.

In what way?

In the way that I can feel things accelerating towards a conclusion that is beyond all of our grasps.

What does that mean? says Mace. That sounds like a riddle.

It means we need to get up this hill and find Steve Rutter.

Are you saying you think Rutter has done Muncy?

I'm saying that anything is possible and nothing is impossible and just when you think you have completed the jigsaw you notice a great glaring hole in the middle of it.

HE HAD PRETENDED she was a deer. It made it easier that way. That same morning or perhaps the one before he had stalked and killed and butchered a deer at daybreak. He had cached its parts and had not yet returned to collect them when he put himself back in the mind of a hunter and stalked her in the early morning snow keeping low. Staying downwind. Leopard-crawling through the brittle heather.

He saw her as a deer hind. Made his mind believe her to be a creature of the woods and moors. A thing of fur and muscle. All instinct. Prey.

The dog had sensed his presence but the girl had had headphones on and ignored its yaps and tugs.

He watched from a distance. Then he followed.

He watched as she walked the hill up to the old stone sheep shed. He had hunkered down and waited for a few moments as she sat and smoked and played with her phone. Oblivious she was.

He thought of Ray Muncy's face. He thought of the sound of Skelton's breathing down the phone line. He thought of Larry Lister in the newspaper. He tried to picture Mr Hood.

When she had left he had left too. He followed her in parallel using the copse as cover. He was glad when she left the valley behind and strode onto the moors. The moors were open but they were not flat. All Rutter needed was a quarry or a scar or anywhere out of sight. Somewhere secret. And then the hunt was on.

But still it was a surprise to him too. He had lost sight of her in the hollows and when the dog appeared from nowhere it went for him. It grabbed a hold of his sleeve but when he unsheathed the knife the simple thing to do was to take that knife and put it in the girl just as he would a fallen deer still writhing with ebbing life and then take it out the girl and then put it in again and keep putting it in the girl until her hands stopped grabbing at his face and the earphones fell from her ears and things fell from her pockets and her screams became a gurgle and then the gurgle became silence but her eyes were still blinking up at him and her fingers were flexing so he had to use his fists and he had to use his feet and it was tiring and in a strange way it felt like a surprise to him too that the girl was just meat – and some of the snow went from white to red and his quick kill was far from quick but in time the heartbeat of this hunted creature began to slow.

The mind plays tricks and the memory plays tricks and life is just a series of cruel tricks and everyone is just meat with a heartbeat but he had done just as Skelton and Hood had told him to do and more than that he had done it with love. The love of a hunter that respects its prey.

Yes.

With love from Rutter.

THEY ARE CUTTING through a dense patch of early

summer ferns just off the Corpse Road above Rutter's farm when they hear something. Something close by. The sound of rustling and panting and stems being snapped and flattened. There is movement in the undergrowth; something is proceeding through the ferns. They freeze.

Then that something is there and then that something is upon him in the clearing and Brindle makes a noise like a sharp inward gasp and he tumbles backwards and he falls but it is just a dog – a small curious dog – and it is trying to lick his face and nuzzle his ear and then another one appears and then another and then there are three dogs on Brindle and he can smell their short excited breaths

Mace laughs and then bends down to stroke them as Brindle says get these things off me.

Bent double the detective stands and brushes himself down and that is when he stops and slowly stands.

These dogs he says. They're running loose.

Yes says Mace.

They're Rutter's dogs.

Are they?

Yes.

Are you sure?

Yes.

Do you think they've escaped?

No. It's impossible. One maybe but not all of them. He usually has them tied up with great clanking chains all hours. These dogs have been turned loose.

Mace scratches one behind its ears.

Terriers he says. They look thin. Can you be certain?

Look – they don't even have their collars on.

Mace is still squatting and stroking the dogs. He looks up at Brindle.

What does that mean?

It means that without their jangling collars on Rutter has

given them a sporting chance to hunt and catch their food.

Mace stands.

But why would he do that?

Because he has gone.

Gone where?

Just gone says Brindle.

Shouldn't we—?

No. It's over.

Over?

It's over says Brindle. All of it is over. He has gone.

And that is when they hear the gunshot far off in the distance.

HE HAS HER teeth in an old metal tobacco tin. It is in his breast pocket. It is just above his heart.

Rutter pulled the rest of them out by hand down in the storm drain a few days back and they came out easy. Yes. Like nails from rotten wood. Yes.

The teeth will span centuries. They will survive the water for a long long time. They will outlast every living creature that dwells in the deepest darkest depths of the reservoir. They'll sink to the floor and they will settle in the dirt there and the dirt will take them it will consume them and hold them and the matter of all other plants and animals will fall and form a sediment on top of the girl's teeth – layer upon layer of it – and maybe they will begin to fossilise and maybe a piece of her will be preserved in stone for the future to find.

And the future will mine her and examine her and worship her just as he has.

Hours he has waited for night to fall and now it is upon him he emerges. Another nocturnal creature of the Yorkshire moorlands.

He walks on. He can see it now. The water.

The moon on it. The boat.

It sits low in the water. Perhaps it is the weight of the breeze blocks he has loaded in. It takes some time for Rutter to find his rhythm with the oars. He seems to be pulling on one harder than the other and this sends him along the shoreline rather than out into the middle. He stops to smoke for a minute and then he tries again and it is better this time. He leans and pulls and leans and pulls. He uses the full force of his arms and aching shoulders. The water is slapping the side of the little row boat and there is a shallow pool of water in the bottom that makes him wonder if there is a leak and whether he will sink and for a fleeting moment he panics but then he remembers that it doesn't matter anyway.

But it sort of does. Because he wants to get this right.

Rutter keeps going until he feels as if he is in the centre of the reservoir. The rhythm he has reached is hypnotic and he has to force himself to focus. There are things he has to do so he does them. Those things are: feed the chains through the holes in the centre of the two breeze blocks and then tie them tight – make sure they cannot come free – and then check that the tarpaulin is sealed as well as he can seal it and then that is it. That is all he needs to do.

All except say goodbye.

Rutter sits for a minute and Rutter sits for two minutes. Three. He is cradling the mushed remains of a girl called Melanie Muncy. He is holding her tight to his chest and a sob sits there inside of him. Trapped. It is unable to escape. He squeezes the mushy molested remains of a girl called Melanie Muncy one more time and he bends and the teeth rattle in the tin in his pockets then he tips it – tips her – over the side of the boat and watches as she silently falls and the water closes in over her. The blackness of it shot through with silver. Scraps of the moon on the surface like an oxygen-starved shoal floating belly up. The slow rock and tip and the slap of the water on the side of the boat.

Then Rutter is reaching for the remaining chain. Then Rutter is reaching for the remaining breeze blocks.

Then Rutter is ready to join her.

YOU'RE RIGHT. CHRIST. It does look like the mouth of hell.

Roddy Mace murmurs this through an intake of cigarette smoke. He says it as much to himself as to James Brindle.

What?

He raises his voice to be heard over the rush of water.

The mouth of hell he says again as curlews dart and dip overhead. You weren't joking.

They birds circle as the reservoir drains down the tiered circular concrete steps of the overflow's spillway. Confused by the unexpected swirling aperture and the atmospheric disturbances it is causing above it the birds depart.

The way the water drops is sculptural says Mace. And fucking scary.

Brindle stands with his hands in his coat pockets.

It has to be done now he says. In summer when the levels are low.

Mace scrapes the sole of his shoe on the shale that sits between the copper-coloured soil of the moor and the foam that has gathered on the shore. He spits and then draws on his cigarette. He inhales deeply.

It's actually pretty nice up here. When the sun's out. The Yorkshire riviera.

Brindle glances at him and then shakes his head.

You've lost weight says Mace. You look fucking ill. How did you even pull this off anyway?

What do you mean?

The draining of the reservoir.

Partial draining says Brindle. And I didn't. It came from up above.

From Cold Storage?

Brindle shakes his head.

Further.

From who then?

The top.

Nearby there are vans parked haphazardly and various representatives of the water board and North Yorkshire Police are standing around. From the back of a minibus men are checking oxygen tanks and adjusting face masks. Some have slowly begun to change into their wetsuits.

The top says Mace as he draws on his cigarette again. What does that mean?

It means what it means. That the command has come down from the top of the chain.

The top of the chain is the government. And the top of the government is the Prime Minister.

Brindle looks at him sideways.

Christ says Mace. Really?

Brindle shrugs.

There have been too many people left embarrassed. A case this big draws people in.

And sucks them under.

Yes. Yes. You're right there.

The water board won't be happy.

No one cares about that says Brindle. No one is happy. Why would you even mention that?

They watch the water fall away as laughter from the police divers echoes across the valley. They appear in no hurry as they continue to check their kit.

Where does it go anyway?

What? says Brindle. Mace can hear the irritation in the detective's voice.

I just wondered where the water goes.

I don't know. Underground.

I would like to know.

There's an explanation for everything. I'm sure you could find it.

Probably down those weird concrete doorways we saw on the way up. I have another question for you.

Then keep it to yourself.

Mace ignores him.

I know what I'm doing here today. But what are you doing here?

Brindle looks at him. He stares at him until the reporter looks away. Says nothing.

You should use the opportunity to have a rest though says Mace. You don't need to be here. Take a holiday.

You call being suspended on medical grounds an opportunity? Having people – your lot – say all sorts.

My lot?

You know who I mean. The press have nailed me. Nailed Cold Storage. I needed to come. Had to. I had to see it for myself.

This time it is Mace who is quiet.

I need to know what happened to her.

Brindle says this so quietly that his voice is drowned out by the flush of the water.

What?

Brindle shakes his head.

It doesn't matter.

Go on says Mace.

Brindle sighs.

I need to know what happened to her. Where she ended up.

And Rutter?

Yes says Brindle. Of course. Him too.

That I understand.

The detective turns to the journalist.

You don't understand. You don't understand anything. You're not the one they're blaming. They all want blood from this. My boss. The press. The government. And you can be sure it's mine they're getting.

It'll pass.

No. No it won't.

Yes says Mace. Yes it will. It wasn't you that killed the girls. It wasn't you who made the films. You're not the copper who was corrupt. The *coppers*. Plural. You're not the Pied Piper who duped entire generations of TV viewers nor did you queue up to award him honours and accolades. That prick Lister used to dine at Number 10. He was about to be made a fucking *knight*.

Doesn't matter says Brindle. Doesn't matter. I was the one who failed. It was my shortcomings that allowed this –

Here he removes a hand from his pocket and gestures out across the dropping water.

– to happen.

They'll have you back says Mace.

Brindle squints across the reservoir.

I doubt it.

The two men stand on the shore and watch as the scuba divers peel on their wetsuits now. They see a goose fly overhead.

A minute passes. Two. Then Mace speaks.

Maybe it just disappears into the centre of the earth. The water. Maybe it really is the mouth of hell. Maybe it just drops away and is drawn down to a place so dark it is beyond our understanding.

Brindle continues to squint at the spillway and the water curling over its edges.

Look says Mace. A rainbow.

He tosses his cigarette.

ACKNOWLEDGEMENTS

Thank you: Claire Malcolm, Anna Disley and all at New Writing North. Stephen May and Arts Council England North. Carol Gorner, Phoebe Greenwood and all at the Gordon Burn Trust. Andrea Murphy and all at Moth. My agent Jessica Woollard at David Higham Associates. For their input in this book: my editor Will Atkins, and Jamie Coleman, Tony O'Neill, Max Porter and Nick Triplow, who all read extracts or early drafts. The Society Of Authors. Emma Marigliano and Lynne Allan at the Portico Library, Manchester. Ian Stripe for the farming stories. Kevin Duffy, Hetha Duffy, Leonora Rustasmova and everyone at Bluemoose Books. Sam Jordison and Eloise Millar at Galley Beggar Press. Michael Curran at Tangerine Press. For general writing support and advice: Nick Small. Rob St John. Jenni Fagan. Paul Kingsnorth. Helen Cadbury. Melissa Harrison. Robert Macfarlane. Kester Aspden. Nikesh Shukla. Jenn Ashworth. Rob Cowen. Jeff Barrett and everyone at *Caught by the River*.

Special thanks to my family and friends, and especially my wife, Adelle Stripe.

ALSO FROM MOTH

Who to trust when everyone's got
something to hide?

HARD WIRED
KATHLEEN McKAY

WINNER OF THE NORTHERN CRIME COMPETITION

WINNER OF THE
NORTHERN CRIME
COMPETITION

Moth Publishing
Paperback: 9781911356011
Ebook: 9781911356042
Available August 2016
£7.99

September 1996. Newcastle United have just bought Alan Shearer for a record-breaking £15 million from Blackburn Rovers and across the city regeneration and investment are reshaping the landscape.

Charlie works in the local bail hostel where, exhausted and made cynical by the job, she expects the worst of everyone. When her friend's son is found dead in the local park she is dragged into the hunt for the murderer. Darren was no angel but as she begins to dig into the crime she sets in motion a series of threats against the hostel. Her attempts to uncover the truth find her probing failures in the justice system and searching for the men who have fallen between the cracks.

Kathleen McKay's stories feature in anthologies *Northern Crime One* (Moth), *Migration Stories* (Crocus), *Light Transports* (Route), *Mountains of Mars* (Fish), and *Arc Short Stories*; and in magazines such as *Red Ink*, www.pulp.net, *Moving Worlds* and *Metropolitan*, and have been broadcast on Radio 4. She is the author of a novel, *Waiting for the Morning* (The Women's Press, 1991); two poetry collections, *Collision Forces* (Wrecking Ball, 2015) and *Anyone Left Standing* (Smith Doorstop, 1998); and one pamphlet, *Telling the Bees* (Smiths Knoll, 2014).